Critical accla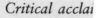

Deadlight

'This is how a crime novel should be written, and it pushes Hurley right to the forefront of British crime writers, where he richly deserves to be'

Mark Timlin, *Independent on Sunday*

'Uncompromisingly realistic ... this series grows in stature with each book'

Susanna Yager, *Sunday Telegraph*

'As serious as ever in its social concerns ... it's got a great plot, rich in detail' Mat Coward, *Morning Star*

Angels Passing

'Splendidly gritty ... most enjoyable' *FHM*

'It is difficult to believe that Graham Hurley could write a better novel than *The Take*. But he has done it. This is tough, gritty, and unsparing'

Margaret Cannon, *Toronto Globe & Mail*

Graham Hurley lives in Portsmouth with his wife, Lin. After twenty years as a TV documentary producer, he now writes full time. More information on www.grahamhurley.co.uk.

By Graham Hurley

RULES OF ENGAGEMENT
REAPER
THE DEVIL'S BREATH
THUNDER IN THE BLOOD
SABBATHMAN
THE PERFECT SOLDIER
HEAVEN'S LIGHT
NOCTURNE
AIRSHOW
PERMISSIBLE LIMITS
TURNSTONE
THE TAKE
ANGELS PASSING
DEADLIGHT

DEADLIGHT

Graham Hurley

ORION

An Orion paperback

First published in Great Britain in 2003
by Orion
This paperback edition published in 2004
by Orion Books Ltd,
Orion House, 5 Upper St Martin's Lane,
London WC2H 9EA

Copyright © Graham Hurley 2003

The right of Graham Hurley to be identified as the author
of this work has been asserted by him in accordance with
the Copyright, Designs and Patents Act 1988.

All rights reserved. No part of this publication may be
reproduced, stored in a retrieval system, or transmitted,
in any form or by any means, electronic, mechanical,
photocopying, recording or otherwise, without the prior
permission of the copyright owner.

A CIP catalogue record for this book
is available from the British Library

ISBN 0 75285 890 4

Typeset at Deltatype Ltd, Birkenhead, Merseyside
Printed in Great Britain by
Clays Ltd, St Ives plc

Deadlight – Hinged metal flap which can be lowered and clamped over a scuttle in order to darken a ship.

Jackspeak – a Guide to British Naval Slang and Usage

– Rick Jolly

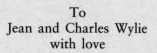

To
Jean and Charles Wylie
with love

Acknowledgements

My thanks to the following for their time and patience:

Jim Allaway, John Ashworth, Ralph Barber, Mark Davenport, Lee Dinnell, Roly Dumont, Alan Estcourt, Diana and Bob Franklin, Alastair Gregory, Barry Hornby, Bob Lamburne, Pete Langdown, Howard Lazenby, Steve McLinn, Clive Morgan, Mary and John Mortimer, Joe Morton, Laurie Mullen, John Roberts, Alfie Saye, Colin Smith, Ray Taylor, Mark Tinker, David Watts, Steve Watts, Tony West, Dave Wilson, Dave Wright and Charles Wylie.

Mark Higgitt's fine book, *Through Fire and Water*, was an indispensable source of reference, and should be compulsory reading for anyone interested in naval aspects of the Falklands War. As ever, I owe an enormous debt to my editor, Simon Spanton, while Lin, my wife, was an unflagging source of comfort and inspiration throughout a long campaign.

Prelude

All the training, all the waiting, all the unvoiced speculation: what it might feel like, how you might cope. And
now, all too suddenly, this.

The first bomb fell aft. His face an inch from the mess
deckplates, he could feel the ship lift, shudder, and then
settle again. Helo deck, he thought. He'd been out there
only hours ago, marshalling Lynx ops in the bright, cold
winter sunshine. Now, in the neon-lit harshness of the
Delta Two mess he raised his head a little, adjusting his
anti-flash, trying to picture the scene above.

'*Second aircraft. Red two zero.*' The PWO's voice on
the main broadcast Tannoy.

The Argie Skyhawks normally came in pairs. Concen-
trating on a single ship was favourite because it narrowed
the odds on a sinking. Nice one.

'*Brace! Brace! Brace!*'

The ship heeled savagely as the Captain tried to throw
the Argie pilot's aim. Then came the fairground boom-
boom-boom of the 20mm Oerliken and a sudden whoosh
as a Seacat engaged. Even with target lock at three miles,
Seacats were famously crap. Loosing one at six hundred
metres, you'd give its little electronic brain a seizure.
Even the PWO admitted it.

The sudden roar of the Skyhawk overhead ground his
face into the deck. He shut his eyes and began to count,
but he hadn't got past one before the mess erupted
around him. Thrown upwards by the blast, he had a
moment of absolute clarity before the world closed in
around him. Small things. The long-overdue bluey he'd

I

started this morning, finished except for a couple of lines at the end. The bet he'd taken a couple of days back with the XO, the date they'd all be home again. And the boy Warren, adrift in the South Atlantic, so much gash.

Smoke, everywhere. And the roar of water blasting out of a ruptured main. Voices yelling, and the clang of metal on metal as men took a Samson bar to the heavy secured doors. All that, plus a licking flame from the yawning gap below.

For a second or two, pure instinct, he checked himself over. His ears were still ringing from the explosion and when his hand came down from his face it was sticky with blood, but he could get up, no problem, and his mind was clear enough to latch itself on to the emergency drills.

According to the book, he was to return to the flight deck to assess the situation. His instincts, though, told him that the ship was finished. Already she'd taken a heavy list. Port? Starboard? He couldn't work it out but the smoke was getting thicker by the second, and judging by the thunder below the fire was spreading towards the Seacat magazine. Situation like this, any sailor with half a brain would be binning the Damage Control Manual and thinking about an orderly evacuation.

On his hands and knees, hunting for clean air, he began to move. Already the deckplates were uncomfortably hot and the upward blast of the fire below drove him to the edges of what remained of the Two Delta mess. Seconds earlier, he dimly remembered three other guys with him in this cramped little space. Where were they now?

He found one of them sprawled beside a yawning locker. Surrounded by packets of crisps, bits and pieces of civvy kit, plus assorted copies of *Mayfair*, the man was rigid with shock but still alive. He slapped his face hard, hauled him into a half crouch, and pushed him towards the jagged hole where the door had once been. A final shove took the man through.

'Out!' he shouted. 'Get out!'

Back inside the mess, the smoke coiled into his lungs. It had a foul, greasy, chemical taste. He could feel his throat burning, his airways beginning to tighten. This is how you die, he thought. This is what the Fire School instructors at Matapan Road meant by suffocation.

He found the next body beside the fridge. Jones. Definitely. He tried for a pulse, spared a breath or two for mouth-to-mouth, all he could muster, then gave up. Taff was very dead.

Two down. One to go.

'Anyone there?' he yelled.

There was a movement in the half-darkness. Someone staggering uncertainly to his feet, shocked but still mobile. He moved towards the man, meaning to help him out, then stopped. Away to his left, beyond a gaping hole in the forward bulkhead, he could just make out the shape of another body.

He ducked low again, sucking in the last of the good air, picking his way through the debris. The casualty was face up. His anti-flash gloves were charred where he'd tried to protect himself, and one of his legs was bent out at a strange angle, but his eyes were open and he blinked in response to the upraised thumb. Yes, I'm still alive. And yes, for Christ's sake get me out of here.

The body weighed a ton. Every time he tried to heave the deadweight towards the mess, towards the passageway and the ladder beyond, the man screamed in agony. Getting him through the tangle of debris would be a joke unless he could find another pair of hands.

The guy he'd glimpsed earlier was still in the mess. He could see his bulk, pressed back against the surviving partition. He had his hands out, trying desperately to follow the billowing smoke, up towards the chill sweetness of the open air.

3

'Hey you!' he managed. 'Come here! Give us a hand!'

The man turned and stared at him. From the main broadcast, faint along the passageway, came a shouted order, repeated twice. The Captain's voice. Abandon ship.

The figure beside the partition was on the move again, faster this time, lunging towards the passageway. Feeling a hand on his shoulder, he spun round. The eyes were wide, letter-boxed in the anti-flash hood.

'There's a guy back there. Give us a hand.' It wasn't a polite request. It was an order.

The man stared at him for a moment, then shaped to take a swing.

'You're fucking joking,' he snarled. 'Piss off, will you?'

One

It took a while for Faraday to make sense of the shape swimming up towards him in the fixing bath. A structure of some kind? Big? Small? He didn't know.

J-J stood beside him, a tall, thin shadow in the tiny darkroom. Despite the pressures of the last three days, he'd been up with his camera before dawn, patrolling the crust of driftwood and debris as the tide fell, and the bitter-sweet saltiness of the harbourside still clung to him.

'Recognise it now?' One bony finger put the question, circling in the gloom.

Faraday rubbed his eyes and peered down as the greys slowly thickened and the ghostly smudge that overlooked the foreshore began to resolve. The big glass doors downstairs, ablaze with the first low rays of the sun; Faraday's study above, still curtained; and a careless arrangement of clouds behind, framing the square, sturdy shape of the Bargemaster's House. The boy must have taken the shot way out on the semi-sunken causeway that dried at low tide, a suspicion confirmed by his mud-splattered Reeboks. Faraday could think of better reasons for this seven a.m. summons but just now he couldn't muster the energy to argue.

J-J reached for a pair of plastic tongs. He gave the fixer a stir, then pointed at another upstairs window on the emerging photo.

'You.' He pillowed his head on his hands, a faintly accusatory gesture. 'Asleep.'

He lifted the dripping print from the fixing bath and

held it up between them, a trophy from his morning's work. Then he turned to one of the lines he'd strung across the cramped little space and pegged the Bargemaster's House amongst the dozens of other prints already hanging in the half-darkness: old, weather-roughened faces; shy smiles; gnarled hands on brass wheels; and Faraday's favourite: an armada of tiny ships, harshly backlit against the June sun, rolling in past the Round Tower, butting against a lumpy ebbing tide.

Faraday gazed at the photo a moment or two longer, aware of J-J's eyes on his face. Then he raised an approving thumb.

'Nice,' he murmured.

Back in bed, enjoying the lie-in he'd been promising himself for weeks, Faraday let himself drift into sleep. The decision to give J-J his mother's camera hadn't been easy, but the pictures he'd managed to conjure from the battered Olympus they'd shared for years had been more than impressive and in the end the decision had made itself. Since then, months back, the photos had got better and better. His deaf son had discovered a new language through the viewfinder of Janna's treasured Nikon, and the installation of the darkroom had given J-J's black and white prints a hard-edged clarity that Faraday found both startling and eerie. These were images that bridged the years, echoes of another life. Just looking at them, he felt nineteen again.

It was gone eleven before his mobile rang. He recognised the voice at once.

'Dave,' he muttered wearily.

Dave Michaels was one of the two DSs on the Major Crimes team. Last thing yesterday, leaving the office, Faraday had made a point of mentioning his rostered rest day, keenly awaited for what felt like weeks. Already, he knew he shouldn't have bothered.

'We've got a body down in Southsea,' Michaels was saying. 'Uniform rang it in thirty minutes ago.'

'What's that got to do with me?'

'Guvnor wants you down there. ASAP.'

'Why can't someone else take care of it?'

Faraday waited until Michaels' soft chuckle began to subside. The last month or so, Portsmouth had become Murder City, the peace of the early summer disturbed by killing after killing. Most of it was rubbish, three-day events, domestic disputes turned into murder by booze or frustration, but every next body in the mortuary fridge triggered a mountain of paperwork as Faraday, above all, knew only too well. There were undoubted benefits to a divisional DI like himself winning a place on the Major Crimes team but a conversation like this wasn't one of them.

For a moment he toyed with having the full ruck, if only to satisfy his own disappointment, but knew there was no point. The rules of homicide – who, where, when, why – took absolutely no account of the rest-day roster.

Michaels was telling him what little he'd gleaned from the uniformed inspector who'd passed on the first report from the attending PCs. Guy in his fifties dead in his Southsea flat. Body discovered by a mate sent round from work. Chummy was naked on the floor, stiff as a board, and someone had given the rest of the room a good seeing-to as well.

'Where's the flat?'

'Niton Road. 7a.'

'Witnesses? Neighbours? Anyone upstairs?'

'Too early to say. Scenes of Crime are there already and they've sealed the premises. No response from the top flat.'

Faraday peered at the alarm clock beside the bed. 11.36. Given the timescale, events had moved extraordinarily fast. How come the referral to Major Crime had come so soon?

'Willard's decision.' Michaels laughed again. 'He can't wait to get his hands on this one. He's talking twenty DCs. He's going to blitz it.'

'Why?'

'Bloke was a prison officer.'

Faraday found J-J bent over the toaster in the kitchen, still enveloped in the harsh, chemical tang of the developing fluids from the darkroom. In a flurry of sign, Faraday explained about the summons to work. Their planned trip to London would have to wait for another day.

J-J was less than happy.

'When?' he wanted to know.

Faraday spread his arms wide. The temptation was to gloss it, to pretend that this latest spasm of violence would be sorted in days, just another settling of domestic accounts, but something in the conversation with Dave Michaels told Faraday to expect a more complex challenge. Detective Superintendents with Willard's experience seldom called out the cavalry in such numbers without due cause.

'I can't say,' Faraday signed. 'Could be next week. Could be next month.'

'What about this woman we're meeting?' J-J's hands shaped the question, then left it hanging in the air between them. He was seriously upset and Faraday knew it.

'I'll phone her. Sort something out.'

'But she's going back next week. You told me.'

'I know. Maybe she can come down here.'

'Really?' A sudden smile brightened J-J's face. At twenty-three, there was still something childlike about the way his mood could change in an instant. Thunder one moment, sunshine the next.

Faraday nodded at the toaster. Smoke was curling from the thick slice of granary that J-J had wedged inside. J-J ignored it.

'When?' he insisted. 'When can she come?'

Faraday signed that he didn't know. He'd arranged the afternoon's meeting months back, after Janna's parents in Seattle phoned with the news. London's Hayward Gallery were planning to mount a major Ansel Adams exhibition, a centenary celebration of the American photographer's finest work, and one of Janna's long-ago college friends had been charged with liaising between the Hayward and the Adams family trust. J-J had inherited his mother's passion for Adams's landscapes, and the offer of a sneak preview – the best prints a month before the exhibition was due to open – was a dream windfall for a young novice photographer as eager and ambitious as J-J.

Faraday rescued the remains of the toast and scraped the worst of the damage into the bin. J-J was looking thoughtful.

'I could go by myself,' he signed at last. 'Go up and meet her.'

'Yeah?' Faraday was checking his watch.

'Of course. You can tell me where and when. And then you can phone her and explain you won't be there.'

'What if she doesn't know sign?'

'Doesn't matter. We're looking at photographs, aren't we? No need for anything else.'

Still preoccupied with what awaited him in Niton Road, Faraday found himself staring at his deaf son. There were moments when J-J astonished him and this was one of them. The boy was right. The whole point of images as dramatic and artful as Ansel Adams's was the way they transcended language. Who needed mere words when a photograph could say it all?

Faraday reached for the butter dish.

'I'll ring her in a moment.' He tapped his watch. 'And then I must go.'

*

Niton Road was one of a series of streets that webbed the eastern reaches of Southsea. The houses were terraced, but generous bay windows gave them a hint of gentility, and a dozen or so trees – recently planted – had so far escaped the attentions of Friday night drunks.

Faraday parked his Mondeo round the corner and showed his warrant card to the young PC guarding the blue tape that sealed the front gate of number seven. The line of vehicles at the kerb included Willard's gleaming new BMW. Seconds later, Willard himself stepped into the sunshine, deep in conversation with the Crime Scene Manager, a youngish DS called Jimmy for whom – on the evidence of the last two murders – Faraday had a great deal of respect.

Faraday met them on the pavement. The CSM was sweating inside the hooded one-piece suit. There was evidently a problem with getting hold of the Home Office pathologist and Willard wanted to know why. The CSM stepped back towards the house, retrieved his mobile from the PC on the door and peeled off a glove to punch in a number. The pathologist lived in Dorset.

Willard turned to Faraday.

'Took your time, Joe. Half day is it?'

Faraday ignored the dig. Willard, as Detective Superintendent in charge of the Major Crimes team, was banged up in his office most of the day, walled in by paperwork, budget-juggling and a traffic jam of meetings. One glance at his diary took Faraday straight back to his own managerial days on division, and it was rare for someone of Willard's exalted rank to make a personal appearance at the sharp end. Yet more proof that dead prison officers got five-star service.

'We've got a name, sir?'

'Sean Coughlin. He's a PO over at Gosport nick. Never turned up for his shift this morning. No phone call. No e-mail. Nothing. The supervisor sent someone round and here we are.'

'He had a key?'

'Didn't need one. He banged on the door a couple of times and then found a window open at the front.'

Faraday followed Willard's pointing finger. One of the small top windows in the downstairs bay had been open overnight. Reaching in, Coughlin's colleague had managed to unfasten the bigger window beneath. The room was still curtained but the smell had been enough to warrant further investigation.

Faraday frowned. Even with the central heating on, it took at least twelve hours for decomposition to set in.

'He's been dead a while?'

Willard shook his head.

'He was at work until five last night. The smell was vomit. Coughlin had puked all over the carpet. His mate thought he must be ill.'

The CSM snapped his mobile shut. The Home Office pathologist had finally responded to his pager and would be putting a call through to the morgue to book a slot for the post-mortem. Since last month, despite the rash of local murders, all post-mortems had been transferred to Southampton General, twenty miles to the west, where the facilities were judged to be better. The fact that this transfer also halved the pathologist's journey time to the dissecting slab was – in Faraday's judgement – no coincidence.

'Today would be good,' Willard grunted. 'Where are we with the body?'

The CSM began to detail progress inside. The police surgeon had certified death and gone on to his next job. The photographer from Netley had burned through five rolls of 35mm film and was now committing the scene to video. Clear plastic bags had been secured around Coughlin's feet, hands and head, and the corpse was about to be readied for transfer to the mortuary. The guys from the undertakers were waiting with their casket in a Transit down the street and the CSM planned the handover inside the shared hall. In the interests of good taste, the neighbours would be spared the sight of a sixteen-stone body bag.

Willard nodded, his eyes following a young WPC up the street, and Faraday realised what a difference a couple of years in charge at Kingston Crescent had made. With his sheer physical bulk, and absolute refusal to accept excuses, Willard had set new standards for the dozen or so men and women at the heart of the Major Crimes team. His insistence on painstaking detective work, allied to the incessant pressure of events, had put a couple of the weaker souls to the sword but over the last eighteen months Major Crimes had posted some famous victories.

Willard wasn't the kind of man to wear success lightly. His taste in well-cut suits now extended to an expensive bespoke tailor in Winchester, and lately – after the attentions of a hairdresser called Roz in a Southsea salon – he'd begun to look positively sleek. Gossip amongst the first-floor suite of offices at Kingston Crescent suggested that there was more to this relationship than a ten-quid tip, but Faraday had yet to be convinced.

Willard took him by the arm and stepped back on to the pavement, pausing beside the BMW for a kerbside conference. Time was moving on. He wanted Faraday back at Kingston Crescent to keep the lid on the pot as the inquiry team gathered. He'd been on to Operational Support at HQ for a couple of dozen DCs to kick-start the investigation. With luck, they'd manage twenty. House-to-house enquiries would be number one, Personal Description Forms for every address, and it would be down to Faraday to fix the parameters. He'd told the Prison Liaison Officer – a DS on division – that he wanted an interview team into Coughlin's nick and he'd just put in a personal call to the governor to smooth the way. Bloke was a hundred per cent on-side, no-nonsense guy, old school. He'd promised to make arrangements for a secure office and would provide a list of Coughlin's work colleagues. Back at Kingston Crescent, they were already firing up HOLMES but there was a problem with the indexers. One of them was on leave. The other was in bed with a migraine. Willard wanted it sorted, priority.

'OK?'

Faraday didn't bother to hide his smile. HOLMES was the major inquiry cross-referencing system, a powerful piece of computer software with a huge appetite for data. It swallowed every shred of emerging evidence, filing it away for the moment when a pattern began to emerge. It was fed by the inputting indexers, civilian operators shackled to their keyboards, and migraine had become one of their milder occupational hazards. PDFs, along with House Occupants Forms and the House-to-House Enquiry Questionnaire, ran to five dense pages of hand-scribbled information. No wonder the indexers were tempted to stay in bed in the morning.

'You want me to go round with an aspirin?'

Willard, scenting a joke, changed the subject. Staffing on this one was going to be tricky. The force had two other Major Crime teams and both were working flat out. The Receiver, Statement Reader and Action Allocator – key HOLMES players – were local decisions that made themselves. Ditto the officers who would handle Exhibits and Disclosure. But Willard never settled for less than the pick of the force-wide talent and he didn't want some knobber turning up as FLO. The Family Liaison Officer mopped up the puddles of grief that every murder left in its wake. A good FLO, winning the trust of immediate family and friends, could also be a priceless intelligence source.

Willard mentioned a couple of names. No way would he give either of them house room. He also wanted a squad briefing, six p.m.

'OK?'

Faraday nodded. Conversations with Willard seldom made allowances for small talk but this morning's exchange was especially blunt. Reviewing his mental checklist – miracles to be worked over the next hour or so – Faraday began to wonder what lay behind this opening barrage.

'You're SIO?'

'Of course.'

'And me?'

'Deputy.' Willard had produced his car keys. 'I'm off on a course tomorrow. Wyboston Lakes. Kidnap and extortion.' Bending to the car door, he glanced back at Faraday. 'Be OK on your own, will you?'

The question was a joke, and Faraday knew it. Wyboston Lakes was up in Bedfordshire, a Centrex training facility specialising in senior command courses, but no way would Willard let a hundred miles come between himself and a job as high profile as this one. Senior Investigating Officers sat on top of every inquiry, responsible for keeping the investigation on track, and having Willard across the corridor at Kingston Crescent was pressure enough. Reporting to him on the phone ten times a day would be a nightmare.

'How long are you away, sir?'

'Five days.' For the first time, a ghost of a smile. 'Unless you fuck it up.'

Willard gone, Faraday stood on the pavement for a moment, enjoying the warmth of the sun on his face. He'd been on Major Crimes for four brief months but already he'd realised how each successive job banged you up in a world of your own.

The need for focus and concentration was intense. Dedicated inquiry teams and six-figure budgets were a luxury beyond the reach of journeyman DIs on division, but the sheer weight of responsibility on Major Crimes was immense. Real life – shopping, cooking, even a snatched half day out on the marshes looking at his precious birds – became a memory. Enquire about the day of the week, and you wouldn't have a clue. But ask about alibi parameters, or forensic submissions, or arrest strategies, or the current state of the overtime budget, and you'd be word perfect, the undisputed king of a virtual world of the murderer's making.

With luck, and ceaseless attention to detail, you'd get a result. And even if you didn't, there still remained a kind of awe at the sheer reach and power of the system. On good days, it did your bidding. On bad days, it could crucify you.

'Sir?'

It was the photographer from Netley. He'd emerged from the house with a bagful of gear.

'You're through?'

'Yep.' He pulled back the hood on his one-piece suit and mopped his forehead with the back of his hand. 'Christ knows what the bloke had to eat last night. It stinks in there.'

Faraday was looking down at the bag. As Deputy SIO it was his right to inspect the room where Coughlin had died, but no detective in his right mind would hazard precious forensic evidence until the CSM declared his work done. More and more often, court convictions turned on a tiny particle of DNA recovered from the scene of crime.

'What kind of state was he in?'

'I've seen worse. He certainly got a kicking. Here and here especially.' The photographer touched his upper body and groin. 'But you're not talking loads of blood.'

'Face?'

'Couple of bruises. Swelling. Nothing more.'

'Weapon?'

'Nothing obvious. As far as the body's concerned, I'd wait until the PM. Maybe the bloke choked to death. There's a bucketful of spew on the carpet.'

'No question about the injuries, though?'

'None. The room's a mess, too. Here.' The photographer bent to the bag and pulled out the video camera. Rewinding the tape, he shielded the tiny screen with his hand until he found the spot he wanted. Then he handed the camera to Faraday.

'Hit play.'

Faraday did his best to make sense of the image but the bright sunlight washed away the detail. Crouched in the back of the photographer's Fiesta van, he tried again.

'Starts with the body. Are you seeing the body? Big bloke?'

'Got him.'

Coughlin was lying on his side on the carpet, his knees drawn up towards his chest, his hands knotted protectively across his groin. He was a big, flabby man, a couple of stones overweight, and there were curls of black body hair across the spread of his belly. The bruising to his rib cage purpled the white flesh and there were more bruises around his thighs and buttocks. A day's growth of beard darkened his lower face and a thin dribble of vomit had caked across his swollen chin. His eyes were open, gazing sightlessly across the soiled carpet. Even in life, he wouldn't have been a handsome man.

The camera offered a couple of extra angles on the body, revealing a serpent tattoo on his left arm. Then came a slow pan around the living room. Faraday wedged himself more tightly against the wheel arch. The photographer was right. The room had been wrecked: chairs overturned, pictures smashed, a bookcase emptied, the tiny hearth full of debris from the mantelpiece above. The shot finally settled on half a dozen magazines, spread in a semi-circle around Coughlin's feet. The images were explicit, stuff you wouldn't buy in W. H. Smith's.

The photographer was squatting beside Faraday.

'Porn,' he said. 'Stuff's everywhere. He had the computer on, too. One of those premium sites. All-night wrist shandy.'

'And it's still on?'

The photographer nodded and Faraday made a mental note to talk to the CSM. The specialist Computer Crime guys at Netley would have to come out and make the disconnection. No way should Scenes of Crime touch the machine.

'Was there more of this stuff?' Faraday had paused the camera on the porn mags.

'Yeah. Whole pile down by the desk the computer's on. Bloke must have wanked for England.'

'And these' . . . Faraday pointed at the spread of magazines on the screen . . . 'you think someone did that little arrangement?'

'Must have.'

Faraday tried to imagine the sequence of events that might have led to this carefully mounted little scene.

'We're talking a flat here? Self-contained?'

'Yep. Two bedrooms. Kitchen. Bathroom. Usual shit conversion.'

'Any damage?'

'None the guys could see.'

'What about upstairs? Who lives there?'

'Dunno.'

'Shared front door?'

'So I'm told.'

'What about entry? Any sign of damage?'

'Not that anyone mentioned. I'd have photographed it otherwise.'

Faraday nodded, releasing the pause button and watching the tiny screen again. The shot began on a magazine cover. Then the sight of two women licking a huge erection receded as Coughlin's body wobbled into view. The camera steadied on the sprawl of dead, white flesh, and for the second time that morning Faraday

17

realised the power of a single image, a moment frozen in time, a man's last gasp celebrated in this sordid tableau.

In the closeness of the tiny van, the photographer began to chuckle.

'Those premium sites charge one pound fifty a minute.' He indicated the body on the screen. 'Bloke's better off dead. Would have cost him a fortune otherwise.'

An hour later, at Kingston Crescent police station, Faraday took the stairs to Hartigan's third-floor office. Recently promoted to Chief Superintendent, Hartigan was now in overall charge of the Portsmouth BCU. Basic Command Units came in all shapes and sizes, but Pompey was one of the biggest building blocks in the force-wide command structure. Heading the forces of law and order was, as Hartigan so often reminded visitors, the dream job. Not just top uniform in the county's most challenging city, but a real chance to make a difference.

'Joe . . .'

Without getting to his feet, Hartigan waved Faraday into a chair. Physically, Hartigan was small and obsessively neat, as precise and fussy in his dress sense as he was on paper. Once, in an unguarded moment in the bar, his management assistant let slip that Mrs Hartigan even ironed the great man's socks.

'Prison officer? Am I right?'

'Yes, sir. Name of Coughlin.'

'Niton Road?'

'Yes.'

'7a?'

'Absolutely.'

'Next of kin?'

'We're still checking.'

Faraday did his best to rein back his rising irritation. He'd watched Hartigan play this game for longer than he cared to remember. It had to do with knowledge and power, and it sent a message that precious little escaped the Chief Superintendent.

'So . . . this Impact Assessment . . .' Hartigan was frowning. 'The beatman tells me it's normally pretty quiet around Niton Road. Unfortunate really, under the circumstances. No?'

Faraday added what little he could. The first of the seconded DCs, half a dozen guys from the local divisional CID strength, had already joined the investigation and four of them were working the house-to-house enquiries, toting their clipboards the length of Niton Road. So far, according to the DS in charge of Outside Enquiries, they'd turned nothing up, no surprise at this time of day.

'Most people are out at work,' Faraday pointed out. 'Won't be back until this evening.'

'Women as well? Mums?'

'Yes, by and large.'

'Typical. Time was when mums stayed at home for their kids.'

'But their kids are at school.'

'Not the toddlers, Joe. That's the age that counts.'

Faraday settled back. Soon enough, they'd come to the meat of the Impact Assessment – the precautionary exploration of ways in which they might keep the inquiry as low profile and non-intrusive as possible. Few householders fancied living in a street blackened by murder. Even fewer relished the prospect of a round-the-clock, high-profile CID operation. Hartigan would doubtless have his views on this, plus a list of neatly pencilled must-action priorities, but for now he was off on another tack.

'Volume crime can be a challenge,' he mused. 'I'm not suggesting you're missing it for one second, not in this new job of yours, but it's true, you know.'

'What's true, sir?'

'The minor key. The small print. That's where we win or lose the battle in this city. Murder? Rape?' He fluttered a dismissive hand. 'That's where the resources go, and maybe that's the way it should be. But tell me this. We have a bunch of kids in Somerstown, tearing around from corner shop to corner shop. They operate mob-handed. They're completely upfront. They go through a shop like a bunch of locusts and nick anything they can get their hands on: money, goods, alcohol, even shop fittings. They're out beyond the law, out beyond society, and they couldn't care a monkey's. Terrifying, eh Joe? So what are Major Crimes proposing to do about that?'

'Nothing. Unless they kill someone.'

'But occasionally they do, Joe, they do. As well you know.'

Faraday ducked his head, trying to work out whether Hartigan had just paid him a compliment. A year back, still on division as DI at Highland Road, Faraday had cracked a case that ended up making national headlines. A fourteen-year-old who'd thrown herself off a Somers-town tower block. And an even younger kid – ten, for God's sake – happy to burn a house down and kill a man to revenge a separate death. The day after the boy had been found guilty, the *Guardian* had caught the mood with its page three feature analysis. 'Fallen', the headline had read.

'About Niton Road . . .' Faraday began. Hartigan ignored him.

'The kids should be at school, Joe. They should be motivated, keen. They should be committed. Instead of which we're chasing them around Somerstown at God knows what expense. Don't get me wrong. I don't resent the resource implications. That's what we're here for. But where does it lead? Where is it taking us as a society? Any ideas, Joe?'

For a moment, Faraday was tempted to believe that this was a prelude to a serious debate, that Hartigan really was keen to follow through on the events of last year, but then the little figure behind the desk gave himself away, mentioning a speech he was due to make to the Government Office for the South-East up in Guildford, and at once Faraday realised that this little outburst of civic concern was simply a rehearsal. Real life goes on, Hartigan was saying. While you guys hog the money.

Ten minutes later, after agreeing that Major Crimes should tread as carefully as possible in Niton Road, Hartigan brought the conversation to an end. Only at the door did Faraday voice his misgivings.

'You're sure that's enough?' he queried. 'Assessment-wise?'

Hartigan, back behind the desk, glanced sharply up.

'It's all about absent mothers, Joe.' He shook his head. 'Kids go off the rails. I'm surprised you can't see that.'

Two

When the bent figure in the stained polyester dress tottered back with yet more refreshments, even DC Paul Winter couldn't manage it. He and DC Dawn Ellis had been sitting in Doris Ackerman's tiny bay window since lunchtime. A fourth pot of Shopper's Choice teabags, and his kidneys would explode.

'No thanks, love.' Winter eased her gently back towards the open door. 'Nice thought, though.'

Ellis looked around the stuffy little sitting room. The furniture had seen better days and there was a powerful smell of cats. A copy of last month's *News* lay folded on the dresser and a limp-looking plant on the mantelpiece badly needed watering. The framed black and white snap beside it showed a much younger Doris arm in arm with a sailor.

Denied a perch in the corner store itself by the nervous Bangladeshi shopkeeper, Winter had phoned Mrs Ackerman first thing from the CID office at Southsea's Highland Road police station. Mrs Ackerman remembered nothing of her previous encounter with DC Paul Winter, but was happy to confirm that her house was right across from Mr Patel's corner shop. She often went over for biscuits and cat food. Saved her legs the trip down Elm Grove to the Co-op.

Ellis, as amazed as ever by the sheer depth of Winter's contacts book, had been curious about this woman's willingness to convert her front room into a CID observation point. In an area as rough and unforgiving as the Somerstown estate, any association with the Filth was a guaranteed brick through the window. So how come she was putting out like this?

Winter, predictably tight-lipped, had shrugged the question aside and only when they'd turned up on her doorstep did Ellis realise that the old lady thought they were from Southern Electric. Quite why a power company should have been interested in mounting surveillance on the Patel store was anybody's guess, but Doris Ackerman was charmed by Winter's smile and happily let them get on with it.

There were, of course, strict regulations about the use of private premises for covert operations. The standard risk assessment called for prior consultation and a sheaf of double-signature forms, but Winter had seldom let procedure stand between himself and the prospect of a modest result. If Hartigan wanted a bunch of scrotey kids off the plot, and if Cathy Lamb thought a stake-out might do the trick, then so be it. With the clock ticking on, and the wastelands of Somerstown a virtual no-go area, then the time had very definitely come for a spot of creative policing.

Personally, Ellis had thought using the cross of St George to camouflage the camera a crap idea. Winter had spotted the big, grubby England flag in a Fawcett Road junk shop, arguing the price down to fifty pence, and back in the car Dawn couldn't believe he really meant to use it, but the moment they'd turned into the Somerstown estate she'd had to give him the benefit of the doubt. These same flags were everywhere, hanging over balconies, draped in front windows, knotted to the rusting bodywork of builders' pick-ups, part of the city-wide carnival that would doubtless carry Sven's boys into the World Cup final.

In three days' time, England were playing Argentina. The entire country was readying itself for an epic encounter but here in Pompey – the city which had despatched the Falklands Task Force – the game already reeked of expended cordite and hand-to-hand combat. Several gallons of lager and a goal or two were bound to kick off the usual mayhem, a source of some anticipatory excitement for the younger uniformed lads who enjoyed – in the parlance – a spot of robust policing.

Winter was morose. The afternoon had come and gone and the expected excitements had failed to kick off. At the morning briefing, Cathy Lamb had put her money on a blag just after lunch. That way, the kids could be ready at school gates across the area, flogging nicked gear to other kids en route home. Accordingly, the corner shop had been rigged with discreetly mounted hi-res video cameras, and the till had been stuffed with marked notes. Only an outbreak of lawful behaviour could keep the likes of Winter, Ellis and the uniformed lads on the pursuit bikes out of the medals.

For the umpteenth time, Winter phoned one of the DCs in the back-up unmarked Fiesta on his mobile. He'd long ago given up on the police net because these days the kids were way ahead in the comms war and routinely used scanners. He knew this because they, too, were nicked and regularly turned up on the shoplifting reports.

The conversation was brief. Winter pocketed his mobile.

'And?' Ellis shot him a look.

'Bored stiff. Plus they've been clocked again.'

'Tell him to move.'

'They're going to.' Winter glanced across at her. 'You want some really bad news?'

'About what?'

'That dead screw in Niton Road.'

Ellis nodded, saying nothing. The Coughlin murder in Niton Road had been common knowledge since mid-morning and there wasn't a Pompey DC who wasn't praying for secondment to Major Crimes. The suspicion that none of them – not Winter, not Ellis, not either of the guys in the Fiesta – had made it on to the squad was galling, to say the least. In overtime alone, a decent murder would pay for a couple of weeks in the Caribbean.

'Well?' Ellis said at last.

'Bev Yates, for starters.'

Dawn absorbed the news. At forty-five, Bev Yates was a veteran DC. His glory days as centre forward on the CID team were long gone and three decades of heavy-duty partying had taken their toll. Nonetheless, with his sleepy eyes and slow smile, he knew he was still a looker and had a recently acquired young wife to prove it.

'They've just had another baby,' Winter murmured. 'Did you know that?'

'Everyone knows it.' Dawn was studying her finger-nails. 'What a waste.'

'The baby?'

'Bev. He was discussing the price of Pampers the other day. Can you imagine that? Bev Yates? Sex god? Into *Pampers*?'

Winter chuckled softly. He'd set up the Minolta from Technical Services on a tripod a pace or two back from the window. The telephoto lens offered a close-up of the Patel shop doorway through a carefully torn rent in the flag and he leaned forward yet again to check the viewfinder. Two Bangladeshi women standing in the sun-shine yakking about God knows what. Absolutely no sign of impending trouble.

'They must do these secondments on purpose.' Ellis yawned. 'They know Bev's really up for the World Cup.'

'He'd be at work anyway, times they're showing these games.'

'Not at half past seven in the morning he wouldn't. And the later games he'd sort somehow or other. You know what he's like when it's something he really wants.'

Winter grunted, saying nothing. Even older than Yates, he had a legendary mistrust of team spirit, chiefly because he'd never seen the point of it. Winter was the detective who belonged in a museum, a bulky, balding, streetwise DC who made his best moves in a suede car coat and a haze of after-shave. He'd always hunted alone and the fact that he was still around was a tribute to his predatory skills. According to the likes of Hartigan, successful detection relied on good intelligence, disciplined teamwork and the scrupulous gathering of evidence. Winter, with his unrivalled city-wide sources, agreed about the intelligence but viewed the rest as bollocks.

Dawn Ellis, who'd learned a great deal from Winter, rather liked him. Looks like hers could be a handicap in a culture as macho as CID, and the fact that she was a born-again veggie didn't help. Why a slim, bright, attractive twenty-eight-year-old was wasting herself in the gloom of a Portchester semi was a source of perpetual mystery in the CID room but only Winter, she suspected, knew the truth. That she was lonely, as well as increasingly nervous.

Earlier in the afternoon, she'd mentioned calls she'd been getting, two o'clock in the morning calls, the kind of weirdo calls where the line stays open and all you can hear is breathing at the other end. They'd been happening a lot recently, two or three times a week, and they were beginning to spook her. Winter hadn't said very much, just the obvious, who might they be, but when she'd shaken her head and said she hadn't a clue, he'd made a little joke about the length of the list and left it at that.

Now, though, he wanted to know more.

'There isn't any more.'

'Doesn't he ever say anything?'

'I don't even know if it's a bloke.'

'Something you're not telling me?'

'Not at all. I'm not saying it's a woman. I'm just saying I don't know. And that's the point really. Two o'clock in the morning, stuff like this starts to get to you.'

Glued to the viewfinder again, Winter changed the subject.

'Tell me about Andy Corbett.'

'What makes you think I know anything about Andy Corbett?'

'Because you're supposed to be shagging him.'

'Who said?'

'You're not shagging him?'

'We've been for a couple of drinks. He's a nice bloke, breath of fresh air. That's not shagging, Paul. That's conversation.'

Winter eased away from the tripod, rubbing the back of his neck.

'Met, wasn't he?'

'That's right.'

'Rides a big bike? Ponces around in black leather?'

'What *is* this?'

'Just curious. He's another one who's copped for the Coughlin job.' He smiled at her. 'I'm surprised you didn't know that already.'

The squad briefing for the Major Crimes team was delayed half an hour until 18.30. The incident room lay at the end of Major Crimes' secured first-floor suite of offices at Kingston Crescent. There was space in here for the dozen or so desks that serviced the voracious demands of the HOLMES system, with a perch or two at the edges for all the other specialist officers who would be ducking in and out of the incident room. Other offices down the corridor already housed the Intelligence Cell and the forensic team, and a management assistant was organising more accommodation in a larger room at the far end. By now, the inquiry had acquired an official codename: Operation *Merriott*.

Deep in conversation with Dave Michaels, Faraday didn't notice Willard's arrival in the incident room.

Michaels was the DS acting as Receiver, the all-important pair of eyes that scanned all incoming reports from DCs out there in the field. It was Michaels who would serve as the inquiry's radar, highlighting the first shadowy indications of an emerging pattern.

On a nod from Willard, Faraday called the room to order. Most of the squad had now gathered, DCs from CID offices county-wide, bunched together on any handy surface, curious to know where this inquiry might lead. Only a couple of HOLMES-trained indexers Faraday had managed to poach from Basingstoke had yet to appear.

Willard wasted little time. The victim was a white male, fifty-three years old, unmarried, name of Sean Arthur Coughlin. He worked as a prison officer in Gosport nick and lived alone in a ground floor flat at 7a Niton Road. The flat upstairs was empty and neither set of neighbours on either side had reported any disturbance the previous evening. One of them, an eighty-seven-year-old, was deaf. The other, a young professional couple, had gone to bed early. No joy there.

An anticipatory ripple of approval ran round the room. Already, these men and women sensed an inquiry with legs.

Willard stilled the murmuring voices with a glance. Cause of death appeared to be assault, with or without some kind of weapon, but the post-mortem had barely started and the preliminary results wouldn't be through until later. The Scenes of Crime team would be knocking off around eight and the premises would be secured for the night. In view of the fact that the house was empty upstairs and down, the SOC boys would be taking their time over the forensic search. Jerry Proctor, the SOC coordinator, was guesstimating a minimum three days for the job.

Proctor himself was in the incident room, a large, bearded, bear-like man who had begun to remind

Faraday of an Afrikaans farmer. Passionate about sailing, his big face was tanned and wind-roughened, and his deep-set eyes had the kind of thousand-yard stare tailor-made for hot, dusty days on the veldt. Willard's news about the protracted forensic search drew a curt nod of agreement. When Willard asked him whether he had anything to add, he shook his head.

'Just the shoeprint,' he said. 'And the porn.'

Prompted by Willard, Proctor filled in the details. Early afternoon, completing their visual search back and front of the premises, one of the SOC team had found a perfect footprint in a flower bed softened by last night's rain. The footprint, directly underneath Coughlin's bedroom window, had been photographed, and a plaster cast had also been made. Early indications suggested a size ten moulded sole, very probably a jogging shoe of some kind.

Willard stirred.

'Wouldn't be Coughlin himself?'

'No, sir. Wrong shoe size.'

Proctor glanced down at his notes, then added a word or two about the magazines on the floor and Coughlin's affection for the rougher end of the porn sites. Late afternoon, a DS from the Computer Crime Unit had driven over from Netley and removed Coughlin's Hewlett Packard for detailed analysis. A phone check with the Eastleigh company who managed the porn site had established that Coughlin – or someone using his computer – had logged on at seventeen minutes past midnight. Given the fact that the site remained live for sixteen hours, Coughlin had run up a bill of nearly fifteen hundred pounds.

The laughter this time was louder. For fifteen hundred quid, a porn site owed you something truly special.

Willard took the briefing back to Coughlin. He'd put a two-man interview team into Gosport prison. They'd spent the afternoon talking to Coughlin's colleagues and an interesting story was beginning to emerge. Willard glanced towards Dave Michaels.

'Yeah.' Michaels took his time. 'Seems the guy was an arsehole. Bev?'

Bev Yates had been one of the interview team. He'd just returned from Gosport and briefly he paraphrased the findings from half a dozen interviews. POs on the same wing as Coughlin were naturally wary of speaking out of turn, but the agreed consensus on the dead man was clear enough. The bloke was a loner, no friends, no drinking buddies, and precious little small talk. On shift, he kept himself to himself, never overtly aggressive, nothing like that, but not the kind of bloke you'd want to pass the time of day with. Nothing seemed to excite him. Not football. Not women. Not DIY. Not even car boot sales. Ask Coughlin the time and you were lucky to get a reply. Ask him for a loan of his *Sun* and he'd tell you to buy your own copy.

'Why does that make him an arsehole?'

Yates looked up from his notes. Willard's was a fair question.

'It doesn't, sir. But one of the blokes I talked to took it a bit further. This guy's off on a transfer to another nick next week so maybe he doesn't mind having a pop.'

'What did he say?'

'He said that Coughlin had a terrible reputation amongst the prisoners.'

'What for?'

'Bullying.'

'And nothing got reported?'

'Apparently not. He seems to have chosen his targets. He knew the weaker ones would keep their mouths shut and he'd take it out on them. But he'd try it on with others too, nothing physical, but little games, wind-ups, you know the way it is inside.'

'You checked this out with the governor?'

'He was away this afternoon.'

Willard nodded, scribbling himself a note, aware of a stir of movement amongst the DCs blocking the open doorway to the corridor. Then the bodies parted and a tall figure in a well-cut suit slipped in. He was young, mid-twenties, with neatly cropped hair, steady eyes and the kind of all-over leanness that suggested regular workouts. Spot him in a magazine, and you'd have said footballer or dotcom entrepreneur. Either way, he wasn't averse to attention.

He nodded at Willard and apologised for the late entrance. Flat London vowels, and a voice pitched slightly higher than you'd expect. Willard, who clearly hadn't a clue who he was, demanded a name.

'DC Corbett, sir. Working with DC Yates.'

'We've been going twenty minutes, Corbett. Where the fuck were you?'

'On the phone, sir. To the nick.'

'That's not an answer. That's an excuse. On this squad, briefings mean just that. You drop what you're doing and turn up. End of story. You understand that?'

'Yes, sir. I apologise.'

Faraday was watching Bev Yates. It had been Faraday's decision to pair them up and send them into Gosport prison, and just now Bev seemed as curious as everyone else to find out what kind of phone conversation could possibly have kept Corbett out of the squad briefing.

'Well?' Willard, too, wanted to know.

Corbett had found himself the corner of a desk by the window. Silhouetted against the light, it was difficult to read his expression. As he produced a pocketbook from an inside pocket and began to flick through, Faraday had the feeling that he was watching some kind of performance. The self-possession, the sheer nerve, was too measured to be spontaneous.

'His name's Ainsley Davidson, sir,' he said at last. 'I've

been going through the list of recently released prisoners, and he's the one who definitely fits the bill.'

'What bill?'

'The job, sir. Coughlin . . .'

For the first time, an edge of uncertainty crept into Corbett's voice. He'd just produced a rabbit from the hat. Where was the applause?

'And?'

'Davidson was one of the guys who'd been getting a hard time from Coughlin. There's a lot of stuff about his conviction. Basically, he never held his hands up to being guilty and Coughlin wound him up. It's a long story. I'm not sure this is the time and place . . .' He tailed off, folding the pocketbook and returning it to his jacket.

It was Dave Michaels who broke the ensuing silence. As Receiver, he took first bite at all incoming information.

'You're going to let me have that?'

'Of course, skip.'

'See me afterwards, yeah?'

The briefing broke up within minutes, stalling on the hard shoulder after a blow-out in the fast lane. Corbett's showboating would doubtless earn him closed-door bollockings from both Willard and Michaels, but the fact remained that Coughlin's prison was an obvious place to find a prime suspect. Whether or not Ainsley Davidson was the name to put in the frame was anybody's guess but for the time being it was Willard's priority to establish a time-line for Coughlin's final hours. He wanted to know where the guy had been, who he'd met, who might have clocked him. A receipt retrieved from the premises already indicated a fifty-pound withdrawal from an ATM at 18.46 on Monday evening, and Coughlin appeared to have spent most of it by the time he met his death. Pubs were an obvious place to start. The city's web of CCTV cameras was another. Willard added the usual health warnings – explore every option, keep an open mind, work like bastards, and always but always think *court* – while afterwards it fell to Faraday to take care of the routine bits of housekeeping.

Only at the end, amongst the closing rustle of papers, did Willard add a final footnote to the briefing. He was off tomorrow on a five-day course up at Centrex. The course had been booked for the best part of a year and he was buggered if he was going to miss out on it. Naturally, he'd be available on the end of a mobile, but he was lodging the Policy Book with DI Faraday, and he had every confidence that the DSIO would drive the investigation forward. With luck, *Merriott* would be sorted by the time he got back. Otherwise, they'd doubtless get to know each other a great deal better.

He glanced across at Faraday.

'OK, Joe?'

A couple of miles away at Highland Road police station, Cathy Lamb was doing her best to make sense of the quarterly overtime allocations when Winter appeared at her open door.

Promotion to DI on division had earned Lamb a first-floor office of her own, accommodation entirely in keeping with the rest of the building. The police station had once been the headquarters of the pre-war bus company, an organisation keen to establish a certain architectural tone, and the oak panelling and lead-light window above Cathy's ample desk had survived acquisition of the premises by Hampshire Constabulary. Indeed, with its heavy oak staircase and imposing boardroom, Highland Road had become one of the county's showpiece stations, living proof that state-of-the-art policing could march hand-in-hand with delicate and painstaking conservation.

Winter wanted to talk about the Somerstown kids.

'We're never going to sort them this way.' He settled

into the armchair Cathy kept for important visitors. 'We're wasting our time.'

In her heart Lamb felt the same, but the last thing you did with Winter was agree with him.

'You found yourself an OP, then?'

'Couldn't have been better placed. But they never showed, did they?'

Lamb, irritated by the ease with which Winter had put her on the back foot, refused to take the bait. Analysis by one of the field DCs in the Crime Incident Management Unit had indicated a definite pattern to the shop blags. Tuesdays and Thursdays, early afternoon, were favourite. Last month or so, you could practically set your watch by them, just one of the reasons Asian shopkeepers were threatening to take things into their own hands. The latter threat, all too credible, had sent Hartigan scurrying for cover. Racial incidents figured importantly in the Home Office performance tables and Asian heavies laying into local white kids could spark all kinds of trouble. The last thing the newly promoted Chief Supt wanted on his precious CV was any kind of race riot.

'You don't get lucky every time,' Lamb insisted. 'You know that.'

'So we do it again? And again? Just tuck ourselves up and wait? How much budget are we talking here?' Winter's derisive gesture took in the spreadsheet on the desktop PC. 'You're telling me there's money to burn?'

Lamb fought the urge to turn the computer off. Lately, she'd noticed a change in Winter. For a while, after he'd lost his wife, he'd beaten a tactical retreat, spending far too much time trying to maintain Joannie's precious garden, but the Bradley Finch job had rekindled the old spirit, revived the old trademark deviousness, and lately he'd taken to playing the elder statesman. With five years to serve, the guarantee of a decent pension and absolutely no prospect of promotion, he could afford to offer a suggestion or two. Like now.

'Suppose you let me talk to a couple of people . . .' he began.

Lamb shook her head.

'Suppose we ask ourselves about this afternoon. Just whose house was this?'

'The OP? A woman called Doris Ackerman. Used to be married to an ex-stoker before he fell under a bus. Nice as you like.'

'And you took her through the paperwork?'

'Of course.'

'So she knew what you were up to?'

'She knew we were in her front room with a camera.'

'Pointing at Patel's?'

'Of course.'

'So who did she phone?'

'No one.'

'How do you know?'

'Because the phone was in the hall and I pulled the jack out.'

'Mobile?'

'She wouldn't know the meaning of the word. She's eighty-seven.'

Cathy gazed at him for a moment. It didn't really matter whether it was true or not about the phone. The only point of pursuing the argument any further was to test Winter's footwork. Could he still match you move for move? Anticipate the traps? Box you in with his case-hardened experience and cheerful contempt for procedure? The answer, she knew, was yes. Banging on about Doris Ackerman would get them nowhere.

'So what's the big idea?'

She waited for Winter's slow smile. It didn't happen. Perhaps, she thought, he's started taking recently-promoted female DIs seriously.

'There's a guy I know runs charlie and smack for Bazza Mackenzie. He's not near the top of the food chain. He's

35

not even halfway up. But he shifts a lot of gear and he's extremely pissed off.'

Lamb reached for a notepad. Bazza Mackenzie had the local Class A drugs market by the throat. Put in a call for cocaine, or heroin, and it was ninety-five per cent certain you'd be buying from him. Not directly. Nothing as silly as that. But the cash you swopped for doing your head in would, one way or another, almost certainly end up in one of Bazza's many bank accounts.

'Go on.'

'I'm due a meet with this guy. He's talking next week but he can be ever so flexible if he tries.'

'You thinking earlier?'

'I'm thinking tonight.'

'And?'

'We have a chat.'

'But why? What's he got to do with kids wrecking corner shops?'

'I dunno but there's a name he keeps using, crops up all over. This kid's fifteen, Cath. And Tuesday lunchtimes, I bet he doesn't go to school.'

Bev Yates and Andy Corbett sat in Faraday's office in the Major Crimes suite. After a punishing fifteen-minute wrangle with Willard, who was less than happy about having his briefing hijacked by some upstart DC, Faraday was in no mood for more showboating. He wanted to know the real strength on Ainsley Davidson. Not hearsay. Not speculation. Strictly the facts.

'Sure, sir.'

Corbett laid it out, date perfect, pausing at every bend in the road in case Faraday couldn't keep up. Bev Yates, a mere spectator, couldn't believe his ears. Maybe this was what they taught you in the Met. Maybe this kind of arrogance came with the turf.

Corbett had just spent another fifteen minutes on the phone.

'Number one, Davidson's a known South London criminal. As a kid, he did a couple of spells in YOIs for robbery, street crime mainly, wallets, handbags, stuff like that. Later he took to TWOCing. According to the screw I've been talking to, he was happy to admit it. Loved motors, loved everything about them, couldn't keep his hands off anything with wheels. He'd steal for the fun of it, for the drive afterwards. Then he got himself in deeper shit.'

'Like what?'

'GBH with intent. By this time, he's twenty-one. His local manor's Balham. He's running around with some serious criminals. Then he makes his big mistake. He nicks an Astra. That's uncontested. He admitted it in court. White M reg from a car park in Wandsworth. Couple of days later, Balham High Road, that same Astra knocks over a woman pushing a pram across the road. The Astra doesn't stop and the woman dies later in hospital.'

'That was down to Davidson?'

'You got it. The car is recovered the following week. Davidson's prints are all over it, he's got a dodgy alibi, plus a witness to the incident IDs him on a parade.'

'So he admitted the GBH?'

'No way. Not then. Not in court. And not afterwards. A hundred per cent not guilty, m'lord.'

'What about the prints?'

'Obviously his. He admits he nicked the Astra in the first place but he insists he never touched the car that day. Never knocked the woman down. Never killed her. Not just innocent, but bitter and extremely twisted.'

'And he went down?'

'Sweet as you like. Trial lasted less than a fortnight.' Corbett paused, glancing sideways at Yates. 'Seven years, six of them in Gosport. Most of the time on Coughlin's wing.'

'And?'

'The screw's saying it was party-time for Coughlin. Guy had a ball. Nothing physical. Apparently Davidson's a tough little bugger. But everything else, every little wind-up you can imagine, access to lawyers, access to computers, stamps for his little envelopes, lots of conversations about food outside the cell when Davidson went on hunger strike, whatever he could dream up to make life a misery. Davidson never stopped trying to prove his innocence. Coughlin did his best to make sure he never could.'

'How come this screw's so forthcoming?'

'Because he hated Coughlin. Like they all did.'

'Hate's a big word.' Faraday reached for a pencil. 'Bev?'

Yates stirred. His face was pouched with exhaustion.

'He wasn't flavour of the month,' Yates agreed. 'I'm not sure about hate, though.'

Faraday nodded, then pushed his chair back from the desk and stared out of the window. Beyond a thousand rooftops, the swell of Portsdown Hill. Finally he turned back to Corbett.

'And your suggestion is?'

There was a longish silence, then Corbett cleared his throat. He sounded pleased with himself, the voice of a man who'd just spared the rest of the squad a great deal of work.

'Davidson was released a couple of weeks ago.' He shrugged. 'Maybe he had a debt to settle.'

Two hours later, nearly dark, Faraday was still at his desk. He'd been long enough with Major Crimes to know that the first two days were the most important, not simply because the majority of cases were solved within forty-eight hours but because of the sheer volume of work that went into bump-starting the investigative machine. Lately, he'd taken to keeping a checklist of must-do reminders in his wallet – everything from elimination strategies and lab submission protocols to poster circulation and funding codes – because rule one on homicide investigations was brutally clear: a single missed detail, a single slip on the rock-face, and you were looking at disaster.

Faraday knew of SIOs and their deputies who'd let their concentration wander in the early stages of an inquiry only to realise – months later in court – that they'd surrendered the verdict to the defence team with the body still warm. Pressure like that, he supposed, was the charm of the job. Major inquiries put you to the ultimate investigative test, chucking up lead after lead, thousands of words on hundreds of forms, daring you to flag a pathway forward, daring you to eliminate a line of enquiry that just might – despite every indication to the contrary – be productive.

What to make of Andy Corbett's little hunch? In truth, Faraday didn't know. The DC was new to Portsmouth. A couple of months on the CID strength at Kingston Crescent hardly qualified him for in-depth local knowledge, yet that wasn't the point. What they were dealing with here, what they always dealt with, were the fathomless mysteries of human interaction. What made one man take against another? What turned impatience, or irritation, or anger into hatred? And what kind of special demons possessed a man to batter someone else to death?

On the face of it, Ainsley Davidson was a strong lead and Faraday would be crazy not to pursue it. Prison was a pressure cooker and if Davidson's belief in his innocence was genuine, then he'd have been putty in the hands of someone like Coughlin. There were individuals on this earth – mainly men – who got their kicks from situations they could control. Prison was an obvious example. Marriage, oddly enough, was another. Bang someone up, make them deeply unhappy, and your pleasures were there for the taking.

But was that sufficient motivation to justify murder? Would you really spend seven miserable years in a six by ten cell and then risk the same nightmare all over again? Faraday rather doubted it, but knew that his own instincts were irrelevant. He'd come across men who'd killed on far less provocation than this. Indeed, the longer he did the job the more mundane the act of murder became. In books and movies, homicide still attracted an aura, an unsettling glamour, an apartness that spoke of something deeply special. In real life, it wasn't like that at all. You lost your rag. You pulled the trigger or raised a fist or reached for the kitchen knife. And that – all too finally – was that.

The Policy Book lay on his desk. This held the record of every decision the SIO made, hour after hour, as the inquiry developed. In days and maybe months to come it would be invaluable as a retrospective source, charting and justifying every tiny investigative shift, and bosses like Willard understood its value. In complex inquiries it was impossible not to make mistakes but this painstaking process of adding a rationale for every decision provided a comforting degree of protection. The Policy Book was the body armour that lay between the SIO and the small army of career assassins who lay in wait down the investigative road. Take care of the Policy Book, and the Policy Book would take care of you.

Faraday uncapped his pen and began to write. He'd authorised Corbett and Yates to drive to London first thing and interview Ainsley Davidson. Corbett had his mother's address from the prison file and an assurance from one of the screws that he'd probably be there. The address was in Balham, well known to Corbett from his previous life in the Met. Three years in the Streatham CID office, he'd assured Faraday, had taught him everything he needed to know about South London criminals.

There was something in Corbett's manner that

sounded an alarm with Faraday. It wasn't simply the arrogance of the man, and his obvious impatience to get a result. Confidence and an appetite for hard work were prized qualities in young detectives. No, it was something else, and Faraday knew that Bev Yates had sensed it too. Yates was far too canny and experienced to discuss these thoughts with Faraday but there'd been a moment in the office after Corbett had gone when they'd looked at each other, and raised an eyebrow.

'Talks a good war, doesn't he?' Yates had muttered, reaching for his jacket.

Three

The Pembroke lay in Old Portsmouth, just round the corner from the Anglican cathedral. Recently, it had become a favourite pub of Winter's. He liked the clientele – an unusual mix of traders, lawyers, churchmen and retired navy matelots – and he enjoyed the beery cheerfulness that came with them. This was a pub for serious drinkers, free from trash music and fourteen-year-old slappers out of their heads on Vodka Ice. Most evenings you could tuck yourself away in a quiet corner and never attract a second glance.

Rooke was waiting for him, sitting bolt upright on a padded bench beneath a tankful of tropical fish. Winter had never quite got over the look of the man – bony face, yellowing skin, wild eyes, scary haircut – but put the damage down to an unusually heavy dose of inbreeding. Rooke was a terrible warning for anyone who spent too much time in Pompey. Stay a generation too long, and you'd end up looking like this.

Winter ordered two Stellas at the bar. Rooke's glass was already empty.

'Awright, Rookie?' Winter slid on to the bench and gave him a nudge. Lager from the glasses slopped on to the table.

'Listen.' Rooke beckoned Winter closer. 'You want to know about the boy Geech, I've got be fucking careful.'

Winter grinned at him. Most of his touts enjoyed the foreplay when they met, the preliminary gossip about mutual associates, the chance to slag the local football team, but not Rooke. Rookie kept the conversational frills to an absolute minimum, partly because he had no small talk and partly because being with Winter made him very nervous indeed. He was here to make a point or two. And then he'd go.

'You know what he looks like, this Darren?'

Winter nodded. He'd seen Darren Geech on countless occasions, mainly around Somerstown. The boy had always been a problem – thin, pasty-faced, vicious – and watching someone like that grow up offered new insights into the crime statistics.

'So what's he up to now, young Darren?'

'Every fucking thing. You want my opinion, it's all down to his brother, Billy. Billy is a couple of years older than Darren and he's been at it for ever. The latest thing is computer games. Billy got a re-writer off of a market geezer and he burns game CDs by the fucking thousand and flogs them round the estates, twenty quid apiece. Only problem is, he ain't got no inserts for the boxes. Don't stop Billy, though. He just goes to that games shop down Commercial Road with his mates and lifts them empty boxes off the shelf. Mob-handed, no one stops them. But then you wouldn't, would you?'

Rooke had a point. Even CCTV didn't seem to deter the likes of Billy Geech. Face a situation like that across the counter, and the loss of a couple of dozen empty CD boxes would seem a small price to pay for staying intact.

'You're telling me Darren learned the trade off his brother?'

'Doing them corner shops? Definitely. Pull a stroke like that once, the rest comes easy. You'd be amazed what a load of blokes can get away with.'

'Fifteen-year-olds?'

'They're the worst. They just don't care. They do it for the laugh more than anything else. It's pathetic really. Totally disorganised.'

Winter smiled, then reached for his glass. Rookie might have been talking about maths or French. The fact that Darren Geech didn't concentrate hard enough really pissed him off.

'Fuck all profit, then?'

'That's right.' Rooke frowned. 'What's the point in nicking crisps and biscuits? Just makes you fat.'

'What about booze?'

'Goes straight down their throats. These kids are off the fucking planet most of the time.'

'OK.' Winter leaned forward. 'So what does all this tell me about Darren Geech?'

For the first time, Rooke ground to a halt. He had the strangest eyes, almost jet black, and Winter – sensing his reluctance to go much further – decided to give him a prod. In these situations, it often paid to bluff your way to the truth.

'He's muscling in, isn't he, young Darren? He wants a slice of that nice pie of yours.'

'What makes you think that?'

'Because otherwise you wouldn't be here. Geech knows what you're up to. He's watched you for months, years. He knows who you flog the stuff to, how much it's worth, and he's worked out a way of cutting you out. Maybe he's into special offers. And maybe he knows more people than you.'

'No chance.'

'More young people? More fifteen-year-olds? Fourteen-year-olds? Kids still in primary school? You'd have a problem with them, Rookie. No offence, mate, but the paedo register was made for people like you. Just imagine. It's bad enough having your kids skagging up at night. Think what it would be like if their mums sussed they were renting their arses out as well. Doesn't matter if it's true or not, does it? It's a hard world, mate. Just the thought's enough. Plus a word or two from the likes of Darren.'

Winter beamed up at the girl behind the bar. Time for

another pint. By the time he got back, Rooke was looking madder than ever.

'That's crap,' he said. 'I'm no paedo.'

'I never said you were. I'm just wondering what other people might think.'

'Well fuck knows why. You're talking bollocks. Where does all this paedo drivel come from?'

'Doesn't matter, my friend. Just let me tell you about Bazza.'

Just the name was enough. Rooke tried to struggle to his feet. Winter laughed, then pulled him back.

'Listen,' he said. 'Bazza's a businessman, right? Businessmen look for bigger and bigger markets and just now you're way off the fucking pace. Especially when young Darren's whispering in his ear.'

'Darren's a kid. Bazza doesn't deal through kids.'

'What makes you think that? Bazza would deal through babies if there was money in it.'

'That's bollocks, too. You don't know the bloke.'

'No?' Winter extended a hand. 'Twenty quid says Darren Geech is trying to deal off Bazza. Another twenty says Bazza's definitely interested. And a tenner on top says you're trying to stop him. That's fifty. Shake on it?'

Rooke ignored the proffered hand. He'd come to mark Winter's card about Darren Geech. That was what they'd agreed and in his view the evening had come to an end. Time to go, pal. Bet or no bet.

'But you've told me fuck all,' Winter protested.

'I've told you he's doing them corner shops. And I've told you he's the little cunt that organises it all.'

'I knew that already. I even know his address. Just like you do.'

'What's that supposed to mean?'

'Nothing, my friend. Except his mother's been scoring off you for years. Is it cash in hand? Or some other arrangement? I know she's a dog, Shelley Geech, but better than nothing, eh?'

45

This time Rooke was serious about leaving. Only Winter's iron grasp kept him seated. He leaned towards Rooke's ear, two old friends sharing a mutual confidence.

'I'm going to turn over young Darren's place tomorrow,' Winter murmured. 'And I need to know where to look. Charlie would be good. Or even smack.'

There was a long silence. Slowly, Winter released his grip. Over in the far corner of the bar, a punch line raised a laugh. Rooke glanced at Winter, then looked quickly away.

'There's a wardrobe in his bedroom.' He swallowed hard. 'That's all you're getting off of me.'

Faraday was exhausted by the time he got home. His precious day off had disappeared under a mountain of paperwork and even now, close to midnight, he wasn't certain he'd planted a tick in every box. Slowing at the end of the harbourside cul-de-sac that led to the Bargemaster's House, the Mondeo's headlights settled on a four-wheel-drive parked outside. Faraday frowned. Did he know anyone who drove a battered Suzuki Vitara?

The lights were still on in the house downstairs, and letting himself in Faraday heard a bark of laughter coming from the living room. He shut the front door. There was a day sack on the table in the hall and a pair of car keys beside it. He looked up to find himself looking at a woman. She was tall and freckled with a mop of curly blonde hair. She was wearing a pink T-shirt with a map of Antigua on the front and a pair of salt-bleached jeans. Barefoot on the carpet, she stepped forward and grinned.

'Hi,' she said. 'You must be Joe's dad.'

For a moment, the name threw Faraday. Joe, he thought. Joe-Junior. My son.

'That's right.' He shook the offered hand. 'And you are . . . ?'

'Eadie. Eadie Sykes.'

The accent was unmistakable, broad Australian, and at

last Faraday made the connection. Eadie Sykes was the video producer who had commissioned J-J over the weekend. She was making a documentary film to celebrate the Little Ships, the armada of tiny craft which had gathered to mark the sixty-second anniversary of the Dunkirk evacuation, and the photos he'd been summoned to see this morning were to accompany the advance publicity.

Faraday found J-J in the living room. The black and white prints were now spread in a wide semi-circle on the carpet around the sofa, and for a split second Faraday saw Coughlin's body again, garnished with photos of a different sort.

J-J was hanging off the sofa. There were three empty cans of Kronenbourg on the table beside him. Faraday wanted to ask him about London, about meeting Janna's friend, but J-J had other ideas.

'She likes them,' he signed up at Faraday, then nodded at the prints on the floor.

Eadie caught the raised thumb.

'They're great,' she said at once. 'Your boy's done well. Exactly what I was after.'

'For God's sake don't tell him.'

'How can I?'

'Good point.'

Faraday stepped into the kitchen. J-J had obviously been cooking because the place reeked of bacon and burned toast. There were two plates in the sink, both smeared with ketchup. Faraday poured himself a large Scotch and returned to the living room.

'J-J cook for you?'

'Yep.'

'You're insured?'

'All risks. Two billion bucks.' The laugh again. 'Your boy says you're a cop.'

'It's true.'

'What kind of cop?'

'A knackered cop.' Faraday glanced at his watch. 'Twelve hours straight. Not bad for a day off, eh?'

'Try showbiz.' Eadie knelt quickly and retrieved a print from the carpet. 'Look at this one. Neat, huh?'

Faraday glanced at the photo. J-J had met the fleet way out off the Isle of Wight, the first time he'd ever been in a speedboat, and he must have transferred on to one of the incoming craft. The shot was taken from midships, and showed the skipper at the wheel with the swell of the open sea behind. The skipper's face was made for a photo like this, his watery eyes narrowed against the morning sun, and Faraday wondered what those same eyes would have seen, six decades earlier. He'd never quite fathomed the national passion for celebrating military defeats.

Eadie was pointing out the bits of the photo she especially loved. She had big-knuckled hands, almost male, and when she looked up at Faraday he noticed how much damage the sun had done to her face. She looked early forties, Faraday guessed. Maybe older.

'You make lots of films like this?'

'Not really. This is for TV. Most of the stuff I do is industrial. Companies mainly, training films, product launches, you name it. TV's sexy but they never have any money. The other stuff sucks but they always pay on time. So I guess you get to have a choice. Groceries or glory.' She put the photo to one side. 'This one's been fun.'

'It's finished?'

'Rough cut. You want to see it? No problem.'

For a moment Faraday thought she was going to produce a cassette and slip it into the video player and his heart sank at the thought of another hour or so trying to stay half awake, but then she mentioned some kind of office she had in the city. Couple of rooms in Hampshire Terrace. Come up any time.

'Thanks.'

'I mean it.'

J-J rolled off the sofa and made for the stairs. It took more than three cans to get him into this kind of state.

Faraday turned back to Eadie Sykes.

'You've been here long? I'm not checking, I promise.'

'Couple of hours. Your son's done me proud.'

'And himself, too.' Faraday looked down at his own drink. 'How do you get through to him, as a matter of interest?'

'I point a lot. But then I do that in real life, as well. Film directors have to stay on top, comes with the turf.' The grin again. 'Sounds sexy, doesn't it? But then you'd have the same problem, being a homicide cop.'

'You think being a cop's sexy?'

'I know it is.'

'How?'

'By looking.'

For a moment, Faraday thought he'd misunderstood her. Then the amusement on her face told him otherwise.

'You should learn to take a compliment,' she said. 'It's really easy once you get the hang of it.'

J-J returned shortly afterwards. Faraday could tell from the splashes across his T-shirt that he'd put his head under the tap. Kneeling on the carpet, he began to collect the prints and slide them into an envelope. Eadie touched him on the arm with her foot, a curiously intimate gesture, and when he glanced up she tapped her watch and then put her hands together and cushioned her head against them. Bedtime.

Watching, Faraday offered to act as translator.

'No need.' J-J had given her the envelope. 'Like I said, we make out just fine.'

J-J was on his feet again. Less awkwardly than Faraday expected, he gave her a little kiss and escorted her across the room. At the door to the hall, she paused and looked back at Faraday.

'See you for the rough cut.' She grinned at him. 'Beer's on me next time.'

Faraday was in the kitchen by the time J-J returned from the front door. Faraday nodded at the debris in the sink and volunteered to wipe. He wanted to know about London, about the Ansel prints, and most of all about the American woman who bridged the years back to Janna and J-J's birth.

J-J set to with the squeegee and a tiny square of scourer. He was the world's worst washer-up and trying to sign at the same time didn't help. The Ansel stuff, he thought, had been fantastic. Huge unpeopled landscapes. Mountains to die for. And an amazing shot of the moon rising over a township somewhere way down south. The way Ansel had framed these photos looked so, so simple but the woman, whose name was Patti, had explained about the sheer weight of equipment Ansel had hauled around, and J-J had come away half ashamed of the dinky little camera he carried today.

'You could talk to her OK?'

'There was someone there who signed. She'd set it up. It wasn't a problem.'

'And what was she like?'

'Pretty. And nice, too.'

'She talk about mum at all?'

'She had some photos.'

'*Photos?*' Faraday gazed at him. 'You brought them back?'

'Yeah. I'll show you.'

Faraday fought a rising excitement, edged with something darker. He had his own stash of photos, a carefully taped package he hadn't opened for years. Everything was in there, every last shred of photographic evidence. He and Janna had spent seventeen months together and many of the best moments had found their way on to film. Faraday wrestling with a dinghy on Puget Sound.

Janna in her high-school bikini stretched out on the lawn of a borrowed summerhouse. The pair of them snapped by a friend at Christmas, bodies entwined, gloriously drunk. Photos like these had become stepping stones across the most important period of his life, a route he knew he could trust. Now came the prospect of a fresh perspective.

J-J dried his hands and disappeared into the living room. When he came back, he was carrying a Jiffy bag. He emptied the contents on to the kitchen table and Faraday found himself looking at the woman he'd never stopped loving.

Young. She looked so young.

He picked up the nearest of the photos. The colour had faded a little over the years but there was no mistaking the firm set of the jaw line, the mischief in the eyes, the way her mouth curled up when she smiled.

He'd first met her in a bookshop in Seattle, the corner on the upstairs floor where they kept the biographies. She'd been looking for something on Tennyson. He'd babbled on about the Isle of Wight. His mum and dad lived a mile down the road from Tennyson's house. Winter weekends he'd walk the three miles out across Tennyson Down to the Needles. The name Tennyson had freighted his adolescence, and here he was, years later, desperately trying to turn all those heavy memories into a conversation.

'You ever read the poetry?'

He'd confessed he hadn't. Poetry had always been difficult, remote stuff. He'd tried hard at school but it had never happened for him.

'No need to apologise.' She'd smiled. 'No need at all.'

They'd gone for coffee to a place across the street. Two weeks later they were living together, her place. She'd read him 'Maud' in the thin, grey light of dawn. He cared nothing for the poetry, just the sound of her voice.

For sullen-seeming Death may give
More life to Love than is or ever was
In our low world, where yet 'tis sweet to live.
Let no one ask me how it came to pass;
It seems that I am happy . . .

He picked up another photograph, Janna snapped on a hiking holiday, and the face of the girl Patti came back to him. She and Janna had been friends at college. She lived down in Oregon, and she'd taken the Greyhound north one weekend, camping on the floor of Janna's tiny apartment. Janna had been pregnant by then with J-J, and the two girls had spent most of the Saturday tramping round the bargain stores, looking for cheap baby clothes. They'd brought back armfuls of trophies to the flat, piling them on the tiny table where they ate, and that night Faraday remembered buying a gallon flask of Californian red. It was the first time the idea of a baby had felt remotely real to him and they'd celebrated for half the night.

J-J pushed another photograph towards him. Janna again, face and shoulders, sitting in a window. Faraday had taken it himself, listening carefully while she talked him through the essentials – F stop, film speed, framing – and he remembered how pleased he'd been with the results. He'd shot a whole roll of them, and this one must have found its way to Patti. He gazed down at Janna's face. In less than a month, they were due to ship out to England. There, on the Isle of Wight, they'd find a place for the three of them. J-J was due in July. Four months later, she was dead.

Faraday looked up, and swallowed hard. J-J was staring at him, his face a blur. He reached for the kitchen roll and tore off a sheet, holding it out. Faraday shook his head, turning hopelessly away.

It took a while for Dawn Ellis to get to the door. Winter

heard her footsteps down the stairs, then the pause as she tried to work out who it might be. Under the circumstances, a midnight knock on the door was the last thing she needed.

'It's me. Paul.'

There was a rattle as Dawn slipped the chain on the door. Then the door swung open and she was standing there in a pair of outsize pyjamas. She suppressed an involuntary shiver at the coolness of the night air. She didn't invite him in.

'Something happened? Something wrong?'

Winter shook his head. The last two pints had been a mistake but he was determined to say his piece.

'Nothing, love, and I'm sorry to get you up.'

She looked at him, bewildered.

'What is it then?'

'Just a little . . . I dunno . . .'

She disappeared a moment, muttering an apology. Winter watched a cat stalking through the shadows. Nice night, he thought. Nice girl. Back again, Dawn had found a dressing gown. She held the door open, asking him in. Winter shook his head.

'What is it then?'

She knew he'd been drinking by now. He could tell by the expression on her face. He beckoned her closer. She didn't move.

'I just wanted to say you've got a friend,' he said slowly. 'It's important, that's all.'

'What friend?'

Winter stepped back a pace, looking up at the moon. 'Me,' he said.

Four

Bev Yates drove north, up the long green sweep of the Meon Valley. The second half was barely minutes old in Kobe, and Russia had just taken a one-nil lead. The commentator on Five Live was gloomy about Tunisia's chances of surviving the attentions of attackers like Igor Titov and Dimitri Sychev but Yates knew they were still in with a shout. Football was funny like that. The experts could stack the odds against you, computing the skills of multimillion-pound players, but on the day there was still room for the odd rogue factor. Like whether or not you really wanted to win.

He slowed for a milk tanker, grinding up the hill out of West Meon. Corbett had phoned him last night. The call had been brief. He was in town, and planned to stay overnight. He'd meet Yates up the road from Ainsley Davidson's mum's place in Balham, half nine. OK? Spared the prospect of sharing the journey to London, Yates had poured himself a celebratory Scotch, checked on Freya, and rolled into bed. Melanie, asleep beside him, had scarcely stirred. One of these days, he thought, it might be nice to get round to a conversation.

Jutland Road, Balham, was home for a cheerless terrace of red-brick houses, gazing sightlessly at each other over the potholed tarmac. Number twelve had been brightened with a lick of yellow paint, and there was a spray of pink carnations in the downstairs window.

Corbett's black Nissan 300-ZX was parked at the end of the street. Yates left his car round the corner and walked back. Corbett was still deep in his morning paper, scarcely bothering to glance up when Yates's shadow paused beside him. Yates stood at the kerbside, wondering about the choice of paper. Only girlies read the *Daily Mail*.

'Two nil,' Yates grunted, when Corbett finally emerged, 'Karpin played a blinder.'

'That right?'

They walked back along the street, avoiding the scabs of dog shit on the pavement. Corbett's bomber jacket looked new. Leather as soft as that, thought Yates, and you were talking serious money.

They stopped briefly outside number twelve. There was a newish-looking Renault Clio with a back wheel up on the kerb. Someone had run a key down the length of the car and one of the wing mirrors had taken a battering. Yates was looking at the house. The windows upstairs were still curtained and no one had taken in the freesheet at the front door.

Corbett had to knock three times before anything happened. Then came the flush of a lavatory deep inside the house and the sound of someone coughing. Seconds later, the front door opened.

'Ainsley Davidson?' Yates offered his warrant card.

Davidson was younger-looking and smaller than he'd imagined. He was wearing nothing but a pair of boxers and his bare toes curled upwards on the wooden floor. The boxers were a startling white against the brownness of his skin and it was more than obvious that he worked out.

He wasn't pleased to see them and refused to step aside when Corbett tried to push past.

'You guys ever ask nicely?'

Corbett gave him a look, then stepped back into the sunshine. When Davidson started on about a search warrant, he made it plain they were coming inside. Easy or hard, it made no difference.

Davidson shrugged, then stooped to retrieve the morning post. He couldn't be arsed to argue. Yates followed him down the narrow hall. The kitchen at the back of the house was bigger than he'd expected, with a conservatory extension into a tiny garden. Whatever else she might have done with her life, Mrs Davidson knew a thing or two about keeping a house together.

Davidson filled a kettle and plugged it in. Corbett was already scanning the contents of a corkboard on the wall.

'Anyone else here?'

'Yeah.'

'Who?'

'Friend.'

'Like who?'

'Listen.' Davidson turned his back on Corbett and looked at Yates. 'What the fuck is this? You guys walk in off the street, no warrant, no explanation, not even the fucking time of day. You don't think I have rights here? You think I'm that stupid?'

Yates smiled at him, then opened the fridge door. Three flavours of yoghurt and an opened pack of bacon. He bent for the carton of milk on the bottom shelf and handed it over.

'Up for the Irish game, are we?'

Willard's first call came in at quarter to ten. He'd made it to Wyboston Lakes and was about to go into the opening kidnap session, a presentation by a negotiator from Control Risks, but first he wanted an update on overnight developments on *Merriott*. What was happening with the house-to-house calls? Who'd made a start on the CCTV? How were the Scenes of Crime boys getting on? What kind of cooperation was he getting from the media?

Faraday shut the office door with his foot and returned to his desk, dealing with the fusillade of questions one by one. The good news was that HOLMES was up and

56

running. The indexers had finished with the first pile of Personal Description Forms from yesterday's house-to-house, and were now waiting for more PDFs. The Outside Enquiries DS had laid hands on a mug shot of Coughlin and organised half a dozen DCs to start on the likeliest city pubs. The machine Coughlin had used to withdraw cash was down in Southsea, and the guys were working outwards from the ATM.

'What about the computer?'

'It's over in Netley. They started work on it last night. They—'

Faraday broke off, listening to Willard speculating on the likely importance of what they might find. First off, the guys had to clone Coughlin's hard drive, a process that could take eight hours.

'My money's on chat rooms,' Willard concluded. 'The guy's a perve. I bet he talked dirty to half the world. What about the PM?'

'Jerry Proctor's due any moment. We've got a management meet at ten.'

'Scenes of Crime?'

'Jerry's got the details.'

'Good. Keep me briefed, will you?' There was a pause on the line, and a snatch of conversation. Then Willard was back again, one last question. 'Davidson?'

At Yates's suggestion, they talked in the conservatory. Davidson had put on a pair of tracksuit bottoms and a sweatshirt from a Brixton gym. Curled in a wicker chair, nursing his third cup of coffee, he went over his movements all over again.

'You're asking me whether I was in Pompey Monday night, yeah? No question. You're asking me who I was with. I've told you. You want to know what we were up to. I've even told you fucking that. And now you're telling me I went round to that cunt's house and gave him a kicking.'

'He's dead,' Corbett pointed out, 'and you don't seem too bothered.'

'Bothered? *Bothered?* I'm fucking over the moon. I am so fucking grade A *pleased* about it I might even go along to the funeral. Just to make sure it's true.' He paused, eyeballing Corbett. 'You got any photos? Video? All that stuff your guys shoot? Only I'll have the full set. Save it up for Christmas. Give myself a treat.' He shook his head, looking away, then launched off again. 'Lots of blood, was there? Bits of him all over the walls? Man I'm telling you, that Coughlin was evil. I haven't a clue what happened to him but he deserved it all. I hope he was conscious for every fucking second. I hope he rots in hell. Good fucking riddance.'

Yates did his best to mask a smile. Anger this righteous, this gleeful, sent a message of its own.

'You didn't like him?' he suggested mildly.

'And I wouldn't, would I? Don't you guys listen? Don't you have any idea what it's like? Banged up for something you never did? With an animal like that making it worse?'

He broke off, gazing down at his coffee, brooding. Already, in graphic detail, he'd tallied the ways Coughlin had made his life a misery. The incoming letters he intercepted. The rumours he spread. The derision he heaped on Davidson's endless protestations of innocence. His talent for making access to a lawyer, or even a phone card, so difficult that the temptation was to give up. Even Davidson's vegetarianism became a weapon in this ongoing war. Days when Coughlin was on the wing, Davidson would find half-chewed bits of meat nesting under his spaghetti.

Now, under Corbett's watchful gaze, he added to the charge sheet.

'There was a young guy, not too bright, not too clever. Coughlin frightened him shitless and that just made it worse. He'd be at him all the time, sneaky stuff, little digs. Guy had a girlfriend, used to come and see him sometimes on a visit. Nothing special, you know, but she meant the world to Gary. Anyway, Coughlin started up about the car she came in. Sports car. Bloke used to leave it in the visitors' car park. Big bloke. Black. Nice gear. Expensive. Showing her a good time. Coughlin would go on about this geezer, how tasty he was, and it drove Gary nuts. Some nights he bawled his eyes out and Coughlin would be on the landing outside his cell having a good laugh, cunt that he was.'

Yates stirred. Davidson could certainly hold your attention.

'And the black guy?'

'Didn't exist. I had my mum check it out after one of her visits. The girl went home on the bus.' He nodded. 'What kind of arsehole does that?'

Corbett, unimpressed, wanted to know more about Davidson's movements.

'I just told you.'

'I meant here. You've been out for three weeks nearly.'

'And?'

'What have you been up to?'

'Is that your business?'

'It might be.'

'Why?'

'Because I hear things, Ainsley. Things that tell me you're keeping company again.'

'*Again?*'

'Yeah, like last time.'

Yates glanced across at him. He was finding this line of questioning as bewildering as Davidson. Just what was he driving at?

Davidson shook his head, more pity than anger this time. He didn't like Corbett and he didn't bother to hide it.

'You got something to say, man, just say it. Otherwise, get the fuck out and leave me alone.'

'Let's talk about Portsmouth again. Monday night. You say you were with Marie.'

'Not say, man. Not say. I *was* with Marie. That's why I went down there in the first place. You think I'd spend a minute more than I had to in that shithole?'

'So why didn't she come up here?'

'Because she works for a living.'

'So what's she doing upstairs?'

'She's got a couple of days off.'

'Then why not wait for that?'

Even Yates admitted it was a fair question. Davidson thought otherwise.

'You ever been in love, man? Head-over-heels, knock-your-socks-off, let's-get-down-to-it love? Eh? Ever been there? Ever felt any of that shit?'

Corbett's eyes were stony. He asked the question again but Davidson brushed it aside. He'd first met Marie in Gosport nick. She taught remedial English. He'd volunteered for her classes and within weeks she'd got to parts of his brain that no teacher ever thought existed. He'd started writing stories, poems. He'd found out about foreign authors, French stuff mainly. He'd even wondered about tackling André Gide in the *original*. Did Corbett have any notion where an adventure like that might take you?

Corbett was unimpressed.

'You fancied her.'

'I fell in love with her.'

Corbett gazed at him, amused.

'Trophy fuck?'

'Wash your mouth out, man.'

'I meant you.' The smile widened. 'You're the trophy fuck.'

For a moment, Yates thought Davidson had lost it. The tiny muscles around his jaw tightened. His mouth became a thin, dark line in his face. Small or otherwise, you wouldn't want to be on the receiving end of whatever might happen next.

Corbett hadn't moved. He was back with Monday night. Davidson had got to Marie's place around half eight, nine. What happened next?

'We drank two bottles of wine.' Davidson was still seething.

'And then what?'

'We fucked on the sofa.'

'How long?'

'Hours, man. Longer than you'd ever dream about.'

'So when did you leave the house?'

'Next day. Yesterday.'

'And drove up here?'

'Yeah . . . taking our time, though. You familiar with that road at all, that A3? All them woods around Hindhead? Sweetest fuck imaginable. Just us and the skylarks.'

Yates turned away. Davidson was taking the piss now. Any more of this line of questioning and they'd be selling the film rights. There was a movement in the hall. Davidson's eyes went at once to the kitchen. A woman in her thirties was standing by the open door, staring down at them. She was tall and pale, with a fall of jet-black hair. The dressing gown probably belonged to Davidson because it barely reached her knees.

Barefoot, she stepped down into the conservatory. She was looking at Davidson.

'I heard voices. What's going on?'

'The Filth.' Davidson waved a hand. 'Never fucking know when to stop.'

Corbett had his warrant card out. He hadn't bothered to get up.

'Marie?'

'That's right.'

'What's your second name, love?'

Yates winced. She very obviously took exception to the

61

question, especially the way Corbett called her 'love'. This was a woman used to taking classes, used to standing up in front of rooms full of hardened criminals. She most definitely didn't respond to 'love'.

'My name's Elliott,' she said at last. 'Marie Elliott.'

'And you're with ... ?' Corbett nodded towards Davidson.

'His name's Ainsley.'

'Where were you on Monday night? Do you mind me asking?'

'Not at all. Ask away.'

'I just did.'

'OK.' She shrugged. 'I was at home in Portsmouth. Eastney, actually. Adair Road. Number 101.'

'Anyone with you?'

'Yes, Ainsley.' She didn't, for one second, take her eyes off Corbett.

'Between when and when?'

'Dunno.' She frowned, trying to remember. 'Mid-evening? Eight maybe? Then right through to next morning.'

'Anyone else in the house?'

'I live alone.'

'No one I can talk to, then?'

'No, except me. What is this?'

Corbett didn't answer. He was good at masking his emotions but Yates detected the merest hint of disappointment in his face. He'd expected, at the very least, the odd dropped stitch. Instead, this woman was the model of composure.

'We're investigating a suspicious death,' he said slowly. 'Someone you may well know.'

'Really? Who might that be?'

'Sean Coughlin.'

'*Coughlin?* From the prison?'

'That's right.'

'And you're telling me he's dead?' She looked at Davidson.

Davidson grinned back, raising a thumb.

'Yeah,' he said, 'and you know what? These guys think I kicked him to death. Can you believe that? Get myself hooked up with all this shit again?' He shook his head. 'Why would I ever do that?'

The first of the *Merriott* management meetings lasted nearly an hour. Faraday chaired it in Willard's office, seating his core team around the long conference table.

After Faraday's brief introduction, Jerry Proctor brought news from the post-mortem. Coughlin had received a number of heavy blows to his face, neck, upper body and groin area. There were no penetration wounds and the damage could equally have been inflicted by boots, fists, or some kind of weapon. Coughlin had three broken ribs and a ruptured spleen but the immediate cause of death, in the view of the Home Office pathologist, had been inhalation of vomit. At some undetermined point, he'd started to throw up and the stuff had been sucked back into his lungs, effectively suffocating him.

'This was after the beating?' Faraday wanted to know about the exact sequence of events.

'Almost definitely.'

'You think he might have been alone by then? Only there could be legal implications here.'

'Manslaughter?' Proctor shook his head. 'We're talking specific intent, aren't we? Whoever whacked him did so for a purpose. And the whacking led to his death. That says homicide to me.'

'But you're telling me he threw up because he got whacked?'

'Impossible to judge. The pathologist's talking lots of alcohol. Tox won't be back for a couple of days but there was an empty bottle of Johnnie Walker on the floor and his gut still stank of booze.'

'So what are we saying? He was pissed out of his head?

He got whacked? He threw up, swallowed it, and choked to death?'

'Something like that. But it's intent again. Without the whacking' . . . Proctor shrugged . . . 'who knows?'

'OK.' Faraday scribbled himself a note then paused, struck by another thought.

'Had he eaten at all? Earlier?'

'Kebab. There were bits of meat and shredded lettuce in the vomit.'

'Fresh? Recent?'

'Couple of hours. Maybe a bit longer.'

'Did he bring the take-out back with him?'

'I'd say not. We've been through the waste bin in the kitchen, and the dustbin outside, too.'

'What about the kebab houses, then?' Faraday addressed the question to a sturdy-looking figure down the far end of the table. Paul Ingham was the DS in charge of Outside Enquiries, a no-nonsense Yorkshireman highly rated by Willard. It was Ingham's job to turn queries like this into individual actions, tasking his two-man teams of DCs.

'This afternoon, boss. They've all got copies of the mug shot but most of these places don't get going until two.'

Faraday turned back to Proctor. 'Let's stay with Coughlin. Any signs of resistance? Did he put up a fight?'

'Seems not. Nothing under his fingernails, nothing we could DNA, and very little blood. That pissed, he'd have been helpless. Time of death was around one in the morning, maybe a tad later. It might all have been over in a couple of minutes. We just don't know.'

'Great.' Faraday looked at Dave Michaels. 'How are we doing with a time-line?'

Michaels consulted an A4 pad at his elbow. Coughlin had definitely made a cash withdrawal in the early evening. The ATM receipt in the pocket of his trousers put him in Southsea's Osborne Road at 18.46.

'We've got CCTV on that?'

'Yes, sir. Guys are down at the suite at the moment. Definitely Coughlin. Definitely Osborne Road.'

'And he went where? After getting the money?'

'Thresher's. It's just along the street, same camera. We're checking on the till records but he definitely walked out with a bag.'

'With the Scotch?'

'Tenner says yes.'

'Receipt?'

It was Proctor who shook his head. The lads at 7a Niton Road had been through Coughlin's clothes and found nothing.

'Must have binned it,' Michaels grunted.

'OK.' Faraday closed his eyes a moment, trying to get a fix on the sequence of events. 'Let's say the Scotch *was* from Thresher's. Are we suggesting he drank it all?'

He opened one eye. Michaels was shaking his head.

'I think we're talking company. No forced entry, remember.'

'We're sure about that? Jerry?'

Proctor nodded. The SOCOs had crawled over everything, front door, hall door, every exterior window and every carpet beneath the window sill inside. Absolutely no sign that anyone had tried to force their way in.

'What about this plaster cast? The footprint?'

'Definitely fresh and definitely worth pursuing. But we found bugger all on the bedroom window above, and nothing on the carpet inside. Whoever was standing in the flower bed never went in through that window.'

'And you're still telling me the cast doesn't fit any of Coughlin's shoes?'

'No, sir. Too big.'

'Shame.' Faraday frowned. 'So whoever got in, Coughlin let in. Is that a safe assumption?' Heads nodded round the table. 'A friend then, is that what we're saying?'

A hand went up. It was DS Brian Imber. A trim, combative fifty-three-year-old, he'd come down from the

Havant-based Crime Squad to head up the *Merriott* Intelligence Cell.

'We have to ask ourselves some questions here,' he said slowly. 'The man had no friends. This is Billy No-mates. It's all there in the statements from the prison.'

Dave Michaels threw down his pencil.

'Yeah ... but Brian, he has to have a friend somewhere, doesn't he? Mates are like ...' He shrugged. 'He had to have *someone* to talk to.'

'OK.' Faraday took the point. 'So who?'

'Haven't a clue, guv. Yet.'

Faraday returned to Imber. The Intelligence Cell was responsible for analysing the calls Coughlin might have made.

'What about his phone? Where are you on that?'

'We've applied for billings on his land line and mobile. The forms are ready for your signature.'

'What about 1471? Any joy?'

'Withheld number.'

'What time?'

'Two minutes past midnight.'

Faraday wrote down the time and gazed at it. Coughlin had logged on to the porn site at seventeen minutes past midnight, a quarter of an hour later. Did that mean he'd only just come in? Or was he so pissed, or so preoccupied, that he wasn't answering the phone beforehand? Had he gone out early, bought the Scotch, stopped for a kebab somewhere, and then gone home for a night in front of the telly? Or had he been out all evening and brought someone back? A stranger, say? Someone he'd picked up? He tabled the suggestion and saw Dave Michaels pull a face. Stranger murders were the toughest of all.

'Well?'

'Could be, boss. You look at the shots from Niton Road, it could easily be some stranger. Coughlin brings him home, gives him a bit to drink, makes a move, gets it wrong, and the bloke takes exception.'

'*Kills* him?'

'Batters him. Smashes the place up. Then leaves the porn mags as a kind of message. You're asking me whether that sounds credible? Yes. You're asking me whether it happened? Impossible to say. For now.'

Faraday nodded, knowing it was true. The wider they cast the investigative net, the greater the chance that something – some interlocking pattern of events – might slowly start to resolve. In the meantime, all they could do was take it a step at a time, making sure they missed nothing.

Jerry Proctor went through his first list of forensic submissions: tapings, the empty Scotch bottle and an abandoned glass that were ready to be shipped to the Forensic Science Service in Lambeth. The SOCOs had lifted good prints from a number of surfaces in Coughlin's front room and they'd all been sent over to the force labs at Netley for possible hits on the NAAFIS database. If any intruder had a criminal record, the system would flag up a name.

Faraday knew that Proctor's SOC team would be spending the next couple of days going through the rest of Coughlin's flat, swabbing door handles and switches, removing items for chemical analysis, applying specialist techniques to floors and carpets in search of tiny traces of protein that might indicate blood. Only when every last square inch of the flat had been searched would the house finally be available for Brian Imber's intelligence team. Bank accounts, building society books and credit card statements often flagged new paths in an investigation like this.

'What about this computer?' It was Paul Ingham. 'Anything useful?'

Faraday pushed his chair back from the table and told them what he knew. The computer guy at Netley had already been on with some preliminary findings from Coughlin's cloned hard disk. It was a relatively old machine, no real decoding problems. They'd taken a preliminary look at his e-mails without turning up anything significant, but a number of conversations retrieved from chat rooms and newsgroups looked a great deal more promising. Coughlin's nickname, it appeared, had been 'Freckler'. More detailed analysis would follow.

It was Brian Imber who asked the obvious question.

'What kind of conversations?'

Faraday flicked back through his notes.

'Pretty nasty,' he said at last. 'Apparently there's a protocol in these newsgroups but he appears to have ignored all that.'

'Nasty how?'

'Obscene. The man had sex on the brain.'

'You've got details? Special friends he might have made?'

'Not yet.'

'It's a thought, though, eh?'

Faces brightened around the table. These men were far too busy to explore the delights of chat rooms for themselves but there was a collective awareness that the internet had added an extra layer of possibilities for anyone determined to make serious mischief. Hence the specialist Computer Crime Unit at Netley.

Imber leaned forward. He had another question. They'd all been at last night's briefing. They'd all heard what Corbett, the new guy, had to say. So what was the latest on this Davidson?

Faraday gazed down at his pad. The truth was that he didn't know, not until Corbett and Yates got back from London. He glanced at his watch, wondering why they hadn't heard already.

'It's an active line of enquiry,' he said woodenly. 'And I'll keep you posted.'

*

Corbett was in his Nissan before he made the call to Dave Michaels. Yates stood at the kerbside, gazing down at him through the open car window. They'd left Davidson and Marie Elliott at number twelve. The two-hour interview had added absolutely nothing to Davidson's first account of his movements on Monday night. He and Marie had been at it most of the evening. Afterwards, on and off, they'd gone to sleep. Next day, they'd driven to London. Their statements, all too brief, gave them absolutely no opportunity to pay a midnight visit to Niton Road.

From the car, Corbett had finally managed to raise Dave Michaels. Briefly, he described the morning's exchanges. When Michaels asked for an opinion, a gut feeling, he began to laugh.

'Davidson's talking bollocks,' he said. 'If he really expects me to believe a word of it, he's even thicker than I think he is.'

'And the girlfriend?'

'In it up to her arse.'

'So what do we have for evidence?'

'Leave it to me, skip. I'll bell you again later.' Corbett grinned to himself and then put the mobile on the dashboard. Yates, watching, wondered whether he'd been somewhere else for the last two hours. He'd only heard one end of the conversation but that was more than enough.

'How do you make that out, then?' He nodded at the mobile.

Corbett gazed up at him. Impatience verging on something close to contempt.

'You're telling me you believed that little twat?' He offered Yates a cold smile, then reached for his ignition keys. 'I've got a couple of calls to make. See you back at the nick.'

Winter got the go-ahead from Cathy Lamb at noon.

Banged up with Hartigan for most of the morning, she returned to Highland Road to find a note from Winter suggesting a search warrant on Shelley Geech's flat. She lived in a block off Somers Road and he had reason to believe it might repay a visit. Face to face, pressed for a reason why, Winter talked vaguely about conversations with a trusted source. Bloke would never let him down. Chiefly because he had so much to lose if he did.

'And what does the source say?'

'The kid's carrying for Bazza Mackenzie.'

'You believe him?'

'I do, boss. And a couple of tenths of smack might put us in the driving seat. We've got a choice, haven't we? Another trillion hours of overtime or a punt on Geech's place. Take young Darren out, and Mr Patel can make a decent living again.'

Cathy Lamb, her head still aching after the ninety-minute harangue from Hartigan, pondered the risks.

'You need back-up?'

'Only Dawn.'

'You're sure?'

'Positive. If we hit the big one, you might want to bring in a POLSA team. In which case I'll secure the premises and give you a call.'

'Do that. And listen,' – she gave him one of her sterner looks – 'watch your bloody step.'

Winter and Dawn Ellis shared a microwaved pasty for lunch, a brief stand-up snack in the first-floor room that served as a help-yourself canteen. Ellis looked exhausted. She'd taken another of the breather calls last night, barely an hour after Winter had appeared on her doorstep. She'd done the usual, tried 1471, but it was number withheld again and she'd not been able to get to sleep afterwards, waiting in the darkness in case the phone should ring a second time. When Winter suggested she do something about it – talk to BT or even have a word with

Cathy Lamb – she shook her head. She'd handle it by herself, she said. She wasn't that feeble.

After lunch, they took Ellis's car, found a magistrate to swear the warrant, and then drove to Somerstown. Early afternoon, the estate was quiet. Leaving the little blaze-red Peugeot amongst a litter of broken bottles in a lay-by off the street, they took the stairs to the third floor. Shelley Geech's flat was at the end of the walkway. Winter's second knock brought her to the door. She was a thin, pallid, harassed-looking woman who refused to return Winter's smile. She wore a 1999 Pompey away top over patched black jeans and inspected the warrant with barely a flicker of interest.

'That'd be Darren,' she said.

The boy's bedroom lay down the hall. The stench of stale chip fat was overpowering and Winter turned to warn Ellis about a puddle of something evil outside Darren's door. Shelley Geech was banging around inside the kitchen but finally reappeared, a cigarette dangling from her fingers.

'He's in here?' Winter nodded at the bedroom door.

'Still asleep. Likes to lie in.'

'Ever go to school, does he?'

'No.'

Winter pushed at the door. The curtains were still closed, but under the Pompey poster on the wall he could see the hump of a body in the single bed. A dog lay in a hollow of the duvet, a small cairn terrier. Apart from an MFI wardrobe with its door hanging off, the room was bare of furniture.

Winter reached down in the half-darkness and shook the boy awake. There was a swishing noise and a sudden flood of sunshine as Ellis pulled the curtains back. The dog yapped and jumped off the bed.

'Geech?'

A face appeared from under the duvet, puffy with sleep. It took a second or two for Geech to work it out, then he was on his feet by the bed. Grubby white boxers. Stick-thin legs.

'Where's my fucking dog?'

'Sit down,' Winter told him.

The dog started up again, in the hall this time, and Geech made a dive for the open door. Winter caught him and threw him backwards on to the bed. There was a sharp, bony crack as the back of his head hit the wall and Geech yelped with pain. The moment he tried to struggle off the bed, Winter sat on him.

'The wardrobe.' Winter had turned to Ellis. 'But watch yourself.'

Ellis stepped across the room, pulling on a pair of heavy-duty gloves, and began to examine the wardrobe. It was virtually empty inside – grubby-looking jeans hanging on the rail beside a couple of identical bomber jackets, brand new, that were probably nicked. She went through the pockets one by one, then fetched a chair and took a good look at the top edge of the door. Even kids knew how to use a router, hollowing out a little cavity to stash gear, but she could see no trace of interference on the scuffed MDF. Finally, she got down on her hands and knees and felt around in the tiny space beneath the bottom of the wardrobe. It took her a full minute to confirm that there was nothing there.

'You're sure?' Winter was frowning.

Ellis tried again, lying full length on the threadbare carpet.

'Nothing,' she confirmed. 'Clean as a whistle.'

'Try inside again.'

She did so, pulling the clothes out this time, checking the seams as well as the pockets. Geech watched her, kicking out against the weight of Winter's body. Geech's mother, meanwhile, had wandered back to the kitchen.

At last, Ellis abandoned the search and put the clothes back in the wardrobe. She'd found nothing.

'OK?' Geech spat the word out. 'Happy now, are you?'

Winter looked reproachful for a moment, then stood up. The warrant gave him the authority to search the rest of the flat but he knew it wouldn't be worth the effort. For whatever reason, Rookie had got it wrong.

Outraged, and still half-naked, Geech followed them to the front door, screaming abuse. Most of it went over Winter's head but the word 'cunt' brought him to a halt. He turned on Geech and told him to shut his mouth. Any more crap like that and he'd turn the place over. Then he bent quickly and grabbed the dog. There was a collar round its neck, with a little silver ID disc. Ellis's eyes were better than Winter's. The dog peered up at her through a fringe of hair. He could feel it shivering with excitement.

'His name's Charlie,' Ellis said. 'There's a local number. 92851933.'

Winter shouted for Shelley Geech. She appeared from the kitchen.

'Who's dog is this?'

She peered at the little terrier as if she'd never seen it in her life before.

'Darren's,' she said at last. 'Never lets it out of his sight.'

'Had it from the off, has he? Got it as a puppy?'

'Fuck knows.' She shrugged.

'Where's your phone?'

'They cut it off.'

'What was the number?'

'92874 . . .' She frowned. 'Can't remember.'

'Excellent.' He beamed down at Geech. 'This dog's nicked. Stolen property. I'm seizing it.'

Geech tried to snatch at the dog. Winter stepped backwards on to the walkway, letting Ellis slip herself between them. The dog was getting even more lively, struggling against Winter's chest. With Winter halfway

73

down the stairs, Geech's thin face appeared over the parapet above, scarlet with rage. He watched them as they crossed the patch of yellowing grass outside the flats and made for Ellis's car.

'You tell that bastard I'll get him,' he screamed. 'Tell that cunt he's a dead man.'

Five

Bev Yates was back at Kingston Crescent by early afternoon. The car park behind the police station was packed with vehicles he didn't recognise, a sure sign of a Major Crimes special event, but he managed to find a space for his Golf before taking a moment to check his mobile for calls in his voice-mail.

Amongst the half-dozen waiting messages was an SOS from Melanie. Her Citroen was on the blink again. Freya had thrown a wobbler about not going over to her friend Kate's and there was nothing in the fridge for supper. Could Bev sort out a couple of readiwarm meals from the supermarket on the way home? And maybe pick up some Ostermilk supplement while he was about it? Any more breast-feeding, and she wouldn't have any bloody nipples left.

She ended the message with a half-hearted attempt at laughter but Yates wasn't fooled. Married life with two young kids wasn't working out at all the way they'd both expected. Living in the country was a pain: no shops, one pub, and few neighbours under the age of seventy. Plus Bev's hours seemed to be getting longer and longer. Last week he'd twice got back the wrong side of midnight, and for the first time ever she'd stopped waiting up for him.

Bev gazed at the mobile, then shrugged. Checking his watch, he wondered whether he could afford to stay with the Five Live coverage of the Ireland v Germany game until the final whistle. According to the commentator, there was only a couple of minutes to go and with the Germans predictably ahead, if only by the one goal, the

Irish were going to be struggling for a place in the next round. He settled down behind the wheel, shifting slightly until the sun fell on his face. Seconds later, he was asleep.

He awoke at half two, tugged back into consciousness by a hand on his shoulder. Half blinded by the sun, he switched off the radio and tried to make out the silhouette of the head and shoulders at the car window. Someone was squatting outside the car, looking in.

'Lucky it was me.'

'Dawn? What are you doing here?'

'Meet with a guy in Traffic. He pulled a young kid on a TWOCing.' She paused. 'So how's the big time? *Merriott*, isn't it?'

'Nightmare. I've got landed with the buddy from hell.'

'Who might that be?'

'Corbett. Andy Corbett. I've been trying to work it out. Either he's taking the piss or he's seen too many movies. I'm telling you, this bloke's not real. Whatever he's on, he should sue the makers.'

'You really think so?'

Bev caught the inflection, the tiny rise in her voice at the end of the question. He struggled upright and took a proper look at her.

'You're joking.' He shook his head. 'You can't be serious.'

'Why not?' She moistened her fingertip with a kiss and then planted it on the end of his nose. 'A girl can't wait for ever.'

Bev wanted her to stay but she was late already. Maybe that drink one night? If he could ever spare the time? She smiled at him again, no kiss this time, then got to her feet. Seconds later, she'd disappeared through the big door that led to the back stairs.

Corbett? Bev shook his head again, reaching for the rear-view mirror, an automatic reflex that was beginning to get on his nerves. The face that stared back at him spoke of too many late nights, too many three-pint conversations, too many bids to turn back the clock. At forty-five, second time round, he had to start learning the knack of making the best of what he had.

There were worse things to be saddled with than two young kids. Pass round photos of Freya and Nathan, and half the world thought you were the luckiest guy alive. Show them some of the holiday snaps of Melanie, topless on the beach at Marbella, and even the younger blokes started paying him a bit of respect. How come a bird that fit, that gorgeous, bothers with the likes of you? He never spoiled these moments with the truth, never even hinted at it, but he knew in his heart that there had to be more than twelve-hour working days and a family life that never seemed to get beyond a list of unfinished jobs. Ostermilk? Readiwarm garbage for the microwave? He rolled his eyes, taking a final peck at the mirror, then reached for the door handle.

Corbett? She must be off her head.

Minutes later, Michaels saw Yates walking past his open office door. He called him in and told him to sit down. He wanted to know more about Davidson and his ladyfriend.

Yates settled into the chair by the door. Sitting here, visitors couldn't help noticing Michaels' thirteen-year-old son, star striker in a local tyro league side. The photograph was tacked up on a wallboard beside a sports-page story from the *News*. 'Four Goal Hero' the headline read.

Yates enquired about the final score in the Ireland game. When Michaels said he hadn't had a chance to see it, Yates changed the subject.

'Corbett back yet?'

'Blow-out on the motorway. He just phoned in.'

'Not badly hurt I hope?'

'Haven't a clue, mate. Listen, he might not be your cup

of tea, and he might not be mine, but there's plenty of this job to go round so don't slag the guy.'

'Did I speak out of turn there?'

'No, but I'm not fucking deaf. OK?' Michaels sounded genuinely pissed off, a rare event.

'You all right, skip?'

'Never better, son. Now why don't you answer the question?'

Yates had been anticipating this conversation all the way home. At some point or other he was going to have to come up with an opinion on the strength of Davidson. That's the way the system worked. Not one pair of eyes, but two.

'There's no chance,' he said slowly. 'Absolutely none.'

'No chance of what?'

'No chance he did Coughlin. Number one, he's got a perfectly sound alibi. The girlfriend's a teacher for fuck's sake, not some Fratton slapper. And number two, no one's that good an actor. You know when someone's trying it on for size. Believe me, skip, he wasn't.'

'Corbett says he hadn't got any regrets.'

'Who hadn't?'

'Davidson.'

'He said that? Davidson had no *regrets*?'

'Just now.' He nodded at the phone. 'When he called in.'

'Then the guy's a dickhead. Regrets is way off the mark. The moment it dawned on him that Coughlin was a goner, Davidson lit up. In fact he was over the bloody moon. Nothing pleased him more than the thought of Coughlin getting it. Regrets suggests he did it. He didn't.'

'Corbett thinks otherwise.'

'Yeah? So why didn't we arrest him?'

'That was my question.'

'Sure, and I'll give you an answer. Because we haven't got a shred of evidence against the guy. If he was that certain about Davidson, why weren't we in there with

Scenes of Crime? Ripping the floorboards up? Seizing his gear? His clothes? The girlfriend's motor? Why turn your back on all that DNA if it's that bloody obvious he did it?'

Michaels made no comment. Instead, he asked again about the girlfriend, Marie Elliott.

'I told you, skip, she's class. If you want the truth, she made us feel that big.' He narrowed the gap between finger and thumb. 'Corbett tried to do the big Met number on her and she just blew him away. Easy really, if you know you're innocent.'

'You're that sure?'

'Yes.'

Michaels leaned forward, his elbows on his knees. Fifteen years on the same force, job in, job out, you get to learn who to trust.

'Off the record, right?'

'Sure.'

'Why is he riding this one so hard?'

'Corbett? Because it's easy. Because it makes him look good. He's a young bloke. He's come down from the big time. He's in a hurry. He's got a reputation to make. We were all there, once, skip. You know we were.'

'Yeah, and look what fucking happened.' He rocked with laughter and gave Yates's knee a slap, suddenly the old Dave Michaels again. An East End childhood and three tough years trying to make his own way in the Met before coming south had given him a shrewd take on life. He knew there was some stuff that would never make it on to paper, never make it into HOLMES, and as a good detective he also knew the value of conversations like these.

He was looking at Yates's briefcase.

'You've got the statements?'

'Yeah.'

He nodded at the desk.

'Stick them on the pile.' He stood up and stretched

while Yates bent to the briefcase. 'And another thing,' he said.

'What's that?'

'The Irish play better without Keane.'

Cathy Lamb wanted an explanation.

'I haven't got one, boss.'

'You told me this bloke of yours was kosher.'

'He is. Was.'

'Have you seen him? Talked to him? Asked for our money back?'

'It was a freebie. He owed me.'

'Terrific. We save loads of money and achieve absolutely nothing.'

Winter looked pained. Apologies were strictly for losers but he was coming dangerously close to saying sorry. It was rare to find DIs with a brain in their heads – in Winter's view, Faraday had frequently been off the planet – and there'd been countless occasions when Cathy, as DS, had covered Winter's arse. These favours certainly didn't come for free. A bollocking from Cathy Lamb could make your eyes water. But the fact was that Winter's more colourful adventures very seldom came to management's attention, thus sparing Winter a great deal of grief. As a newly promoted DI, though, Cathy *was* management. And that put their relationship in an altogether different light.

They were sitting in the unmarked Skoda on the edge of Somerstown. Cathy had asked for a tour of the targeted corner stores and Winter had obliged with a drive-by past all three Asian shops. The presence of Geech's dog on a square of old plaid blanket on the back seat appeared not to surprise her. In fact Winter was beginning to wonder whether she'd even noticed the little cairn terrier.

'We have to get one or two things sorted,' she said.

'Whatever you think of PIMS, it's there for a purpose. Use it.'

The PIMS system was the official filter through which every informant was supposed to pass. Just registering a tout – paperwork alone – could take half a day. Winter, who resented having to fight the crime war with both hands shackled, largely ignored it.

'I just talk to these guys,' he protested. 'We get on fine. It's like a love affair. Why ruin it by getting married?'

'Because that's what the book says.'

'You never complained before.'

'You always delivered before.'

'But it's not going to work every time, Cath. PIMS or no PIMS, it never does.' He smiled to himself. He rather liked the comparison to marriage. He hadn't thought of it in those terms before. He glanced across at Cathy. 'How's Pete?'

'He's fine. Don't change the subject.'

'I'm not. I'm serious. Bloke told me he was doing really well the other day. Got a promotion, didn't he?'

With some reluctance, Cathy nodded. Pete Lamb, her husband, had once been a uniformed sergeant across at Fareham. Both his police career and his marriage had hit the rocks after he'd shot a major drugs supplier and tested positive for alcohol afterwards. Three years later, back home again, he now headed the investigations department in a big Portsmouth-based insurance company.

'We've got a new boat,' Cathy said. 'A twenty-eight-footer. Pete's over the moon. You should see it.'

'Ah . . .' Winter at last began to understand. 'New job, thirty-five grand a year, and a boat to go with it. No wonder you're getting nervous.'

'Pete doesn't earn that kind of money.'

'No, but you do.' Winter put a hand on her arm. 'Apologies, boss, about Geech. Won't happen again.'

Cathy seemed not to have heard him. She wrinkled her nose, then twisted round in the seat.

'Jesus Christ!' She sounded resigned as well as incredulous. 'What's that bloody dog doing in the back?'

Corbett went straight to Faraday. His office door was open and Corbett didn't bother with the usual precautionary knock.

'Yes?' Faraday was reading some material sent down the corridor from Brian Imber's Intelligence Cell. The first of the phone billings had come in, confirming the state of Coughlin's social life. Last quarter, nearly eighty per cent of his calls had gone to premium-rate porn sites.

Corbett closed the door behind him. He'd been to see Dave Michaels about Davidson and his girlfriend and he wasn't a happy man.

'What's the problem?'

'Difference of opinion, sir. I was there. In my view, Davidson needs further development.'

'DS Michaels has discussed it with me. We agree.'

'Agree what?'

'That Davidson needs further development.'

'So why put me on house-to-house?'

'Because that's the way the cards fall. Paul Ingham's got a pile of actions need attention. Last time he counted it was past sixty. You're one of the squad. Some of those actions go to you. This isn't rocket science, Corbett. That's the way the system works.'

'But I talked to Davidson. And I flagged him up in the first place. Why put someone else on to him when I've got the inside track?'

'Who said we're talking this afternoon?'

'We're not? I'm sorry, guv, I thought this was a murder inquiry.'

Faraday looked him in the eye, letting the silence stretch and stretch.

'Do you want to apologise for that?' he said at last.

'I'm sorry, sir, I'm just concerned about—'

'Did you hear what I said?'

'Yes, sir.' His face was a mask. 'And I apologise.'

'Good. Now fuck off out of here. Ingham works in the incident room. Big guy. Yorkshire accent. Can't miss him.'

Corbett held his gaze. This was a declaration of war and both men knew it. Out beyond the car park, a flock of pigeons wheeled over the rooftops of Stamshaw. Finally Corbett stood up.

'They told me it would be different down here,' he said softly. 'But you know what? I never believed them.'

Faraday watched him leave the office, letting his anger slowly subside. When he picked up the phone and dialled, Dave Michaels answered on the second ring.

'I'm off to the prison.' Faraday was already struggling into his jacket. 'Back in an hour or so.'

HMP Gosport was over the water, a ferry ride away across a busy stretch of Portsmouth Harbour. A sprawling Victorian red-brick pile, as martial as many of the other institutions that littered the area, it towered over the surrounding terraces. According to the latest count, it was now home for nearly six hundred prisoners.

Faraday had visited the place on a number of occasions and hated it. It was institutions like these where the people he hunted would probably end up, but in the strangest of ways Faraday had nothing but regrets for putting them there. Most of the villains he saw through to conviction were young, male, unmarried, ignorant, jobless and suffering from varying degrees of mental disturbance. Lock them in a cell twenty hours a day, get them used to the smell and sight of failure, and they'd quickly lose what little interest a decent life had ever held for them. Prison, in his view, was the very best way of turning an inadequate into a lifetime criminal.

He stepped out of the cab and showed his warrant card

at the gatehouse. A phone call confirmed his appointment and he followed a burly prison officer through a warren of corridors towards the administrative block. This was Sean Coughlin's world, he kept telling himself. The constant jangle of keys as warders patrolled the echoing wings. The jarring clang of steel on steel as they shepherded prisoners from floor to floor, opening and closing the big metal grilles. This was where you could take a serious liberty with people too frightened or too bewildered to make a fuss. This would be close to paradise for someone as predatory and ruthless as Coughlin appeared to have been.

Or would it?

The prison governor thought not. He was a small, squat, red-faced man with a toothbrush moustache and bad breath. He wore a brown tweed jacket with leather patches at the elbow. In another life, thought Faraday, he might have been a prep school headmaster.

'Coughlin? Never had a problem with him. Exemplary would have been too kind but effective, certainly. We'll miss him, I'll tell you that. More Coughlins and life might be a great deal quieter.'

Faraday frowned. He'd come here with an open mind. One or two of yesterday's interviews suggested that Coughlin wasn't the most popular of prison officers. True?

'He keeps himself to himself, certainly, but I'm not aware of any Home Office regulation against that. If a man can get by without company, good luck to him.' He patted the file on his desk. Coughlin's timekeeping was spot-on and he'd taken just three days sick leave over the last couple of years. He'd never make management but that had never appeared to worry him. All in all, he was dependable, conscientious and effective, virtues by no means as common as people like Faraday might suppose.

Faraday nodded. It was the second time the governor had used the word 'effective'.

'Effective how, exactly?'

'Effective with prisoners. Especially our more challenging guests.' He paused, expecting a smile, but Faraday didn't oblige.

'You're talking about physical restraint?'

'God, no. By the time you get round to talking about physical restraint, you've lost it. But that's the point, you see. Prison officers like Coughlin have a knack of setting the boundaries. Like it or not, prisons are very black and white. Have to be. That's the nature of the beast. Coughlin understands that. It might be his service background.'

Faraday raised an eyebrow. The governor's use of the present tense was beginning to irritate him.

'Coughlin's dead,' he pointed out. 'That's why I'm here.'

'Of course. And that's something I deeply, deeply regret. You know my number one problem in this place? Not the prisoners. Not overcrowding. Nothing like that. It's staff morale. The politicians think we can work miracles and the fact is that we can't. Not on the kind of budgets they give us. I've got good blokes, *good* blokes, the best, but it doesn't take much to get to them. What happened to Coughlin was a real blow. That kind of thing sends a message to the rest of the staff. We need it sorted. Fast.' He stared at Faraday for a moment, then patted the file again. 'I understand you want to take a look at this.'

'I want to take it away.'

'No can do. I'll get you a photocopy but you'll have to sign for it.' He stood up and shouted a name through the open office door. A prison officer appeared and scooped up the file. He must have been listening, Faraday thought. The entire interview will be round the prison within minutes. This man's not talking to me. He's addressing the bloody staff.

'Tell me about Davidson,' Faraday suggested.

'You know about Davidson?'

'I know he was released not long ago. And I know he always contested his sentence.'

'Then you know it all, Mr Faraday. Davidson, excuse my French, was a little shit. I don't expect prisoners to enjoy themselves here. Far from it. That wouldn't be the point, would it? No, but I do expect them to buckle down. The man got caught. Justice followed. The least he could do was keep his head down and get on with it. Least said, soonest mended.'

If only, thought Faraday.

'What if he was innocent?'

'He wasn't. We don't do innocence.'

'OK.' Faraday tried to hide his smile. 'Then tell me what kind of man he was.'

The governor sat back and stroked his moustache. The question appeared to have taken him by surprise.

'Clever,' he said at last. 'Intelligent. I grant you that.'

'Intelligent enough not to do anything silly?'

'Like what, Mr Faraday?'

'Like have a go at Sean Coughlin. If Coughlin had been' . . . Faraday was choosing his words carefully . . . 'especially effective.'

'You mean Monday night?'

'Yes.'

'*Kill* Coughlin? Murder him?'

'Yes.'

'Good God, no.'

'Not even pay him a visit? For old times' sake?'

'No.' When he shook his head, his whole face wobbled. 'I saw a lot of young Davidson. One of the perks of the job. Every time he got in a muddle with the appeals procedure, or had a run-in with his latest lawyer, he'd be up here like a shot. I knew him. I knew him well. He wouldn't have done anything like that. Davidson looked after number one. You don't do that by knocking off prison officers.'

'You said he was a little shit just now.'

'He was, he was. The man was a pain. Wouldn't lie down. Wouldn't take his punishment. What would happen if the whole bloody prison did that? How would we cope? It's all right for you, Mr Faraday. Putting them away's the easy bit. We pick up where you blokes leave off. But let me tell you something. This job of ours isn't easy.'

The prison officer had returned with Coughlin's file. The governor checked through the photocopy page by page before inserting it carefully into an A4 envelope. The prison officer produced a form. Faraday signed it, then glanced up.

'So I can strike Davidson off my list, can I?'

'What list?'

'My suspect list.' He tapped the file envelope, spelling it out. 'Coughlin's would-be killers.'

'Christ, yes.' The governor stood up. 'In my view, the man was never into serious crime in the first place.'

By late afternoon, Winter and Charlie had fallen in love. The little cairn terrier he'd seized from Darren Geech had accompanied him back to the first-floor CID room at Highland Road, and had now found a home under Winter's desk. The dog was obviously hungry, probably hadn't been fed for weeks, but when Winter popped out to the Londis across the road they had no pet food so he returned with a tin of Fray Bentos steak and kidney, spooning half the contents into a saucer and watching while the dog demolished it.

Afterwards, Charlie set out on a little tour of the office, much to the the disgust of the duty DS. A stolid, humourless Scot from Aberdeen, he told Winter to find somewhere else for the wee hairy shite. The Lost Property store was unlocked or he might try the cupboard down the hall where the cleaners kept their mops. Winter ignored him, laying hands on a length of blue and white

Police No Entry tape and converting it into a makeshift lead. Moored to one leg of Winter's desk, Charlie settled down for a nap.

The number on the ID disc round Charlie's neck was local but so far Winter hadn't managed to get through. Finally, he put a call into the control room at Netley, and had the desk supervisor check the reverse phone directory. Charlie evidently belonged to a household in Old Portsmouth but when Winter tried the name Czinski on the dog it failed to raise a flicker of interest. He was beginning to wonder about taking the animal home for the night when one of the uniforms from downstairs appeared at the office door.

'Serious assault in Somerstown,' he called. 'Anyone interested?'

By the time Winter got to Fraser Road, the ambulance had gone. A small crowd was still gathered in the road, mainly older people and young kids. A WPC met Winter as he got out of his car.

'Bloke was lying on the pavement, just here. Cabby spotted him and called in.'

Winter was following her pointed finger. There was a lot of blood, still fresh.

'Anyone see what happened?'

'No one we've found so far.' She nodded at the houses across the road. 'We've started knocking on doors but no one's at home.'

'What about this lot?' Winter indicated the faces staring down at the pavement.

'Half of them don't speak English and the kids think it's a laugh.'

'No one saw anything?'

'What do you think?'

Winter took the point. What you didn't do in Somerstown was volunteer any kind of help. A formal statement could land you in court as a witness and who needed that kind of grief?

'We've got a name?' Winter was looking at the blood again.

'Yes.' The WPC produced a creased envelope. 'We found this in the guy's back pocket.'

Winter took the envelope. Inside was a demand for payment on an electricity bill. If the recipient didn't come up with £57.16 in seven days he'd face the risk of disconnection. Winter peered at the name. David John Rooke.

'Shit,' he said quietly. 'How badly was he hurt?'

'Badly, I'm afraid. The blokes on the ambulance were talking brain damage. He was unconscious when I got here and he was still out when they took him away.'

'Head? Face?'

'Total mess. Someone had given him a right battering.'

Winter nodded. He had no idea whether Rooke had been intercepted on the street, or dragged out of some nearby house, but either way the beating had happened in broad daylight. Mid-afternoon, in the heart of a major city, there had to be witnesses and you'd have thought that someone – *someone*, for God's sake – might have the bottle to come forward. He'd put a call through to Highland Road now, and ask Cathy Lamb for Scenes of Crime and extra bodies for a proper house-to-house, but even so he knew that their chances of finding someone brave enough to come forward were zilch. Putting someone in the frame for this wouldn't be easy, but already he knew exactly where to start.

The WPC was curious about Winter's reaction to the name on the electricity bill.

'You knew the guy?'

'I did.'

'Friend of yours?'

'No, love.' He pocketed the envelope. 'Client.'

Six

Faraday found Nick Hayder in the top-floor social club at Kingston Crescent police station. The club doubled as a bar, but late afternoon Hayder was sitting by himself at a table by the window, sipping at a coffee while he trawled through a disclosure schedule.

He looked up as Faraday approached.

'How's it going?'

'Slowly.'

'Not short of bodies, though, eh?'

Hayder was one of the other two DIs on Major Crimes. A decade younger than Faraday, he'd already helped the newcomer out of a dodgy corner or two and Faraday had come to rely on his support. Slightly built, with prematurely greying hair and a quiet wit, Hayder had acquired a well-earned reputation for playing his cards extremely close to his chest. The first time they'd had a proper conversation, he'd muttered something in passing that Faraday had treasured ever since. *Wherever you are*, he'd said, *whoever you're with, think enemy*.

At the time, Faraday had rather liked that. It smacked of exactly the right kind of paranoia. View the world through Hayder's slightly wild eyes, he thought, and you wouldn't go far wrong.

Now, Faraday wanted advice. He'd taken a couple of minutes in the prison car park to scan through Coughlin's Home Office file. Everything about this case convinced him that the key lay in getting inside the dead man's head. What had he done with his life? Where had he been? Who had he seriously upset? The governor had already mentioned a service career. Now, thanks to the file, Faraday knew more.

'Coughlin was in the navy,' he said briefly. 'Did seventeen years. Who do I talk to?'

Hayder put his papers to one side. Recently, as Faraday knew, he'd been conducting a long-term inquiry into a series of stranger rapes in the Southsea area. The time-line and one or two other indicators pointed the finger at a possible link to a serving matelot. As a direct result, Hayder had got to know a great deal about, in Willard's dry phrase, the MOD interface.

'You need to be bloody careful,' he said at once. 'Go through proper channels and you may end up with some real twat. Formal inquiries can take for ever. Christ knows why.'

'So what do I do?'

'Depends what you want.'

'His service file, for starters.'

'Not a problem.' He picked up his pen. 'Give me the guy's full name.'

Downstairs in his office, Faraday found a scribbled note from Dave Michaels. The Outside Enquiry team had struck lucky on the kebab joints. Faraday reached for the phone, wanting to know more.

'Third one they visited, bloke behind the counter recognised the mug shot.' Michaels was sounding pleased with himself. 'Apparently Coughlin used the place a lot. Couple of times a week. They'd started giving him extra pickles so maybe that helped.'

'Where is this place?'

'The Strand, across from the newsagent's. Monday night they reckon he was there early, seven, seven-thirty, something like that.'

Faraday nodded. The Strand was up the road from Thresher's, a ten-minute walk at most. Time-wise, this thing was beginning to hang together. After the cash withdrawal, a bottle of Scotch and a kebab. Then what?

'Was he alone?'

'Afraid so.'

'No one outside waiting for him?'

'Christ knows. These guys get really busy. But Coughlin definitely ordered just the one kebab. Bloke was sure about that.'

'OK. Anything else?'

'Yeah. We've confirmed the Thresher's end of it. Till receipt matches the time on the CCTV. Bottle of Johnnie Walker and some Doritos. There's an empty packet of chilli-flavoured on the SOC log.'

'They recognise the mug shot, too?'

'Different girl behind the counter but it has to be him. The times match exactly.'

Faraday remembered watching the video of Coughlin's body in the back of the Fiesta in Niton Road, the vomit pooled on the carpet around his open mouth. Chilli-flavoured Doritos would never taste the same again.

Michaels had more news.

'Willard's been on twice,' he announced cheerfully. 'Best give him a bell if I were you.'

The Detective Superintendent was sorting out his lecture notes at the conference centre when Faraday rang. An afternoon exploring the investigative challenges of product extortion had done nothing for his temper.

'What the fuck's going on?' he said at once.

Faraday gazed at the phone, listening to Willard detailing a call he'd taken earlier. Apparently the Davidson lead was really strong. So why wasn't Faraday piling on the pressure?

'Davidson was one of a number of recent releases. We're looking at them all.' Faraday paused. 'Who was this call from?'

Willard refused to answer the question. He wanted

facts. Was it true that Davidson had been interviewed up at his mum's place?

'Yes.'

'And the girl was there, too?'

'Yes.'

'Mirror alibi for Monday night? No other corroboration? That says dodgy to me, Joe.'

Faraday began to explain about Bev Yates. According to Yates, there was no chance that Davidson was down for the Coughlin hit, not the way he'd reacted to the news. In Faraday's view, it paid to trust an opinion like that, especially from someone with Yates's experience.

'But who's saying he necessarily did it himself?'

Faraday blinked. Davidson part of some bigger conspiracy? This was a new development, even more bizarre.

'I'm not with you, sir.'

'No, you're not, are you?' Willard took a breath or two and Faraday wondered whether there was anyone else with him. Willard was a good boss, a fair man, but occasionally liked to demonstrate his grip on an inquiry. Not easy, when you were a hundred miles away.

'I understand there's intelligence,' Willard was saying. 'Have you seen it?'

'No, I haven't.'

'Comes from the Met. Sources at Streatham nick. Davidson's name's come up in a surveillance op they're mounting. Something to do with a bunch of guys sorting themselves out a Securicor job. The way I hear it, Davidson knew them before. Now he's back on the team.'

'Before what?'

'Before he went away. He's a driver, Joe. Well thought of. Sorts out a motor and does the business on the day.' He paused. 'Why is it me has to tell you all this?'

Faraday didn't answer. Streatham was Andy Corbett's old patch. He'd done three years there as a DC before applying for a transfer to Hampshire. Dave Michaels had told him only hours ago. Faraday sat back in the chair, beginning to sense where all this came from. His turn now to ask the questions.

'Has Corbett been on to you?'

'Yes. Should he have done? No. But where were bloody you?'

'In Gosport prison. Talking to the governor.'

'Why?'

'Because it pays to get a second opinion. And a third. And a fourth. It's called keeping your options open.'

'Don't you have a team to do that? Or aren't twenty blokes enough?'

Willard was really angry now, not least because Corbett's recklessness had driven a horse and cart through the management hierarchy. There were rules here, strokes you should and shouldn't pull, and Corbett had broken them all.

'Corbett should have talked to me,' Faraday insisted, 'or Dave Michaels. He had absolutely no right to go mouthing off to you.'

'Of course he shouldn't, but that's not the point.'

'It's not?'

'No, not here and now it isn't. I'll deal with Corbett later. What bothers me at the moment is this Met intelligence. If it checks out, we're looking at a conspiracy.'

'Is that Corbett's line?'

'He's saying one of these heavies is a professional hit man.'

'How convenient.'

'Listen to me, Joe. Davidson's spent seven years banged up for something he says he didn't do. Coughlin's made all that much, much worse. There's no way he's going to whack Coughlin himself, but the guys up in town want him back behind the wheel. Odds are he'll say no. Odds are they'll look for ways to persuade him. Money's one. A favour or two might well be another.'

Faraday could hear Corbett's voice behind Willard's version of events. It must have been one of the longer calls.

'You're telling me Davidson's price is a contract killing? On Coughlin? You think he's brainless enough to think he'd get away with something like that?'

'I'm telling you that's a possibility. Seven years inside does strange things to people. And I'm also telling you we should be actively developing this intelligence.'

'A pleasure, sir. I'll talk to Brian Imber and get the FIB on to it.'

The Force Intelligence Bureau was at force headquarters in Winchester. It would be their job to contact the Met's S11 Intelligence Branch and get the ball rolling.

'Anything else, sir?'

There was a long silence. Maybe Willard's having second thoughts about bollocking his DSIO, thought Faraday. Maybe he might even credit his deputy with a little intelligence of his own.

'No,' Willard grunted at last. 'But keep me in touch. At this rate, Perry's holiday's going to be shorter than he thought.'

Faraday put the phone down. For the second time that day, he fought to contain the scalding waves of anger lapping at his brain. Perry Madison was the DCI on Major Crimes. Under normal circumstances, he'd have been DSIO on *Merriott* but a pre-booked fortnight walking up and down mountains in the Lake District had put Faraday in the hot seat. Whether Willard meant it or not, the threat was now explicit. Another fuck-up, and Faraday would be off the case.

Paul Ingham, the DS in charge of Outside Enquiries, would know about Corbett's movements. He answered on the second ring. Corbett, he said, was busy on house-to-house.

'You've got his mobile number?'

'Yes, sir. But I tried a couple of times just now and he's not answering.'

Winter wanted Dawn Ellis to come back with him to Shelley Geech's flat. This time they were going through the whole property. Ellis still had the original warrant and Winter knew it would get them in. At length, the door opened. Shelley Geech looked wrecked.

'Where's Darren?' Winter pushed inside.

'Dunno. You can't just come in here.'

'Yes, I can. Where is he?'

'Fuck knows. Listen—'

Winter rounded on her. Instinctively, she took half a step backwards, colliding with the wall. Her eyes kept losing focus and she was having trouble with her balance.

'When did you last see him?'

'Hours ago.'

'We were here hours ago. And so was he.'

'He went out.'

'And?'

'That's all I know. Why don't you just fucking leave us alone?'

'Us?'

Ellis had been in the kitchen. She emerged for long enough to gesture to Winter.

'Come in here, Paul.'

Winter stepped into the tiny kitchen. KFC wraps were spilling out of the swing bin under the window and there was a half-eaten slice of toast abandoned on the side. Beside the gas cooker, neatly arranged on a cracked saucer, was a heat-blackened spoon and a plastic syringe. The length of rag she'd used as a tourniquet was lying on the floor. Winter held the back of his hand against the spoon. The metal was still warm.

'Get her in here.' Winter slipped on a pair of gloves and gestured back towards the hall.

Ellis left the kitchen and Winter heard the beginnings

of a bleary argument before Shelley Geech appeared at the open door.

Winter nodded at the syringe.

'That yours?'

Shelley Geech stared at it, glassy-eyed. Then she reached for the wall to support herself.

'What if it is?'

Winter took her left hand and pushed up the sleeve of her sweatshirt until her forearm was fully uncovered. She made no attempt to stop him. She'd made a botch of the injection, and there was a fresh bruise spreading around the dot of drying blood in the crook of her elbow.

'Let's talk about Darren,' he said softly. 'Only this is the last time, the last chance. Where is he?'

Ellis had disappeared again. This time she shouted Winter's name. Winter turned Shelley Geech around and marched her out of the kitchen. The narrow little bathroom was up the hall, the door open. Ellis was standing over the bath, gazing down.

Winter wedged himself beside her. There was an inch or two of water in the bath, pinked with blood from a pair of jeans. There was more blood seeping out of a pair of black runners. Even Winter, with half a lifetime's experience of Pompey crime, was amazed at the find. Subtle, this wasn't.

'Your boy's in serious shit, Mrs Geech. They've just transferred the bloke he did to the neuro unit in Southampton. If you're lucky, he might not die.'

Shelley Geech was looking dazed.

'They belong to a mate of Darren's,' she managed. 'Had an accident. Fell over.'

'You'll have to do better than that, love. Accessory to murder will put you inside for a very long time. Last chance. Where's Darren?'

'I don't know.' She shook her head. 'I ain't got a clue.'

It occurred to Winter that she was probably telling the truth. Like so many mothers on this crap estate, she'd just let her life fall apart. The fathers had long gone. The kids were out of control. Only those consolatory little wraps would offer the promise of some peace and quiet.

He backed her out of the bathroom. The sitting room was bare except for a broken-backed sofa, a dodgy-looking beanbag and an upturned plastic drinks crate to support the telly.

Winter indicated the sofa. Shelley Geech sank on to it without a word. Even an armful of heroin couldn't soften the trouble she knew she was in.

'Tell me about Rookie,' Winter suggested. 'How often is he round here?'

The name seemed to make an impression.

'As often as I needs him. I calls his mobile from the box on the corner. Good as gold, he is.'

'Charge you for it, as a matter of interest?'

'You mean money?' Her eyes were struggling to focus. 'Yeah, sometimes.'

'The rest in kind?'

She looked at him, then shook her head from side to side with infinite care, as though it might fall off.

'He may as well move in, Rookie. There ain't enough smack in the world the way I'm getting through it lately.'

'Darren wouldn't like that, though, would he?'

'Darren can fuck off. I've had enough of Darren. It's Darren's got me in this state in the first place.'

'And Rookie?'

'Rookie helps. Rookie always helps. Strange-looking bloke, ain't he? Not that looks matter. Good heart, that man. Yeah . . .' She sighed. 'Rookie.'

For a moment, Winter thought she was going to sleep. Ellis had appeared at the door. She was shaping something with her hands, holding them maybe a metre apart, but Winter signalled her that he was busy. They were getting close, now. The next couple of minutes might save a lot of time in the interview room.

'There's something you ought to know, love.'

Shelley Geech tried to smile. It made her look even older.

'Yeah?' she said vaguely. 'What's that, then?'

'The bloke Darren did was Rookie.'

'Darren didn't do no bloke. I told you.'

'He did, love. And we can prove it.'

'Bollocks, can you.'

Winter waited for her to draw a line between the two dots. When she finally made the connection, sensing the trap she was in, she closed her eyes and sighed. Then came the tears, welling up beneath her eyelids and trickling down her cheeks.

'Little bastard.' She sniffed. 'What did Rookie ever do to deserve that?'

'You tell me.'

'Fuck knows.' She shook her head again and then wiped her nose on the back of her hand. Her words were beginning to slur. 'Dependable bloke, Rookie. Good gear.' She nodded, as if reaching out for some distant memory, then closed her eyes again, slumping back against the single cushion. For a moment, Winter thought the sofa was going to collapse. He leaned forward and gave her a little shake. She stirred.

'What was that for?'

'Your Darren came back. Was he alone?'

'Yeah. No. I can't remember.'

'Try.'

'I'm trying.' She gave another little sigh. 'Must have been a friend of his. Dunno.'

'You're still telling me the jeans aren't Darren's?'

'Yeah ... fuck knows ...' She trailed off, her eyes closing again.

Winter tried to rally her, reaching for every trick in the book. A deal on what might happen next. Even the possibility of more smack.

'I need some clues, love. This mate of Darren's. Other mates of Darren's. Names. Addresses.' He waited for a response. Nothing happened. He leaned forward, whispering in her ear, 'Remember who they've done, love. Remember Rookie. Eh?'

It was no good. She was out to the world, her head lolling back, her face still shiny with tears. Another couple of months like this and she'd look about ninety.

Winter got to his feet and went to the window. In the street outside, a bunch of kids was standing around Dawn's Peugeot, peering in. He opened the window and shouted at them to push off but they just laughed at him. There wasn't a kid round that car older than ten, he thought, but they'd all long ago sussed the odds. No one could touch them. Not their teachers. Not their parents. Not even the police. Put a finger on kids like these, and they'd be running to Pompey's small army of social workers with some wank story about paedos.

He stepped back into the room, thinking about Rookie. It wasn't that he'd ever liked the man. In fact he couldn't remember giving that aspect of their relationship a moment's thought. It was just that there was a protocol here, stuff you could and couldn't do, and one of the definite no-nos was attacking a man three times your age and turning him into a vegetable. Winter had very little time for mission statements from the likes of Hartigan but on occasions like these even he had to admit that the man had a point. Let the Darren Geeches of this world get away with it, and you were looking at anarchy.

Ellis wanted to show him something. They went into Darren's bedroom this time. She'd been through the wardrobe again. Propped at the back, behind the handful of hanging clothes, was a baseball bat. Winter squinted at it in the gloom. Even an hour later, the blood looked fresh.

'I haven't touched it,' Ellis said.

Winter nodded. Scenes of Crime could handle this. He struggled to his feet. Then, struck by a sudden thought, he asked about Dawn's new Peugeot. Did it, by any chance, come with a first aid kit?

'Yeah,' Dawn said.

'And does the kit include smelling salts?'

'I don't know. Shall I have a look?'

She was away less than a couple of minutes. When she returned, she handed Winter a small, white tube.

'I had a go.' She pulled a face. 'Makes your eyes water.'

Winter took the tube into the living room. Shelley Geech hadn't moved. He propped her head up, uncapped the tube, and waved the open end under her nose. For a couple of moments, nothing happened. Then her eyes shot open and she grabbed Winter's arm.

'What's going on . . . ?'

'That dog of Darren's. The one we found on his bed. Remember?'

She was fighting to make sense of the question. At length, she muttered, 'Charlie?'

'Yeah, Charlie. Attached to Charlie, is he, Darren? Fond of the dog?'

For a second or two, Winter thought he'd lost her again. Then she gave an involuntary little shudder and the grip on Winter's arm tightened even further.

'Loves him.' She swallowed hard. 'Loves him to death.'

Faraday looked up to find a figure at his open office door. Black trousers and a crisp white short-sleeved shirt. Hand raised, about to knock, and a big, round face that Faraday was sure he'd seen before.

'Mark Scott. Nick Hayder said you wanted a word.' He paused. 'Scottie ring a bell?'

Faraday had it now. Scottie was Nick Hayder's navy contact, the chisel he'd been using to prise open various bits of the RN bureaucracy. Nick had mentioned him in the bar when they'd talked earlier. Scottie had been appearing in the Major Crimes suite for months, slipping into Hayder's office and closing the door behind him. If Faraday really wanted a peek at Coughlin's service file, then Scottie was the man to ask.

Faraday got up. Scottie had a firm handshake. He settled himself in the spare chair and looked up at Faraday's wall board. Beside the RSPB calendar were a couple of photographs. One, taken at ground level, was an upward shot of an enormous tower block, twenty-three floors climbing into the bluest of skies. Beside it, Faraday's favourite, was a big colour blow-up showing a seabird plunging into an angry sea.

Scottie wanted to know about the flats.

'Chuzzlewit House, isn't it? Big block over by the station?'

'That's right.'

'So why . . . ?' Scottie nodded at the photo.

Faraday hesitated a moment, wrongfooted. This brand of candour – cheerful nosiness – obviously came with the job. According to Hayder, Scottie was a Reggie, a member of the navy's Regulating Branch. As a seagoing policeman, he understood the thrust and demand of major CID investigations and had won himself an official attachment to Nick's stranger rape inquiry. More to the point, with barely a year to serve, he had his eye on a second career in the civvy police.

Scottie still wanted to know about the flats.

'Job I was on last year.' Faraday was looking at the photo. 'I ended up on top of that lot with a kid of ten. There's a little parapet runs round the edge of the roof. The rest you wouldn't want to know.'

'This wasn't the kid who torched the house in Stamshaw?'

'Afraid so. Some people know no fear and he was one of them. The trick with a drop like that is never to look down.'

'And you?'

'Looked down.' Faraday shook his head. Even now,

more than a year later, he could feel the swirl and tug of the wind as he fought for balance on top of the parapet. J-J had been up there, too, at the mercy of the ten-year-old, and there'd only been Faraday to come between them. That was the night he'd first understood that fear was something you could physically taste.

Scottie, impressed, wanted more details but Faraday passed over the rest of the case. Infinitely more interesting was the other photo. Scottie got up and inspected the bird at close quarters.

'Gannet, isn't it?'

'Yes.' Wings folded back, the bird's dive was near vertical. J-J had snapped it years back on a birding trip they'd shared to the Bempton Cliffs in Yorkshire, getting lucky with an 80–200 zoom. Maybe that moment was a portent of all the other shots to come, thought Faraday. An even better reason for posting it on his office board.

'Nick told me you were a bird freak.' Scottie had sat down again. 'I used to do a bit myself when I was down in Plymouth. Strictly dude.'

'Whereabouts?'

'Up the river there, Tamar Valley, little place called Bere Ferrers. Low water, right time of year, you'd get to see all kinds of stuff.'

Faraday, who'd never visited the Tamar Valley, guessed at curlew, mallard, widgeon and teal, with maybe avocets in the winter. Mention of avocets drew a frown from Scottie.

'Black and white jobbies? Long legs? Funny upturned beak? Yeah, copped them by the shedload. Listen, about this bloke of yours, Coughlin. It's his service file you want, yeah?'

Nick had been right. Official channels, you might wait days for a result but Scottie had talked to a mate in HMS *Centurion*, over in Gosport, and with luck he'd have a photocopy by first thing tomorrow. *Centurion* was where they kept personnel records. Coughlin's was bound to be there.

'Do I need to talk to anyone else?'

'Not now you don't. If you get really stuck in I'll give you a number, my boss in the dockyard. Any luck, and he'll just sign me off on it.' Abruptly, he stood up and pumped Faraday's hand. Then his eyes returned to the soaring tower block. 'Nick said you did brilliant on that job. Must have been scary, though, eh?'

Scottie gone, Faraday returned to the paperwork on his desk. Amongst the dozens of messages was a call one of the management assistants had fielded. It had come from an Eadie Sykes. She'd left a number and wanted Faraday to call back. First time he'd seen the message, the name had meant nothing but now he realised who she was. Just why was J-J's new employer going to the trouble of tracking Faraday down? He picked up the phone, glad of a moment's respite from stroppy bosses and pain-in-the-arse DCs.

She picked up the phone on the first ring.

'Sykes.'

Faraday smiled. He didn't know too many women who introduced themselves so bluntly. She might have been Willard.

'It's Joe Faraday. J-J's dad. You rang.'

'I did. You're a hard man to find. I just wanted to say what a clever son you've got. Deserves a drink.'

'I'm sure he'll be delighted.'

'I meant you, Joe.'

'Me?' Faraday began to laugh. 'How come?'

'Just some things it might be good to discuss.'

'About J-J?'

'Maybe. Listen, tonight would be best. You name it. I'm buying.'

Faraday paused, trying not to think too hard about the million and one boxes he still had to tick.

'I'm not sure . . .'

'You gotta scheduling problem? Don't even talk about it. Come round when you're ready. You know those flat conversions on the seafront? Next to South Parade Pier? Mine's number thirty-three, top floor. There's a squawk box on the front door. Hit the button marked Sykes and we'll take it from there. Be good to talk, eh?' She laughed and then hung up, leaving Faraday gazing at the phone.

Seconds later, he turned to find Brian Imber at the door.

'Just had the computer unit on from Netley,' he said. 'They've got something they think might interest us.'

Winter was still at the city's Central police station with Dawn Ellis when Cathy Lamb caught up with them. Winter and Ellis had arrested Mrs Geech and driven her down to Central. The Custody Sergeant had booked her in and phoned the police surgeon for formal medical checks. In her state, there'd be no question of interview until the heroin had left her system. With Mrs Geech locked up for the night, and the police surgeon yet to appear, Winter and Ellis were about to head back to Highland Road.

'See you there,' Cathy said.

She'd already pulled a squad together and the meeting had begun by the time Winter and Ellis walked into the CID office. Winter counted nine bodies perched on desks and chairs, a mix of uniforms and CID. It was a decent turn-out for a force stretched to breaking point, ample proof that the bosses had decided to draw a line in the sand.

Cathy Lamb confirmed as much.

'Hartigan's had enough,' she was saying. 'And frankly I don't blame him. I've had the *News* on twice already. We're talking broad daylight with a middle-aged man beaten half to death. They've got a couple of quotes off some of the locals. It's going to look like Beirut in the paper.'

'It *is* Beirut.' It was Rick Stapleton, called in on a leave-day. Judging by the state of his hands, he'd been working on his Kawasaki again.

'Thanks for that.' Lamb sounded knackered. 'The problem's going to be witnesses. We'll have to crack that somehow but at least there's a name in the frame. Paul?'

Winter settled himself on the table beside the electric kettle. He and Dawn Ellis had paid two visits to a flat in Somerstown. The boy's name was Geech. He was well suss for the corner shops and also had his fingers in Bazza Mackenzie's pie, much to the irritation of one of the older dealers.

'Who's now in neuro?' Stapleton again. 'Surprise, surprise.'

A ripple of laughter went round the room, stilled by Cathy Lamb. She wanted Winter to explain about the first search and the surprising absence of heroin wraps in the boy's wardrobe. Stapleton followed him word for word.

'So you knew where to look?'

'Yeah.'

'Because Rooke had told you?'

'That's right.'

'And the kid was watching when you looked in the wardrobe?'

''Fraid so.'

'Don't you like this Rooke bloke? Or were you sending a message?'

Winter looked pained. He'd trusted Rookie implicitly. He'd expected a decent stash of smack, enough to lift the boy from the streets for a while. Without Geech, the rest of the kids who were doing the corner shops would go off the boil. Wasn't that the whole point of the exercise?

'Sure.' Stapleton nodded. 'But you know the score with kids and the law. A word from some social worker, and Geech'd be out on bail and back to give this Rooke a smacking. As it is, the bloke just got it early. Great result.'

Winter feigned outrage. He didn't see it that way at all.

'One street dealer off the plot? One fifteen-year-old lunatic on the run? That's double top, isn't it? Brilliant darts.'

Cathy Lamb intervened. She wasn't interested in family rows. Hartigan was right. They had to get out in Somerstown in substantial numbers and start sending a message. First priority was the boy, Geech. The forensic haul from his mum's flat would, fingers crossed, be more than enough to put him away. First, though, they had to find him.

There were murmured suggestions from the assembled squad – putting the word round the usual places, issuing mug shots to units city wide, staking out his top mates – but it was Winter who came up with an alternative. He had ground to make up and on these occasions he liked nothing better than an audience.

He signalled to Cathy, then pointed down the office. The cairn terrier was still curled under Winter's desk, cocooned in Police No Entry tape.

'Young Darren's got a real thing about his bloody dog. Can't live without him.' Winter smiled. 'Why don't I work something out?'

Seven

In the end it was the DS who drove over to Kingston Crescent from the Computer Crime Unit at Netley. Faraday convened a small impromptu meeting in Willard's office – just Brian Imber and Dave Michaels – and let the DS have first shout.

Frank Stockley was a short, broad-shouldered forty-five-year-old with a greying crew cut and an impressive tan. He and his wife had just come back from three weeks in Florida and couldn't wait to put down a deposit on a house out there. Gulf Coast was favourite. Ten miles inland from Tampa and property was still a steal. Who needed another wet winter in Fareham when your biggest problem was buying a fridge big enough for all those ice-cold lagers?

He spread his papers out on the conference table. The analysis of Coughlin's hard disks was in its early stages, he said, and there were a lot of problems still to be cracked, but a pattern was beginning to sort itself out and he only thought it right to flag up one or two preliminary leads.

'First off, we've got a confirmed on the man's handle. That's the name he used, his alias if you like. It was definitely Freckler. Second, we had a dip into the hard disk during the cloning process, just to see what came up, and he's definitely been using newsgroups. We're still burning stuff from the cloned disk on to CDs but in the meantime we thought we'd check out the archive. This is techie stuff, I know, but there's a site called DejaVu, holds the records for every newsgroup conversation ever, and we've been into that, searching under Freckler.'

Imber was no stranger to cybertalk but Michaels was as fascinated as Faraday.

'And?' he said.

'Lots of stuff.' He patted the pile of print-outs in front of him. 'Keep you going for weeks.'

Faraday nodded. Duplicating data like this was standard procedure. Coughlin's original hard disk had itself become vital evidence, its preservation for court purposes as important as the state of the room where he'd met his death. A virtual crime scene, Faraday thought, full of hidden pointers.

Imber wanted to know about Coughlin's manners on the internet. There were protocols here, many of them unspoken, but a very definite code to which you were expected to conform. Had Coughlin behaved himself? Or did the print-outs tell a different story?

'He was an animal,' Stockley said at once. 'The guest from hell. Threw his weight around wherever he went. If you're after a list of guys he's offended, I can give you thousands.'

'Great.' Faraday glanced at his watch. Despite the messages he'd left, Corbett still hadn't been in touch.

Stockley was passing round examples of Coughlin's contribution to newsgroups. The groups themselves were categorised under headings. 'Rec.', for instance, catered for hobbies and pastimes while 'sci.' was reserved for scientific exchanges. Traditionally, all the oddballs, misfits and hippie refugees headed for the cyber-hills, getting together in newsgroups under the 'alt.' heading, and this had been Coughlin's favourite destination. Here, at least, he stood some chance of bumping into like-minded folk, the cyber equivalent of a dodgy bar, yet even in these newsgroups he seemed determined to bust every rule.

Faraday was looking at an exchange from a couple of years back. A guy calling himself Dozer had told a joke about three priests on a 747. The joke was far too involved and not very funny but had nevertheless attracted a small round of applause from others logged on. Then, abruptly, in steamed Freckler. He hated fucking priests. The only good priest was a dead priest. He'd seen enough of the cunts to last him a lifetime and a half. When the chips were down, and you really needed someone to talk to, away they went with their Bibles and prayer books and you'd find them days later screwing some poor fucking choirboy to death. This outburst, totally out of keeping with everything else that had happened in the group, earned a mild rebuke from a couple of fellow contributors. 'Hey, fella,' one of them had typed, 'if that's what you do for openers, hate to be around later in the day.'

Indeed. Reading on through more of the print-outs, Faraday began to wonder whether Coughlin had been drunk during these tirades, or whether the privacy of 7a Niton Road had simply offered him the chance to get one or two things off his chest.

Whatever the drift of the newsgroup conversation he encountered, he seized the smallest opportunity to blaze off at a tangent, attacking a series of seemingly random targets. A couple of minutes with stuff like this and there was absolutely no doubt about the length of his personal hit list.

Leaving the priesthood to one side, Coughlin had hated Jews, blacks, Hispanics, every Home Secretary who'd ever lived, politicians in general, football fans, social workers, smart bastards who drove BMWs and thought they owned the fucking world, girlie weather forecasters, people who ponced around in Waitrose, and the dozy old bitch at the school round the corner who saw the kids across the road and kept grinning at everyone like she was some kind of idiot.

In judicial terms, this stuff was of zero evidential value – there was no law against spoiling someone's evening in a newsgroup – but Faraday sensed it was priceless in terms of what it told him about the inner Coughlin. There was a madness about this man that you'd want to avoid, an inner darkness that enveloped every single one of his conversations. Not once did anything amuse or gladden him. Not once did he offer anyone a compliment or even a greeting. In a real-life bar, this was a voice that would empty the place in minutes. No wonder Davidson, banged up with no prospect of escape, had hated the man.

Faraday asked Stockley what he thought. Coughlin, on this evidence, was a monster. No?

Stockley counselled caution.

'You have to be careful with all this stuff,' he said. 'The internet's a strange place. It's not face to face, and that's the point. Lots of people pretend. They adopt a persona. They change their age, change their sex. Sometimes they become what they've wanted to be all along. A lot of it's straight fantasy.'

'But Coughlin *was* horrible. Everyone we've talked to says so.'

'I know, Dave told me on the phone.' He shot Michaels a look. 'Mr Nasty? Am I right?'

'Spot on,' Dave Michaels confirmed. 'You read those statements from his fellow screws and no one had a good word for him. Tell me something, Frank' – he had his finger anchored in one of the print-outs – 'what's this?'

He passed the print-out around the table. In July last year, after someone in the States had taken violent exception to Coughlin's views on the US navy, Coughlin had told him to get down on all fours and do himself a favour. This invitation had been followed by a strange footnote. Faraday gazed at it. O X? What did that mean?

Stockley obliged with a translation.

'It's like a smiley.' He reached for a pen. 'This' – he drew :-) – 'means you're happy, someone's made you laugh. This' :–('means the reverse. People use it all the time in newsgroups and chat rooms.'

'And OX?'

'I'm guessing but I think it means kiss my arse. That's one of the things about Coughlin. He seemed to make these things up. Here. He used to type this sometimes, too.'

Stockley drew another series of characters and passed it across. Faraday frowned. What did O''''''''''''''\: mean?

Stockley laughed.

'Work it out. In conversation, he'd probably say "Fuck you".'

Faraday peered at it again: the big 'O', the eager line of apostrophes, the erect little backslash.

'Nice,' he said at last.

Brian Imber wanted to know about Stockley's time-frame. This stuff was very interesting but it didn't really get them any further. They'd all assumed that Coughlin was a monster and now they knew it for sure. When might they expect hard leads?

'Like what?'

'Like people he might have pissed off recently.' Imber picked up a handful of print-outs and let them fall through his fingers. 'I don't know how personal this stuff gets but I suppose it's possible that someone might have come looking. No?'

It certainly happened, Stockley said. There came moments when individuals crossed the cyber-divide, heading back into real life. Some of these newsgroup encounters ended in bed. There was no reason to suppose that others shouldn't lead to the mortuary.

'And Coughlin? You'll be checking that out?'

'Of course. The next stage is for us to go through his recent conversations. The newsgroups should all be archived and accessible. Chat rooms are dodgier. Depending on the server, these conversations often fall off the end and disappear within hours. Then there's the problem of tracing particular subscribers. If it's a foreign-based ISP, it could take for ever.'

Faraday was lost again. Like Imber, he wanted a name, an address, hard data, a door he could knock on, not a bunch of fantasists in la-la land.

Dave Michaels held up a hand.

'Why Freckler?' he said.

Stockley admitted he didn't know. He'd never heard the nickname before. Was Coughlin a ginger by any chance?

'No way.' Michaels had seen the SOC photos, full colour. 'Not a freckle on him.'

Michaels glanced down the table. They'd all heard the trill of Faraday's mobile. Faraday dug it out of his jacket pocket, then frowned and glanced at his watch.

'So how come it's taken you so long?' he muttered.

He bent to the phone again, the frown deepening. At length he nodded.

'Make it half seven. My office.' He snapped the phone shut and looked at Michaels. 'Corbett,' he said briefly.

Winter, helping himself to another chocolate biscuit, couldn't believe his ears.

'Tell me that again.'

The woman readily obliged. She'd taken the Audi to the car wash at the Jet station in Green Road. She'd gone for the once-a-month shampoo and wax, buying a couple of pounds' worth of tokens from the cashier in the garage. She'd given the car a good hosing with the foamy brush and followed up with a high-pressure rinse but the token had run out halfway through and she'd had to go back inside to buy another one. There'd been a bit of a queue at the counter but she hadn't given the car a second thought. Yes, it had been unlocked, and yes, the keys were still in the ignition, but the last thing she'd expected was to go back round the corner and find the bloody thing gone.

'And the dog? Charlie?'

'Inside on the back seat. He loved it when I used the car wash, especially the soap cycle.'

'And you reported the car missing?'

'Of course I did.'

'What about the dog?'

'I mentioned it, certainly.' She frowned. 'Maybe it never got written down.'

Mrs Czinski lived around the corner from the Camber Dock, in Old Portsmouth, a newish house with a red door and a now-empty garage. She worked as a part-time teacher in the local grammar school, a job for which she was eternally grateful because her Polish-born architect husband had lost a battle against alcoholism and was currently hospitalised with suspected cirrhosis. Losing the car had been a real bind but what she most wanted in the world was her dog back.

Winter, who had Charlie in his Subaru outside, wanted to know more about the car.

'Audi, you say?'

'That's right. Audi A4. It used to belong to my husband but it's not much use to him these days. I was wondering whether to tell him about it but there's no point at the moment, is there? Not if you're going to get it back?'

Winter was asking himself why all this had come as a surprise. The details of the theft would have been input on to the force automatic crime recording system, presumably under this woman's name. A simple search on the ACR database through his own PC would have highlighted the Audi's disappearance. Shame he hadn't done it.

'What colour was the car?'

'Red.'

'Registration?'

'XBK 386 . . .' She half-closed her eyes. 'W.'

'Any identifying marks?'

'Not when I last saw it.' She paused. 'You will get it back, won't you?'

Winter assured her they'd be doing their best. Charlie ending up with Darren Geech wasn't proof that the boy had nicked it in the first place but Winter, given Geech's track record, didn't need much convincing that this was probably the case. His mum's flat was barely a quarter of a mile away from the Jet station in Green Road, and if you had the right connections there were countless places where you could stash a motor like that. No wonder the boy had disappeared. He was probably squatting in some lock-up, keeping an eye on Mrs Czinski's precious Audi.

'This dog of yours, Charlie,' Winter began, 'we've definitely retrieved him.'

'You have?' She clapped her hands and for a moment Winter thought he was in for a hug. 'Where? Where is he?'

'At the station,' Winter said. 'Good as gold, he is.'

'My Charlie? You're sure it's my Charlie? Little pink bows on his collar?'

Winter smiled. The thought of Darren Geech out and about in Somerstown with a dog sporting pink bows was irresistible.

'The bows have gone, I'm afraid. But he's a champion eater.'

'He is? Thank God for that. Wonderful. You've made my day.'

Winter helped himself to another cup of tea from the pot on the low table between them. He'd be bringing Charlie round a bit later but first he had a favour to ask. The police were forever on the look-out for good-news stories. Charlie's return was a natural. If he talked to a contact on the *News*, might Mrs Czinski be willing to pose for a photo? Charlie makes it home again? Something like that?

'Of course I would, of course I would. Only too pleased.'

'They might name you in the paper. Is that a problem?'

'Absolutely not. Why should it be?'

'No reason at all, Mrs Czinski.' Winter smiled. 'Just asking.'

Corbett was late for his appointment with Faraday. Nearly eight o'clock, the Major Crimes suite was emptying fast. One of the indexers in the incident room was still inputting data into HOLMES, and Paul Ingham was reprioritising his undischarged list of actions for tomorrow morning, but the offices either side of the long central corridor were largely empty.

Faraday hooked the spare chair towards him with his foot and told Corbett to sit down. They could do this quietly, get it over with, or Corbett could throw his toys out of the pram. His choice.

'I'm not with you.' Corbett's eyes were the colour of slate. 'Sir.'

'You went to the Detective Superintendent behind my back. That was pretty silly.'

'Was it?'

Corbett held Faraday's gaze. The motorcycling leathers looked brand new. The white full-face helmet in his lap was decorated with a long, scarlet lightning flash, and when he shifted position in the chair Faraday caught sight of the neatly stencilled medical details on the back. This man, thought Faraday, belongs in a kids' cartoon. The Warrior King. Blood group O.

'Why didn't you come to me? Why go to Mr Willard?'

'Because you weren't here.'

'I was away for a couple of hours. You could have written me a note if it was that important. Rung me on my mobile. Left me a number to get back on.'

'You could have been anywhere. How was I to know you'd be back so soon?'

'Did you bother to check with DS Michaels?'

'No.'

'Shame, he'd have told you where I was.' Faraday let the silence grow between them. It didn't bother Corbett in the least. 'So tell me, what makes you think you've got the right to go straight to the top like that?'

'I had some intelligence. I thought it was materially important.'

'Thought?'

'Think. The reason I phoned Mr Willard was simple. Stuff gets lost in the system. That's no surprise. Happens everywhere. Get yourself plugged in the way I've done, keep your ear to the ground, and you don't want that kind of intelligence just dribbling away . . .'

His eyes never left Faraday's face. What he thought of the SE Hants Major Crime team couldn't have been clearer.

'So why didn't you take it to DS Imber?'

'I don't know DS Imber.'

'You should do. He heads our Intelligence Cell.'

'I know that. I meant I don't know him personally. Never had the pleasure.'

'What difference is that supposed to make?'

In spite of a determination not to rise to this kind of provocation, Corbett was making Faraday very angry indeed, and the realisation made him angrier still. A tiny smile puckered the corner of Corbett's mouth. When he didn't answer the question, Faraday asked him again. At length, he shrugged.

'No difference at all, sir. I just thought it best to go to the top.'

'Then you were wrong. When Mr Willard's away, I am the top. Do you have a problem with that?'

'Not at all.' He gestured idly at the space between them. 'It's not me who's got the problem here.'

For a moment, Faraday fought the urge to take Corbett by the throat and wipe the smile off his face. Then he leaned forward, gesturing the DC closer.

'You know something, my friend? You're even more

reckless than I thought. On this unit, there are things you do and things you don't do. We have a system here. It depends on teamwork. You have intelligence to offer, you take it to DS Michaels. He's our Receiver. That's what he does. And if Dave's not around, you try the Intelligence Cell. Or me. It's not rocket science, OK?' Faraday held his gaze for a long moment, then eased back in the chair. 'It's too late for an apology so there's no point making one. You were a dickhead to phone Mr Willard and Mr Willard will doubtless be making the point in his own way later. I'd wish you luck but I wouldn't want to raise your hopes of staying on this investigation. If it was down to me, you'd have been out of the door hours ago.'

For the first time, Faraday detected a reaction, the merest flicker of a nerve beneath Corbett's left eye. Anxiety? Anger. He didn't know.

'Tell me about this intelligence,' Faraday said. 'Pretend I know nothing.'

Corbett amplified what Willard had already said over the phone. Before he'd gone to court on the GBH, Davidson had been one of the in-demand drivers around the Streatham/Balham area. He'd been nicking motors for most of his young life and was extremely good behind the wheel. A couple of gangs, to Corbett's certain knowledge, had hired his services on quality jobs and he'd built himself a sweet reputation with the people who really mattered.

'So how come he was stupid enough to run the woman over?'

'He may not have done. In my view, Davidson was right to kick up a fuss about not driving the car.'

'The ID parade?'

'One woman picked him out. Three other witnesses didn't.'

'The forensic from the car?'

'He held up his hands to nicking it. Never denied that

for a moment. Hair, prints, fuck knows what else, the motor would have been full of it. No, the point about the car is much simpler. Say he did run the woman over. Given the fact he drove off sharpish, got away with it, why didn't he torch the car afterwards? That way, there'd have been no forensic at all. Just one woman's word at the ID parade.'

'OK.' Faraday conceded the point with a nod. 'Say he didn't do it. Say someone else was at the wheel when the woman got run over. Where does that take us with Coughlin?'

There was a creak of new leather as Corbett shifted in the chair. He crossed one leg over the other, making himself comfortable.

'The way I read it, Davidson was stitched up. The bloke at the wheel that day was tied in with the firm Davidson was working for. Someone higher up. Someone with clout. He blew it on the crossing and ran the woman over. His arse was more precious than Davidson's. Davidson took the fall.'

'And knew it?'

'Yeah. Either knew it or worked it out later. He had plenty of time.'

'And now?'

'He's back in Balham, back on the scene.'

'Picking up where he left off? Same firm?'

'More or less. One or two of the faces have changed but it's the same blokes calling the shots at the top.'

'And you're telling me they owe him?'

'Yeah, big time.'

'Conscience?'

'That plus he's the same old Ainsley Davidson. Good at nicking motors. Even better at driving them. He's broke. He needs money. As well as something on deposit.'

'A contract on Coughlin?'

'A roughing-up that went too far.' He paused, inspecting his fingernails. 'Coughlin inhaled his own puke, didn't he? That doesn't sound like a contract to me.'

'And the state of the room? The porn mags?'

'They smashed the place up and sent a little message. Coughlin was a wanker. Par for the course.'

Faraday was still wondering where Corbett had picked up the details on the post-mortem. Maybe Paul Ingham, he thought. Or even Dave Michaels.

'All this intelligence . . .' Faraday waved a hand at the space between them. 'Where does it come from?'

'I worked at Streatham, CID,' he said. 'You get to know a lot of blokes in three years.'

'You've been tapping them up?'

'Of course I have. That's what I get paid for.'

'You're paid to share information, spread it around. It's called teamwork.'

'You weren't here,' he repeated. 'So I went one better.'

'Of course you did.' Faraday got up and went to the window. Gone eight, it was still broad daylight. The car park below was nearly empty but a queue of lorries was still heading into the nearby ferryport. 'DS Imber is processing a formal request through channels,' he said at length. 'When we see what comes back, we'll be in a better position to make some operational decisions.'

'Meaning?'

'Meaning I don't place that much reliance on hearsay. You've got anything on paper? Officers you've talked to? Sources? Names?'

'You know I haven't. That's not the way it works. Not in the real world.'

Faraday didn't even have to force the smile. Wind-ups this obvious were easy to deal with. He glanced at his watch and turned back into the office.

'Dunno about you,' he said, 'but I've got better things to do than hang about here all night. I take it you've checked in with DS Ingham?'

'Of course.'

'Glad to hear it.' He nodded towards the door. 'We're widening the house-to-house parameters tomorrow. Good luck with the PDFs.'

Winter had more trouble than he'd anticipated convincing the *News* about Charlie. His best contact was a journalist who occasionally did week-long stints as a stand-in for the news editor. She was youngish and extremely pretty and she'd come to Winter's attention during the course of a long-running investigation into arcade robberies.

Gangs were running round the country with some very expensive tools that got them inside the latest gaming machines. They'd work arcades, clubs and pubs mob-handed, the women distracting the security staff while the pointmen did the business. It took barely a minute to empty a machine of all its cash and the beauty of the scam was that no one knew any different until the next big jackpot was due and the punter found himself looking at an empty tray.

A good team would net hundreds of pounds a night, and Winter had spent several very happy weeks gathering intelligence from outlets the length of Southsea seafront. Coincidentally, a routine *News* enquiry for tasty background information on current inquiries had been OK'd by Hartigan, and the reporter who'd turned up with her notebook and scoop-necked Elle T-shirt had, by some welcome twist of fate, been directed Winter's way. He hadn't bothered her with any of the operational details on the machines scam, but he'd told her enough to whet her appetite and she'd gone off very happy. The resulting feature had been embargoed until the case came to court but she'd still wound up with her name in lights and a nice memo from the editor.

Now, she seemed to be having trouble spotting Charlie's news value. Was this a rare breed of dog? Had it just had a heart transplant? Or was she missing something here? Winter started going through the whole thing again, then realised there were better ways to bait the hook.

'You'll know about the guy kicked half to death in Somerstown . . .' he began.

'Sure. Front-page lead in tomorrow's paper. What about it?'

'Just some enquiries we're making. Might interest you.'

'Yeah? Like what?'

'Can't say just now but when I can, you might be the first to know.'

'Is that a promise?'

'It most certainly is.'

'Are we talking tomorrow?'

'We might be.'

'And Charlie?'

'He's here now, love. I can meet your snapper outside the owner's place. A Mrs Czinski. Heart of gold and extremely photogenic.' He paused. 'Do I hear a yes?'

Eight

It was nearly dark by the time Faraday made it to the long terrace of apartments overlooking South Parade Pier. Pre-war, most of these buildings had been well-kept family hotels, catering to the thousands of holidaymakers who took the train down from London and stayed for weeks on end, but vacation tastes had changed and the hotels had got seedier and seedier until the developers stepped in, sorted out the crumbling stucco and Victorian plumbing and turned the entire parade into a lifestyle statement. Instead of tour coaches, there were BMWs and sleek Mercedes saloons at the kerbside. Instead of high tea and an evening of bingo, the new residents preferred digital TV and designer cocktails.

Eadie Sykes lived at number thirty-three. Faraday inspected the intercom and pressed the button against her name. After a couple of showers in the late afternoon, the weather had cheered up again and the tiny cap of cloud over the Isle of Wight was pinked with the last rays of sunset.

'Joe? Hi. Come up.'

Faraday took the lift to the fourth floor, trying hard not to look at himself in the mirrored glass. The last twenty-four hours had been even more brutal than usual and he knew it showed on his face. Keep up this kind of pace and he'd need more than a couple of snatched extra hours in bed before the city delivered another corpse to Major Crimes.

Eadie Sykes had left the door to her flat open. She must have heard the lift arrive because she shouted for him to come in. First sight of her flat took Faraday's breath away. The interior space stretched the full depth of the building, acres of maplewood flooring dotted with rich oriental rugs. The walls were painted a fashionable green – a shade or two lighter than sage – and the scattering of chrome and leather furniture was arranged to make the most of the view.

Tall glass doors opened on to an ample balcony. Standing in the coolness of the dusk, Faraday gazed out over the Solent. A pattern of lights against the dark hump of the island resolved itself into a cruise liner. Inshore, much closer, he could hear the putter-putter of a fishing boat pushing out against the flooding tide.

'Don't be too impressed. I'm only camping.'

Faraday didn't believe her. Spend a single night with this view, and you'd never want to leave.

He stepped back into the room and looked round again, wondering how he'd alter things. A change of sofa, definitely, and pictures on the walls that didn't look so impersonal. Whoever had furnished this place had never got beyond the second floor at John Lewis.

'Where do you sleep?'

'Through there.' Eadie indicated a connecting door. 'Bathroom and two bedrooms. Poky compared to this.'

There was a fitted kitchen at the back of the room, lots more chrome. Everything looked brand new, barely used, a page ripped straight from the brochure. There was nothing on the big ceramic hob but hints of garlic and rosemary suggested something bubbling in the oven.

'I thought you were taking me out for a beer?'

'Afraid not.' Eadie shook her head. 'I thought I'd test your sense of humour and do some cooking. You're not a veggie, are you?'

'Never.'

'Thank Christ for that. There's a butcher I just found in Fratton. Lamb to die for. Change your life.'

She swept him on to the sofa and poured a huge glass

of wine. Given any kind of choice, Faraday would have preferred a beer but never had the chance to ask.

'Rioja. Bloody wonderful. Try it.'

Faraday did what he was told. She was right. The wine was delicious. She went back to the kitchen and rummaged around in a cupboard before returning with a bowl of cashews. She was a big woman, broad shouldered, and moved with the easy lope of a serious athlete. Conversationally, she seemed to ride wave after wave as they caught her fancy and she radiated an energy that lit up her entire face. Someone like this around, Faraday thought, and you'd never bother with central heating.

He'd noticed a pair of worn Nike runners in the hall.

'You go jogging?'

'Every morning.' She dipped in the bowl for another handful of cashews. 'Get out there early and there's no one around. That way you keep your secrets.'

'Which are . . . ?'

'I'm too bloody fat.' She slapped a thigh. 'You know something about your boy? He's going to have hair just like yours.'

She reached up and touched the greying curls at Faraday's temple. It was a cheerful, artless gesture, completely devoid of sexual overtones, and it made Faraday feel curiously at home. Another glass of wine and he'd forget he'd ever met Andy Corbett.

'So who owns this place?'

'Guy called Doug Hughes. He's got the whole block.'

'And you rent it from him? Must cost a fortune.'

'Not really. We've got an arrangement.'

'What kind of arrangement?'

'I keep an eye on the other tenants. Throw little soirées when he wants to impress someone. Go away for the weekend and leave him the key when he fancies a discreet shag. Works OK most of the time.'

'You know this guy well?'

'Should do.' She laughed, reaching for the wine bottle. 'He used to be my husband.'

'You're serious?'

'Always.' She recharged his glass, and then handed him the bottle. 'Call me Sykes, by the way.' She was on her feet again. 'Everybody else does.'

They ate supper on stools in the kitchen. The lamb was delicious, a half-shoulder with the meat still pink round the bone. Afterwards, picking fat green olives from the salad, Faraday wanted to know more about her film-making. He'd noticed a pile of stationery next to the phone. The stationery was headed Ambrym Productions, and carried her name. Why Ambrym?

'You know the New Hebrides? Bunch of Pacific islands next to Oz? Ambrym's where I was conceived.'

Her father had been an English teacher in the Australian government service. He'd volunteered for a posting to the New Hebrides and stayed a while. Sykes had been eleven before the family had returned to Melbourne and still carried the happiest memories of her island childhood. Faraday, eyeing the remains of the lamb, was impressed.

'You want to be careful.' Sykes laughed. 'I might get the album out.'

After secondary school in Melbourne, she'd won a scholarship to the University of Sydney. Three years' intermittent study had given her a degree in French studies and a lifelong passion for surfing. Waiting table in the evenings at a posh harbourside restaurant, she'd met Doug Hughes. Even then, at twenty-three, he'd known exactly what he wanted in life.

'Which was?'

'Me, for starters. That was easy. Then he wanted money, serious money. That took a while longer.'

She'd flown back with him to the UK and a year later, days before her visa expired, they'd got married. By now,

Doug had passed his accountancy exams. Six months with a big city firm had cured him of any desire to work for other people and so they'd come south, to Portsmouth, where his brother was already running an interior design business.

Times were tough in the early eighties but Doug had taken a gamble, setting himself up as a chartered accountant and slowly building a worthwhile list of clients. They'd lived from hand to mouth for a couple of years, renting a two-up, two-down in Fratton, but as credit began to ease they'd taken the plunge and acquired their first mortgage, a cosy little house in central Southsea. Forty grand had been way beyond their means but within a couple of weeks Doug had struck lucky with a new client, and from that point on he'd never looked back.

'Who was the client?'

'A builder. Young bloke. Ambitious. Just like Doug. They've stuck together ever since. Brothers-in-arms.'

She and Doug moved twice more. The houses got bigger and bigger until the nineties arrived, by which time Doug was fast becoming the rich man of his dreams.

'That's when it all went wrong, if you want the truth. Broke, we were really happy, kids living from hand to mouth, but money gives you choices, doesn't it? Doug used to call it making the most of life. Still does when he gets pissed.'

'What kind of choices?'

'Everything, you name it. I'd give you a list but we haven't got time.'

'Women?'

'Of course, by the hundreds. Sometimes I think he found safety in numbers but he's got married again recently so it can't be true, can it?'

For the first time, Faraday sensed a wistfulness, the hint of an ache between this tumble of reminiscence, and it occurred to him that her sex life with her ex-husband might not be quite over. There were lots of ways to pay for a flat like this and an occasional shag for old times' sake might well be one of them.

'You haven't told me about Ambrym Productions,' he said gently.

'I haven't?'

She cleared the plates away and then poured more wine. Divorce had given her a good financial settlement – more money than she'd ever had in her life – but she bored easily and knew she had to find something to do with her time. The local poly ran a production course for aspiring film directors and she'd enrolled. After a couple of years running round with a cheap VHS camera, she'd pretty much mastered the basics and Doug had been happy to stake her when she decided to chance her arm and set up a small production company. Ambrym Productions still occupied the same two rooms in premises in Hampshire Terrace and though she'd never make a fortune, she'd certainly managed to pay her way.

'It's fun,' she said. 'How many jobs can you say that about?'

Faraday smiled, toying with his wine glass. He liked this woman. She was vivid and gutsy and this story of hers seemed totally in keeping with the warmth of her physical presence. Unlike so many people he knew, she didn't waste time on regrets or blame. Life, he suspected, would never intimidate her.

'That film you're making at the moment. The one with J-J. You were going to show me the . . .' Faraday frowned. He couldn't remember the term.

'Rough cut. I dubbed a copy and brought it home. Kick off your shoes. I'll put it on.'

She pulled out a video cassette from a satchel on the floor and slipped it into the player under the big wide-screen television. Faraday made himself comfortable on the sofa. There were worse things in life, he'd decided, than a couple of bottles of Rioja and conversation that had absolutely nothing to do with DNA and cloned hard disks. It had been this way when he'd first met Marta – a pleasure uncomplicated by any kind of commitment, physical or otherwise – and in the long, empty months since she'd ended the relationship he'd realised just how much he missed the chance to let his guard down. Women, he'd decided, were brilliant at cracking one of life's toughest challenges: how to relax.

'Comfy?' Sykes threw him the remote control and returned to the kitchen to make coffee.

Faraday thumbed the play button and settled down. Expecting shots of tiny launches bucketing in across the Solent, he found himself watching a slow pan across acres of white headstones. There were hundreds of them, bone-white under the bluest of skies. On the soundtrack, haunting flute notes dipped to make way for a man's voice. It was an old voice, bitter and reflective, and as he began to talk the cemetery on the screen resolved into a single headstone. 'An Australian Soldier of the 1939–1945 War' went the inscription. '20th – 27th May, 1941'.

Faraday felt a stir of movement beside him. Sykes had returned from the kitchen and was staring at the screen.

'Shit,' she said. 'Wrong cassette.'

She reached for the remote but Faraday shook his head.

'Leave it,' he said. 'I want to watch.'

Dawn Ellis was in the bath when she heard the knock at the front door. She reached for her watch. Quarter past ten. She listened for a moment or two, then sank back into the water. Whoever it was could come back some other time, preferably at a respectable hour. If it turned out to be Winter again, she'd kill him.

'Dawn?' It wasn't Winter. No way. 'Dawn?'

The voice was familiar, though. Not a stranger. Reluctantly, she climbed out of the bath and towelled herself dry. Wrapping herself in a dressing gown, she made her way downstairs. The knock again, louder this time. He's been round the side, she thought. And seen the light in the bathroom window.

She put the chain on the door and opened it. Through the gap, she could see a figure silhouetted against the street lights. He had boots on and shiny leathers. He was cradling a helmet.

'Andy?'

'I knew you were in.'

'What's the matter? What is it?' For a moment she thought he must have had an accident.

'Just fancied a chat.' He flashed her an uncertain smile. 'Can I come in?'

She didn't know what to say. They'd had a drink on a couple of occasions, it was true, but that hardly qualified for a full-on relationship. What on earth possessed him to turn up so late like this?

She pulled the dressing gown more tightly around herself. It wasn't that cold with the door open but she knew she was shivering. Pathetic, she told herself. I'm being pathetic.

She slipped off the chain and opened the door. Corbett gave her a nod and stepped round her as she shut the door behind him. He smelled of fresh air and new leather.

'Coffee?'

'Please.'

He waited in the chaos of the lounge at the front while she boiled water in the kettle. He must have put the television on because she could hear the round-up of the day's World Cup scores at the end of the BBC news.

'Milk? Sugar?'

'As it comes.'

He was sitting on the tiny sofa, stiff as a board. He'd moved all her magazines up to one end and found a nest for his helmet amongst the laundry she'd been meaning to dump in the washing machine. The sight of her thong wound in with assorted knickers and tops brought the colour to her face.

'You hungry? Want anything to eat?'

Corbett shook his head. He still hadn't looked up at her. In fact he'd barely moved.

'No, thanks. Sorry to barge in like this.'

She began to tell him it didn't matter but he held up a hand. He wanted to pick her brains, get one or two things off his chest.

'About what?'

'Faraday.'

'What about him?'

She passed him the coffee and at last he looked up at her. His face was drained of all expression. She'd never seen such dead eyes.

'He's a disgrace,' he said softly. 'The man shouldn't be let anywhere near a major crime.'

'What makes you say that?'

The question, innocent enough, set him off. He told her about Davidson, about going to London, about the intelligence stuff he'd put together with the help of old mates. He told about the interview he'd done and the conclusions he'd drawn. He'd got Davidson by the bollocks, worked the whole thing out, saved the inquiry trillions in overtime, and now, as a thank you, Faraday had put him on house-to-house. The man, he said again, was a disgrace. He had no experience, no proper grip. He played everything by the book. He was ignoring a lead other governors would have given their eye teeth for. He was terrified of stepping outside the rules.

'Really?' Dawn had her own quarrels with Faraday but would never have accused him of over-respect for his bosses. On the contrary, the bloody man was forever going his own sweet way. 'He's new to Major Crimes. It's a big challenge.'

'Yeah, and wasted on people like him. In the Met, I'd

give him a week, maybe two, then they'd find him something more suitable. School crossings, if he was lucky. You want to know what I really think? I think he's got something on Willard.'

'And Willard protects him? That's daft. Willard wouldn't protect anyone he didn't think was doing their job.'

'Yeah, unless he had no choice.'

'You're being paranoid. You really are. You ought to watch yourself on that bike.'

'Yeah? And what's that supposed to mean?' He stared at her and for a split second she saw something in his face that made her feel deeply uncomfortable.

'Joke?' she said. 'Listen, I sympathise, I really do. I don't know what you expected down here but it's obviously not working out. It happens sometimes, we all know that, but you just have to ride with the knocks. Blokes like Faraday are doing their best, just like the rest of us. We may not be as cool as the guys you're used to, and most of the jobs are pretty crappy if you want the truth, but at least you've got something half-decent for a change.'

'Yeah, and look what's happening. Maybe he's just trying to string it out. This Davidson's well-sus, believe me. He's a hundred per cent totally in the frame and we haven't even rattled his cage yet. So how do you explain that?'

'Faraday has a strange way of doing things sometimes.'

'Tell me about it.'

'Yeah, but it may not be the way it looks. You think he's lost interest but often it's the reverse. You ought to talk to some of the other guys. Bev Yates is good on Faraday, reads him like a book.'

'He's another one.'

'Who?'

'Yates. Should have been pensioned off years ago. If he

bangs on about bloody football again, I'll fucking throttle him.'

'You *are* getting paranoid.'

'You really think so?' His voice sank to a whisper and he began to knot and unknot his hands, staring down at the carpet, avoiding Dawn's eyes. She gazed at him for a moment, wondering what really lay behind this strange visit. Was he lonely? Was it as simple as that? Or did career frustration do strange things to you? She sat down beside him, clearing a space for herself. When she put an arm around him, she realised he was crying.

'Andy? What's the matter?'

'Nothing.'

'Tell me.' She could feel him trembling through the thick leathers.

He shook his head, then began to wipe his nose on the back of his hand.

Dawn pulled a Kleenex from a box on the floor.

'Here.'

He looked at the Kleenex, his eyes glazed, then took a deep breath.

'I can't hack this, you know, I really can't. I thought I could but I can't.'

'Hack what?' Dawn waited for an answer. 'Andy?'

'This. Us. The job. Everything. Sometimes, some mornings, I wake up and I'm fucking superman. Other times, like now, I can't get a single thing straight. You want the truth, it's all just falling to pieces.'

'What is?'

'Every bloody thing.'

Dawn smiled at him, and touched his face. The news that someone else was as confused and bewildered as her was a huge relief.

'Things work out,' she said softly. 'In the end, they do, I promise.'

'Yeah? You really think that?' It was a little boy's question, voiced through a blur of tears.

Dawn gave him the Kleenex. She had some vodka next door. She'd fix up a couple of drinks. She'd put some music on, nothing hectic, and they could just chill out on the sofa. There was no pressure, no deadlines, no crimes to solve, just the two of them. Whatever else he wanted to get off his chest, she was here to listen.

She slipped off the sofa and eased the side zips on his boots. When she glanced up at him, he was trying to force a smile.

'OK?' she said.

The video had long come to an end. Faraday stood at the big glass doors, nursing his third cup of coffee. Down the road, queues were forming round the block for one of the clubs by the pier.

Eadie Sykes was folded into a corner of the sofa, her knees tucked beneath her chin. Faraday studied her for a moment. Behind the laughter and the repartee, he'd just glimpsed an altogether different woman.

'Your dad fought in Crete? 1941? He was part of all that?'

'Yep. Got the last boat out. Bombed stupid for five days then nearly swam back to bloody Egypt. Tell me something, Joe, why do the Brits always fuck it up?'

To Faraday's shame, he hadn't known the full story. He'd heard about Crete, of course, known that it hadn't been the army's finest hour, but the shaming weight of detail, the sheer scale of the catastrophe, had never dawned on him. Allied commanders who'd lost their nerve. Counter-attacks that were never properly developed. Thousands of men, poorly led, chucking in the towel against a handful of German paratroopers then legging it through the mountains for yet another botched evacuation. Brilliant.

'What possessed you to make the film?' he asked.

'My dad. He died a couple of years ago. It was a kind of tribute if you like.'

'Has it been seen anywhere? Have you sold it?'

'Oz, New Zealand.' She smiled. 'And Germany.'

'Not here?'

'Not yet. The Brits are odd. They like to celebrate their defeats. That treatment might be a bit close to the bone.'

Faraday joined her on the sofa, thinking of the Dunkirk film she was making with J-J. She was right about the Brits. There was nothing they treasured more than a military disaster.

'Did your dad talk about Crete a lot?'

'Not until very recently. In fact it was only when he was in a home in Oz and I went back to see him that I realised he'd been in the war at all. He never mentioned it when I was a kid and I was away most of the time after that.'

'And was he bitter?'

'Resigned. Maybe even amused. He saw a lot, my dad. I only knew what he chose to tell me.'

'What about the Brits? Did he like them?'

'Not much. On a good day he'd say he felt sorry for them.'

'But you married one.'

'Yeah.' She pulled a face. 'Not my cleverest move.'

'You're telling me you regret it?'

'No, but my dad did, big-time. Me? I never give it a moment's thought. Looking back's a waste of time. What's done is done. Only the Brits bang on about the past. There . . .' She grinned at Faraday. 'How's that for an insult? Bet you're really glad you came now.'

Faraday said it didn't matter. He'd had a great evening, totally unexpected, and one day soon he'd try and repay the hospitality. In the meantime, he'd tell J-J the Dunkirk video was going well.

'True?'

She didn't answer him. Instead, she got to her feet and looked him in the eye.

'We haven't talked about you at all, have we? Your wars?'

'No.' Faraday was trying to find his car keys. 'And thank Christ for that.'

Nine

Faraday was at his desk early next morning, the worst of the hangover gone. He'd been out first thing, tramping north on the path that skirted Langstone Harbour, glad of the wind on his face. Clouds were piling up to the west, the promise of rain in the air, but the rich orange spill of dawn had brought him to a pause and he'd lifted his binos for a sweep across the gleaming mud flats.

June was a dead time for birds but he'd caught a glimpse of shelduck, way out on the harbour, and later en route back towards the Bargemaster's House, he'd taken a brief detour to check out one of the fresh-water ponds that dotted Milton Common. He loved this time of the morning, no one around, the first fat drops of rain on his face, and he'd paused in the cover of a blackberry bush, checking on a family of reed warblers nesting in the bulrushes at the water's edge.

For days now, mother and chicks had been sharing the nest with a cuckoo. One by one, the cuckoo had expelled the other chicks, hogging the mother's food for itself, and Faraday asked himself yet again what the shy little warbler made of this huge baby with its ever-open gape. Something deep in her brain made sure that she kept supplying the food but surely – at the very least – she'd be resentful that this greedy stranger had taken over her entire world. Could reed warblers feel resentment? he'd wondered. And, given this ever-diminishing family, were they able to count?

Now, gazing down at the Policy Book still open on his office desk, he heard a knock on the door. It was one of the management assistants. She held out a big manila envelope.

'The navy bloke,' she said. 'Dropped it off earlier.'

Faraday opened the envelope. Inside was a thick stapled photocopy headed 'In Confidence'. From the top left-hand corner, a younger, thinner face swam out, staring at the camera, backed by the pleats of a photo-booth curtain. Coughlin, Faraday thought, remembering that same face, swollen and purpled, on the SOC video.

The Divisional Officer's Report ran to a dozen pages, tracking Coughlin from his days as a sixteen-year-old junior seaman through to his discharge seventeen years later. Faraday flicked through it, skipping from posting to posting, trying to distil the essence of the man from the various handwritten comments.

Early on, the training officer at HMS *Raleigh* had talked of 'disappointment' and warned that Coughlin 'must temper his undoubted energies with a degree of self-discipline if he is to realise his full potential'. A couple of years later, at sea aboard HMS *Edinburgh Castle*, another officer had written guardedly of 'compe-tence' and 'occasional flair', a judgement heavily qualified by a Lieutenant Commander reviewing his progress on his next posting. 'CK Coughlin,' he'd scrawled, 'still requires a significant degree of supervision, disappointing after nearly five years in the service.'

Faraday eased back in his chair, gazing out as the first drops of rain smeared the view. He'd need a translator to properly understand a document like this – what did 'CK' mean? – but twenty-two years in the police force had left him fluent in the stilted bureaucratic prose reserved for career assessment.

Coughlin, without doubt, had been a handful, a judgement amply confirmed by more or less every officer who'd crossed his path. He seemed to have survived, just. He'd obviously been canny enough to avoid a major disciplinary drama. But nowhere was there any evidence that he'd happily submitted to the demands of teamwork. 'Coughlin can be a solitary individual,' another Lieutenant Commander had written in 1976, 'and sometimes he appears unaware of the needs of others. Confronted with his shortcomings, he finds it difficult to accept or even acknowledge blame.'

Solitary individual? Faraday leafed on through the report, pausing a page or two before the end. By 1982, Coughlin had become a 'LCK' aboard HMS *Accolade*. The ship had obviously been part of the Falklands Task Force because the posting had come to an abrupt halt in the middle of the hostilities. 'The loss of a ship can be profoundly traumatic,' a Commander Wylie had written, 'and it is to LCK Coughlin's credit that he seems to have been less affected by the sinking than many of the ship's crew. This strength of resolve should stand him in good stead in future drafts.'

Faraday put the report to one side, suddenly swamped by memories of the Falklands Task Force. For the moment, HMS *Accolade* rang no bells – so many ships had gone down – but April 1982 had found him on leave from the CID training school in Lancashire, and back in Portsmouth he'd taken J-J down to the harbourmouth to watch *Hermes* and *Invincible* leaving for the long passage south.

The crowds had been ten deep on top of the Round Tower overlooking the harbour narrows, but with his three-year-old son perched on his shoulders Faraday had found the perfect spot, wedged against a big retaining wall. The ships had seemed enormous – *Hermes* in particular – and Faraday remembered the choke in his throat as he watched the battered old aircraft carrier slip slowly seawards. The flight deck, crammed with helicopters, had been lined with sailors – feet spread, heads held high – and it was impossible not to wonder how many of these men wouldn't be coming home. The crowd, mainly women and kids, had been strangely muted, not a hint of the brash tabloid jingoism that had gripped the rest of the nation, and watching the television news that night, Faraday had tried to explain something of this puzzle to his infant son. The country, he'd signed, seemed only too glad to go to war. Only cities like Portsmouth were anticipating the bill.

'Sir?'

It was Dave Michaels' head around the door. He was looking unusually cheerful. He'd just had a call from Dave Stockley at the Computer Crime Unit. They'd been working flat out on the analysis of Coughlin's hard disk and had come up with what Stockley termed 'good news'.

'Like what?'

'Like a name.'

Stockley himself appeared forty minutes later. He'd driven over from the CCU at Netley and brought yet more print-outs. Faraday borrowed Willard's office again, spreading the paperwork across the conference table. Brian Imber had abandoned the Intelligence Cell up the corridor to join them. Dave Michaels made the coffees.

Since the last meet, Stockley's analysts had isolated a number of more recent newsgroup conversations involving Coughlin. Still using the nickname 'Freckler', he'd thrown his weight about, doing his best to antagonise whoever might have dropped in. None of this had been the least bit surprising, not after his earlier performances, but another factor had entered the equation, something new.

Faraday looked at him, waiting.

'Well?'

'Coughlin was being stalked. There's another guy, follows him around from site to site, logs on, gets stuck in. Here.'

Stockley selected a print-out and slid it along the table.

Faraday noted the time and date: 23.12, 17.11.01. Seven months ago. He peered at the lines of text beneath. Coughlin had embarked on one of his more violent riffs, slagging off a subscriber from Heidelberg who'd evidently been making enquiries about a Led Zeppelin album. In Coughlin's view, the guy was a total wanker. Only cretins and Nazis liked that kind of crap. This diatribe, increasingly explicit, had been interrupted by a new voice, even more savage than Coughlin's. 'Freckler' deserved a bomb up his arse. And if he didn't watch his manners, the new arrival would be only too happy to oblige. This threat naturally sparked a reaction from Coughlin and over the next half an hour or so this corner of the newsgroup was wrecked by a full-scale brawl. Even on paper, the violence felt all too real.

Faraday looked up.

'And there's lots of this?'

'Loads.' Stockley gestured at the print-outs at his elbow. 'We haven't had a chance to go through absolutely everything but it seems to have started last year. The new guy obviously checks in through DejaVu, runs "Freckler" as the prompt, and tracks Coughlin from newsgroup to newsgroup.'

'Is that easy?'

'Time-consuming. You have to want to do it. It has to matter to you.'

'And the stuff is all like this?' Faraday lifted the print-out he'd just read.

'Worse.' Stockley was trying to find another example. 'The last couple of weeks it's virtual death threats.'

Dave Michaels' grin flagged the pun. Virtual indeed. Until you knocked on a door in Niton Road and found an overweight fifty-three-year-old dead on the floor.

Faraday was still looking at Stockley.

'So who is he?'

'He calls himself Guzza.'

'Guzza?'

'That's his nickname, his handle. That's what we start with.'

It was Stockley's turn to smile. He opened his briefcase again and took out a file. Tracking down a subscriber name and number could often take weeks. With foreign-registered ISPs it would often be even longer. On this occasion, though, they'd struck lucky. The duty inspector had signed the RIPA and data protection forms and the ISP had come up with a subscriber number.

'In the UK?'

'In Pompey.'

Faraday blinked. Dave Michaels had been right. Good news at last.

'And they gave you a name?'

'No, but BT did.'

The duty inspector had obliged by signing another DP2 and the form had gone to BT's Police Liaison department. Thirty minutes later, Stockley was looking at their response. He passed the fax to Faraday. Kevin Pritchard. Alhambra Hotel. Granada Road. Southsea.

Faraday stared at it. Granada Road ran from the Strand down to Canoe Lake, an expanse of brackish water reserved for mute swans, pedalos and model yachts. There were lots of hotels down Granada Road, thirty pounds a night B and B, the kind of place you wouldn't take anyone you wanted to impress.

Faraday looked up.

'Niton Road's five minutes away.'

'Exactly.' Dave Michaels was already on his feet, collecting the mugs. 'I took the liberty of phoning Scenes of Crime.'

Paul Winter had been waiting nearly half an hour before Dawn Ellis turned up. The CID office was virtually empty. Cathy Lamb had organised massive house-to-house checks in the vicinity of Rooke's beating, the squad bulked out with uniforms poached from every corner of the city. Chief Superintendent Hartigan, who had an appetite for Wild West metaphors, had decided that this was high noon. One way or another, he was going to re-establish the rule of law in Somerstown.

Dawn Ellis looked awful. She normally had a flawless complexion, a tribute to her diet and her arm's-length relationship with tobacco and booze. She went weeks without touching a proper drink, never smoked, and regularly worked out at a Port Solent gym. But this morning, for reasons that Winter could only guess at, her normal sparkiness had gone. She went straight to the electric kettle and then spooned Nescafé into an empty cup. Her face was drawn, the skin beneath her eyes smudged black with exhaustion.

Winter looked pointedly at his watch.

'Traffic bad, was it?'

Ellis ignored him. She wanted to know what Scenes of Crime had sussed last night.

'They finished late, round ten, closed off the whole street. Jerry Proctor was in here first thing with Cathy.'

'And?'

'Nothing much. The blood's got to be Rookie's.'

'All of it?'

'Yeah.' Winter reached for the last of the biscuits. 'This wasn't a fight. Just a bunch of kids handing it out.'

'Bunch? Who says?'

Winter explained about the mobile phone SOC had retrieved from the pocket of Rooke's denim jacket. The last stored message to come in had invited him to a meet on the street where the beating had taken place. The presumption was that Rookie had gone along in the expectation of a drug deal. At Proctor's request, Winter had listened to the voice and confirmed it wasn't Darren Geech. Not that Geech wasn't squarely in the frame.

'So probably two of them,' he said. 'At least.'

'What about Rooke's mobile?'

'They got a number off that last message. Traced it to another cell phone.'

'And?'

'Stolen off a kid from the school down the road last week. He was in class yesterday afternoon.'

'Does he know who nicked it?'

'Of course he does.'

'Is he telling?'

'No bloody chance – and no one else has come forward either. Cath organised a speaker tour last night, and put a media appeal out this morning. The house-to-house started at seven to catch the early risers. Hartigan seems pretty up about the prospects but he's old-fashioned that way. Thinks the uniform still opens mouths. Amazing, isn't it? Couple of years behind a desk and you'll believe anything.'

Ellis was pouring hot water over the coffee and Winter noticed that her hands were shaking. Nothing heavy, just the slightest of tremors.

'Good night?' he enquired.

'Wonderful,' Ellis said bleakly. 'So where do we find young Darren?'

Willard phoned Faraday mid-morning, between lectures. Faraday was in his office, waiting for Bev Yates to return from the magistrates' court with a search warrant for the Alhambra Hotel. Scenes of Crime had already got themselves organised, calling in reinforcements from Southampton. The last twenty-four hours, in Jerry Proctor's dry phrase, had been a challenge: a full day's work still waiting at Niton Road, a near-murder in Somerstown, and now every prospect of the full monty on the premises in Granada Road. If you were looking for career experience in forensics then Portsmouth wouldn't let you down.

Willard wanted to know more about Kevin Pritchard. The impatience and irritation of yesterday had vanished and he was back to his old, measured self, following the story step by step, interrupting Faraday's account with an occasional grunt.

Faraday brought him up to speed. He'd put a car out front of the Alhambra, two DCs, and stationed another one round the back. Orders had gone out that everyone leaving the hotel was to be discreetly stopped and ID'd. For the time being he had no idea whether Pritchard was in residence but he wasn't taking any risks. By lunchtime, with Scencs of Crime, they'd be inside giving the place a thorough shake. Pritchard too, with luck.

'Pritchard got any previous?'

'Nothing on PNC.'

'Anything else we know about him?'

'No, apart from his manners on the internet.'

Willard's chuckle took Faraday by surprise. Twenty-four hours without another head-to-head with Corbett had done wonders for his sense of humour.

'What about Niton Road? Any hits on the print lifts?'

'None. I phoned Netley this morning. They've run the whole lot now.'

'That doesn't sound like Davidson to me, then.' He paused. 'What about FIB? Have they got anywhere with SO11?'

'No.' Brian Imber had already fed Corbett's hearsay into the headquarters Force Intelligence Bureau and was still awaiting an assessment. Whatever happened, there were very definite limits to the covert information other forces were prepared to share. Individual sources were fiercely protected and the most that FIB could probably expect from the Met was a nod or a shake of the head in Davidson's direction.

There was a brief silence on the other end of the line, then Willard was back again. Famously manic about good housekeeping on major investigations, he wanted to know about media strategies, about the appointment of a Family Liaison Officer, about the state of the overtime budget after the first blitz. Faraday jotted down the questions one by one. Photos of Coughlin had been released to local press and television. There was still no sign of a Family Liaison Officer on the inquiry but that was just as well because Coughlin didn't appear to have any family.

'None at all?' Willard sounded incredulous.

'Just a mum. She's in her eighties in a home somewhere near Emsworth. Coughlin never saw her. Not even at Christmas. His dad died young and there were no brothers or sisters.'

'Wives? Kids?'

'Never married.'

'OK.' Willard seemed mollified. 'What about the overtime?'

'I checked again this morning. We've caned it over the last couple of days but we're still within the allowance.'

'Thank Christ for that. You know about this Rooke business?'

'Yes, sir.'

'Fella died an hour ago. Under the circumstances, I'm hoisting it into Major Crimes but there's going to be resource implications. You'll be looking at a smaller squad on *Merriott*.'

Faraday was still thinking about Willard's reference to 'circumstances'. Dave Michaels' account of the Somerstown beating had left little to the imagination. Paul Winter had found a bathful of blood in some nearby flat and Scenes of Crime had allegedly picked up brain tissue from the pavement. Any more kids turning executioner on city streets and the top corridor at force HQ would be thinking hard about early retirement.

Willard was musing aloud about personnel. He'd already put a call through to Operational Support for yet more bodies but he knew the cupboard was nearly bare and Faraday should start drawing up a list of DCs to be transferred to the Rooke killing. Nick Hayder would be SIO until Perry Madison got back on Monday.

'Any ideas, Joe? People you might want off your hands?'

'No problem.' Faraday kicked his office door shut. 'Let's start with Andy Corbett.'

From the unmarked Skoda, Winter had a perfect view of Mrs Czinski's house. Off to the left, in the heart of Old Portsmouth, was the picturesque muddle of yachts and fishing smacks that filled the Camber Dock. Look to the right, where the road curved away between rows of new-looking town houses, and the red front door of number twelve was unmissable. Soon, if Winter had this right, young Darren would appear.

Dawn Ellis sat in the passenger seat, reading the first edition of the *News*. Winter's contact had been as good as her word, penning a brief three-paragraph story about Mrs Czinski's precious Charlie. The dog had unaccountably gone missing. Pompey's finest, in the course of their duties, had scooped the little terrier up. And here was Charlie, bedecked once again in big pink bows, sprawled on his owner's lap.

'So what makes you think Geech is going to see this?'

Winter didn't take his eyes off the rear-view mirror. The street was one-way. He was looking for a red Audi A4, XBK 386 W.

'Has to. Celebrity's a big thing with these kids. They like seeing their efforts in the papers. That's why they'll all be buying the *News*, to check out Rookie.'

'But what makes you think Darren can read?'

'Doesn't have to.' He leaned over and tapped the colour shot of Mrs Czinski. 'A picture's worth a thousand words.'

His eyes returned to the mirror again. If he'd got it right, the Audi would appear first beside the pub up the road, slowing for the speed bumps. Darren would be at the wheel, looking for number twelve. That left them plenty of time to ready themselves for the moment when he found the address, stepped on to the pavement, and left himself wide open to what would inevitably follow. Game, set and match. Drinks in the bar and a herogram from Willard.

Dawn wasn't convinced.

'You really think the dog matters to the boy that much?'

'I know it. You were there. You heard what his mum said. Geech loves the bloody animal to death.'

'His mum was off the planet. She'd have said anything.'

'Nonsense.' Winter shook his head. 'Darren's found himself a little friend. This is a kid who's probably never loved *any* living thing in his life. If all that stands between him and Charlie is a couple of pink bows he'll be round here like a shot. Guarantee it.'

Dawn tried not to laugh. Winter was at his least credible when he tried to sound like a social worker.

'Since when have you cared about kids like Darren?'

'Never. You asked a question. I gave you an answer.'

'That's not an answer. That's wish fulfilment. How long has Cathy given us?'

'As long as it takes.' He hesitated a moment, then frowned. 'Three hours.'

Faraday decided to accompany Bev Yates and the Scenes of Crime team to the Alhambra Hotel. Strictly speaking, he should have stayed at Kingston Crescent, chained to the precious Policy Book, tallying his latest decisions and fielding the incessant stream of incoming calls, but there had to be compensations for this crippling sequence of twelve-hour days and a potential breakthrough like this was undoubtedly one of them.

Yates had the search warrant in his hand when the door opened to his second knock. A small, dark woman of uncertain age peered out at them. She was wearing a black wig and far too much eyeliner. A thick layer of make-up masked a face that might once have been pretty.

'Can I help you?' West Country accent, softer than Pompey.

Yates introduced himself. He was investigating a major crime. He wanted to talk to a Mr Kevin Pritchard.

'You can't, my love.'

'Why not?'

'Because he's not here.'

'Where is he?'

'Gibraltar.'

The woman held the door open and stepped back to let them in. The smell of the hotel hit them at once, years of damp and neglect anointed with gallons of the cheapest spray deodoriser. Stay here for more than an hour or two, Faraday thought, and you'd live with that smell for ever.

The woman took them into a small lounge. The patterned nylon carpet felt greasy underfoot and most of the tables were cratered with cigarette burns. The net curtains were yellow with nicotine and there was a gust of stale beer from the tiny bar at the far end as the woman closed the door behind them.

Faraday's eyes strayed to the framed photographs hanging on the wall. Most of them were sepia or black and white and all of them featured warships. HMS *Hood* nosing out through the harbour narrows. HMS *Repulse* nudging the quayside in some faraway port, officers in tropical gear peering down from the bridge, sweating matelots making fast below.

'And you are?'

'Jackie Pritchard.'

'Mr Pritchard's wife?'

'Sister. He doesn't have a wife.'

While Yates made a note in his pocketbook, Faraday eyed one of the chairs but decided not to risk it.

'How long has Mr Pritchard been gone?' he enquired.

'Since' . . . she frowned . . . 'Tuesday morning. Went early. Took a taxi to the airport. Knows one of the firms, like, but still a terrible price. Seventy quid there and back? You have to be joking.'

Faraday and Yates exchanged glances. By Tuesday morning, Coughlin had been dead for barely hours.

'You live here too?'

'On and off I do, yes. Not permanent, like, not for ever, but I help out when I can.'

'Were you here on Monday night?'

'Yes.' She nodded. 'I was.'

'And your brother? He was here, as well?'

'He was serving in the bar down here. I was upstairs in my little room.'

'Was the hotel busy that night? Booked out?'

'Booked out?' Just the thought of it made her laugh. 'We're never booked out. Couple of guests a night, maybe. Never more.'

Faraday wandered over to the bar. There was room for three stools and maybe an extra body standing. He peered into the gloom beneath the line of optics, making out a display of photos pinned to some kind of board. The tiny sink beneath the bar was blocked with sodden cigarette ends.

'The switch is on the wall, my love. Over to the right.'

Faraday found the switch. Two of the spotlights were blown but there was enough illumination to make out a trophy collection of parking tickets nesting amongst the snaps on the board.

'D'you mind?' He gestured at the photos.

'Go ahead. Help yourself.'

Faraday stepped behind the bar and took a closer look at the photos. Big, beery, cheesecake grins, arms around shoulders, faces bloated with drink. Guests might not kip at the Alhambra but they certainly liked a pint or two. He was still wondering which of these faces might belong to Pritchard, when a photo tucked between two others caught his attention. He reached forward and pulled it out. Two men in make-up were locked in a big pantomime embrace. Both were clearly pissed. One of them had the strangest face: receding hair, huge forehead, wet eyes. The other one, beyond doubt, was Coughlin.

Faraday called the woman over. Yates came, too.

'Who's that?' Faraday pointed to the man with the lips pressed to Coughlin's cheek.

The woman took her time, taking the photo over towards the window then shading her eyes against the light.

'That's my brother,' she said at last. 'Kevin.'

Scenes of Crime started upstairs. Kevin Pritchard had a three-room bachelor flat on the top floor, and Proctor's team sorted methodically through the chaos while Yates and Faraday remained downstairs, questioning Pritchard's sister.

Kevin, she admitted at once, lived like an animal, totally disorganised, world of his own. He'd barely packed a thing for Gibraltar and most nights he was so drunk she'd had to remember to put the alarm on to get him up in time for the taxi Tuesday morning. Asked about where he might be staying in Gibraltar, she said she hadn't a clue but she thought he'd made the booking a while or so back through the internet so maybe there'd be something on his computer. Either way, she'd come over from Plymouth to keep an eye on things. She'd certainly be staying for a bit because Kevin didn't seem to be quite sure when he was coming back. He'd mentioned a couple of weeks on one occasion, a month on another. Faraday's guess was as good as hers.

'What about Tuesday morning? When the taxi came? Did he say anything then?'

'No fit state, I'm afraid. Still pissed as a rat. Must have been drinking all night, poor love.'

'So you've really no idea when he'll be back?'

'None.'

'Does he have a mobile? Can you call him?'

'That was another thing. He forgot to take it with him. I found it behind the bar Tuesday morning after he'd gone.'

'And you've still got it?'

'Of course.'

'Used it since?'

'Wouldn't know how to.'

Faraday began to relax. Better and better, he thought. First a prime suspect who does a runner within hours. And now an abandoned mobile phone, potentially priceless in terms of evidence. He showed her the photograph again.

'You know this other man?'

For the first time, Pritchard's sister hesitated. Yates saw it, too, trying to catch Faraday's eye. At length, she nodded.

'Sean,' she said briefly.

'A friend of your brother's?'

'He comes in here a lot, yes.'

'But friends, are they?'

She bit her lip. There were things here she didn't want to say. Not without being pushed.

'Do you like him, this Sean?'

This time there was no hesitation. She shook her head.

'No,' she said. 'I don't like him at all, and that's God's truth.'

'Why don't you like him?'

'Because . . . because . . . he takes advantage.'

'Of you?'

'Of Kevin. Kevin doesn't know it. That's Kevin's problem. He's stupid that way and I've told him, too. That man only wants one thing out of Kevin and poor Kevin just goes along with it. I've got nothing against them, mind, if that's what they prefer. But not with someone like that Sean. Ugh . . .' She shuddered.

There was a silence. Then Faraday told her that Sean Coughlin had been found dead several streets away first thing Tuesday morning. Any possible link with her brother seemed to pass her by. She was genuinely astonished.

Yates leaned forward.

'You didn't know? Didn't read it in the papers?'

'I never read the papers.'

'Television? The radio?' He gestured round. 'Someone in here?'

'No.' She shook her head. 'You're sure it was him? Sean?'

Faraday heard footsteps down the hall and then the bang of the front door as one of the SOC team went out to the van. The gate to the hotel had been taped off now, a PC keeping guard beyond it.

'I know this is hard, Jackie.' Yates could be surprisingly gentle when it mattered. 'I was wondering about what you said just then. About your brother.'

'What about him?'

'I take it you're suggesting he's gay.'

'Of course he is. And it's not a suggestion, either. He *is* gay. He's always been gay. Not that he doesn't like women. He does. But he just doesn't like them . . . you know . . . in that way.'

'Whereas . . . with men . . . ?'

'Yes, dear. Definitely.'

'And with Sean Coughlin?'

'Yes, my love. Even him. In fact, especially him.'

She bit her lip. Faraday took up the running. There were things he didn't understand here. If Kevin Pritchard had been making life so tough for Coughlin on the internet, how come they'd ended up as lovers?

'This Coughlin and your Kevin,' he began, 'have they known each other a while?'

'A few years.' She nodded.

'You're sure about that? Seen it for yourself?'

'Only too often. All the times I've been here.' She nodded at the photo. 'I knew from the first time I saw him he was horrible. But you can't tell Kevin anything. Never could.'

Faraday looked at the photo one last time, then left it on the table between them. There were dozens of other questions he wanted to put – about Monday night, about Gibraltar, about the man Coughlin – but his mobile had started to ring.

It was one of the SOC team from upstairs in Pritchard's flat. Jerry Proctor had come and gone, leaving Faraday's number with instructions to get in touch should they find something of major importance.

'And?'

Yates glanced towards him, sensing the excitement in Faraday's voice. Faraday listened intently, then muttered his thanks and brought the conversation to an end.

'You remember that shoeprint under Coughlin's bedroom window?' He was looking at Yates. 'The lad upstairs thinks they've got an exact match.'

Ten

It was Ellis who saw the Audi first. Paul Winter, busy trying to open a new packet of Werther's Originals, felt her hand on his arm. After three hours without any kind of result, he'd been on the point of packing the ambush in.

'Coming round the corner,' she said. 'Now.'

Winter's eyes went to the mirror. She was right. The squat red saloon was coasting slowly past the pub. W reg. Two up. Winter dropped the Werther's in his lap and reached for the ignition key. Parked on the right-hand side of the road, it was Ellis who'd be exposed to any chance sighting as the Audi drew level.

She picked up the paper and ducked her head, letting the fall of black hair mask her face. The Audi, clear of the speed bumps, was still dawdling along. It was barely yards away now and a single glance in the mirror told Winter that it was definitely Darren Geech at the wheel. He had another youth beside him – baseball cap, gangster shades – and they were both wearing blue Pompey tops.

Winter's fingers tightened on the ignition key. He could hear the Audi now, the low burble of the exhaust. They must have fitted special mufflers, he thought. No way would Mrs Czinski go in for boy-racer extras. He ducked his head as the Audi drew level, aware of the shape of the car slowing even more. Beside the unmarked Skoda, it paused.

'Shit.' It was Ellis. 'He's seen us.'

Winter looked across at the Audi. Geech was leaning forward, the thin, pale face contorted in a manic grin. A couple of derisory flips of his wrist, a middle finger raised in salute, and then he was gone. Through the inch or two of open window, Ellis could smell the burning rubber.

'Fuck.' Winter hit the ignition and stirred the Skoda into life. Already the Audi was halfway down the road, still accelerating towards the T-junction at the end. 'Get on to control. Ask for a marked car. He's going left. St George's Road.'

Ellis reached for the radio. The Skoda's call sign was Kilo Sierra Nine Two. Control took a moment or two to respond.

'What now?' She was looking at Winter as the car began to move.

'We go after him.'

'You're joking.'

At last, an acknowledgement from control. Ellis gave them the facts. Red Audi. W reg. Two white males. Heading west on St George's Road.

'We need a marked car,' she added.

There was a brief pause at the other end and Ellis tried to picture the scene in the control room as the Skoda slid sideways on to St George's Road. Hot pursuit had become a big policing issue recently, especially in urban areas. Far too many pedestrians had died for the sake of keeping tabs on some sus vehicle and there were strict rules about what you could and couldn't do. Chasing anyone in an unmarked Skoda was very definitely off-limits, not least because the target driver could – with some justification – plead harassment. Not that Winter seemed to care.

'Traffic lights at Gunwharf.' He was sweating now. 'Little bastard's jumped them.'

The Skoda was still travelling at speed but the Audi was way ahead. Beyond the traffic lights, where the road went left under the railway bridge, it disappeared completely. The lights turned green. As the waiting traffic began to move, Winter thumped the horn and barged past, accelerating hard again. Ellis grabbed for the dashboard as a bus swung towards them under the railway bridge, filling the windscreen.

'Paul,' she muttered. 'This is not a good idea.'

Winter ignored her. As the bus swerved to avoid a collision he darted back into the traffic queue. Ahead lay the big coach park beside the harbour station.

'Kilo Sierra Nine Two.' It was the control room, a different voice this time. 'State your position. Repeat, state your position.'

'Portsea Hard. Travelling west.'

'Target?'

'Out of sight.'

'Tell them Queen Street.' Winter had spotted another break in the traffic. 'He'll be going for the motorway.'

Ellis relayed the message, pressing herself back against the seat as Winter took the onrushing mini-roundabout at speed. A taxi driver coming at them from the left hit the brakes, then gave them the finger.

'Paul. Please.'

Winter ignored her. To the left, the long black hull of HMS *Warrior*. Ahead, the ten-foot brick wall that curtained the dockyard. The road swung abruptly to the right here, and Winter changed down to second, reaching for the handbrake. The force of the turn threw Ellis against the passenger door, the side of her head smacking the window. She gasped with pain, then the car was accelerating again, back in a straight line.

'Got him.' Winter nodded at the radio. 'Traffic lights, Edinburgh Road junction. Definitely the motorway.'

Ellis passed on the message. The Audi was no more than a scarlet dot in the distance, hundreds of yards down the road. No way would they ever get anywhere near it.

'Paul,' she shouted. 'Jack it in!'

Winter, crouched behind the wheel, was back in top

gear. Seconds away from the pedestrian crossing, he was nudging fifty again.

'Paul . . . for God's sake.'

The bent old figure on the crossing seemed oblivious of the Skoda. Winter, his hand on the horn, pulled hard right to take the central refuge on the wrong side. An oncoming lorry was a blur of flashing headlights. The Skoda started to slide sideways again, then Winter overcorrected and they were over the crossing and heading for the nearside pavement. There was a huge bang as they mounted the curve – both front tyres gone – then Ellis's world slipped into slow motion as a shopfront raced towards them. She closed her eyes, bracing herself for the impact, aware of Winter still fighting the wheel beside her.

'Fuck,' he said again.

Willard was in his office at Kingston Crescent, the Centrex course abandoned. He'd baled out after his mid-morning phone conversation with Faraday, pleading pressure of work. To Faraday's surprise, he didn't seem the least bit upset.

'I've been talking to the Gibraltar boys,' Faraday said. 'They sound bloody helpful.'

'What are they offering?'

'More or less anything. I gave them the name of the hotel and they're sending someone round to make sure Pritchard's there.'

'They'll keep an eye on him?'

'So they say.'

'Good.' Willard was still studying the booking details recovered from Pritchard's flat. 'Best if they don't arrest him, eh?'

Faraday agreed. He'd talked at length to Nick Hayder. He'd had months of dealings with the Gibraltar police over a series of potentially linked incidents and had given Faraday a couple of contacts to phone. Gib, he'd said, was Pompey with palm trees. Everyone knew everyone else and most of them seemed to be interrelated.

Willard, with two murders on his hands, was clearly relishing the resource battles to come. In these situations, he was at his best, the marauding robber-baron with a talent for grabbing the lion's share of whatever was going spare. Budget, bodies, it made no difference. At his command level, a man was measured not simply by results but by the size of the investigatory army he could put into the field. Two squads servicing separate major inquiries was the stuff of dreams.

He reached for the *Merriott* Policy Book and began to leaf through it.

'You'll be on reduced rations for a while,' he said. 'But if Pritchard is as strong as it looks then we might be home and dry. You'll have to build the case afterwards, of course, but then you can take your time.' He paused, frowning. 'Have you talked to Ludgate Hill?'

Faraday nodded. Ludgate Hill was home for the branch of the Crown Prosecution Service specialising in foreign jurisdictions. Pursuing inquiries abroad could frequently turn into a nightmare, especially if you got ensnared in extradition proceedings. According to the CPS, if Pritchard dug himself in at Gibraltar then extradition might be the only way of getting him back.

'Extradite the guy, and we're buggered,' Willard warned. 'We'd have to make the case against him in Gibraltar and once we'd done that, and they'd agreed extradition, then we wouldn't be allowed to interview him. You with me?'

'Yeah.' Faraday nodded again. 'The way I see it, the key is talking to him. We go for first account there and see where it takes us. Fingers crossed, we avoid extradition.'

'Good.' Willard looked up. 'Who's going with you?'

'Bev Yates.'

'I thought he was up to his knees in shit and nappies?'

'He is, sir. Can't wait.'

The phone began to ring. Willard picked it up and then slowly revolved in his chair until the conversation was shielded from Faraday. A couple of grunts later, he hung up.

'Bloody Winter's just demolished a newsagent's in Queen Street.' He glanced at Faraday. 'Can you believe that?'

In his office, Faraday summoned a conference. Willard had been in the building less than an hour but already he'd taken the Rooke job by the scruff of the neck, reallocating ten of the *Merriott* squad on to Nick Hayder's blitz on the Somerstown murder, an inquiry now codenamed *Hexham*. To Faraday's immense satisfaction, one of the first DCs to be transferred had been Andy Corbett, an executive decision that Faraday interpreted as a small but important vote of confidence on Willard's part. Corbett, it turned out, had done himself no favours by turning up in the Major Incident room an hour and a half late. Quizzed by Paul Ingham, he'd pleaded overnight vomiting and diarrhoea, implying that he could have swung himself a couple of days off had he bothered acquiring a sick note from his GP.

'Aren't we the lucky ones,' Ingham had grunted, allocating him a particularly scrotey block of flats for house-to-house in deepest Somerstown.

Now, Faraday made room in his office for Brian Imber and Dave Michaels. Both men would be helping out with the Rooke job but their prime allegiance was still to *Merriott*.

Faraday summarised developments at the Alhambra Hotel. Kevin Pritchard, according to his sister's statement, had been on duty at the hotel throughout the evening on Monday night. She'd checked the bookings, and he'd served two dinners for guests between half six and eight. The rest of the time, he'd been behind the bar in the front lounge. Monday nights, she'd said, were usually quiet. There was a handful of regulars who drifted in and out, many of them retired navy, but these were the kind of people who liked to be in bed by ten. After that, the bar was generally dead.

Brian Imber was sitting by the window, jotting down the odd note.

He looked up. 'And last Monday night?'

'She can't say. She was in bed herself by then because she knew Pritchard was already pissed and she had to be up at five to make sure he was ready for the taxi.'

'Taxi?'

'To take him to Gatwick. It was an Aqua cab. Bev Yates is checking the driver out.'

'So this holiday was prearranged?' Dave Michaels picked up the booking form. Like Brian Imber he'd somehow assumed that Pritchard had done a runner, fleeing the scene of crime and buying himself a one-way ticket at the airport.

'I'm afraid so,' Faraday said. 'Pritchard sorted it out weeks ago. According to the sister, he was a bit vague about the return flight but the evidence is pretty plain. The bloody holiday was pre-booked. The paperwork we seized proves it. And that, I have to say, is a problem.'

'But we're still sure about all this newsgroup argy-bargy?' Dave Michaels let the booking form flutter to the desk.

'Absolutely. His computer has gone over to the CCU for cloning but there was a pile of print-outs up in his living room, little souvenirs, choice quotes underlined. Pritchard is definitely Guzza.'

'And the footprint?'

'Ninety-nine per cent sure it's his. The sole looks identical to the cast and they should be able to match the soil, too.'

'So why the long face, boss? We've got motive, the newsgroup stuff. We've got opportunity, the shoeprint.

And now we find the bloke's flown off with no definite plans to come back. I might be thick, but where's the problem?'

Faraday leaned forward, his elbows on his knees. A number of loose ends had been worrying him since he left the Alhambra and this was the opportunity to tease them out.

'OK,' he said slowly. 'What do we actually know? We know that Pritchard's been slagging Coughlin off for ever on the internet. We have proof that he's threatened to ram all kinds of goodies up his arse. And then we find a photo of them snogging. That says best mates to me, and that's exactly what his sister confirms in her statement. She couldn't stand Coughlin but it obviously made no odds to Pritchard because the pair of them have been shagging for years.' He gazed down at his hands. 'So how does all that work? Anyone care to tell me?'

Michaels said the question was irrelevant. In his view, their job was to put the bad guys away. Explaining why one man killed another was down to the psychiatrists.

Brian Imber was looking more thoughtful.

'Lovers' tiff?' he suggested. 'Coughlin giving Pritchard a hard time about his holiday? Couldn't bear the thought of life without him? They're both pissed? Things get out of control? You know the way it goes with these people . . .'

'So why the footprint in the flower bed round the back?'

Imber looked at Faraday a moment, then got up and stepped across to the window. Every day of his working week he faced questions like this, trying to figure out the likeliest pattern amongst all the dots.

'Pritchard couldn't raise Coughlin at the front door,' he suggested at last, 'so he goes round the back, taps at his bedroom window.'

'Scenes of Crime say the bed hadn't been slept in.'

'Sure, but Pritchard didn't know that. He knocks a

second time. No response. So round the front he goes and tries the front door again. This time Coughlin opens up and hey presto . . . he's in.'

'And then what?'

'They have a row, a tiff, like I said just now.'

'And?'

'There's a fight.'

'But Coughlin's twice Pritchard's size. You can tell in those photos behind the bar. Pritchard's skinny.'

'Sure, and Coughlin's pissed.'

'But so is Pritchard.' Faraday stared up at Imber. 'You're telling me a bloke like that could really damage Coughlin?'

Dave Michaels intervened again. The expression on his face suggested they were missing the obvious.

'Happens all the time, boss, you know it does. Pritchard gets lucky, whacks Coughlin where it hurts, gives him a kicking.'

'You might be right.' Faraday nodded. 'But there's another problem.'

'Which is?'

'The shoes they've recovered. Absolutely no sign of blood or tissue.'

'Proves nothing. How many times have we sent shoes away, clean as you like, and the report comes back, list as long as your arm, blood in the lacing, blood in the stitching, blood under the uppers?'

'OK. So why haven't they found bloodstained clothing in Pritchard's flat? They've been through all three rooms, first trawl. Crap everywhere but absolutely no sign of what you'd expect.'

'He's hidden it.'

'Doesn't work, Dave. According to his sister, this is a guy who can't organise his way downstairs. His brain's gone. That's why he ends up with a pile of parking fines. He gets pissed, abandons the car, then can't remember where he left it. Monday night was like that. She says

Pritchard was out of his head. Are you really telling me he'd be in any fit state to bury the evidence?'

'He binned it on the way home.' Michaels wouldn't give up. 'He stuffed it into someone's dustbin, chucked it over a hedge, left it in a skip, whatever. We ought to retrace his route, have a poke about.'

'I've organised a POLSA.'

'Great. Then let's wait and see.'

'Sure. But say he's got blood on his jeans? On his shirt? What does he do? Walk home half-naked? Come on . . .'

Michaels was beginning to look concerned. He'd never had Faraday down as a manic depressive but this conversation was going absolutely nowhere.

'You're still up for Gib, boss? Only if you're not, I know just the bloke—'

Faraday stayed him with a look. Discussions like these were invaluable. Better to shake the wrinkles out now, before they got anywhere near a defence lawyer.

Brian Imber had sat down again.

'This mobile you gave me. We've applied for priority billing but we've also managed to access the last number he dialled.'

'And?'

'It was Coughlin's. Pritchard tried to phone him at some point before he left.'

'Bingo!' It was Michaels. 'That'll be the call we retrieved from Coughlin's message tape. Number withheld.'

Faraday looked from one to the other.

'OK,' he said slowly, 'so where does that take us? Pritchard calls from the hotel? Wants to make sure Coughlin's in? Goes round to find out for himself? Or say he's outside the flat? Can't get in? Tries to raise Coughlin on the mobile?'

'Whatever, take your choice.' Michaels was still grinning. 'Right now it doesn't matter a toss except it's yet more evidence. We want to tie Pritchard to Coughlin

Monday night? We've done it twice. Once with the footprint, and now with the phone.' He paused, searching for the right words. First Davidson. Now Pritchard. He leaned back in the chair, his hands clasped behind his neck. 'Hate to say this, boss, but how many times do you want to solve this fucking crime?'

Faraday offered him a bleak smile, acknowledging the justice of the question. Then he knotted his hands again.

'Once would be good,' he said quietly. 'In court.'

Cathy Lamb found Paul Winter in a ward on the third floor at the Queen Alexandra Hospital, his bed wedged between a consumptive-looking eighty-year-old and a younger man being prepared for a heart operation. She pulled up a chair and found a space for herself beside the tiny bedside cabinet. According to the nursing sister behind the desk, Winter had been admitted for 'observation'. X-rays had confirmed two broken ribs and a fracture of his upper right arm but neither need keep him in hospital for more than twenty-four hours.

'This is a welfare visit,' she said at once. 'In case you were wondering.'

Winter offered her a weak smile. A bandage round his head covered the wound they'd stitched in Casualty and he was still convinced they'd left tiny splinters of glass in his face. Maybe, after all, it might have been wiser to have worn the seat belt.

'Here, Cath.' He reached for her hand and took it on a little journey across his right cheek. 'And here and here. See anything?'

Cathy withdrew her hand, not even bothering to look.

'You'll be glad to know that Dawn's OK,' she said. 'In fact they've already discharged her. Shock and multiple bruising. I'm insisting she take the rest of the week off.'

'She's an old toughie, Dawn. Good as gold in the ambulance.' Winter was still exploring his face.

'You could have killed her, Paul. Easily. Plus God knows who else.'

'Who told you that?' Winter tried to frown but frowning hurt. 'I had it completely under control, Cath. There was absolutely no problem.'

'Until the old lady appeared on the crossing.'

'Exactly.'

'But that's what old ladies do, Paul. They appear on pedestrian crossings. And you know something else? That's what crossings are for.'

Cathy folded her arms. She'd brought fruit and a jumbo bag of Werther's but she wanted a good deal more contrition before she parted with either.

Winter sighed. He knew what was coming next. It wouldn't be today, or even next week, but sooner or later the suits were going to reach for the big stick. Pursuit in unmarked cars was strictly verboten. Even slipping behind a suspect and quietly tailing him for a mile or two required a full-blown risk assessment. Paperwork, he'd long concluded, was the working criminal's best friend.

'You've forgotten the big one, Cath.'

'And what might that be?'

'Darren Geech.' He lifted his good arm again and wiped his nose on the back of his hand. 'Anyone nail the little bastard?'

Cathy shook her head. According to the control room log, it had taken a full eleven minutes to sort out a traffic car for the slip road on to the M275, by which time the red Audi had long gone. There'd been a couple of possible sightings since – one in Fareham, another in Portchester – but nothing that anyone wanted to stake their careers on. Geech would doubtless surface in God's good time but for now he'd disappeared again.

'Shame.' Winter was peering down at Cathy's bag. 'Back to the drawing board, then?'

'Not for me, Paul.'

'No?'

''Fraid not.' She shifted her weight on the chair. 'Your mate Rookie died this morning.'

'No one told me that.'

'You asked for radio silence, remember? All those scanners? Otherwise I'd have let you know. We're looking at a murder charge.'

'And Major Crimes have nicked it? Set up a squad?'

'As of lunchtime.'

The news seemed to sober Winter. He struggled to make himself comfortable against the pillows, then closed his eyes. Watching, Cathy Lamb began to wonder quite what the dead informant had really meant to him.

At length, Winter sighed.

'That's terrible, Cath,' he muttered. 'I'd have been a definite for that squad. I know I would. You're right about chasing after Geech. If I'd known earlier about Rookie dying, I'd have let the little bastard go.'

It was gone seven by the time Faraday left the Major Crimes suite and clattered down the back stairs to the car park. The tickets had come through for the Gibraltar flight – 06.25 out of Gatwick – and he had a mountain of calls to make before he could even think about packing a case. Normally he'd stay at the office to finish the day's work, but he'd promised J-J a prawn curry and a decent look at the prints he'd finished on the job for Eadie Sykes, and he knew he could sort out the calls in his office at home.

Hurrying across the car park, he spotted a familiar figure. Scottie was getting out of a battered Fiat with an armful of documents. For a moment, Faraday thought that the bundle of files was for him. The last thing he wanted just now was yet more paperwork.

'These are for Nick. Stuff on the rape case.'

'Thank Christ for that.'

'You busy? Time for a drink?' Scottie nodded up towards the top-floor bar.

Faraday made his excuses, fumbling in his pocket for his car keys. Then he paused.

'That file you left me this morning, Coughlin's naval records. I should have rung you.'

'Any use, was it?'

'Yeah. Guy really was a loner, wasn't he?'

'He was,' Scottie said, then beckoned Faraday closer. He'd had a spare hour or two this afternoon and he'd taken a peek at a couple of other files, stuff to do with *Accolade*. Something had rung a bell, something from way back.

'*Accolade?*' Faraday knew this conversation had been a mistake.

'Coughlin's ship in the Falklands. The one that went down.'

'Ah, yes, yes, sorry.' Faraday forced a smile. 'And?'

'Turned out I was right. You sure you don't want that drink?'

For a moment Faraday was tempted. Then he thought about J-J waiting at home, and Pritchard, down in Gibraltar, and everything else he had to cram into the handful of hours in between. Reaching out a hand, he patted Scottie on the shoulder.

'Next time,' he said. 'And the first pint's on me.'

Eleven

Faraday was asleep when the British Airways 737 banked low over the Bay of Algeciras, readying for the final approach into Gibraltar. Bev Yates, who'd lost the toss for the window seat at Gatwick, abandoned his copy of *Jet-Ski Monthly* and gave Faraday a shake.

'Gib,' he muttered. 'Pilot says it's raining.'

Faraday did his best to stretch his legs beneath the seat in front, then pressed his face to the cold perspex. Through rents in the cloud he glimpsed the sea, gun-metal grey, the long Atlantic rollers capped with foam. The aircraft bumped down through turbulence and yawed wildly before steadying again. Streaked with raindrops, the view was suddenly full of breaking waves. Then came a second or two of scruffy beach, a pile of boulders and a heavy lurch as the plane settled on the racing tarmac. Out beyond the airport, beneath the lid of cloud, Faraday could see the sprawl of the dockyard, grey again, at the foot of the towering Rock. Pompey, he thought, reaching down for his seat belt.

Frank Melia was waiting for them inside the terminal building. Back at Kingston Crescent, Nick Hayder had dubbed him Mr Smiley and now Faraday could see why. A small, round man with inspector's pips on the epaulettes of his crisp, white, short-sleeved shirt, he pumped Faraday's hand and led them across the concourse towards the big glass exit doors. He'd obviously done his homework because the first news he gave Bev Yates was the final score in the Kobe game.

'Two one.' He beamed. 'To Sweden.'

The drive to police headquarters took less than ten minutes. The rain had eased now, and Faraday sat in the back of the Toyota Landcruiser, gazing out. The streets beneath the looming Rock were choked with traffic: pickups with Spanish plates, piled high with boxes of fruit; a bored-looking sailor at the wheel of a Bedford truck; an old man on a bicycle, nut-brown face, oblivious to everything.

Police HQ turned out to be a colonial-style building down by the docks. The Landcruiser dropped them outside and Melia led them beneath an archway, keying a number into the big gate that led through to the inner courtyard. Palm trees dripped the last of the rain on to the surrounding flagstones and it was warmer than Faraday had expected, a hot clamminess that pricked at his skin.

A first-floor veranda ran around all four sides of the courtyard and Melia gestured up towards a half-open window.

'Coffee?'

Two other men, both plain clothes, were waiting in Melia's office. Melia did the introductions. He had a courtliness and a charm that Faraday had long ceased to associate with policing, and he could see that Yates noticed it too. Eager to please, this man could have been a hotelier in one of those discreet establishments that used to soften the harder edges of empire. They were welcome in Gibraltar. The weather would cheer up in an hour or so and he hoped they'd have a profitable stay.

Faraday was keen to get on with the business. Was Pritchard still at the Panorama Hotel?

'As of this morning,' Melia said, 'yes.'

He'd assigned a two-man squad to keeping tabs on Pritchard. The Panorama was one of a chain of hotels catering for the cheaper end of the package tour market but the manager was well known to them and had been more than helpful.

'We have a log of all Mr Pritchard's phone calls and access to his room whenever you need it. It seems that he's is a regular at the hotel. He came here last year, and twice the year before. He normally stays a couple of weeks and does pretty much the same thing every day. The manager says you can set your clock by him.'

'Meaning?'

'The same bars. The same restaurants. Your Mr Pritchard, it appears, is a creature of habit.'

Faraday, impressed, returned the smile. Nick Hayder was right. These guys had Gibraltar taped.

'So this morning . . . ?'

'He'll have taken breakfast in his room. Normally toast and coffee and a little drink on the side. He buys Scotch by the litre from a shop round the corner. It's cheap here, duty free. Currently, he's getting through a bottle a day.'

'Including breakfast?'

'According to the chambermaid, yes. She knows him, too, and likes him. She says he likes Johnnie Walker best of all. He drinks the stuff by the tumblerful.'

Faraday and Yates exchanged glances. Conducting interviews under caution when the subject was pissed was a non-starter. Given Pritchard's consumption, they'd have to allow hours for him to sober up.

'What's he up to the rest of the morning?'

Melia glanced across at the older of the two detectives. The man produced a notebook. According to the manager, another friend of Pritchard's, their guest was planning a little light shopping followed by a session at the Nelson Bar.

'It's down on Main Street,' Melia added. 'Very popular with the matelots. The management have put in extra screens for the World Cup. I understand our friend is keen on football.'

Yates had been gazing at the prints on the wall, sepia

studies of Gibraltar between the wars. Now he reached across to Faraday and touched him lightly on the arm.

'England versus Argentina,' he murmured. 'Kicks off at twelve-thirty.'

Faraday was still looking at Melia.

'Pritchard'll be there for that?'

'Undoubtedly. The chambermaid says he's brought three England shirts. He thinks they'll be enough to get him to the final.'

'Then he *is* a pisshead.' Yates's aside drew a laugh from both detectives.

'What do you think, then?' It was the younger man this time. 'Draw?'

'No way. I think Argentina will stuff us.'

'Seriously?'

'Yeah. Unless Owen gets cranked up we've got no chance. The Argies are world class. Eriksson talks a good game but we were pathetic against the Swedes.'

Faraday brought the conversation to an end. Already, thanks to Frank Melia, he could sense the outlines of a battle plan. It was close to ten. Pritchard, according to the hotel manager, was due at the Nelson within the hour. He'd settle in, down a lager or two, and prepare himself for the big game. A setting like this would provide the perfect opportunity for Yates and himself to study the man. The game over, they'd approach him with a view to a chat. The invitation would be there for him to accompany them back to police headquarters. If Frank Melia would be kind enough to provide Pritchard with somewhere he could sober up, Faraday and Yates would take a cab to the Panorama and have a good look at his room. Later, once Pritchard was in a fit state, they'd go for a first interview under caution.

Yates couldn't believe his ears.

'You mean we get to watch the whole game?'

'I'm afraid so. We need this guy onside. You see any problems, Frank?'

'Plenty. What if he refuses to talk?'

'We hope he won't.'

'But what if he does? You want us to arrest him? If so he's bound to ask for legal representation – and that might be tricky. What if he goes for extradition? You could be looking at months.'

'Sure.' Faraday nodded. 'And even if we got it we couldn't interview him afterwards.'

'Precisely.'

There was a long silence. Frank Melia suggested the possibility of swearing the pair of them in as special constables, giving them powers of local arrest and interview, but Faraday knew this would only lead to the same legal impasse, the entire investigation stalled while they plodded through extradition proceedings. On balance, he'd prefer to busk it, letting the situation develop, searching for a relationship with Pritchard that might ease him back to police headquarters without the need for arrest.

'We have to take a chance,' he said finally. 'Make it good cop–good cop and he might be up for a chat.'

Paul Winter was released from hospital at half past ten. The ward manager arranged for transport to take him back to Bedhampton and a nurse helped him get dressed. Walking slowly down the long central corridor towards the lifts, he was astonished how old he felt. Every movement required a conscious effort and he watched the way everyone seemed to make a big, respectful detour as they walked towards him. Even the women waiting for the lift stepped aside at his faltering approach.

Home was a modest post-war bungalow off the island on the lower slopes of Portsdown Hill. The minibus dropped him at the kerbside but he refused the offer of a helping hand up the garden path. Only when the bus had gone, and the street was empty again, did he investigate the huge bunch of flowers on his front doorstep. The cellophane wrapper was the giveaway, embossed with the name of the florist the CID office at Highland Road always used. A tiny card was tucked between the stems of iris and chrysanthemums. He bent slowly to inspect it. 'Heartfelt sympathies,' it read, 'from all your friends at the Skoda Preservation Society.'

Bastards.

Winter fumbled for his key and let himself in. Despite the improvement in the weather, the bungalow felt cold and unloved. Lately, he'd been toying with getting a pet of some kind, maybe a dog, and he'd been sorely tempted to hang on to Charlie. Nursing his throbbing arm as he made for the kitchen, he now regretted trying to bait a trap like that. Sometimes, he told himself, you can be just too fucking clever.

There was a pack of Nurofen in one of the kitchen cabinets. He swallowed three and then filled the kettle. Plugging it in one-handed was trickier than he'd expected, and he ended up by slopping most of the water on to the tea tray. This little battle, comprehensively lost, made him gloomier than ever and he wondered quite how he was going to kill the days that stretched before him. The consultant at the hospital had muttered something about a complex fracture and warned him to be patient. He had an appointment in three weeks' time for an assessment, and the plaster might be off by the end of July, but there'd be lots of physio sessions before he could expect a full range of movement.

The tea brewing, Winter sank on to one of the kitchen stools and gazed glumly out of the window. Physio or no physio, he knew he was in even deeper shit with the job. Just now, his injuries qualified him for sick leave but Traffic were bound to investigate his pursuit of Darren Geech and if the evidence sustained a dangerous driving charge then he'd be off the road until the case was resolved in court. Office-bound, without wheels, he'd be fuck-all use to CID and he knew that Hartigan would have him back in uniform within seconds. That was bad enough. What was even worse was the possibility of losing the court case and facing a lengthy period of disqualification, a handicap that would keep him in uniform for the foreseeable future.

Would that matter? He rocked back and forth on the stool, waiting for the tablets to kick in, knowing that the question answered itself. Of course it would bloody matter. He was a detective, for God's sake. He'd spent the last twenty years chasing the bad guys, befriending them, tickling their fat tummies, setting them up for the inevitable fall. He did this better than any detective in the city and had the scalps to prove it. That was what he was good at, that was what earthed him, and the prospect of a lengthy spell in uniform was unthinkable. Would he really be able to survive a couple of years as Community Beat Officer, plodding up and down Fratton Road, protecting an eternity of teenage mums and half-arsed charity shops? The answer, he knew, was no but even now, deep in his heart, he still believed that no corner was tight enough not to offer the prospect of escape.

In bed, at the hospital, he'd gone over the chase time and again. The blow to his head had muddied his recall but he seemed to remember the major stepping stones that had bridged the mile or so from Old Portsmouth to the onrushing prospect of the newsagent's front window. The bus under the railway bridge. The old lady with the stick on the pedestrian crossing. Any of these witness statements would be another nail in Winter's coffin, and Traffic would doubtless move heaven and earth to dig them up, but the trick in situations like these was to ignore the small print. What he needed now was a change of perspective. Politicians had a word for this. They called it spin. First, though, he had to make sure they'd both got the story straight.

Balancing the tea tray in one hand, Winter made his way through to the lounge. The curtains were still drawn, the room in semi-darkness. He left the tray on the low table beside the telephone and headed for the window but then changed his mind. The sight of Joannie's precious garden would only depress him more. The last thing he needed just now was a reminder of everything he should be doing, now that summer was in full bloom.

He switched on the standard lamp over his recliner and dug in the breast pocket of his jacket for his address book. Left-handed, it took an age to hook it out. Dawn's number was under E for Ellis. The number rang and rang, before an answerphone finally cut in. Callers were to leave a message.

Winter tried to ease his position in the chair. The tablets weren't working at all.

'It's your favourite cop, love. Give us a ring?'

The Nelson Bar was nearly full by the time Faraday and Bev Yates walked in. Frank Melia had given them a lift from police HQ, leaving his mobile number in case something cropped up. Faraday had done his best to express his thanks but Melia had silenced him with a hand on his arm.

'Pleasure, my friend,' he'd said simply. 'I just hope we win.'

Inside the bar, Yates managed to find them a couple of stools, wedged beneath a fading print of HMS *Victory*. The view of the game from here would be far from perfect but there were two TVs plus a big screen so one way or another he'd pick up most of the action.

'And Pritchard?' Faraday enquired drily, emerging from the scrum around the bar with a couple of pints of Carlsberg.

With the help of the photo from the Alhambra, Yates had located him at a nearby table. Faraday found a shelf for the lagers and followed Yates's eyes as they flicked left, recognising the huge white dome of Pritchard's forehead. Without the pantomime make-up, oddly enough, the man looked even weirder: moist, bulging eyes, full mouth and a nervous habit of rubbing at a reddened patch of skin on his right cheek where he must have caught the sun. There was a bunch of young sailors seated around him, already several pints down, and Pritchard seemed happy enough to be trapped in the conversational crossfire.

Faraday raised his glass to Yates, and the promise of the next couple of hours. Nick Hayder had been right. Half close your eyes, and they could easily have been back in Portsmouth.

The game kicked off ten minutes later. By now the pub was bursting, a solid mass of people, most of them standing, all of them determined to put the Argies to the sword. The sheer volume of noise was unbelievable, the crowd swaying as one, and Faraday – used to the busy silence of the New Forest, or the sigh of the wind across the salt marsh at Pennington – began to ask himself whether this was such a bad idea. If England managed any kind of result, he'd reasoned, then Pritchard might well be predisposed towards a celebratory chat. Add the warming effects of a couple of gallons of lager, and their worries about extradition might magically disappear.

The first twenty minutes or so, to Faraday's untutored eye, were inconclusive. Play switched from end to end, then the English goalie made an impressive-looking save, sparking a hundred raised glasses and a chorus of '*Sea-man . . . Sea-man . . .*' This was obviously good news for the English fans but Faraday, watching Pritchard, couldn't help wondering about the almost permanent smile on his face. For someone who may well have kicked his lover to death, he seemed to be having a fine old time.

Seconds later, Yates was on his feet. One of the English players had evidently been clattered by an Argentinian and Yates, along with every other male in the room, wanted blood. The chant this time sent a chill down Faraday's spine. '*Bel-gra-no!*' they roared. '*Bel-gra-no!*

We nicked your fucking islands and you'll never get them back.' Faraday turned away, taking a long pull on the lager, wishing he was anywhere but here.

'Owen Hargreaves.' Yates had caught Faraday's eye. 'They'll have to sub him.'

As the injured Hargreaves left the field on a stretcher, another English player came on, black, West Ham. According to a pimply youth at Faraday's elbow, this would make all the difference. Scholsie would shift back to his midfield position alongside Butt, and the fucking English would start stroking it around. Faraday followed this prediction as best he could, trying to decide about the wisdom of another pint. He'd got to second in the queue at the bar when a through pass found Michael Owen in the Argentinian penalty area. A defender stuck out a leg and the Nelson exploded. Seconds later, Faraday felt a tug on his arm. It was Yates. Whatever he felt about football, Faraday couldn't possibly miss the penalty. This had ceased to have anything to do with sport. This was history in the making.

Even Faraday recognised David Beckham. A howl of protest greeted an Argentinian's attempt to shake his hand as the English captain sat the ball on the penalty spot. Then Beckham was walking backwards, his face in huge close-up as he turned to eyeball the Argentinian keeper. The bar fell silent. Yates ducked his head and shut his eyes. Someone, in a low, urgent whisper, appeared to be praying. Beckham hesitated a moment, took a tiny breath, then five quick steps and the ball was in the back of the net.

The bar erupted. A glass flew across the room and smashed against the far wall. '*Argies are shit!*' went the chant. '*Argies are shit . . .*' Faraday, no longer interested in another pint, checked out Pritchard and then beckoned to Yates. If Pritchard left the Nelson, then Yates was to follow him and keep Faraday posted by mobile. For his part, Faraday had seen more than enough of England's finest hour. He'd sit out the second half elsewhere and be back in time for the final whistle.

Yates looked bemused.

'You're *leaving*? When we're one nil up?'

Faraday nodded, stole a final look at Pritchard, and then headed for the door.

He found the Trafalgar Cemetery exactly where the tourist map had indicated. The sun was out now, blazing from a near-cloudless sky, and it was very hot. Sweating after the climb from Main Street, Faraday slipped his jacket off and loosened his tie. Entrance to the cemetery was through a big iron gate, pitted with rust around the hinges. As far as Faraday could judge, the place was empty.

Ahead lay a litter of tombstones, bleached white teeth bunched together in the tall grass, one seeming to lean against another. Two hundred years of scouring Atlantic weather had reduced many of the dead to the ghost of a name on the crumbling sandstone but here and there it was possible to pick out the details. *Marine Johnny Press. Died of Wounds. Lt Henry Kettle. Died of Wounds. Seaman George Christian. Died of Wounds.*

Indeed, thought Faraday. He walked on, head down, trying to rid himself of the roar of the crowd in the Nelson. He'd never had any taste for mob violence. He loathed the kind of patriotism that wrapped itself in the cross of St George. Why? Because it could so easily lead to places like this.

Just now, in Pompey, it was impossible to drive a hundred yards without another outbreak of English flags or English T-shirts, but privately Faraday shuddered at the message they sent. Football was war by other means, a very welcome substitute, but it carried the same celebratory whiff of cordite and spilled blood. Easy, he thought, if you'd never fought in a war, never seen your shipmates blown apart. He paused in the shadow of the cemetery wall, hearing the chant of the sailors again. All that aggression. All that lager. All that drunken innocence. *We nicked your fucking islands and you'll never get them back.*

He shook his head, feeling the warmth of the stones through his shirt, thinking once again of Pritchard.

Winter hadn't a clue who'd come knocking at his door. Wakened from a deep sleep, he struggled out of the recliner and made his way down the hall. Maybe Cathy, he thought, with something nice to drink. Or bloody Traffic, with a firing squad.

It was Andy Corbett. Winter had seen the face in the bar at Kingston Crescent, asked someone else for a name. Now, on the doorstep, he looked him up and down. Wearing leathers like that on a hot day must be a real pain.

'Yes?' he said blankly.

Corbett pushed past without a word. Winter caught up with him in the lounge. The standard lamp was still on, the room curtained, the recliner pooled in light.

'Something on your mind, son?'

Corbett turned to face him. He was a couple of inches taller than Winter and made the most of the extra height.

'You're a fucking disgrace,' he said. 'You could have killed her.'

'Really? And what's that to you?'

'None of your business, but I'll tell you something else. If you weren't such a pathetic old bastard, I'd sort this out here and now. You know what you've done to that girl? You've turned her into a basket case. Can't think straight. Can't sleep properly. Can't stand the thought of going back to work.'

'You'd know that, would you?'

'Yeah, I would.' He poked a finger in Winter's face. 'And if I were you I'd shut my mouth and just fucking listen for a change. You know what the blokes on the job say about you? They say you're fucking bent. Well, I can live with that. That gives me no fucking problem whatsoever, Mr Winter, but what I can't stand is fucking Mickey Mouse blokes like you thinking they're big-time cops and pulling a stunt like that. Where I come from, you'd be pensioned off. You'd be put out to grass. You'd be down in the West Country somewhere in a field of donkeys where you can't do anyone else any damage. And good fucking riddance.'

Winter eyed him for a moment, amused.

'Finished, have you?'

'No.' Corbett stepped across to the window and tore the curtains back. Sunshine flooded the room. 'You live like this all the time? Dossing in the dark? Only Dawn said you had some strange habits.'

'Sure, like she'd know.'

'But she does, Mr Winter, she does. And what makes it even more pathetic, she actually likes you. Can you believe that? Some fat old git can't even keep a car on the road?' He came very close, pushing his face into Winter's. 'Fucking Skoda, wasn't it? Just about sums this place up.'

He stepped back, looking round the lounge. Only last week, Winter had come across an old photo in one of the bedroom drawers next door. It showed a much younger Winter, flares and leather jacket, posing on the seafront half a lifetime ago with a couple of other DCs. He'd propped it on the mantelpiece next to his lottery tickets, meaning to find a frame. Now Corbett picked it up, holding it out at arm's length.

'Sad.' He shook his head. 'What is it about this place? Half the guys I meet have never been off the fucking island.'

'Maybe we like it. Maybe we're that simple.'

'Yeah, maybe you are, too. You know how I spent most of yesterday? Running round Somerstown after a bunch of inbreds. And that's just the blokes I have to work with.'

'Their privilege, son. I'm sure you'll teach them lots.'

'Fat fucking chance. You think I'm staying here a day longer than I have to? I signed up for CID, not Punch and fucking Judy.'

'Do you mind?' Winter reached for the photo and put it back on the mantelpiece. His arm was throbbing again and he had a splitting headache.

Corbett wanted to know what Winter intended to do about Dawn.

'Do?'

'Yeah. She's talking legals. She wants compensation. Money.'

'You mean you've been talking legals.'

'No, Mr Winter. I mean she's fucking angry, and fucking hurt, and she's not about to sit around and let you get away with it. Neither should she. The way she tells it, you were off your head, totally unreasonable, wouldn't listen to a word she said. That says serious money to me and I'll bloody make sure she gets it. People like you should come with a health warning. You're dangerous, Mr Winter. And that's another reason they shouldn't let you anywhere near the job.' He nodded at the photo. 'How they ever took you on in the first place is beyond me. They must have been fucking desperate.'

Winter gazed at him a moment, then took him by the arm and steered him towards the door. He'd had quite enough of Andy Corbett but the last thing he was going to offer was the satisfaction of a full-blown row. On the front doorstep, Corbett shook him off. He'd said his piece but that wouldn't be the end of it. Just now he was off to work, but Winter shouldn't think for a minute that this was the end of the story.

'I'll be back,' he promised. 'Bend your fucking ear again.'

'Really?' Winter offered him a cold smile. 'And what makes you think I'm interested in listening?'

Twelve

It was half an hour after the final whistle before Faraday and Bev Yates could get close enough to Pritchard to have a decent conversation. The Nelson Bar was still packed, knots of swaying sailors toasting Michael Owen, toasting David Beckham, toasting Sven Goran Eriksson, toasting each other. The English had stuck it to the Argies, no more than those bastards deserved. After Maradona's hand of God and Beckham's sending off at St Etienne, justice had finally been done.

Pritchard looked up as they approached. His eyes were brimming. Faraday counted four empty glasses stacked at his elbow.

'Brilliant, or what?' he mumbled.

He made a long, expansive gesture with his right hand. Yates, accepting the invitation, sat down beside him.

'Man of the match?' he enquired.

'Owen. Has to be. Hadn't got a fucking answer, had they? Couldn't touch him.' Pritchard shook his head, gazing at the mill of sailors. 'Magic. All the way, now, all the fucking way.'

Yates was pressing the claims of Nicky Butt. In his view, he'd never played a better game in an England shirt. He'd worked his socks off, tackling, harrying, probing forward, passing, containing.

'He took Veron out of the game,' he concluded. 'Marked him off the pitch. Wonderful. Wonderful.'

Pritchard had his arm round Yates now, hugging him. After the solitary excitements of the last couple of hours, he'd finally found a friend.

'You back here tomorrow, are you? Fancy the Brazil game? Few bevvies?'

'No question, mate. It's Italy–Croatia, too. That Robert Prosinecki is something else.'

Faraday, suspecting Yates could keep this up all day, took the spare seat across the table. Pritchard squinted down at the proffered warrant card. Clearly, he hadn't a clue what it was.

'We're policemen,' Faraday said slowly. 'CID. From England.'

'Yeah?' Pritchard was trying to digest the news. 'On holiday, are you?'

'I'm afraid not.' He leaned forward across the table, aware of a couple of sailors watching them. 'We need to talk to you, Mr Pritchard.'

The fact that this stranger knew his name caused Pritchard more confusion.

'I don't get it. Do you want a drink or something?' He fumbled in the pocket of his jeans and produced a crumpled twenty-pound note. 'Here. My shout.'

Faraday shook his head. Yates likewise.

'Not for me, mate.'

'But . . .' Pritchard was frowning now. 'We won, didn't we? Stuffed the bastards?'

'We did.'

'Let's all have a drink, then.' He looked slowly from one to the other. 'No?'

'Afraid not.' Faraday glanced at his watch. 'We really do need a little chat.'

Pritchard stared at them a moment longer, then shrugged and struggled to his feet. Faraday had phoned ahead, asking Frank Melia for transport, and a white minibus was waiting at the kerbside. There were two policemen inside and they helped Pritchard clamber into the back. The sight of the uniforms clearly puzzled him.

'Mates,' Yates muttered.

'They see the game, too?'

'Yeah. Loved it. Eh, guys?'

The taller of the two policemen nodded, flinching when Pritchard squeezed his leg.

'Fucking one nil.' He closed his eyes and let his head fall on to Yates's shoulder. 'Magic.'

Pritchard was still asleep, minutes later, when they turned into police headquarters. The chance of a decent kip with someone to keep an eye on him, and the man would be ready to accompany Faraday and Yates to the Panorama Hotel for a search of Pritchard's room. After that, back at police headquarters, would come a formal interview.

It took Pritchard a couple of hours to sober up. When Faraday and Yates stepped into the cell where Pritchard had been sleeping it off, the Alhambra's manager was sitting on the single iron bed, rubbing his eyes. Only the stench from the lavatory in the corner of the cell suggested any aftermath from half a gallon of export-strength lager.

Pritchard gazed up.

'What is this?'

'A CID investigation, Mr Pritchard.' Faraday once again offered his warrant card.

'CID?' Pritchard looked startled. 'Am I under arrest?'

'Absolutely not. But we do need to talk to you.'

'No problem. Be nice to know what's going on, though, eh?'

Faraday hesitated a moment. Then he suggested that Pritchard come with them to the hotel. Pritchard shook his head at once.

'No chance.' He nodded at the lavatory. 'Dodgy gut. The lager here gives you the shits.'

'All the same, we still need to take a look at your room.'

'Be my guest – but do us a favour, eh? Come back here and tell me what the fuck this is all about?'

Faraday glanced across at Yates. Pritchard wasn't exhibiting the least sign of guilt. On the contrary, Faraday had rarely met anyone so peaceably disposed after a couple of hours in a police cell.

'You're sure you don't want to come with us to the hotel?'

'Positive.'

'Do you mind putting that in writing? Just for the record?'

'I'll do any fucking thing.' Pritchard got up and stepped towards the lavatory. 'Just give me a moment, though, eh?'

The Panorama lay at the far end of Line Wall Road, a three-storeyed confection in pre-stressed concrete that did nothing to raise the architectural tone. Frank Melia drove them down in the Landcruiser and introduced them to the manager. Pritchard's room was on the third floor. On Melia's instructions, it hadn't been cleaned since yesterday and Faraday was welcome to the key.

The room, like the rest of Pritchard's life, was in a state of some disarray. There was bedding on the floor and a pile of dirty clothes beside the door to the tiny balcony. An unzipped holdall on the dressing table held two six-packs of Guinness and the uncapped remains of a bottle of Johnnie Walker was wedged upright against the bedhead by a pillow.

'Where have we seen these before?'

Yates had found a pile of soggy gay porn magazines on the bathroom floor, same titles as the stuff in Coughlin's flat. Last month's edition of *Blade* featured a full-lipped white youth playing flautist on a sizeable black erection. Yates began to leaf through, then tossed the magazine back into the bathroom with a sigh.

'At least it makes him happy,' he muttered.

Faraday smiled. Last night, at home, Yates had been

up late with the baby, scarcely bothering to go to bed. Faraday had got the full details on the plane.

'You want to get a nanny. Takes the pressure off. That's what I did with J-J. Worked a treat.'

'Yeah, but you were on your own, weren't you? I've got this marriage thing all wrong. I thought babies were down to the wife. Maybe I should have a word with Pritchard. Turn gay.'

Faraday was going through the drawer in the bedside cabinet. Pritchard had yet to get lucky in Gibraltar because the pack of Durex Gossamer was still intact but what interested him more were the postcards underneath. There were three of them. They all showed the same view – Barbary apes preening for the visitors – and two of them had already been stamped and addressed.

'Listen.' He turned to Yates. ' "*Terrible fucking weather but whoever came to this shit hole to lie on the beach? Two ships in off exercise and skates everywhere. Someone's got to fancy it sooner or later, even if I have to pay. Look after yourself. Be good. Big G.*" ' Faraday looked up. 'Any guesses on the address?'

Yates stared at him for a moment.

'Don't tell me.' He paused. 'Coughlin?'

'Dead right.'

'So who's "G"?'

'Guzza. Has to be. That's the name he uses in the newsgroups.'

'Shit.'

Yates read the postcard for himself. The other one was addressed to Pritchard's sister. Faraday had sunk on to the bed. No wonder Pritchard had been so cooperative. He didn't even know Coughlin was dead.

'Pritchard's mates with the manager,' Yates suggested. 'The manager knows we're interested because Melia's told him and now he's blown us to Pritchard. Pritchard writes the postcard and leaves it for us to find.'

Faraday gave it a moment's thought, then shook his head.

'No,' he said. 'No way.'

'The maid, then. Same deal.'

'Doesn't work. Pritchard's not that organised. You've seen the guy. He's Scotch on legs.'

'Drunks can be fucking devious.'

'Not this one. I just don't believe it.' He took a final look at the postcard, then returned it to the drawer. Full length on the bed, Faraday stared up at the ceiling, giving the jigsaw yet another shake.

'Tell me about the taxi again, the one he took to Gatwick.'

'Tuesday morning?' Faraday nodded. 'He spent the entire journey asleep. He was in the back, crashed out. Car stank of booze. Driver said he had to have the window open the whole bloody way.'

'Great.' Faraday shut his eyes. 'Does that sound like guilt to you?'

En route back to police headquarters, Faraday and Yates snatched a meal at a cheap seafood restaurant recommended by Frank Melia. They ate in silence, picking at plates of hake and chips, and Faraday left Yates chasing peas with his fork while he went outside to the tiny car park and put through a call to Willard.

Willard, if anything, was even more despondent. The Darren Geech inquiry was going absolutely nowhere. No one was talking, there was no CCTV, zilch leads, and someone with a twisted sense of humour had plastered most of Somerstown with dozens of trophy front pages from that day's *News*. The headline ran alongside a big colour photo of Winter's wrecked Skoda embedded in the Queen Street newsagent's. 'Neighbourhood Policing,' went the headline, 'Portsea Style'.

'The kids just think it's a laugh,' Willard growled. 'This fucking city's out of control.'

Faraday gave him the bad news about Pritchard. Willard wasn't having it.

'You're telling me he hasn't got questions to answer? The footprint? All that stuff on the internet?'

'No, sir. I'm just telling you he probably didn't do it.'

'That's no way to start an interview. What if Yates is right? Anyone can plant a postcard. You don't have to be fucking Einstein to pull a stroke like that.'

'I just think—'

'Yes, Joe. I know what you think. Just keep an open mind, OK?'

Willard rang off moments later without bothering to say goodbye. Operational Support were denying him more bodies and he'd spotted a 140-hour overspend in the overtime budget. One day he might knock some sense into this job of his but just now Faraday got the impression that he wished he was back at Centrex, exploring the possibilities of a new career in kidnapping and extortion.

Yates had been watching Faraday's face through the restaurant window.

'We could always nip into Spain,' he suggested when Faraday walked back in. 'Lie on the beach for a week or two.'

Winter took a taxi to see Dawn Ellis. Portchester was a fifteen-minute drive west along the coast. Neat post-war semis wound up the lower slopes of Portsdown Hill, and there was a big, thick-walled Roman castle on the foreshore that drew visitors by the thousands. Portchester was the kind of place that seemed to offer a refuge from the street crime and social anarchy that had had engulfed so much of the city itself. In reality, as Winter well knew, the crime stats were as alarming as anywhere else in the suburban sprawl that Hartigan liked to call Greater Portsmouth, but pull up your drawbridge and tend your roses, and you could kid yourself that life really was a breeze.

Dawn took for ever to answer the door. Winter knew she was in because he'd taken the precaution of phoning ahead. Ignoring her pleas to be left alone, he told her to get the kettle on. The notion of the Skoda Preservation Society had rather taken his fancy. They were, he announced with a chuckle, founder members.

'You think that's funny?'

They were sitting in the garden, waiting for the next patch of blue to drift across. Dawn was sporting a pair of Ray-Bans a size too big for her face. She'd done her best to mask the bruise on her cheek with a dusting of Boots No. 7 but Winter couldn't help wondering what else lay behind the sun shades.

'How are you, love?' He touched his own face.

'Fine.' Her voice was a mumble, not the usual Dawn at all.

'Seriously.'

'I'm fine.' She turned her head away. 'Seriously.'

For a moment, Winter wondered whether to apologise. Taking the odd physical risk or two was, in his view, all part of the job but he could quite understand that a full-scale RTA might seem a bit extreme. Ending up in a Queen Street shop window wasn't an experience for the faint-hearted.

'What did the medics say?'

'Not much. Bit of bruising. Bit shaken up, you know, inside. Nothing that a couple of aspirin can't sort out. Just as well I had the seat belt on, really . . .'

Dawn's head was still turned away, her voice even lower. She hadn't offered tea, or anything else for that matter.

'And you?' she said.

'Bored stiff, love. I was wondering whether you might be up for a bit of convalescence. Saga do some nice coach trips.'

The joke fell flat. Dawn sat in the deckchair, her arms crossed, plainly waiting for him to go. Winter adjusted his weight, making himself comfortable. In these situations, it was silence that would do the trick.

'Anyone been round to see you?' she enquired at last.

It was an innocent enough question. Winter shook his head.

'No, love.'

'No one at all?'

'No. I've been expecting a Traffic skipper but nothing so far.' He raised his plastered arm. 'Not that I can sign any confessions at the moment.'

The quip at last raised a smile. She turned on him.

'What on earth were you doing?' she said hotly. 'I know you're not keen on the rules and stuff but there were two of us in there, Paul, not just you.'

'I know, I know.'

'But you don't, do you? You come round here like nothing's happened. We could have been killed. Easily. Hasn't that crossed your mind at all?'

Winter considered the proposition for a moment, then shook his head. Immortality, he'd long concluded, came with the job.

'We had a little accident,' he said mildly. 'You ever want to buy me a present, don't make it a Skoda.'

'You're blaming the *car*?'

'I'm blaming nothing. I'm not even thinking about it. What's done is done.'

'Great. So what do we say when they come asking questions?'

Winter smiled. He liked the 'we' a great deal. Corbett, as he'd suspected, had been making it up.

'We tell them the truth. We tell them we had the place staked out. We tell them Geech clocked us and drove off. Naturally, we followed.'

'Chased.'

'Followed. This is Pompey, love. The traffic's awful. You don't chase, you dawdle.'

Dawn said nothing for a moment. Miles above them, the whine of a jet.

'What about witnesses? You nearly put a bus on the pavement for starters.'

'I don't remember any of that.'

'The taxi driver at the Hard?'

'Gone.'

'You mean it? You really can't remember?'

Winter looked back towards the house. He could murder a drink.

'I've got amnesia, love,' he said at last. 'I find it helps no end.'

'I bet. And what about me? Am I supposed to have amnesia too?'

'Pass. For all I know you might have been busy on the radio. Or maybe you'd dropped something and you were trying to find it in the footwell.' He smiled at her. 'Does that sound likely?'

Dawn stared at him. Moments later, her mobile began to ring. She picked it up and bent forward in the deckchair. As the conversation developed, she began to tug nervously at the sleeve of her sweatshirt.

'No,' she kept saying. 'Really, I'd prefer not. Leave it a couple of days . . . please.'

Winter was looking at her forearm, trying to work out how she'd got the marks around her wrist. The skin was angry and roughened, a series of scarlet welts. Maybe seat belts weren't as effective as people claimed.

At last she brought the conversation to a close. The pallor in her face only emphasised the bruising. She struggled to her feet, then gestured at the phone.

'Cathy. Wanted to come out for a little chat but I've managed to put her off.' She paused, biting her lip. 'Lager be OK?'

*

At police headquarters in Gibraltar, Pritchard appeared to have made a temporary peace with his bubbling gut. One of the duty sergeants had given him tea and biscuits and assured him once again that he wasn't under arrest. By the time Faraday and Yates stepped into the interview room, he'd even had a wash.

Pritchard watched as Yates stripped the cellophane from a packet of audio cassettes and slipped one into each of the recording machines. He said he was sorry about the state of his hotel room but taking holidays alone turned you into a slut.

'Know what I mean?'

Faraday smiled at him, noncommittal, then explained the official caution. Pritchard waved away his right to free legal advice. What concerned him more was exactly what Faraday was after.

'We're here on a murder investigation,' Faraday said slowly. 'And we think you may be able to help us.'

'Help you how?'

'There's someone we think you might know,' Faraday began. 'He was killed late Monday night, early Tuesday morning.'

'Where?'

'In Portsmouth.'

'*Pompey?*'

'Yes.'

'And who was he?'

'Sean Coughlin.'

Pritchard rocked back in the chair. The big, flabby mouth fell open, then closed again. He reached for the table, steadying himself. Not for a second did he take his eyes off Faraday's face.

'You're joking,' he said. 'Tell me you're joking. Sean? You can't mean it.'

'I'm afraid it's true, Mr Pritchard.' Faraday nodded at the audio machines. 'It would help us if we could record this interview. Do you mind?'

'God, no. Anything. I'll do anything. You go ahead.
Sean dead? Christ . . . that's unbelievable.'

Faraday glanced at Yates. The machines began to roll
and Pritchard watched the tiny sprockets going round,
seemingly mesmerised, as Faraday announced the date,
time, location and names of those present. From time to
time, Pritchard's hand would stray to that same patch of
skin on his cheek, the little nervous tic Faraday remembered from the Nelson Bar.

'What do you want to know?' he said at length.

'Tell us about Monday evening. Where were you?'

Faraday waited while Pritchard hauled himself backwards through the week. Finally, he got to Monday.

'I was at home.' He frowned. 'I run a hotel. The
Alhambra. Granada Road. I was there.'

'You don't sound that sure.'

'No, I was, I was.' The frown deepened. 'Monday was
the night before I flew out, yeah . . . ?' Faraday looked at
him, saying nothing. 'We were quiet. In fact we're always
fucking quiet. There were a couple of overnights—' He
broke off. 'You want me to check all this? Only I can
always phone my sister. She's looking after the place
while I'm away. Jackie her name is. She'd know.'

'We've talked to your sister already. She says she was
in bed by ten but you were still downstairs in the bar.
You'd had a few drinks, right?'

'Yeah, of course.'

'So what happened then?'

Pritchard was deep in thought again, trying to work it
all out, and as far as Faraday could judge this confusion
of his was real. Neck a bottle of Johnnie Walker a day, he
thought, and your brain would turn to sponge.

'Three blokes,' Pritchard said at last. 'There were three
of them.' He counted them on his fingers. 'Yeah,
definitely three.'

'Three blokes what?'

'Came into the bar. Late it was. Past eleven. The

highlights were on.' He shifted slightly and stared at Yates. 'Brazil–Turkey?'

'That's right . . . and Croatia–Mexico,' Yates told him. 'One nil to the Mexicans.'

'Crap game.'

'Yeah? I never saw most of it.'

'OK.' It was Faraday again. 'So tell us about these three blokes. You knew them? You've got names?'

'Never seen them in my life. They'd had a few, mind. Ex-skates, definitely.'

'And?'

'They settled in. Stella and Bacardi chasers for a couple of them. Scotch and water for the other bloke.' He looked up, pleased with himself. 'They obviously wanted to make a night of it.'

'So you stayed up with them? Is that what you're saying?'

'Had to. No choice. There was only me behind the bar.'

He took a deep breath, then sat back in the chair and stared up at the ceiling. After a while, it occurred to Faraday that he was crying.

'You're serious, aren't you, about Sean? You're telling me he's really dead? Only . . . shit.' The chair tipped forward and he buried his face in his hands, sobbing.

'Mr Pritchard?' Faraday was being as gentle as he could. 'I know this is difficult—'

'Difficult? Do you know how much I loved that man?' The face came up, contorted with grief. 'He was fucking everything to me, everything. No one else saw it, no one else knew him. Not like I did. This has to be some kind of joke. Who'd ever kill Sean?'

Yates had found a paper tissue from somewhere. He slid it across the table. Pritchard stared at it, numbed.

'Tell me something, Mr Pritchard.' Faraday changed the subject. 'How come you chased Coughlin round the internet the way you did?'

At first the question seemed to baffle Pritchard. Then he reached for the tissue and blew his nose.

'Freckler? Guzza? You know about that crap?' Faraday nodded. 'It was a game we played. We were at it for months, just slagging each other off in front of all those tight-arsed twats. Americans were the best. We really got to some of them. It was a laugh, the way they'd always react.'

'So it was make-believe? Is that what you're saying?'

'Yeah. Freckler and Guzza. The terrible twins. The lunatics from hell. Fucking brilliant.' His eyes were brimming with tears again but there was defiance in the stare.

Yates had produced a notebook.

'Why Guzza?' he enquired.

'Guzz is Plymouth. Jackspeak. I was born there, grew up there.'

'You were in the navy, too?'

'Twenty-one years.'

'You met Coughlin in the navy? Served in the same ship?'

'No.' He sounded regretful. 'We met a couple of years back. Pure coincidence. He came into the Alhambra one night, wanted a quiet drink. It all kicked off from there.'

'You were lovers?'

'Too fucking right. Best shag on the planet.'

'Coughlin?'

'Me.' He shook his head and blew his nose again. 'Hard, this. Fucking impossible.'

Faraday took the interview back to Monday night. The three guys had arrived late. Pritchard was by himself in the bar. They were all drinking. Then what?

Pritchard was leaning forward, angry now. He hadn't heard a word.

'You don't get it, do you? You just don't get it.'

'Get what, Mr Pritchard?'

'About Sean. He came in that Monday night. He came

in when those blokes were there. They knew him. It was fucking obvious they knew him. He was out of that bar – bang – just like that. Didn't even stay for a drink.'

Yates had stopped writing. Faraday blinked.

'Did they say anything, these blokes?' Faraday was leaning forward across the table. 'Did they talk about him at all? After he'd gone?'

'They were in a huddle round a table in the window. I can see them now. One stood up and watched Sean walking off. Then . . . you know . . . gave him the finger.' He lifted his hand, repeating the gesture. 'They hated him. Ask me why, I don't know, but they did. And after that, they really went for it.'

'Went for what?'

'Got really pissed, and I mean really pissed.'

'Can you describe these guys? Young? Old?'

'Old, two of them. Our age. Scan's age. The other one looked slightly younger. Bigger, too. Fat bastard.'

'Can you remember names? Did they call each other anything?'

'I couldn't hear. I was down one end of the lounge and like I said they were in the bay window.'

'Would you recognise them again?'

'Definitely.' He nodded, making the point. 'I was really upset, really, really upset. For Sean, not me. Fuck knows why but they really got to him, these guys. Sean's not the kind of bloke to . . . you know . . . duck out like that.' He sniffed again. 'I tried to phone him after he walked out, to make sure he was OK, but he had the machine on.'

'You used your mobile for that call?' Yates again, pencil poised.

'Yeah. I phoned him from the hall. I didn't want those bastards listening.'

Faraday was trying to get a fix on the exact sequence of events. Three strangers had driven Coughlin back into the night. Afterwards they'd got very pissed. What time did they leave?

'I dunno. I got them a cab in the end. And that was a performance, too, because I couldn't find my mobile. Had to use the proper phone.'

'So where was your mobile?'

'I must have left it behind the bar.'

Yates wanted more details on the cab.

'Which company?'

'Aqua.'

'In whose name?'

'Mine. It was easier. These blokes didn't really want to go but I called it anyway.'

'And they all got in?'

'As far as I know.'

'What time was that?'

'Fuck knows. Late. Way past midnight. Aqua would have it.'

Yates glanced at Faraday, and grinned. Flying to Gibraltar hadn't, in the end, been such a bad idea.

Pritchard reached out across the table. He wanted to finish the story, tell them everything he knew. His touch was clammy on the back of Faraday's hand.

'After they'd gone I had a bit of a sort out, cash from the till for my spending money, I remember that. Then I went up to bed but there was no way I could sleep, not leaving Sean like that, so I got dressed again and went round to his place.'

'What time was that?'

'Haven't a clue. Three in the morning? Dunno. Anyway, I knocked at the door, our special knock, rap-rap-rap, but I couldn't raise him. Then I went round the back, thinking he must be in bed. I hammered on the window, really hard, but nothing happened. Then I went round the front again, tried the front door, knocked on the front window, but . . .' He shook his head, not wanting to go on, overwhelmed by the thought of what he might have found inside.

There was a long silence. Yates was about to ask

another question but Faraday stilled him with a tiny shake of the head. Finally, Pritchard's hand strayed to the patch of reddened skin on his cheek and he looked away, the tears streaming down his face.

'You're seriously telling me he was dead by then?' He swallowed. 'I can't believe it.'

Thirteen

It was Bev Yates who volunteered to drive Pritchard home from the airport. They'd managed to book three seats on the early evening flight from Gibraltar, hanging grimly on to their supper trays as the plane bucketed through a vicious thunderstorm over the Bay of Biscay. Pritchard, who had gulped three hasty pints of Harp lager in the departure lounge, ignored the Fasten Seat Belt signs to stagger to the loo. When he returned, he was pale and sweating, and Yates thought he could smell vomit on his breath.

Accompanying them back to the UK had been Pritchard's idea. The thought of staying on holiday when his mate was lying in a mortuary fridge was, he'd said, totally out of order and he'd insisted on a lift to the Panorama and five minutes up in his room to throw his kit together. Yates had gone with him, not because he thought Pritchard might do a runner, but because he was genuinely concerned. The man was inconsolable. He'd shuffled around like a sleep-walker, slow, dream-like movements, absolutely no idea what he was doing, and watching him trying to repack his life into the grubby old holdall, Yates had come to the conclusion that Coughlin had been blessed with at least one solid relationship. No one, no matter how talented, could put on a performance like this.

Now, with Pritchard asleep in the aisle seat, it occurred to Faraday that Coughlin's body still hadn't been formally ID'd. There'd been no relatives to attend the morgue and a conspicuous lack of volunteers from his fellow screws at Gosport prison. With the coroner's officer eager to get the paperwork squared away, maybe Pritchard could do the honours.

Yates wanted to know about the Family Liaison Officer.

'There isn't one. We never got round to it.'

'So who goes along with him?'

Faraday glanced sideways at Yates and smiled. Once the plane stopped shaking itself to pieces, the drinks trolley might appear again.

'Small gin?' he suggested. 'Lots of tonic?'

An hour and a half later, with Yates off hunting for his Golf, Faraday and Pritchard stood in the orange loom of one of the long-term car parks, watching the incoming queue of aircraft swaying down the glidepath into Gatwick. In the morning, once Pritchard had caught up on his sleep, Faraday would send someone round to the Alhambra to take a formal statement. He wanted an account of exactly what had happened that last Monday night. Maybe there was stuff – little points of detail – that might have slipped his mind. He must have spent at least an hour with the three guys in the bar. Physical descriptions would be important and maybe a nickname might come back to him. Anything, he repeated, anything that would make the hunt for Coughlin's killers just that little bit easier.

Pritchard turned to him, his eyes wide.

'You think they did it, those blokes?'

'I think they've got some questions to answer.'

'But you really think they might have done it?'

'It's possible, certainly, but in my line of work, Kevin, it doesn't always pay to draw the obvious conclusions.'

It was the first time Faraday had used Pritchard's Christian name and the smile that lit his face was a reminder of just how vulnerable this man was. Coughlin would have loved that, Faraday thought. He'd have scented the weakness, the almost childlike hunger for affection, and turned it into a relationship. That Pritchard had come to depend on Coughlin was no longer in doubt. With Coughlin gone, this strange, gauche, awkward figure was utterly lost.

Yates arrived with the Golf and made room for Pritchard in the front. Faraday could see his own Mondeo several rows away. He dumped his bag in the boot and sent a text message to J-J, announcing his imminent return. Within seconds, still in the car park, he had a reply. *One hotel on Old Kent Road*, went the message. *And loads of houses on the blue streets.*

Driving home, Faraday waited for updates. By Chichester, J-J had won the first game and started another. Half an hour later, Faraday found him sprawled across the carpet, deep in negotiations over a Get Out Of Jail Free card. Cross-legged on the other side of the Monopoly board was Eadie.

'Sykes.' Faraday realised he was pleased to see her. 'This is becoming a habit.'

'Yep. Just a shame I'm not winning.'

She nodded down at the board. J-J had built himself a small estate around the Old Kent Road and secured an equally substantial presence around nearby Islington. Throw virtually any number in the vicinity of Go, and the boy would clean you out.

'You good at this too?' Sykes was still looking up.

'Used to be. How come he conned you into playing?'

'I dropped by with the rough cut. Right bloody cassette this time.'

'You showed J-J?'

'Yep.'

'And?'

She reached across and gave J-J a nudge, touching her own eye, nodding at the television, and then making a tiny inquisitorial movement with her hand. Learns fast, thought Faraday, as J-J glanced up at his father.

'Not bad,' he signed. 'Needs more pictures, though.'

Faraday began to laugh. A weekend at sea, and J-J was unforgiving.

'You understand what he's saying?'

'Yeah. He thinks bits of it are OK but the rest is crap. We've had the conversation.'

'I'm impressed.'

'You needn't be. He wasn't.'

J-J, who realised he might have gone a bit too far, was trying to repair the damage. The soundtrack, of course, was a mystery to him and to be fair he probably put too much emphasis on the visuals. He got this thought across to Faraday in a blur of sign, and Faraday began to offer a translation.

'I know what he's saying,' Sykes interrupted. 'That's exactly what he told me earlier and you know the real problem? He's right. People like me get waylaid by what these old guys say, the stuff they come up with. Movies should be about pictures.'

'Exclusively?'

'Of course not. But look at it through Joe's eyes and you've got nothing else to go on. That's why he takes a good photo. He *sees* the world. We're cursed with these.' She plucked at her own ear and then tossed the jail card on to the board. 'I have to go. There's a message for you by the phone. I wrote it down.'

Faraday was still trying to get over someone calling his son Joe. He couldn't remember when anyone had last done that. It sounded so different, so grown-up.

'You want to stay for something to eat? I'm starving.'

'No, thanks.' She tapped her watch. 'Early start.'

Faraday shrugged, then retrieved the message, trying to decipher Sykes' boisterous scrawl. He was to phone someone called Nick. There was a mobile number and a time: eight thirty.

'It sounded important.' Sykes was halfway up the hall. 'Give me a call. You owe me a beer.'

There was the sound of the door opening and closing, and then she was gone. J-J was still on the floor, counting his money. Faraday gave him a poke with his shoe.

'You eaten yet?' he signed.

'No.'

'Want to get something together?'

J-J nodded and disappeared into the kitchen with a handful of Monopoly notes. Faraday dialled the mobile number. Nick Hayder was still up.

'How did it go?' he asked at once. 'Gibraltar?'

'It rained a bit but it was OK in the end. You into football at all?'

'Loathe it.'

'Wise man.'

Hayder had a problem with the Somerstown inquiry. The job, he said, was fast turning into a nightmare. A couple of possible witnesses to the Rooke killing, both of them kids, had been on the verge of volunteering for interview but had abruptly decided to withdraw after visits from Geech's mates. Hayder had put together background intelligence from a number of other sources only to discover that Darren's little gang, shapeless and ever changing, seemed to reach into every corner of the estate. The real challenge, therefore, was to try and figure out just who Geech normally knocked about with. Which was where J-J might come in.

'J-J?' Faraday said blankly.

'You remember last year? That drama thing he was doing with the kids before it all kicked off?'

'Yes.' J-J had teamed up with a local theatre producer, an ex-marine called Gordon Franks, in a bid to channel offending behaviour into cutting-edge on-stage perform-ance. Faraday had been dubious about the enterprise but on some strange level J-J had connected with the kids at once, winning their respect as well as their affection.

'Well,' said Nick, 'theory is he'll probably know as much as anyone else about who runs with who. The whole place is tribal. You can practically hear the tom-toms.'

Faraday found himself laughing. There'd been nothing remotely funny about the events that had led to the top of Chuzzlewit House, but when it came to kids scuffling around, giving life a good kicking, tribal was as good a description as any.

'You want to talk to him?'

'Please.'

'Tomorrow OK? Only he's not great on the phone.'

'Sure. You'll be there? Help me out?'

'Pleasure.'

Faraday stole a glance at the kitchen. J-J was rummaging in the cupboard where they kept the packets of pasta and Faraday wondered just how much J-J would be prepared to say. He owed a loyalty to these kids, no matter how wayward they might be, and Faraday had seldom come across anyone to whom loyalty was so important.

Hayder was having a final grouch about the Somerstown job. Nightmare was probably too small a word because he seldom let anyone else this close to an ongoing inquiry.

'We've had it all,' he concluded. 'Murder. Attempted kidnap. Extortion. Multiple assault. The lot. At least it can't get any worse.'

Faraday, still watching J-J, smiled to himself.

'If only,' he said.

Winter was contemplating a trip to the kitchen to finish the remains of the Glenfiddich when his mobile began to ring. He rolled over on the big double bed, cursing when his plaster snagged on the rough edge of the blanket. With the bedside light on, he peered at his watch: 02.14.

'Yeah?'

It was Dawn Ellis. She sounded hysterical. She could barely manage a sentence.

'Where are you?' Winter asked.

'At home.'

'What's happened? What's the matter?'

'Just come, Paul. Please . . . just come.'

Winter was already out of bed, hunting for his trousers, the phone clamped to his ear. His arm hurt like a bastard.

'Is there anyone there with you? Neighbour?'

'Just come, Paul. *Please.*'

The phone went dead. Winter gazed at it for a moment, trying to remember which cab firm was favourite this time of night. 92838888.

'Aqua? Soon as you can, love.' He gave her his home address, then went looking for his trousers again.

The cab seemed to take an age and Winter was out by the garden gate when it finally turned up. The driver was a young guy, hyper. He stared out at Winter's plaster cast, half hidden by the suede car coat he'd managed to drape over his shoulders.

'Man, you've had an accident.'

'Brilliant. Portchester, son. As fast as you can.'

The main road west was virtually empty. They sped through the long ribbon of suburbs, slowing only for roundabouts and the occasional traffic light. Turning right in the centre of Portchester, Winter was already looking for clues that might explain Dawn's phone call, but even when they rounded the corner into her road there was absolutely nothing out of place. Cars parked neatly, nose to tail. The occasional light in an upstairs window. The lurking shadow of a cat.

'Number . . . ?'

'Twenty-two, son. Up on the left-hand side. Behind the Volvo.'

They came to a halt. At first, Winter couldn't see anything. Then he spotted curtains in the downstairs front window stirring in the breeze and he realised that the glass had been smashed. He gave the driver a twenty-pound note and hauled himself awkwardly on to the pavement. Dawn had already opened the front door. She met him halfway down the path. She was wearing a sweater over a pair of men's pyjamas but she was shaking with cold. Winter put his good arm round her.

'What's that smell?'

'Petrol. Thank God you've come.'

He followed her into the house. The smell was overpowering now, thickened by the aftermath of what seemed to have been a sizeable fire. Dawn pushed at the door into the lounge-diner and then stepped back to let Winter through.

'Christ.'

There was a big, black hole in the carpet, a pace or two in from the window. The pile had burned through to the backing underneath. Some bedding nearby, heavily charred, was still smouldering.

'How did—?'

'Someone threw a bottle of the stuff through the window. Look, I haven't touched it.'

She pointed to shards of glass beside the coffee table. Winter bent to inspect them. Milk bottle, he thought, two thirds full of petrol, stuffed with old rags. Put a match to the rags, chuck it as hard as you can, and the chemistry of four-star would do the rest. He straightened up and looked around. The curtains were still intact, no sign of burning, and there wasn't a mark on the furniture.

'You were bloody lucky, love. How come—?'

'I put it out myself,' she said quickly.

'Just like that?'

'Yeah.' She swallowed hard. 'I was still downstairs, still in here. I heard a car stop outside and thought nothing of it. Then . . .' She looked at the window and shuddered. 'You know that wooof sound? It's true. It's just like that. The window came in and then . . . wooof. I couldn't believe it.'

Winter was still interested in the bedding.

'You were kipping down here?'

'Yes.'

'Got guests, then?'

'No.'

'Redecorating the bedroom?'

She shook her head, offering no other explanation. Winter stepped over to the window, produced a pen and poked at the broken glass. The hole was surprisingly small. Best to leave it till the morning. He turned back into the room. Dawn had wedged herself into a corner of the sofa, hugging her knees. She looked about twelve. Winter perched himself beside her and did his best to give her a cuddle. His efforts to shield the plastered arm at last brought a tiny smile to her face.

'This is getting beyond a joke,' she muttered. 'First we nearly get killed and now this.' She shook her head, staring down at the carpet, still not quite able to believe it.

'Any ideas? About the car?'

'None. I never saw it. I can't imagine . . .' She shook her head again. 'These calls I've been getting. Maybe it's to do with them. I just don't know, Paul. One minute you think you've got a grip. The next, this happens. What are they trying to do? Frighten me? See me off? Why would anyone want to do that?'

'Good question.'

Dawn's hand was icy cold. Winter began to massage it, trying to restore the circulation, but stopped when he felt her flinch.

'That hurts?'

She nodded, fighting back tears. Winter folded back the sleeve of her sweater. Her wrist and forearm were circled with angry red welts. He'd seen them earlier, in the garden.

'Was this from the accident?'

'Yeah.' She nodded. 'Your fault.' She looked away. She was a terrible liar.

As gently as he could, Winter took her other hand. He felt her resisting and told her to relax. The sleeve rolled back, he found more marks, the same pattern, the flesh inflamed and scarlet.

'Matching set,' he murmured. 'How come?'

'Dunno. Just happened. Can you stay? Please?'

'Of course, love. Have you rung anyone? Fire brigade? Our lot?'

'Just you.'

'Andy Corbett?'

'Just you,' she repeated.

Winter wondered whether to press it, whether to try and get to the bottom of whatever was really troubling her, but knew from the expression on her face that this wasn't the time to ask.

He found the Bacardi on a shelf in the kitchen. There was Coke in the fridge. He half filled two tumblers, tucked the Coke bottle under his arm, and returned to the living room. The smell, sour and acrid, brought him to a halt.

'Upstairs, then?'

Without waiting for an answer, he began to climb the stairs. Near the top, where the stairs turned right before the landing, he paused. Dawn was staring up at him.

'Don't go up there,' she said.

'Why not? You think I'm going to sleep in the kitchen?'

'No. It's just—' She bit her lip, then shrugged. 'OK,' she said. 'Door at the end.'

Still juggling the tumblers and the Coke, Winter made his way along the landing and pushed at the door with his foot. Inside was a tiny bedroom largely occupied by a double mattress on the floor. Dawn must have used it as a dumping spot for stuff she couldn't find a home for. Amongst the assorted debris on the mattress was an open suitcase. Beside it, a pile of new-looking clothes, mainly beachwear.

Winter was trying to find somewhere for the glasses and the Coke.

'I'm sorry it's such a mess.'

Dawn was standing behind him in the open doorway, gazing in. She took one of the Bacardis and there was a moment of near candour as their eyes met. Winter raised his glass.

'Big bathroom, is it? Only anywhere's better than here.'

'Paul, don't—'

'Don't what?'

'Be difficult.'

'Is he still here, then?' He nodded beyond her. 'Gone back to bed?'

'No. He went this morning.'

'Hasn't been back since?'

'No.'

'Quite sure about that? Doesn't fancy his chances with half a pint of four-star?'

'He's a policeman, Paul. One of us.'

'Sure, but that doesn't make him sane, does it?' He swallowed half the Bacardi without bothering with the Coke, then peered down at the suitcase through swimming eyes. Tucked neatly into the folds of an aubergine sarong was a bottle of factor 10 sunblock. 'Anywhere nice?' he inquired.

'Seychelles.'

'Kept that quiet, didn't you?'

'It was meant to be a surprise.'

'Lucky old us.'

'Me, actually. Not that I'll be going.'

She was quieter now, Winter thought, definitely getting a grip.

'We've got a choice here,' he said affably. 'Either we find somewhere a bit cosier or we start sorting the serious business.'

'What are you saying, Paul?'

'I'm suggesting we have a little drink in your bedroom, one because it's probably the only decent room in the house, and two because I'm bloody uncomfortable standing here. The alternative is a phone call.'

'To?'

'Jerry Proctor. Someone's tried to firebomb your house. You need Scenes of Crime. You're a serving CID officer. It's not just you, love. It's all of us. And in case you think it's me saying this, it's not. It's Willard. I can hear him now. He'll go ballistic.'

'Can't it wait until tomorrow?'

'Sure. And that would give us time to have that little drink.'

'You'll sleep in here?'

'Of course I will.'

'But we still need to talk? Is that what you mean?'

Winter nodded but said nothing. Dawn eyed the open suitcase a moment then did her best to summon a smile.

'Shit,' she said. 'Why not?'

Fourteen

Faraday was dressed and out of the house early next morning. He'd woken at six, slipping into his study and stealing a precious ten minutes or so to sit behind his Coastguard binos and follow a single turnstone, rust-coloured in his summer plumage as he scampered busily across the mudflats, poking at little mounds of bladder-wrack. Just the sight of this little bird hunting for food brought a smile to Faraday's face. For the first time since *Merriott* got down to business, he felt that the investigative log jam was beginning to shift. Not, after all, a vengeful ex-con with a debt of blood to settle. Nor a drunken lover confusing sex with homicide. But three strangers, nameless shadows ghosting into the HOLMES files, a new lead that seemed – to Faraday at least – to promise a great deal.

The Major Crimes suite was already busy by the time Faraday arrived. Saturdays, the offices were usually deserted, but it was Nick Hayder who happened across Faraday in the tiny kitchen and told him the news.

It seemed that Winter had woken Willard at six and told him of an incident at Dawn Ellis's place, over in Portchester. What Winter was doing there was by no means clear but someone had chucked a petrol bomb through Ellis's window in the middle of the night and now Willard was demanding even more bodies to find out why. One of the SOCO blokes from Fareham had started work on the scene only minutes ago but already he'd retrieved a good lift from the broken bottle and was waiting on a van to despatch the lot to Netley for a possible hit on the NAAFIS database. On Willard's insistence, they'd called someone in specially to process the print, and with luck they'd be looking at a result before the nine-thirty squad meet on the Somerstown job.

'You're thinking there's a connection?' Faraday couldn't find any sugar for his coffee.

'Has to be. Ellis and Winter were the ones who gave Geech a hard time at his mum's flat. They're also the ones who went back after Rooke got battered and found the stuff that puts Geech at the scene. We haven't seen Geech since, of course, but these kids watch too many movies. This one's called revenge.'

'How would they know where Dawn lived?'

'No idea. There'd be a way.'

'There's a time on this incident?'

'Two in the morning. Give or take.'

'CCTV? Number plate recognition?'

'We'll be checking as soon as we're cranked up.' He spotted a cupful of sugar and slid it across to Faraday. 'Do Audis show up well in the dark?'

Back in his office, with Willard drawing up the wagons around his precious Major Crime team, Faraday had time to track down Scottie. A call to his mobile found the naval regulator stuck in a monster traffic jam on the M275.

'Builder's Transit lost a wheel,' he said cheerfully. 'The body count's in double figures.'

'You're serious?'

'No.'

Faraday explained they needed to get together. There was a new lead they ought to discuss, three blokes in town on the night of the murder, all of them allegedly ex-navy, none of them big fans of Sean Coughlin. It was early days but Faraday could use some advice.

'I'm not surprised.' Scottie was laughing. 'I told you we ought to have that pint.'

Just now, he was en route to sort out his mother-in-law's leaking overflow. After lunch, he'd pop over.

'No sooner?'

'Sorry. More than my life's worth.'

Faraday looked up to find Willard at the door. He got a promise of two o'clock from Scottie and then hung up. Willard was looking for scalps. In certain moods he could be truly intimidating, and this was one of them.

'Where's Corbett?'

Faraday's heart sank. He hadn't thought about Andy Corbett for at least twenty-four hours. Now this.

'I've no idea, sir. You transferred him to the Somerstown job the day before yesterday.'

'I know I did. And the job's called *Hexham*, by the way. Corbett's been back up to Streatham. Did you know that?'

'No, sir.'

'I've got an e-mail from FIB. They've talked to SO11 and the intelligence checks out.'

'Meaning what?' Faraday was beginning to get irritated. 'Sir?'

'Meaning Davidson may be at it again with his old mates. Securicor job. Just like Corbett told us.'

'And the inference is?'

'We ought to be working a fuck's sake harder on Davidson. Pull him in. Have another chat. The last thing we need is some little scrote like him giving us the runaround.'

'And Corbett?'

'According to the bloke at SO11, he was due a meet with one of the Streatham intelligence DCs last night. I've left a message on his mobile. He's still on the *Hexham* squad. And if he doesn't show at the squad briefing, I'm going to kick his arse so hard he won't be sitting down for months.' He paused. 'I've nicked half a dozen more of your blokes, by the way. Just so you know.'

He offered Faraday a thin smile and then he was gone.

Bev Yates began to wonder whether Pritchard was ever going to make it downstairs. He'd phoned ahead to the Alhambra, and had a brief conversation with Pritchard's sister. Jackie confirmed that Pritchard was awake and promised to have him on his feet by the time Yates turned up. Nearly an hour later, though, Yates was still waiting in the poky little room at the back that served as a restaurant. He'd turned down Jackie's offer of a full breakfast on the house but was now beginning to regret it.

At length, Pritchard appeared at the door with a mug of tea. He was wearing a shirt with stains down the front and a pair of black trousers that were too big round the waist. He tottered across to the table and collapsed in the other chair. Half the night seeing off the remains of the Johnnie Walker had made him look gaunter than ever.

'I'm not sure I can do this.' He put the tea down and his hands shook as he tried to light a cigarette.

'Kevin, mate, you have to. Without a statement we're fucked. In fact without a statement, we needn't have gone to bloody Gibraltar at all.'

'I meant the body. Sean.'

'Ah . . .'

Coughlin's corpse had been returned from the post-mortem in Southampton and was now in a fridge in the local mortuary. The senior technician at the mortuary was a soccer fanatic called Jake. He turned out every Saturday afternoon for a decent Pompey League side but Yates had assured him that they could have Coughlin sorted by midday at the latest. Now, Yates glanced at his watch. 10.14. Say an hour for the statement, and they'd still be through by twelve.

'First things first, Kev.' Yates stationed an ashtray under the cigarette. 'Let's start with Monday evening. You do the talking and I'll write it all down.'

Yates bent to his briefcase and produced a statement form. Pritchard lurched to the door and pleaded for more tea. Back at the table, he put his head in his hands.

'Monday night?' he began.

The statement turned into one long ramble. If anything, he seemed to have forgotten most of the facts he'd been so certain about less than a day ago. Monday night had lost all shape, all meaning, just a string of random impressions. A couple of guest meals early on. Some crisis with the wrong tin of soup. The empty bar and the prospect of a quiet night with the football highlights. The three guys crashing in from nowhere – fucking *nowhere*, you understand that? – and turning on poor Sean. The way they'd looked at him. The stuff they must have been saying. The fat one standing there in the window, giving Sean the finger as he shot off into the night. What did these guys have on Sean? What had he ever done to *them*? If only he'd answered the phone when he'd rung. If only he'd had a chance to say goodbye. If only. If only.

'Fat one?' Yates had his pen poised.

'Big bastard.' Pritchard nodded. 'See the weight on him.'

'Face? Hair?'

'Skinhead. Baldilocks.'

Yates put the pen down.

'Clothes?'

'Jacket. Tie. Blue tie. Blue tie with a crest on it.' This was turning into a quiz show, Yates thought. Or a séance. Did Pritchard expect voices? Sean Coughlin swaying in with a fresh pot of tea and a kiss? He picked up the pen again and started writing while Pritchard had a fresh think about Monday night, the fog slowly lifting.

Half an hour later, to Yates's relief, most of it was there, right facts, right order. Far more often than he should, he'd had to prompt and suggest, playing the driver at the wheel of Pritchard's clapped-out memory, using his own recall of the Gibraltar interview to provide a map, but in the end – everything considered – it made a good solid five pages, the last one initialled in Pritchard's wavering hand.

'Now then.' Yates got to his feet and consulted his watch. 'We up for it, Kevin?'

It was the first name again. The eyes began to swim with tears.

'How important is this?'

'Very, mate. What you're going to do is grace Sean Coughlin's death with a little dignity. That make any sense?'

Yates had once heard Faraday use exactly this phrase. He watched Pritchard clambering slowly back over the sentence, sorting out the words, cocking his huge head, trying to understand exactly what difference a visit to the mortuary might make. Grace? Dignity?

At length, he took a deep breath and nodded.

'Let's do it,' he said.

The mortuary was at the back of St Mary's hospital, a big Victorian institution with an outer keep of modern, post-war blocks. Recognising Jake's boy-racer Escort, Yates pulled in behind it. Jake was waiting for them in the sunshine. He kept a special suit for occasions like these, a dark two-piece from Austin Reed with narrow lapels and a sombre cut. On other occasions, Yates had seen him mistaken for an undertaker.

'This way, gentlemen.'

He led them into a waiting room. It was immediately colder, a perceptible chill, and it was obvious that Jake had been busy with the air freshener. Not that Pritchard appeared to notice. His face was quite blank, a mask. Clasped together in front of his body, the knuckles of his hands were white with tension.

Jake had a quiet word. Sean Coughlin was next door in the chapel. There were chairs by the body and absolutely no pressure on time. Pritchard could go in there alone, or with Yates, or with both of them. It was his decision, his call. All the occasion demanded in terms of formalities was a confirmation that this was, indeed, Sean Arthur Coughlin.

Pritchard was having trouble with his eyes. He rubbed them a couple of times with the back of his hand, then sniffed. Jake appeared at his elbow with a box of tissues. They were pink.

Pritchard shook his head. He wanted Yates to go in there with him. He needed support, a hand, anything.

'Help me,' he said quietly. 'Please.'

Yates took his arm and steered him gently towards the door. The chapel was even darker, pricked with light from two candles. Coughlin lay on a trolley. The trolley was draped with a sheet, and the long hump of his body was softened with a funeral pall. Coughlin's head lay on a pillow. There were still signs of bruising around his cheek and jaw, shades of yellow and purple, but the swelling had gone down and he looked – to Yates – remarkably peaceful. He had a big face, like Pritchard, and there was barely any trace of grey in the thick, black hair.

'He never wore it like that. Never.' The hair was combed low on the forehead. Pritchard seemed outraged. 'Who did that?'

Yates muttered something about post-mortem procedures but Pritchard wasn't listening. He knelt by the body, his face inches from Coughlin's. He wanted to kiss his lover. He wanted to say goodbye. Yates stepped backwards and turned away, giving him a little privacy, then came a tiny gasp, almost animal, a strangled noise deep in Pritchard's throat. Yates looked round. Pritchard had tried to backcomb Coughlin's hair with his fingers, but pushing away the funeral pall had revealed a crude line of stitches across Coughlin's scalp. They were big stitches and they puckered the flesh, a terrible reminder that this lover of his wasn't, after all, asleep.

Yates stepped quickly forward, taking Pritchard's arm again. He could feel his whole body trembling.

'Sorry, Kev . . .' he murmured. 'But is this Coughlin?'

Pritchard was staring down at Coughlin's face. He wanted to say no. He wanted to rub those hideous stitches out. He wanted to put the time machine into reverse, go back to Monday night, leave the three guys in the lounge bar, and be there for the moment when this man of his needed him most.

Instead, he turned away, sobbing.

'You see why I loved him?' he said.

Winter did his best to hurry the SOC boys along. Once they'd finished with Dawn Ellis's lounge, they moved out into the front garden. Neighbours, intrigued by the sight of two men in baggy white suits crawling all over Dawn's front lawn, lurked behind curtains and made a series of unnecessary trips to the pillar box at the end of the road, curious to know what lay behind this dramatic little flurry of activity. Dawn, who'd always kept her job to herself, gave them a tired smile. The SOC van at the kerbside was unmarked. Challenged for an explanation, she'd decided to blame an infestation of killer bugs.

Winter loved this thought. After a sleepless night in the tiny spare bedroom, he'd been up since six. He'd got Willard's weekend off to a flying start with a brisk phone call, checked the fridge for milk for the SOC team, and then decided to treat Dawn Ellis to a proper breakfast. Cooking one-handed was a new challenge, but he'd made a fair job of eggs on toast, loading the tray with a huge mug of tea and spilling barely a drop as he juggled his way up the narrow stairs. After last night, the least the girl deserved was a little TLC.

Dawn was still asleep when he knocked at the bedroom door and though her face told him the last thing she wanted was food, she was touched by the gesture and told him so. Perched on the edge of her bed, Winter had cheerfully demolished the eggs, enquiring whether she had any preference when it came to glaziers. There were umpteen firms in the city who'd charge the earth for an insurance job but he knew a bloke in Fratton who'd do it cash for thirty pounds and he'd be happy to give him a ring. Dawn, bewildered by Winter's matter-of-factness, told him she was past caring. The SOC van had arrived shortly afterwards, both blokes gagging for tea.

Now, Winter wanted to know when they'd be through. The glazier went to his allotment Saturday afternoons and was getting tired of waiting for the phone call. Hang on much longer, and Winter would be back with the cowboys from the city.

The older of the two SOCOs told Winter thirty minutes. Apart from the print they'd lifted from the remains of the bottle they'd drawn a blank, but Proctor had made it absolutely plain that Willard would be going over every line of their report and Proctor didn't make that kind of stuff up. Winter, back inside the house, heard the cheep of a mobile. Moments later, one of the white suits came tramping down the hall. He'd had a bit of news. The NAAFIS guys at Netley had scored a hit on the print.

Winter, still trying to remember where he'd put the glazier's number, shot an enquiring look at the SOCO.

'Bloke called Darren Geech?' The SOCO was looking at the teapot again. 'That mean anything to you?'

After Bev Yates had left the office, Faraday remembered the photo album. It had formed part of the forensic seizure from the Alhambra Hotel, the morning Jerry Proctor's boys had gone through Pritchard's flat, and Faraday had hung on to it in case he needed to evidence the relationship between Pritchard and Coughlin. Now, deep in thought, he went down the corridor to the exhibits cupboard and retrieved it for a second look.

A lot of the photos went back years – a younger,

happier Pritchard mugging for the camera with a series of men – and some of them featured excursions on a new-looking mountain bike. To Faraday, these snaps came as a surprise. He'd never associated Pritchard with physical exercise but he'd certainly invested a bob or two in the right gear – cycle helmet, Lycra shorts – and the wooded slopes that filled the background of shot after shot suggested some serious terrain.

It was this same landscape that reappeared in many of the more recent shots. By now, Pritchard had met Coughlin. The bike had disappeared and the pair of them were clad in walking gear – Berghaus anoraks, proper boots. Most of the photos featured either one or the other, a clear indication that they'd been alone on these outings, and Faraday lingered on a particular shot of Pritchard. He was lying on his side, a blanket spread beneath him. The remains of a picnic lay scattered beside an open Ordnance Survey map. It was obviously hot, because Pritchard had his shirt off. Peering up at the camera, he'd propped his sunglasses on the very end of his nose, camping it up for Coughlin's benefit, but there was something about the expression on his face, something in the eyes maybe, that spoke of a total dependence. Love would be too gentle a word. Enslavement was much closer.

Returning from the mortuary, Yates had reported on Pritchard's state of mind. Taking him to ID Coughlin had been a really bad idea. Coming away in the car, the bloke had been inconsolable. Only Jackie, back in the hotel, had been able to do anything about the tears.

Now, turning the photo upside down to get a better look at the Ordnance Survey map, Faraday felt the slightest twinge of guilt. Given his own conviction that Pritchard was telling the truth – both about Monday night, and about his feelings for Coughlin – Faraday began to wonder about the damage he might have done. Death, in his own experience, was incomprehensible.

Experts who spoke of the psychiatric benefits of viewing the deceased, of accommodation and closure, had obviously never visited a mortuary. Had he been over-hasty with Pritchard? Should he have ignored the coroner's officer's pleas to get the paperwork sorted? In truth, he didn't know.

He gazed down at the map in the photo, then suddenly realised where these two men had been. Queen Elizabeth Country Park, he thought. Just up the A3.

'Mr Faraday?'

Faraday looked up to find Scottie standing at the open door. He was carrying a B&Q plastic bag. Work on his mother-in-law's dodgy overflow had obviously drawn blood because he had a fresh plaster wrapped round his forefinger.

'Here.' He took a buff file from the bag and gave it to Faraday. 'Before we do anything else, you ought to read this.'

It was Winter's idea to take Dawn Ellis to the supermarket. At his insistence, she drove him to the big Sainsbury's down the road from his bungalow at Bedhampton. Saturday afternoon, the place was packed. Dawn pushed the trolley while Winter criss-crossed the aisles, plucking items from the shelves. Dawn, who had been a veggie for longer than anyone could remember, watched the pile of pre-packed meat grow and grow. Pork chops. Bacon. Sausages.

'Is any of this for me?' she said. 'Only you really needn't bother.'

Winter didn't reply. By the time they were heading for the check-out, the big trolley was full. Winter added a litre bottle of Scotch, another of Bacardi, paid with his Switch card and lent Dawn his good hand for the push across the car park to her little Peugeot. Only when she'd packed everything away in the boot did he volunteer any kind of explanation.

'We're laying in supplies,' he said. 'Think siege.'

'We?'

'You're coming to stay with me for a bit. We'll nip back to your place and pay off the glazier. The place should be secure once you've locked up. You'll need some clothes, of course, but we'll be OK for food.'

'Do I get a choice in any of this?'

'Not after last night you don't.'

'But there's no way Geech is coming back. Even he's not that stupid.'

'It's not Geech you should be worrying about, love.' He looked her in the eye. 'Is it?'

It took a while for Faraday to get to grips with the file. HMS *Accolade* had been a Type 21 frigate. An attached photograph showed a sleek grey warship with a flared bow. A single gun turret lay forward of the bridge and there was a small flight deck with room for a helicopter aft.

In 1982, according to the section of the file flagged by Scottie, *Accolade* had been on exercises in the Mediterranean when Galtieri invaded the Falklands. With Argentinian forces pouring into Port Stanley, she'd been ordered to join the Task Force, pausing at Gibraltar to refuel and replenish, and again at Ascension to pick up extra stores plus six Stingray anti-submarine missiles. On 12 May, she'd entered the Total Exclusion Zone. Nine days later, she'd been on picket duty in San Carlos Water when she was attacked by Argentinian Skyhawks. Three bombs registered direct hits. Within twenty minutes, irrecoverably damaged, she'd sunk with the loss of nineteen lives.

'Coughlin's ship,' Scottie reminded Faraday. 'Big-time trauma.'

Faraday nodded, still uncertain why he was reading the file. They knew already that *Accolade* had gone down in the Falklands. They knew, too, that the loss of a ship was a uniquely terrible experience, akin to nothing else. Your home, your reputation, your pride, your belongings, your very identity, all gone. But what did any of that have to do with an overweight prison officer, killed at home twenty years later?

'Go back a couple of pages. The yellow sticky.' Scottie nodded at the file. 'Fifteenth of May?'

Faraday did his best to concentrate. Any time now he was due a conference with Willard. Briefly surfacing from the swamp of *Hexham*, the Det Supt wanted an interim review on *Merriott*. Live lines of enquiry were the key to any investigation and Faraday knew there were questions he'd have to answer about Davidson. Aside from anything else, Willard was still keeper of the Policy Book.

'Halfway down. Look.' Scottie was on his feet beside Faraday, his bandaged finger indicating two paragraphs towards the foot of the page. The rating's name was Matthew Warren. He'd been a steward. Between 23.30 on the fourteenth and 06.00 on the fifteenth, he'd unaccountably gone missing. A search had been ordered of the entire ship. His absence confirmed, the Captain had ordered *Accolade* turned around. For five hours, the frigate had backtracked, making allowances for wind and current. At noon, with no sign of a body or even a lifejacket, Warren had been declared lost at sea.

Faraday looked up.

'And?'

'Warren was a youngster, a kid, just eighteen. He served as a steward in the wardroom. Coughlin was a killick chef, cock of the walk. They'd have worked together, messed together.'

'But what's your point?'

Scottie wouldn't sit down. He went to the window, looked out, glanced back, looked out again, and watching him Faraday realised he'd probably been rehearsing this moment for days. For a naval regulator with one eye on a subsequent career in the CID, this was the answer to Scottie's dreams.

'You think any of that's a coincidence?' he said at last. 'Coughlin? A bloke with his reputation? Young kid? Baby of the mess? Still in nappies?'

'I'm not with you. Blokes go missing at sea all the time, don't they?'

'No way. Guy goes over the side, it's a major drama. Ship's Investigation. Board of Inquiry. The lot. The only reason this one never made the headlines was the war. Six days later nineteen blokes were dead, Christ knows how many were injured, and they'd lost the ship as well. No wonder no one spared a thought for Matthew Warren.'

'But Coughlin . . . ?' Faraday left the rest of the question unvoiced.

'Coughlin was a bad bastard, you know that. Listen.' Scottie sat down again, leaning forward, his elbows on his knees. 'I had a little ring round last night, trying to find blokes who were in *Accolade*. I've left messages and someone's bound to get back to me but one of the blokes I did talk to had been on Coughlin's last ship. He was the Joss.'

'Joss?'

'Master-at-Arms. Sheriff. Seagoing police chief. And he told me that Coughlin was at it all the time. Give him half a chance, he'd screw anyone.'

'Literally?'

'Yeah. Bloke was a real shagnasty. It's funny on a ship, especially on something like a 21. They're small, two hundred blokes, maybe less, and in a ship that size there's no way you'll ever keep a secret. There are buzzes everywhere, all the time, it's what keeps the blokes going, and the buzz on Coughlin was always the same.' He nodded. 'Shagnasty. A hundred per cent. Fuck anything on legs. Women, blokes, donkeys, never mattered. Take a run ashore with him and apparently you got to see it first hand, just couldn't wait to stick it in.' He paused a moment. 'You take a look at his personal file? The one I gave you?'

'Of course.'

'Well, that's the authorised version. When blokes are transferred from ship to ship, a discharge note goes with them. Their Divisional Officer gets to see it – and so does the Joss. There's a little code we have, pencil, strictly eyes only. When you see WTF on the top right-hand corner of the discharge note, you know you've got a problem.'

This time Faraday simply raised an eyebrow.

'WTF?'

'Watch This Fucker.' Scottie was grinning.

'And Coughlin?'

'WTF in spades. Bloke like that can make life aboard a misery. Believe me, I've been there. We used to have a Coughlin aboard a Type 42 I was on, big bastard, really nasty, drank like a fish. He used to go off his head at the slightest provocation, totally violent. Blokes were terrified of him. The strokes he used to pull he should have been straight in the rattle, but you do your job, try and troop him, and you've suddenly got a very big problem with evidence. He's decked someone, maybe even seriously hurt them, but you know what? The moment you want to sort the man out, the bloke he's assaulted doesn't want to know. He wasn't decked after all. He fell off a ladder or walked into a stanchion, or some other fucking nonsense, just to avoid standing witness when it comes to trial at the Captain's table. At the hearing. Don't get me wrong. Blokes like Coughlin are rare now. The navy's done a bloody good job. But back in 'eighty-two it certainly happened. Which is why we should be looking hard at Warren.'

Faraday was thinking about ship's procedures. This was a new world and it took time to get your bearings. Surely there'd have been *some* form of inquiry after the boy went missing?

'Ship's Investigation Board.' Scottie nodded. 'The

Captain organises two officers and maybe a senior rate. The Joss gathers the evidence, puts the facts together, and the Ship's Investigation Board do the rest. They interview various people and try and work out what happened. Then they put their conclusions into a formal letter for the Captain.'

'And in Warren's case?'

'Definitely happened, *had* to happen, even with a war on.'

'So what did the report say?'

'Ah!' Scottie at last sat back. 'Now there's the mystery. I went looking for it yesterday. It should have been at *Centurion*, along with that.' He indicated the ship's file. 'But you know what?'

'What?'

'It seems to have gone missing.'

Half an hour later, Willard couldn't see the point.

'You're telling me we should be looking at a twenty-year-old suspicious death?'

'That's the general drift.'

'Because some sailor falls off the back of a ship?'

'Yes, sir.'

'And that's somehow down to Coughlin? Is that the allegation?'

Faraday said nothing. Willard rarely made a move without the comfort of solid evidence. All Faraday could offer was an excited naval Reggie with his eyes on a second career.

Willard was brooding.

'How old was this kid?'

'Eighteen.'

'And he was off down to the Falklands?' Faraday nodded. 'So who says he wasn't cacking himself? Who says he didn't get pissed one night and think too hard about the Argies? Who says he wasn't homesick? Missing his mum and dad? Missing the girl he'd been shagging?'

'No one, sir, but that's the point. There's an inquiry procedure the navy go through, and a report at the end of it.'

'So what does it say?'

'It doesn't.'

'Why not?'

'Because no one can find it.'

It took a moment for the implications of this to register. Then Willard visibly brightened. Nothing on the job gave him more pleasure than the prospect of a turf battle. In this respect, as in many others, Willard was programmed for a fight.

'You're telling me we can't see it?'

'I'm telling you it's gone missing.'

Faraday explained about Scottie's search at HMS *Centurion*. Most naval records were held there. Except, it seemed, this one.

'Put in a formal request, then,' Willard grunted. 'And if they give you grief let me know. We're supposed to be on the same bloody side, aren't we?'

Without waiting for an answer, Willard changed the subject. Nick Hayder had mentioned the possibility of Faraday's son lending *Hexham* a hand. The way things were going just now, he'd take help from any bloody where.

'That's nicely put, sir, if I may say so.'

'I didn't mean it that way, Joe. Don't be so bloody touchy. Get the boy in, you'll be doing us a favour. You think he might know this Geech?'

'He may do. I've no idea.'

'You hear about that Audi Geech stole?' Faraday shook his head. 'Recovered on a trading estate in Hilsea first thing this morning. Burned out. We've been through the CCTV tapes for late last night and the timings are a dream. Portchester, A27, at one fifty-seven. Bottle through Ellis's front window soon afterwards. Back down on the main road at two ten. Into the city eight minutes later. Then someone puts a match to it up at Hilsea. Beats me why Geech bothered. His prints are all over the bottle. Had to be him.'

'Bored, I expect. Arson's fun but kids like that always want to go one better. Ironic really, his teachers would probably call it ambition.'

'Yeah. If the little fuckers ever went to school. Where are we with Davidson?'

Faraday had seen the question coming for the last ten minutes and ignored it. Just now, thanks to Darren Geech, he had an acute manpower problem. With his squad down to four DCs, he needed every pair of hands he could muster to develop the Pritchard interview.

'You're happy with that statement of Pritchard's?'

'Perfectly. Remember I was there in Gib when we first talked to him. He wasn't trying it on.'

'You don't think so?'

'No, sir. In his own way, he loved the man. That's why Coughlin's death has hit him so hard.'

'I'm not questioning his passion, Joe. I'm just asking you whether he might have killed Coughlin. With these guys, the one goes with the other. Straights, too, for that matter. You love someone enough, you're capable of anything.'

'I know. I just don't think it works. Not here. Not with Pritchard.'

'You're sure, Joe? He goes round to Coughlin's late? Leaves a footprint in the flower bed? Maybe has his own key? Lets himself in? Gives Coughlin a whack or two? All that stuff on the internet? I know juries that would put him away for a lot less than that.'

'Of course. But we have to make decisions, too. And I just don't think he did it.'

Willard broke off to take a call on his mobile and in the silence that followed Faraday told himself that sessions like these were one of Willard's ways of testing the evidence. If a particular line of enquiry couldn't survive a ten-minute conversation, what chance would it ever have in court?

Willard finally pocketed his mobile. He'd obviously read Pritchard's statement in some detail.

'So what are we left with? Three guys he can't name? Two he can't even describe? And a third who turns out to be a big bastard with a grudge? Shit, Joe, that could be anyone in this city.'

'He's a drunk. He's got a memory problem. We have to take what we're given.'

'Sure, but my point is we've been given fuck all.'

'That's not true. I've got a couple of DCs talking to Aqua. Pritchard called a cab for the guys in the bar Monday night. What they did next is critical.'

'OK.' Willard scribbled himself a note. 'What else?'

'CCTV. Pritchard thinks they walked from wherever they came from. There are cameras both ends of Granada Road.'

'And Pritchard thinks he can recognise them?'

'So he says.'

'Hmmm.' Willard was gazing at his notepad. 'So what about Davidson?' he asked again, pointedly.

'We'll talk to his girlfriend. Bev thinks she's the way in – and she's local, too.'

'When do you plan the interview?'

'Soon, sir. Today maybe.' He paused. 'What happened to Corbett, as a matter of interest?'

'He's back, behaved himself all morning, sweet as pie. Says he can't wait to work with you again.'

'Sense of humour, then?'

'I doubt it, Joe.' Willard got up and stretched. 'I made that last bit up.'

Fifteen

Marie Elliott lived in a tiny terraced house in Eastney, a close, tight-knit extension of Southsea, five minutes' walk from the beach. Someone had recently had a go at the front of the house with a tin or two of Weathertex, cream with a hint of yellow, and there were fresh flowers in a vase in the front window. While Bev Yates rapped at the door, Faraday gazed absently at a black and white cat which had appeared beside the flowers.

Bev had drawn a blank on the taxi driver who'd picked up the fares from the Alhambra on Monday night. They'd managed to trace the guy through the taxi firm, only to find that he'd just left for a long weekend in Amsterdam. Half a week on from his aborted day off, Faraday couldn't remember feeling so tired.

Elliott recognised Yates at once. The long fall of raven-black hair was gathered in a twist of scarlet ribbon and she was knotting a green sarong. Judging by the blush of sunburn on her bare shoulders, she must have been in the garden for a while.

Yates had offered his warrant card, then introduced Faraday. Elliott barely gave him a second glance.

'What do you want?' Straight to the point.

Yates mentioned the Coughlin investigation. They had a couple of things they'd like to clear up. It wouldn't take long.

'It's Saturday. You know that?'

Faraday was trying to smother a yawn. Too right, he thought.

She let them in without another word. The front door

led directly into a little sitting room, rugs on carefully stained floorboards, interesting prints on the wall, the smell of freesias hanging in the air. The cat watched Elliott as she padded barefoot through to the back. Yates was inspecting a newish-looking mountain bike, propped against the dresser.

'Ainsley's.'

Elliott was back from the kitchen. Leaning against the door jamb, she was nursing a glass of something long and cool. Faraday could hear the clink of ice cubes as she moved.

'You want to talk in the garden? Or here?'

'Wherever.' She shrugged. 'I don't want to talk at all but I don't suppose I've got a choice.'

They settled for the sitting room. Yates and Faraday perched awkwardly on the two-seat sofa, Elliott sitting on a beanbag on the floor. Yates had produced the notes from their last encounter and, watching the woman's face as he began to go through her statement, Faraday sensed a certain softening in her attitude. She had nothing against Yates personally. Only the implications of this abrupt intrusion into her otherwise peaceful weekend.

After she'd confirmed everything she'd said before, Yates started on her movements since.

'Where have you been?' he asked.

'Work. As you might expect.'

'In the prison?'

'Of course.'

'And Ainsley?'

'He's been in London.'

'Still with his mum?'

'As far as I know, yes.'

For the first time, Faraday spotted an opening. Yates saw it, too.

'You're not sure?' he said.

'It's not that. It's not that I'm not sure. It's just that he does his own thing. This is a man who's just spent the last seven years inside. I imagine he might treat himself to the odd night away from his mum, yes.'

'But not with you?'

'Of course not, he does what he does. I'm not his keeper.'

'But you are his' ... Yates hunted for the word ... 'girlfriend?'

'I like to think so, yes.'

There was a long silence. She never took her eyes off Yates's face. There was still resentment there, but something else as well. She wasn't as sure about Ainsley as she might like.

'Blokes, then?' Yates suggested. 'He's off with mates.'

'More than possible.'

'Have you met these people?'

'One or two of them.'

'What are they like?'

'*Like?*' She tipped her head back, rolling her eyes. 'They're black. They're young. They all hang around together. And they're probably up to all kinds of' – she shrugged – 'stuff. I don't know. Like I say, I'm not Ainsley's keeper. Or his social secretary.'

'You don't approve? Is that what you're saying?'

'Whether I approve or not is immaterial. I . . .' She frowned. 'Disappointment? Does that make any sense?'

'Disappointment how?'

'With this.' She indicated the space between them. 'With all of it. Ainsley's paid his dues. Seven years wipes the slate clean, at least for me it does. Spend time in that place, like I do, and you get to know what those blokes go through.'

'But you're telling me that Ainsley's back into it. You're telling me that—'

'Back into what?' She was getting angry now, a flush that had nothing to do with sunburn. 'I'm telling you that Ainsley has been banged up for seven years. That's most of his adult lifetime, probably for something he never did.

He's out now. He's trying to make his way. And yet everyone does their best to put him right back on square one. You guys included.'

'Meaning?'

'Meaning that friend of yours. The other bloke. The one that came up to London.'

'Corbett?'

'I can't remember. Tall. Loved himself.'

'What about him?'

She was staring at Yates now, frank disbelief.

'You're telling me you don't know?'

'Know what?'

'Following Ainsley around? Night after night? Trying to make life tough for him? That's not even intimidation. It's laziness. Ainsley wouldn't go anywhere near Coughlin. He never wanted to see the guy ever again. Yet here you are again, same old questions, same old routine, trying it on. Haven't you got anything better to do? No one else to hassle?'

Faraday stirred on the sofa. He didn't feel quite so tired any more.

'These friends of Ainsley's. It's important we know a little more,' he said quietly.

'Like what?'

'Like whether or not they're criminals.'

'Of course they're criminals. Everyone up there's at it. That's how you make a living.'

'Sure. But you know what I mean.'

'Serious criminals? Serious enough to kill someone? No.' She shook her head. 'Ainsley's mates are kids. Lots of attitude, but kids. They'd no more kill someone than get a regular job.'

Faraday ducked his head for a moment. Even kids were capable of murder, as he knew only too well.

'But you're worried?' Yates had put his notebook to one side. 'About Ainsley?'

Elliott studied him a moment, trying to gauge where

this encounter might lead. Not an interview any more, but a conversation.

'Yes,' she said at last. 'To be frank, I am.'

'Why?'

'Because it's so hard. Me? I'm middle class. I've got qualifications, a good job, all this . . .' She gestured round. 'I also love Ainsley. That's not a small thing, believe me. So I want to share it with him. I want all this to be ours.'

'And Ainsley?'

'Shows willing. Of course he does. Christ, he even did the bloody front the other day. Had a proper discussion, chose the paint, did a nice job, even cleaned the brushes. But it's not him. It's not his world. And I'd be mad not to admit it.'

Another silence. Faraday, impressed, wanted to draw certain threads together, but Elliott beat him to it. She was on her feet again and up the stairs. Faraday could hear her moving around above them. Then came the scrape of a drawer closing and footsteps down the stairs.

'Here.'

Faraday found himself looking at a sheaf of typescript. They were poems.

'Ainsley's?'

'Yes.' She was standing over Faraday. 'Most of them he wrote in prison. You're looking at three years' work. Some of them are very good. In fact some of them are excellent. We wanted to get something together, find a publisher, get some publicity. We even had a title. *Periscope Depth*.'

'And Ainsley?'

'Doesn't want to know any more.' She shook her head. 'Can't be fucking bothered.'

Faraday stole a glance at the top poem. Something about seagulls. Finally he looked up at her.

'But that doesn't make him a murderer.' He held out the poems. 'Does it?'

*

Late afternoon, Cathy Lamb appeared at Winter's bungalow. Winter and Dawn were sitting in the garden,
enjoying the sunshine. Dawn, after two hefty shots of
Bacardi, appeared to be asleep. Winter was reading the
Daily Telegraph.

'Convalescence, is it? Or have you two got it on?'

Cathy had made her own way round the side, letting
herself in through the garden gate. Winter struggled to
his feet, making a mental note to buy a new padlock.
Dawn hadn't stirred.

'Sweet of you, Cath.' Winter was eyeing the huge
bunch of flag irises. 'I'll sort a vase out.'

'They're for Dawn, Paul. Much though I love you.'

'I'll still find a vase.'

'Really?' Cathy raised an eyebrow but didn't pursue it.

Back inside, Winter dumped the flowers in the sink and
went through to the lounge for another tumbler. He was
clueless about Cathy's taste in spirits but the next half an
hour was already shaping up nicely and a slug or two of
Bacardi wouldn't do any harm.

Through the kitchen window, he could see Cathy squatting on the lawn beside Dawn. By the time he joined them,
she'd obviously been through the events of last night.

'Geech, little toerag.' Cathy shaded her eyes, peering
up at Winter. 'Has to be him, doesn't it?'

Winter nodded, splashing Bacardi over the ice he'd just
brought from the kitchen.

'You want a Coke with it?'

'Nothing at all, thanks. I'm driving. Give it to the
invalid.'

Dawn took the tumbler. She and Cathy had been close
for a couple of years now. After Cathy had thrown her
husband, Pete, out it had been Dawn who had provided
the listening ear, cementing a friendship that had survived ever since. Cathy and Pete were now back together
and they'd recently moved to a neat thirties pebbledash in

leafy Alverstoke, but Dawn and Cathy still managed the occasional girlie night out.

Dawn wanted to know how Cathy had screwed the time off to drop by. The way she was hearing it, every detective in Portsmouth had been press-ganged into the hunt for Darren Geech.

'Yeah.' Cathy nodded. 'Every detective except me. It's mad out there. You don't need that kind of grief, not on a Saturday.' She looked up at Winter again. 'So how come Geech knew where Dawn lived?'

Winter had been asking himself exactly the same question for most of the afternoon. There were a number of options but most of them were far too sophisticated for the likes of Darren Geech. Instead, he favoured the obvious.

'He'd clocked her car.'

'The red racer?'

'Yeah. Car like that, brand new, stands out a mile in Somerstown. We parked outside the flats when we turned his mum's place over. When we seized the dog and came out, he watched us getting in. I remember him doing it.'

'And he followed her later?'

'Yeah. The kids know where we operate from. Car park round the back at Highland Road, they'd just wait in one of those little next-door streets.'

'In a nicked car? That's not very bright, is it?'

'*Bright?*' Winter snorted with laughter. 'We're talking Darren Geech, Cath. The boy knows no fear. Couldn't care a fuck about anything.'

Cathy nodded, saying nothing, and Winter wondered whether now was the time to ask how the inquiry was shaping up. To his own surprise, he'd yet to receive as much as a phone call from the likes of Hartigan.

Dawn took another sip of Bacardi. There was still something bothering her.

'But why try and burn my house down? I don't understand.'

'Because we hurt him, love.'

'*Hurt* him? How?'

'By nicking his dog. And then making it tough for him when he tried to snatch it back.'

'That's an assumption. We don't know he was going to do that, not for sure.'

'You don't think so? You don't think him and his mate were after stopping at number twelve? Tapping on the door? Taking Charlie for a little ride? Maybe you're right, love. Maybe he was out for an afternoon drive.'

Dawn dismissed him with a wave. Winter in these moods wasn't worth the effort of a conversation. Cathy, too, favoured a change of subject. She told Dawn she didn't want to see her until Tuesday at the earliest. That would give her time to sort her place out, contact the insurance, get a new carpet laid. After an experience like that, the last thing she needed was the smell of charred viscose.

'You'll be all right on your own?' Cathy enquired. 'Only you can always stay over with us. It's pretty chaotic but we've got a mattress and a spare bedroom.'

Dawn and Winter swapped glances. After putting up a spirited fight, she'd finally accepted Winter's offer of a bed for the night.

'I'm fine,' she said, swilling the ice cubes round in her glass. 'Paul's being stern with me.'

Cathy laughed.

'You'd like that.'

'Really?' Dawn glanced up, no trace of a smile. 'You think so?'

Cathy stayed nearly an hour. Winter broke open a packet of crumpets from the supermarket and slipped them into the toaster. He was disappointed they'd never got round to discussing what remained of his CID career but he sensed the two women had more important things to gossip about. Through the open window in the kitchen he could hear the low burble of conversation, and once or twice he thought he caught the name Andy, but the moment he appeared with the crumpets they quickly changed the subject. Cathy and Pete were contemplating a maiden voyage in their new boat. Cathy would have been happy with a trip down to the West Country but Pete fancied something more ambitious.

'Britanny at least,' she said, licking Marmite from her fingers.

Cathy left shortly afterwards, making Winter promise he'd take care of Dawn. Winter walked her to the front gate, ever the gentleman. They paused by the car.

'She's had a very big shock, hasn't she?'

Winter nodded, reaching down with his good hand and opening the car door.

'Too right, Cath.' He smiled. 'And then someone tried to burn her house down.'

Faraday was contemplating going home when Scottie called back. Excitement had become his trademark.

'Listen,' he said. 'Are you sitting down?'

Faraday grunted something about calling it a day. He was starting to suspect this eager Reggie belonged in Hollywood, pitching wild ideas to fat-cat producers. Scottie was still at full throttle.

'You know in the navy we have these little associations? Old shipmates getting together? Well, there were loads from the Falklands, specially the ships that went down. *Coventry. Ardent. Antelope.* They all have a meet, usually once a year, little church service, couple of prayers, something to eat and drink, happens all the time, especially round May and June.'

'And?'

'The *Accolade*s have one, too. And you know when it took place?'

'Tell me.'

'Monday night.'

'Where?'

'Here, in Pompey, Naval Home Club.'

Faraday at last sat down. The Naval Home Club was a big, post-war building down the far end of Queen Street, a spit from the Victory Gate. Skates and ex-skates used it for cheap accommodation and a pint or two in the bar. Evidently it did functions, as well.

'You're sure about this?'

'Certain. One of the guys I'd called belled me back. He was in *Accolade* when she went down, and he was there on Monday night.'

'How many people are we talking about?'

'Around sixty.'

'He's got names?'

'No, but I got the secretary's number from him, the guy who organised it all. He lives in Drayton. Local.'

'You've talked to him?'

'He wasn't in. Gone to Lord's to watch the cricket. His missus expects him back late.' He paused. 'You want the good news, too? The Home Club have CCTV. Sixteen fucking cameras. I've checked. Can you believe that?'

Winter took a taxi to Gunwharf, a big, forty-acre lifestyle development on a prime harbourside site. Misty Gallagher occupied one of the coveted waterfront apartments, a £600,000 opportunity for Bazza Mackenzie to unload some of his carefully laundered drugs money.

Winter, blinking in the sunshine, found her name on the entry speakerphone.

'Mist? Paul.'

She buzzed him into the lobby and he took the lift to the third floor. To Winter's delight, the lift opened directly into the apartment. He felt like he'd stepped into a movie set.

'Awright, Mist?'

She was standing in the kitchen, doing something complicated to a glistening pile of monkfish. Winter could smell garlic and fresh chopped ginger. He examined the fish, dipped his finger into a bowl of Thai sauce, and then gave her a peck on the cheek.

'What happened to your arm?' she asked.

'Got in a fight. The other guy died.'

'Bullshit.'

Misty reached for a tumbler of white wine and took a long pull. Life had written a story or two on her face, but for a woman in her forties she still had an amazing body. Winter knew that Bev Yates had been all over her in his younger days, and knew as well that half the CID office had kidded themselves they were next in the queue.

'Bazza OK, is he?'

'Mad. Never bloody stops. You know Bazza.'

Winter was at the window now, gazing out over the harbour. Most of Bazza's money had, in the end, gone into bricks and mortar. Class properties like these. Nursing homes. Some of the seedier hotels. Restaurants. Café bars. Estate agents. Plus God knows what else abroad. Each of these businesses gave him a chance to wash money through the till. Add in all those freeholds, and a rising market made Bazza richer by the minute.

'I hear he offered for the Saracen's Head the other day.' The Saracen's Head was a big eighteenth-century hotel with harbour views. Lack of maintenance over the years had brought it to its knees, a prime target for wealthy barrow boys like Bazza.

'That's right.' Misty nodded. 'Bought and sold in half a day. Lawyers line up the paperwork, bank supplies the loan, and Bazza walks out with three hundred grand profit. Makes you wonder, doesn't it?'

'Wonder what, Mist?'

'Why anyone bothers working for a living.'

She cackled with laughter and then Winter caught the slurp of wine as she emptied the rest of the bottle. Across the harbour, he could see a big yacht easing out from the Camper and Nicholson marina. Closer, one of the early evening cross-Channel ferries was making its way uphar-bour.

'Been anywhere nice lately, Mist?'

'No. Baz is talking about the Caribbean again but I'll believe it when it happens. Be lucky if Trude and me make Bognor this year.'

Winter smiled to himself. Trudy was Misty's seventeen-year-old daughter. Mackenzie had set them both up in a Gunwharf maisonette more than a year ago, tired of shagging Misty in the back of his Mitsubishi 4Runner, and more recently – after months of nagging – Mist had managed an upgrade to this magnificent view. Arethusa House was one of the best addresses in Portsmouth, but Winter knew that Misty's days in the sun were num-bered. Bazza had lately been screwing a young Italian woman from Siena. She had an education, as well as huge knockers, and Misty was heading for early retirement.

'I'm going to open a new bottle. Chianti be OK?'

'Fine.' Winter hooked a stool towards him and sat down. 'I'm here on an errand, Mist. Little message to deliver.'

'Yeah?' She struggled with the cork a moment, then out it came.

''Fraid so.' Winter pushed a glass towards her. 'There's a kid called Darren Geech. You might know him.'

'Of him, yes. Somerstown? Wild child?'

'Off his head, Mist, a real liability. Problem is, he's been working for Bazza, or says he has.'

'You're sure? Baz is normally fussy that way. Doesn't take head-cases.'

'Doesn't matter, love. True or not, everyone believes he runs gear for Bazza. Including my boss.'

Misty abandoned the fish. Winter had her full attention now. Winter relaxed, sipping the wine. Perfect tempera-ture. He could take his time over this. He knew he could.

'Problem is, Mist, young Darren has got himself in serious shit. Number one, he gave a bloke called Rookie a whacking. Rookie died soon after so we're looking at murder.'

'That was in the paper.'

'You're right, but get this. Number two, Darren cranks it up a notch, tries his hand at arson, and chucks a bottle of four-star through someone's window up in Portchester.'

'Why? Why would he do that?'

'Complicated. The place didn't go up in the end but that's not the point. The owner is one of us. CID. And my guvnor's not best pleased.'

'So . . . ?' Misty was trying to open the curtains on this little mystery. 'What's this message you're supposed to be delivering?'

Winter struggled off the stool and went through to the big lounge. The window was enormous, the room flooded with sunshine, the Isle of Wight ferry almost close enough to touch. Winter gazed at the view a moment longer, then took in the rest of the room. He hadn't seen Misty since Christmas but the intervening months had done nothing for her taste. Teletubbies propped on the drinks cabinet. A hideous African sunset in oils on the wall. Two stuffed pandas wedged in respective corners of the long leather sofa. Living in Gunwharf, with its bijou shopping opportunities, crap like this was only a five-minute stroll away.

'Well?' Misty was leaning through the kitchen hatch.

'Nice.' Winter gestured round with his glass. 'Handsome.'

'I meant Geech.'

'Ah, yes . . .' He frowned a moment, deep in thought, then grinned at her, old mates. 'No point in dressing it up, Mist. My guvnor's laid hands on a huge squad. If he can't find young Darren, he's going to start looking at Bazza.' He raised his glass in a toast. 'Cheers, Mist. Here's to the view.'

*

The general manager of the Naval Home Club was a small, fit-looking Scot with three teenage daughters and a passion for golf. His office lay towards the back of the building, the single window barred against the kids from the neighbouring estate. Faraday had phoned him from Kingston Crescent, expressing an interest in Monday night's function. Might Derek Grisewood have time for a chat?

Grisewood had been only too happy to oblige. He had a full house tonight but was free for the time being.

'HMS *Accolade*? Am I right?'

Grisewood nodded. The Home Club regularly laid on functions like these. The navy had several similar associations and it would be the membership secretary who'd normally phone up to make the booking. Once the details were straightened out, the thing went like clockwork.

'Details?'

'Numbers. Accommodation. Whether or not wives are coming along. What kind of scran they fancy. Special requests. Any VIPs. It's all pretty routine.'

Yates was sitting beside Faraday. He jotted down the odd note from time to time but in between he couldn't take his eyes off the line of framed photographs on a shelf behind Grisewood's desk. Three lucky sons-in-law were going to have the time of their lives.

Faraday wanted to know about numbers on Monday night.

'Sixty-three. No wives.' Grisewood's finger was anchored in a file. 'About half of them stayed with us. The rest were either local or kipped over with mates.'

'And times? How does an evening like this go?'

'They muster in the main bar around seven. Seven-thirty they go through to the Nuffield Room. They get a tot of rum at the door, then more drinks in a little bar at the side. Round eight we sit them down.'

'One long table?'

'No. Round tables of ten.'

'There's a seating plan?'

'That's up to the secretary. They sort themselves out.'

'OK.' Faraday nodded for Yates to make a note. 'Then what?'

'We serve the meal.' He peered at the file. 'That night it was Crofter's Soup with a roll. Roast beef, Yorkshire pudding, all the trimmings. Then trifle . . . plus wine, of course, red or white. After they've eaten they generally have a speech or two, what's happened over the year, that kind of thing. Then a toast.' He looked up. 'Normally, it's Absent Friends.'

Faraday glanced at Yates again. Since Scottie's phone call, he'd thought of nothing else but the images that came back from that long-ago war. The bows of a sinking frigate, silhouetted against the flare of a huge explosion. The burned-out hulk that had once been HMS *Sheffield*. Welsh Guardsmen staggering ashore at Bluff Cove, their flesh hanging off in ribbons. Absent Friends, he thought. And then some.

Grisewood was waiting for the next prompt. Yates supplied it.

'They stay in the Nuffield Room afterwards?'

'No, they go back to the main bar. More drinks, more dits, lots of catching up, maybe a hug or two if they talk about the old days. You'd be surprised. These occasions can get quite emotional, especially if there aren't any women around.'

I bet, thought Faraday.

'What time did the bar close?'

'Twelve. Last orders, ten to.'

'And then what?'

'People drift away, go up to their rooms, share a bottle, get cabs, go home.'

'Or go off somewhere else, maybe? Carry on drinking?'

'Of course, if they fancy it.'

'Were you there yourself that night?'

'No, I was up in Scotland as a matter of fact. Troon. Wonderful course if the rain holds off. Back in harness Wednesday morning.'

'So who looked after the reception?'

'Young lady called Bella. My XO.'

'Is she around now?'

'I'm afraid not. Back Monday.'

'What about CCTV? I understand you're state of the art.'

Grisewood nodded, confirming the set-up. Eight internal cameras, covering everything from the lobby to the ground-floor toilets. Plus another eight external cameras, offering all-round surveillance. The cameras fed live pictures to a matrix system, monitored from a small security office next to reception.

'What about the main bar?'

'One camera.'

'The Nuffield Room? Where they had dinner?'

'Same.'

'And no one can leave without being taped?'

He shook his head and closed the file.

'We keep the recordings for seven days.' He smiled. 'And you're welcome to take a look.'

A single glance at the monitor screens in the security office was enough for Faraday. There were moments in any investigation when the door at which you were pushing began to open, and this was very definitely one of them. The CCTV system looked new. The resolution, even on replay, was excellent, faces easily recognisable.

Faraday took Yates by the arm and stepped outside.

'Get hold of Pritchard,' he said. 'Bring him down here. I'll hang on.'

Yates nodded and disappeared while Faraday returned to the bar. The general manager set him up with a pint, made a couple of calls of his own, then came back. It turned out he knew a great deal about birds, as well as golf, and they were deep in a discussion about Scottish tidal estuaries when Faraday's phone began to trill.

'Boss?' It was Yates. 'I'm at the Alhambra. Pritchard seems to have gone missing.'

'Missing?' Faraday put his drink down.

'His sister hasn't seen him since mid-afternoon. She thinks he might have gone to the Isle of Wight. Apparently he does that sometimes.'

'Why? Why would he have gone?'

'She says he was very upset. And she's right, he was.'

'Any idea where on the island?'

'Ryde, probably. He knows somebody who owns a drinking club.'

'You're checking it out?'

'As we speak. If he is over there I can get a local DC or a uniform to walk him on to the hovercraft. He'll be back here in no time.'

Faraday glanced at his watch. The possibilities of Scottish crossbills, ptarmigan and golden eagles over Speyside would keep them going for at least another half-hour.

'Keep me briefed,' he said. 'I'll stay here.'

With the light beginning to fade, Pritchard stepped out of the trees and made his way slowly down the path that led to the fence at the bottom of the hill. He'd spent the last hour or so up in the little shadowed glade where they used to picnic. He'd sprawled face down on the warm grass, the scent of leaf mould in his nostrils, looking for a place amongst his memories where he might rest for a while.

They'd spent whole afternoons here, often. They'd made love in the hot sunshine, oblivious to the curiosity of strangers. They'd crawled all over each other, trying it this way, that way, stretching the moment as long as they could. And afterwards, like now, they'd closed their eyes and drifted away, exhausted.

He felt half dead already. Every movement, every breath, every next image that swam back to him was agony. He treasured those moments, of course he did. That was what had given him purpose and the courage to go on. That was what had brightened the darkness that threatened to swamp him. But with Sean gone, with nothing left but the hideously stitched dummy in the mortuary chapel, the candle had flickered and died.

He hurt. Everywhere. And worse than that, he was frightened. What would he become? How could he spend the rest of his life, that worthless currency, without the man he loved?

He shuddered, remembering the chill waxiness of Sean's dead flesh under his fingers. That wasn't a memory he wanted to take with him. No way. You had a choice here. The women on daytime television, the armchair pundits, all those self-help magazines, they were right. Time to take charge. Time to establish ownership. Time to tell your life just who was boss.

Would it be hard? Of course not. Because, with a certainty that quickened his footsteps, he knew that Sean would be waiting. His Sean. The old Sean. The Sean from up there in the woods.

At the bottom of the hill, he clambered awkwardly over the wire fence. The railway line was down in a cutting, the grassy bank falling away to the bed of the track below. He looked down at the rails. The one on the far side was the one to avoid. That was no way to die, not if you wanted Sean to be proud of you, to be ready and waiting, with a smile on his face. No, for that you needed something a bit more outrageous.

He steadied himself at the top of the bank, then skidded down on his backside. For a moment, in a heap at the bottom, he thought he'd broken his ankle but upright again he stamped the pain from his foot and set off. The tunnel was barely two hundred metres away. With every limping step, the darkness grew bigger and bigger. He broke into an awkward half-run. I'm glad, he thought. Glad for Sean. Glad for both of us. His breath was beginning to rasp in his chest. He could feel his heart pumping and pumping. Moments later, the darkness enveloped him. But still he stumbled on.

Sixteen

It was late before news of Pritchard filtered back to Major Crimes. A London-bound train had made an emergency stop in the Buriton Tunnel. The driver, traumatised, reported hitting an object at speed. There was blood and tissue on the buffers and the lower surfaces of the front of the cab. The train was inched slowly backwards, revealing a severed leg. Searching the side of the track by torchlight, emergency crews found a clothed upper torso, pulped beyond recognition. Current was switched off and passengers were led out of the tunnel and along the track to buses waiting in a nearby village. All services on the main London–Portsmouth line were cancelled until further notice.

It was a young SOC officer who made the connection to Pritchard. Going through his clothing for ID, he came across a battered colour photograph, six by four. It showed a face he'd seen only days ago, sprawled on a carpet in a ground-floor flat in Southsea. He'd got through to his skipper, Jerry Proctor. Coughlin, he'd said. Definitely the bloke in Niton Road.

Faraday was at home when Jerry Proctor phoned with the news. It was late by now, gone eleven, and Faraday was thinking of going to bed. Since there'd been no sign of Pritchard in Ryde, he'd told Bev Yates to pack it in for the night. They'd start again tomorrow. Pritchard should be back by then.

Evidently not.

'Is there any point me giving you a physical description?'

Proctor, who hadn't seen the body, could only go on reports from the scene. Bitten nails. No rings. Black trousers. Plaid shirt with button-down pockets. Cheap runners.

Faraday, who'd sensed already that it had to be Pritchard, gave Proctor the number of the Alhambra Hotel.

'His sister's name's Jackie. She'll be able to ID the clothing.' He turned to look out at the darkness of the harbour. 'Was there a note or anything?'

Proctor said he didn't know. His blokes at the scene hadn't mentioned a note but he'd be organising a POLSA search first thing tomorrow, working outwards from the mouth of the tunnel, and it was possible they might turn something up. Suicides were often obsessively neat, leaving a little cairn of treasured belongings.

'Pritchard wasn't like that,' Faraday muttered. 'Pritchard was chaos on legs.'

He brought the conversation to an end and put the phone down. Outside, down by the harbour, the night air was still warm and Faraday turned his back on the house, walking slowly north. The tide was high, lapping softly at the crust of seaweed heaped at the foot of the sea wall, and from way out across the water came the distant cry of a curlew. It had long been Faraday's favourite call – plangent, haunting – and tonight it seemed especially apt.

Pritchard's final moments didn't bear contemplation. To walk into a tunnel, to hear the faraway rumble of a train, to feel the ground beneath your feet beginning to shake, and then to summon the courage to stand there, feet planted between the rails as the light on the cab lurched into view. There'd come a moment, thought Faraday, when your every instinct was to move, to step sideways, to throw yourself flat, to turn and run, but by that time the monster would be on top of you and it would be far, far too late. Would you feel the impact? The smack of steel against bone? Would you be aware of the wheels slicing through sinew and flesh before your body – your heart – surrendered?

Faraday paused above a tiny crescent of pebble beach. He could see shapes out on the water in the moonlight, mallard and shelduck, and he watched for a moment until they disappeared into the darkness. He could think of a million reasons why Pritchard might have given up on life – the loss of his lover, the ravages of alcoholism, the depressing treadmill of trying to run the world's worst hotel – but what really troubled him was his own part in Pritchard's death. Was he somehow complicit in this decision of Pritchard's? Had the sight of his dead partner driven him into the Buriton Tunnel? Should Faraday, in short, have found someone else to ID Sean Coughlin?

The knowledge that there'd never be an answer to these questions was deeply troubling. Faraday, in the end, was a copper. His job description imposed certain duties and he'd always done his level best to discharge them. To that degree he was simply one party to a contract. He'd signed up to enforce the law, to detect wrong-doing, and to put away the bad guys. But lurking in the spaces between the small print were numberless other responsibilities, stuff that no training sergeant ever mentioned, and one of them was a kinship – a sympathy – for your fellow man.

Evil was a big word, and the older he got the less Faraday understood it. All the evidence they'd gathered to date – hearsay from the prison, accusations from Davidson, hints from the naval files – suggested that Coughlin was a bad, bad man. But somehow or other, God knows why, he'd brought comfort to this lover of his, a little pool of warmth that had kept Pritchard just this side of total collapse. Had Coughlin manipulated him? Taken advantage? Bullied him? Stolen his body as well as his heart? The answer to all those questions was probably yes. But there remained a greater question,

overshadowing everything else. If Coughlin made Pritchard happy, did any of this other shit matter?

Eadie Sykes was still up when Faraday buzzed her on the
speakerphone. She recognised his voice at once.

'Sure,' she said. 'Come up.'

Barefoot, she was wearing an old paisley-patterned
dressing gown when Faraday walked into the flat, and
there was a pile of papers scattered around the laptop on
the sofa. She offered him wine from an opened bottle of
Chablis from the fridge, but he settled for coffee.
Exhausted to the point where sleep was no longer an
option, he needed to talk.

'Go ahead.' She tidied the papers on the sofa, making
room for him. 'You want anything to eat? I haven't got
much, I'm afraid, but you're more than welcome.'

Against his better judgement, he found himself telling
her about Pritchard, about the tunnel, about Coughlin.
He tried to put it all in perspective, to touch on the wider
context of *Merriott*, to tease some payback, some
investigatory advantage from the human remains heaped
by the side of the track. But try as he might, it made no
sense. All he was left with was a thickening residue of
guilt. He should have been more aware, more sensitive.
Amongst the million decisions demanding the deputy
SIO's attention on a major inquiry, he'd got this one
badly wrong.

'You want sympathy?'

The curtness of the question brought his head up.

'No,' he said at once.

'You want something else? Comfort?'

'No.'

'You think we ought to go to bed? See whether that
works?'

'No.'

'Then why are you here?'

It was a question Faraday had been dreading. To have

253

to ask it was confirmation enough. He'd thought she might understand and she didn't. She was as hardened by life as everyone else.

'I just . . .' He shrugged, then shook his head and made to get up. He was wasting her time. He should never have bothered her. It was far too late for all this nonsense.

'Don't.' Her hand was firm on his shoulder. 'Just tell me what's the matter.'

He looked at her a moment, feeling the evening beginning to slip out of focus. Maybe she did understand, after all. Not one misjudgement, but two.

'You really want to hear?'

'Yes, please.'

'OK.' He fingered the hem of her dressing gown where the stitching had begun to go. 'It's just that sometimes . . . it makes no sense. You look for patterns, you look for justice—'

'And there isn't any?'

'No. None. We go through the motions. We clear up the mess. We attend to the walking wounded and sometimes we bang them up. But no matter how clever we are, how ruthless, how kind, it never makes any difference.'

'You want to make a difference?'

'Yes.' He nodded. 'I suppose I do.'

'And you think you ever will?'

'No. Never.'

'Because . . . ?'

'Because there's too much of it. People don't know who they are any more.'

'That's a strange thing to say.'

'Not really, not if you look. It used to be simpler. People belonged. They belonged to families, to jobs, to a local church, to their own sense of decency, to whatever gave them solace, and direction. That's all gone. There is no solace. There is no direction. And people find that . . .' He frowned, hunting for the word.

'Bothersome?'

'Yes. That, certainly, but bewildering, too. We're on a mountain here. We climb and climb and climb. It's relentless. It never ends. And don't think I'm talking about the job. It's not just that. It's everything, all of it. The journey used to have a purpose.'

'And you think we've lost it? You think we don't know where we're headed?'

'Yes.'

Sykes looked at him a moment, then got up and took a packet of cigarettes from a drawer. It was news to Faraday that she smoked.

'You know what my dad used to say? Back in Oz?' She found a lighter for the cigarette. 'He used to say it was down to the weather. One of the reasons he went to New Caledonia was the sun. He loved it. He said it was like treacle. He said it sweetened his life. The Brits, he used to tell me, are fucked. They think too hard. They worry too much. They get wound up in themselves. And you know why? Because it rains all the bloody time.'

Faraday gazed up at her. Maybe she had a point. May excursions to the Spanish Pyrenees, you'd find the sky full of red kites and columns of Griffon vultures. With the meadows full of wild orchids, and the sun hot on his face, he was close to heaven.

'Maybe I should move,' he said. 'Would that do the trick?'

'It might. If you were really serious.'

'You think I'm not? You think I'm making this stuff up?'

'Not at all. I think you're in a muddle. But I think that matters, too.'

'I'm not with you.'

'Yes, you are. You're in a muddle because you like being in a muddle. You question yourself all the time. That's what makes you you. It probably makes you a fucking good detective, too, though I wouldn't be the

255

judge of that. The principle's simple, though. No muddle, no you.'

'Is it bad, then? Being in a muddle?'

'That's a kid's question. This is a grown-up conversation. You should be ashamed of yourself.'

She sat down beside him and kissed him on the nose. Faraday was thinking suddenly about his son.

'You know what J-J did today? He came into the office to talk to a colleague of mine. It's another job, another murder. They think J-J probably knows about a particular kid and they're probably right. But you know what happened?'

'Tell me.'

'He refused to say a word.'

'That's because he can't.'

'No, you don't understand. I was there. I was translating. Nick put the questions, I signed them for J-J. But whatever Nick said, whichever way he put it, J-J didn't want to know. Blanked him. Just shook his head. More than that, he was outraged, took it really personally.'

'Because he had no information?'

'Because he thought the whole thing was wrong. They were taking advantage. Both of me and him. That's a moral judgement. I still don't know whether he knew this kid but that's not the point. J-J had made up his mind. He *knew* what to do. He'd made a decision. That's rare and you know something else? I was proud of him. Not just proud, but envious.'

'Maybe he gets it from his dad. You ever thought of that?'

'Never.' Faraday lay back on the sofa, aware of her physical presence beside him, letting his eyes close at last.

'You want to stay?'

He thought about the question, his eyes still closed. At length, he felt for her hand.

'I've no idea.' He smiled to himself. 'Muddle's a very good word.'

Winter used Dawn's key to let himself into the house. Past midnight, the street was deserted, curtains drawn. Closing the door behind him, he lingered for a moment in the hall. The place still stank of petrol and last night's fire. It reminded him of squats he'd checked out in his uniformed days, places where dossers kipped at night, foul air and little piles of charred wood.

He closed the door without securing the chain and made his way upstairs. He'd brought a small overnight bag but he'd already decided to sleep in his clothes. Dawn, listening to this little plan of his, had been less than happy but the best part of a bottle of Bacardi had blunted her better judgement and by the time he'd left she was tucked up in the spare bedroom at the back of the bungalow, dead to the world.

Dawn's bedroom was at the front of the house. The floor was still dotted with little piles of discarded clothes and the bed had been stripped where she'd carted the top sheet and the duvet downstairs. There were a couple of blankets and a spare duvet in the airing cupboard outside the bathroom. Winter hauled them back along the landing, kicked off his shoes, and made himself as comfortable as he could. The ache in his arm and ribs had eased during the day but now he seemed to be hurting all over. Dawn's pack of Nurofen was still on the floor beside the bed. He swallowed three.

Sleep came slowly. Lying with his head on Dawn's pillow, he could smell her, an extraordinarily intimate experience for which he'd made no allowances. It wasn't that he kidded himself he'd ever be in with a chance. It wasn't even that he especially fancied her. It was simply the thought that he was this close to her, and that she was that vulnerable.

Vulnerability was the key to it, he thought. Vulnerability, that need for other people, for touch, for company, was the kind of temptation that certain blokes just couldn't resist. He'd seen it time and again on the job. He knew where it could lead. But never had he come across it this close to home.

Policemen, of course, were famously violent in their private lives. The job had its fair share of frustrations and he'd known a number of blokes who'd taken it out on their partners, or their wives. But this kind of lashing out, too many late nights, too much booze, was instinctive, just happened – bam – while this story of Dawn's was in a different class altogether.

The way she'd told it last night, he'd been pushed to believe her. At first she'd been reluctant to even talk about it but Winter was world class in situations like these and the more he probed the more he realised how cleverly she'd been manipulated. The things the guy had done were pretty bizarre, pretty disgusting, but the really clever trick was the way she'd ended up blaming herself.

'It's my fault, Paul,' she'd said. 'My bloody fault entirely.'

Wrong, he thought. Wrong, wrong, wrong.

A car whined past and he stiffened for a moment, wondering whether you'd do a little drive-by recce first to make sure the coast was clear. This whole thing was a punt, of course, and he was already half resigned to a sleepless night and fuck all to show for it, but there was another small voice in his head that told him he'd got it exactly right. Spend an entire career poking around the insides of other people's heads, and you learned a thing or two about the way they behaved, the way they circled and circled, always returning to that one still point. There was no chance Dawn could have brought all this on herself, he thought. In the words of the rape manuals, she was simply a target of opportunity.

It felt like minutes later when Winter awoke. He lay in the darkness for a moment, trying to work out what the noise had been. Then it happened again, footsteps in the hall below. He held up his wrist, peering at his watch.

02.49. Just about right, he thought, reaching into the space below the bed and fumbling for the on/off switch before pulling the duvet over his head.

The footsteps were closer now, easing up the stairs. At the top, they paused. He'd left the door open a crack and he could hear the sound of someone breathing hard. Not physical exhaustion, it couldn't be that. Far more likely to be something much nastier. Like excitement.

There was movement again, and the long pull of a zip. Then came a series of other noises, moist little slapping sounds that Winter couldn't place. Lying in the hot darkness under the duvet he tried to imagine what might be happening. Had Dawn gone through this? Was this the trailer before the big movie?

At length, he heard the creak of a door opening. There was a stir of air in the room and then he sensed the presence of someone standing over the bed. He shifted his weight a little under the bulky duvet, gladdened by this little trap of his, then rolled over entirely, his face still hidden. Live bait, he thought.

'Dawn?' He felt a hand giving him a gentle shake. 'You awake?'

Winter resumed his position, breathing regularly, feigning sleep. The voice again, a voice he recognised.

'Dawn? It's going to be all right this time, I promise, love. Look. Look at me.'

Winter threw back the duvet, a theatrical gesture that he immediately regretted. In the spill of light from the street, there was no mistaking the tall frame of Andy Corbett, looming over the bed. He was wearing his motorcycle leathers, unzipped from neck to groin. He was naked underneath and an uncertain erection was already beginning to flag. Winter thought he recognised the faint scent of body lotion.

Corbett, for a moment, was struck dumb. Then he took a tiny step backwards and reached down for the zip.

'What the fuck . . . ?'

Winter reached across for the bedside light.

'Disappointed?'

Corbett, at first, didn't answer. He zipped himself up, then extended a bony finger, inches from Winter's face.

'You're weird. Seriously fucking weird.'

'And you?'

'What's that supposed to mean?'

Winter plumped a pillow and did his best to make himself comfortable.

'How about we start with the cable ties?' he said peaceably. 'You want to have a little chat about those? Or shall we go straight on to the truncheon? Your dad's, wasn't it? I know psychiatrists who could write whole books about you.'

'I don't have to listen to this shit. Especially from a sad old git like you.' Corbett was heading for the bedroom door.

'You do, son. You have to listen very hard. And you know why? Because sad old gits like me could make life very difficult for you. I'm not Dawn's only mate. And the others are much younger.'

Corbett stopped and turned round. 'Is that some kind of threat?'

'Of course it is. But I notice you're not leaving so why don't you sit down?'

Winter nodded at the end of the bed. Corbett remained on his feet.

'Suit yourself.' Winter shrugged. 'First off, let's get down to the facts. A couple of nights ago, you stayed here, right? You weren't quite yourself. Things hadn't been going quite your way. You felt you needed a little TLC. And guess who was silly enough to believe you?'

'I was feeling shit. You don't make that kind of stuff up.'

'We all feel shit, son. It goes with the turf. What we don't do is cop a moody like that to get someone like Dawn into bed.'

'It was her idea.'

'Of course it was her idea. She's just that kind of girl. She's naïve, and she's kind, too, and she meant it. God knows what she's doing in a job like ours. Anyway, she's taken pity on you. She gets you something to drink. You talk for a while. You tell her how unfair the world is, how you're not getting a fair crack of the whip, and sweet, generous guy that you are, you let her take you to bed. The way Dawn's seeing it, that's a definite result. Number one, she's fancied you for weeks. Number two, she's playing the Christian. Fellow cop in dire need. Help yourself, she says, it'll make you feel so much better. But it didn't, did it? And why not? Because you couldn't get it up. Or that's the way it looked, anyway. So how does Dawn feel about this? My friend, she feels exactly the way you want her to feel. She feels totally fucking useless. Literally. There she is, stark naked, fresh from the shower, and the todger doesn't want to know. She thinks she's ugly. She thinks she doesn't turn you on. She thinks she's failed. So somehow she's got to do better.' Winter eased his arm, working a finger under the plaster for a scratch. 'Am I getting warm?'

Corbett didn't say a word. His face was pale, his mouth compressed. Under his left eye, a tiny muscle was beginning to flutter.

'So . . .' Winter beamed up at him. 'You unpack the goodies you've brought along. You've got these cable ties, just by chance. You think it might help if she lets you tie each of her wrists to this bedhead here, these little knobs along the top. Now Dawn's not sure about that, she really isn't, but you're in some distress, some need, and after all it was her idea to begin with, and so she says yes, doesn't she? She says yes, and you get right down to it, big black cable tie round each wrist.' He paused a moment. 'Did you bring the pliers tonight, as a matter of interest? Or are you through with the ties?'

Once again, no answer. Just the dead eyes, staring down.

'No? Don't you want to help me out here?' Winter pressed on. 'OK, so there she is, lashed to the bedhead, but you haven't quite finished yet because – surprise, surprise – you just happened to have found two more ties, this time for her ankles. By now, Dawn's having serious second thoughts. What seemed like a great idea, you stepping in through the door and changing her life, has turned into some kind of porn movie. The wheels have come off, Andy, big-time. And there she is, kippered, totally fucking laid out for you, and she can't help wondering what treat you're planning next.'

'I tried to fuck her.'

'You did, Andy, you did. And I suppose that might have been acceptable, just. But again, it didn't work, did it? Either because you really have got a problem or because you didn't want it to work.'

'You're telling me that's my fault?' he said hotly. 'You think I didn't *want* to fuck her?'

'I haven't got a clue, mate, but I tell you what I do think. I think you're one sick bastard. I think you knew exactly what you wanted when you knocked on her door that night, and the shame of it is you got it. Where are the kicks in that kind of stuff, do you mind telling me? How do you get off on raping women with a bottle of wine? Then with a truncheon? Is it a control thing? Is that your bag? Or is it just plain old aggravated rape? Only I'm just a bit confused.'

'It wasn't rape.'

'You want to tell a court that? Only Dawn might.'

'It was' . . . he bent low over the bed . . . 'just a thing between us. You wouldn't understand that. You wouldn't begin to understand. I came over to apologise. If you really want to know.'

'Sure. And you turn up here in the middle of night with

your knob hanging out. That's hardly an apology, is it? Or am I missing something here?'

Winter let the thought sink in, then he nodded at the door.

'I haven't a clue why you really came round tonight but I'm fucking glad it wasn't Dawn in this bed. I might be a year or two older than you but I'll tell you something for free, son. If you come anywhere near this place again, or so much as lift the phone to Dawn, I'll make fucking sure you're on the next train back to London. You understand me?'

'No, I don't.'

'Then let me spell it out. You leave Dawn alone. You forget all about her. If you really can't control that truncheon of yours, I'll give you a list of phone numbers. There are women in this city who'll sort you out. It'll cost a bit but you never know your luck. Bloke like you might score a discount for being so pathetic. OK? That clear enough?'

For a moment, Winter thought he'd thrown one insult too many. Corbett had the look of a man about to do something very silly indeed. Then he visibly straightened, trying to turn all that boiling anger into contempt.

'You know my big mistake?' he said softly.

'No, son. Tell me.'

'Coming round your place and telling you what a daft old cunt you are. I should have left it, shouldn't I? I should have kept my mouth shut and waited till the next time.'

'Next time?'

'Yeah.' He drew the zip up to his neck. 'Because next time you'll probably kill the poor bloody woman.'

Winter gazed up at him, lost for words. Finally he nodded.

'That's right,' he said. 'Big fucking mistake coming round to my place. You know something, son? You want to learn to control yourself.'

Corbett dismissed him with a cold smile, some tiny shred of dignity reclaimed, then turned on his heel and left the room. Winter heard the stamp of his boots on the stairs and the slam of the front door as he headed back to the street. Faintly, minutes later, came the roar of a big motorbike. Must have parked a couple of streets away, Winter thought. Sly bastard.

He turned from the window and made his way downstairs. The girl on the all-night shift at Aqua promised him a cab as soon as she could. Only when he'd got his shoes on, waiting downstairs, did he remember the little Sony under Dawn's bed. The cassette was still recording, at least a couple of minutes left.

Seventeen

Next morning, Faraday felt infinitely better. Even Bev Yates noticed it. His own Saturday night had been a disaster. He'd got home late to find a crusty lasagne in the oven and Melanie asleep on the sofa in the sitting room. Turning on the TV and settling in for a review of the day's play in Japan and South Korea had been the last straw. Mel had left him to the highlights of Brazil versus China and gone to bed without a word.

Faraday was already at his desk at Kingston Crescent. Yates appeared at the open office door.

'We're sure it was Pritchard?' Yates stifled a yawn.

'Definitely.' Faraday had been talking to the DC he'd seconded to the SOC operation in Buriton Tunnel. 'His sister ID'd the shirt. They'll be digging out the dental records first thing tomorrow but that's just to be on the safe side.'

'She hasn't had a look at the body?'

'There isn't one. And anyway, we're not going there again.'

Yates nodded. He'd had his own qualms about marching Pritchard along to the mortuary but had told himself it wasn't his decision. Now, he wanted to know how they were going to sort out the three guys in the hotel without the benefit of their only witness.

'Get hold of the association secretary,' Faraday said briskly. 'We'll start with him.'

Yates gone, Faraday phoned Willard. A message on his mobile had established that the Det Supt was spending the morning at home and Faraday wondered whether –

like Yates – he was trying to keep some kind of private life together. Willard had a long-term partner in the shape of a psychologist called Sheila. She lived and worked in Bristol and often drove down at weekends.

Willard was gruffer than usual on the phone.

'OK to talk, sir?'

'Go on.'

Faraday told him about Pritchard. Willard, as usual, had his own take on this latest development.

'So why did he do it?'

Faraday said he didn't know. In the absence of a note, anything else was pure conjecture.

'Might guilt come into it?'

'Guilt, how?'

'Guilt for killing his mate?'

'You mean Coughlin? You're serious?'

'It's a suggestion, Joe, something you might have to consider. In my view, the guy was by no means eliminated and chucking himself under a train tells me he had something on his conscience.' He paused to answer a question. Faraday could hear a woman's voice. Then Willard was back.

'What's the status on Coughlin's flat?'

'Jerry finished yesterday. He's got a pile of stuff he's thinking of submitting for SGM-plus and he did every room with the bacofoil.'

'Any hits?'

'Nothing.'

Willard grunted. SGM-plus was the standard DNA test while bacofoil was the Major Crimes code for a forensic technique that laid thin sheets on carpets and flooring. An electrical charge would reveal footprints and other impressions with remarkable clarity.

'Nothing at *all*?'

'Nothing to connect the scene to Pritchard. He had soil all over his runners, remember. Had he been in the flat, Scenes of Crime would have picked it up at once.'

'Maybe he took the runners off.'

'He was pissed, sir. He was out of his head. Even sober, he wasn't the kind of guy to wipe his feet.'

'OK, OK. It's a thought, that's all. Cases like these, it doesn't pay to dismiss the obvious.'

'Quite.'

'What does that mean?'

'Nothing, sir. Coughlin was up to date with his mortgage payments and no one else has got a claim on the flat so Jerry's decided not to release the scene. He's changed the locks and put alarms in. We can go back any time we like.'

Willard wanted to know where Faraday was headed next. Mention of the association secretary and the Home Club video sparked another query.

'That's resource-intensive,' Willard said. 'We're doing a major push in Somerstown today. There might even be some dads around. Where are you getting the bodies?'

Faraday explained that he and Yates would be doing the bulk of the leg work. Priority was a list of guests for last Monday night and a proper sort through the CCTV. With luck, by lunchtime, they might have some names in the frame. He hesitated a moment, expecting another wrangle, but the conversation was evidently over.

'Good luck.' Willard had obviously been summoned. 'And keep me briefed.'

Half an hour later, in Somerstown, a blue Sierra estate coasted to a halt in Fraser Road. Two men got out and opened the tailgate at the back. They pulled out a shape wrapped in a blanket, lowered it roughly to the pavement, and drove away. Minutes later, a paperboy gave it a cautious poke with his foot. The blanket moved.

The HMS *Accolade* association was run by an ex-radio operator called Stanley Wallace. He lived in Drayton, a suburb off the island, and saw no objection to a Sunday morning meet. He had an office five minutes' walk from his house. That's where he kept the association records and he gave Yates the address.

'Over there.' Yates had driven Faraday up from Kingston Crescent. 'Above the fruit and veg.'

They were parked on the main road, across from a parade of shops. The fruit and veg evidently opened on Sunday mornings, admitting a steady trickle of elderly shoppers. Yates and Faraday crossed the road and enquired in the shop for Stanley Wallace. A door at the back led into a storeroom. Turn left by the sacks of potatoes, negotiate boxes of lettuce and cucumber, and a flight of dusty stairs led up to the first floor.

Wallace was waiting in a tiny kitchen, a small, neat man with a wisp of greying moustache. Faraday judged him to be in his fifties. Three mugs were lined up beside a steaming kettle.

'Tea? Coffee?'

Yates and Faraday settled for coffee. Wallace took them through to a bigger office next door. After the navy he'd re-trained as an accountant and now ran a modest business servicing mainly local clients.

While he disappeared to fetch the coffees, Faraday inspected a framed photograph hanging on the back wall. This time, HMS *Accolade* was side-on to the camera, pictured against the immensity of the ocean. It was a beautiful shot – her bows carving through a huge green wave, the sunshine gleaming on the wetness of her flanks as she began to roll – and there was something in the image that reminded him of J-J's work. The photographer had managed to capture a special kind of essence. The image spoke of energy and speed, of direction and purpose. No wonder Wallace had hung it on his wall.

'Bloke shot that from one of the auxiliaries. We'd just taken fuel off him.'

Faraday glanced round. Wallace was shutting the office door with his foot.

'Was that 'eighty-two?'

'Yes. Ten days later that ship was history.'

Faraday looked at the photo again. This man has been living with a ghost, he thought.

They settled into office chairs. Faraday began to explain the background to this visit of theirs but Wallace was way ahead of him. On the phone Yates had merely mentioned a major inquiry.

'This has to be Coughlin, doesn't it?'

'What makes you say that?'

'I had a couple of the blokes on during the week, local guys. They read about him in the paper.'

'And?'

'And nothing. He wasn't someone we ever thought about a great deal. He never turned up at any of the functions. In fact it was news to us he even lived here.'

Yates had been examining the line of accountancy certificates on another wall. Now he turned to Wallace.

'Coughlin wasn't there on Monday night?'

'Good Lord, no.'

'But you still remembered his name?'

'Yes.'

'Why's that?'

Wallace was sitting at his desk. A fabric roller blind softened the morning sunshine through the window.

'All ships are special,' he said at last. 'Lose one, and they become precious. So do the blokes you've served with. Names? Faces? You don't forget them.' He offered a wan smile. 'Ever.'

'Is that why you organise the association?'

'Yes. But then someone has to.' He paused, toying with his coffee. 'You want to know about Coughlin? He was in my mess . . .'

His voice trailed off and Faraday realised how awkward this conversation had suddenly become. Wallace was guardian of *Accolade*'s last voyage, keeper of the ship's secrets, and the last thing he wanted to do was tarnish those cherished memories.

'Which mess was that?' Faraday enquired.

'The S and S mess. Two Delta. Port side, forward.'

'And you say Coughlin was in there?'

'There were thirty-six of us.' He nodded. 'Writers. Radio ops like me. Stores assistants. Chefs. Stewards. The Canteen Manager. Odds and sods really.'

'And Coughlin?'

'Was a killick chef, three-badge man.'

Yates was lost. Faraday, too. Wallace obliged with a translation. A Killick, he said, was a Leading Hand, often one of the older ratings, and Coughlin had earned himself three good-conduct badges.

Faraday raised an eyebrow.

'Behaved himself, then?'

'Hardly. Twelve years of undetected crime. That's not just Coughlin, that's more or less everyone, but Coughlin was . . .' Again, he failed to finish the sentence.

'Unpopular?'

'Certainly. A loner, too. And liable to go off without warning. You didn't wind a bloke like that up. Not if you didn't want to risk the consequences.'

'You're telling me he was violent? Physical?'

'Could be. I never saw it myself but you hear things.'

'Like what?'

Wallace was getting agitated now. This, Faraday sensed, was close to betrayal.

'Runs ashore,' he said at last. 'Twenty-ones were very close. We belonged to the Fighting Fourth, the Fourth Frigate Squadron, and we'd be alongside in Amsterdam or Hamburg or some place like that. There was even a club, the 21 Club. We had T-shirts printed, ties too. Runs ashore could get hectic, believe me.'

'And Coughlin?'

'Coughlin was out ahead of us. Put drink in him and

he'd push it to the limit. His speciality was the young skins.'

Faraday and Yates exchanged glances. Skins?

'Kids. The babies of the mess. Coughlin saw to it they had a good time. Insisted, actually.' He studied his fingernails for a moment, and Faraday began to suspect that he'd been waiting for a conversation like this for years. Coughlin had been a stain on *Accolade*'s memory and now was the time to get rid of it.

'I remember the last run ashore in Amsterdam. We all ended up in this crap bar, most of the S and S mess. Coughlin had been drinking all night but he could handle it, big guy, had the weight on him. They got up to all kinds of stuff in this bar and a couple of the girls had a stunt they used to pull. They had stools at the bar. You sat on a stool looking out from the bar, then leaned your head back so it rested on the top. You put a note in your mouth, ten guilders, twenty, whatever, and then one of these girls squatted over you, stark naked, and took the note – you know – with her fanny. They were Indonesian. Real lookers, some of them.'

'And Coughlin?' Faraday said again.

'He'd got hold of one of the youngest lads, real nipper. He lifted him on to the stool and then put a fifty-guilder note in his mouth. For fifty guilders you got a bag-off afterwards.'

'A bag what?'

'A shag. Jackspeak.'

'So what happened?'

'The girl did the business, got the note, then came round the bar for the nipper. There was a place out the back, little cubicle, it never took long. We were all of us cheering, of course, giving it some, but then Coughlin stepped in. He wouldn't let the nipper go out with the girl. I can see it now. He just stood there, blocking the way.'

'Why?' Yates was entranced.

'Because it was his money. And because it was his money he said he had a right to decide how the thing should go. He wanted the girl to do it there, on the floor, with all us lot watching.'

'She agreed?'

'Not at first. He had to give her another fifty.'

'And then?'

'Then she got down to it. Stripped the nipper. Laid him on the floor. It was awful, just dreadful, poor kid.'

'Why?'

'Because he wasn't up for it. Not his fault, Christ. All those blokes ogling you? Bellyful of lager? And this bint doing her best to stir you up? Coughlin loved it. You could see it on his face. He'd humiliated this poor lad and he just couldn't get enough of it. All the guys thought it was a hoot, of course. They were all telling the nipper to jack it in and let them have a go. Coughlin ended up raffling her. Got half his money back.'

'Didn't have her himself, then?' It was Yates.

'No way. He'd shag anything, mind, but not that night. That night he was just after making this kid's life a misery. It was horrible.'

There was a long silence. Faraday's gaze had wandered back to the photograph on the wall.

'That wouldn't have been Matthew Warren, by any chance?' he said at last.

Wallace looked startled.

'You know about Warren?'

'I know he went over the side, yes.'

'I see.' He looked away a moment, then nodded. 'You're right. It was Warren.'

Willard, outraged, sent two DCs to the Queen Alexandra Hospital. One of them was Andy Corbett. He led the way through the big sliding door into Accident and Emergency and flashed his warrant card at the woman behind the reception desk. He wanted a word with someone about a Darren Geech. She scribbled a note and told him to take a seat. Corbett headed for the drinks machine.

Ten minutes later, he and the other DC were summoned to a desk in the Major Injuries reception area. The duty registrar, a middle-aged Kenyan, told them that Geech had been admitted with suspected fractures to both legs and severe bruising to his face and lower body. He was currently in X-Ray and would be kept on a ward for at least a couple of days for a thorough assessment. He was fully conscious, but for the time being there was absolutely no prospect of any kind of interview. Corbett did his best to push it, talking pointedly about a homicide inquiry, but the registrar was already shepherding them back towards the waiting room. The unit was very busy just now. He was glad he'd been able to help.

Outside, where the ambulances backed in, Corbett put a call through to Dave Michaels.

'Definitely Geech.' He was watching a nurse walking away down the hill. 'Someone's given him a whacking.'

Faraday and Yates took Wallace down to the Naval Home Club. The general manager, alerted by a phone call, had prepared Monday night's video tapes and made available an empty bedroom upstairs. A television and a video player lay on a table beneath the window. Tea and coffee was just a phone call away.

The bedroom was tiny. Wallace perched himself on the single bed. They were still talking about Coughlin.

Back in 'eighty-two, the man had been chef in the wardroom galley, preparing meals for the ship's officers. The hours were long but you fancied you were a cut above the chefs down aft, cooking for the rest of the ship's company in the big dining room, and you were also left on your own, no one else in your way.

'That suited Coughlin down to the ground,' Wallace said. 'Most chefs throw a wobbler from time to time because they've got that kind of temperament but he was a really moody bastard.'

There was a sliding door to the wardroom galley, Wallace explained, and even the officers themselves thought twice about intruding into the chef's space. That meant he had the place entirely to himself. Not only that, but he had access to virtually limitless spirits.

'Scotch, gin, whatever you like. He'd just nick it from the wardroom supplies. Coughlin's tipple was Scotch. Weeks when he was really drinking, he'd carry it around in a Coke can, just keeping himself topped up. That's when blokes avoided him. When they saw the Coke can.'

'You're saying he was a drunk?'

'Not all the time. He'd go without it completely some weeks, just use the spirits for currency, buying favours. Thinking back, he was a control freak, no doubt about it. He wanted to be in charge. Top dog.'

Faraday was watching Yates spooling back through the first of the tapes. He couldn't get the sliding door out of his mind.

'The galley you mentioned. The one where Coughlin worked. That space was completely his own?'

'Totally. It was up forward, one deck, nice and private. That's rare on a warship, believe me.'

'And you say he worked with Warren?'

'Every day. Depending on the watches we were keeping, Warren would be up first thing, helping Coughlin flash up for breakfast, laying the table in the wardroom, sorting out the cereals, all that. Even if he wanted to, there was no way Warren could avoid the man.'

'Which suited Coughlin?'

'Down to the ground. He had the boy exactly where he wanted him.'

Faraday nodded, watching the screen. According to Wallace, Warren had been the baby of the mess.

Accolade was his first ship and though he did his best to hide it, everyone knew he was terrified of Coughlin.

'How do you want to play this?' Yates had cued the first tape.

Faraday glanced at Wallace. The secretary had brought his membership lists with him, together with a note of exactly who had attended the function on Monday night. Twenty years on, Faraday sensed he'd been disappointed at the turn-out.

'Some of the guys have just had enough,' he'd said in the car. 'They ring me up and tell me they can't put their lives on hold for ever but somehow I never think of it like that. A lot of our blokes died and twenty years on is a good time to remember them.'

Now, Faraday sought his advice. If they started with the tape from the main bar, half seven in the evening, they'd get a feel for the occasion. Wallace could maybe point out the odd characters, people who might have had a thing about Coughlin, younger ratings who might have buddied with Matthew Warren.

'That OK?'

Wallace nodded, transferring to a chair Yates had found for him from a room up the corridor. Yates hit the play button and the first tape rolled through. The screen offered a grid of four pictures, each fed from cameras in different locations around the building, and Faraday watched the top right-hand picture as the bar slowly filled: portly men of a certain age, with blazers and ties and a ready handshake for friends and shipmates.

By eight o'clock the room was full. The camera offered a high shot from way up on the wall and the faces easing themselves into the scrum at the bar kept changing as the *Accolade*s bought fresh rounds for each other. It was strange watching these pictures mute. This is the way J-J sees everything, Faraday thought. What would life be like without ever hearing laughter?

'There.' Yates paused the tape. Wallace was pointing

at a figure on the screen. Slightly taller than everyone else, he was locked in conversation with two younger men.

'That was our Jimmy,' he said. 'The XO. Mark Harrington. Hellava guy. Lives in the Meon Valley now, Corhampton way. Drives a desk at the MOD during the week so it was nice of him to turn up.'

Faraday glanced at Yates. Corhampton was a stone's throw from Bev's place. Bev peered at the screen, then shook his head.

'Never laid eyes on him,' he said. 'But then I wouldn't, would I? I'm never bloody there.'

Seconds later, the bar began to empty as the *Accolade*s made their way into dinner. The bottom right-hand picture was fed from a camera in the Nuffield Room and Faraday's heart sank as he watched the tables filling up. He wasn't counting but sixty-three blokes represented a lot of interviews, especially with a squad as depleted as *Merriott*'s.

'Tell me about the night Warren went missing.' Faraday was still gazing at the screen. 'Do you remember any of that?'

'Very well. Like I say, the lad was in our mess. You keep an eye on the kids, it's just something you do, and it seemed all the more important down south because none of us had been to war before and no one had a clue what it was really going to be like.'

'You were nervous?'

'Not really. More thoughtful than nervous. *Belgrano* had gone down by then, and so had *Sheffield*, so you couldn't kid yourself it was an exercise any more.'

Well inside the Total Exclusion Zone, they'd been on defence watches the night Warren had disappeared, six hours on, six hours off. It was winter in the South Atlantic, not much daylight, and you quickly lost all track of time.

'But you remember when he went missing?'

'I remember when the alarm was raised, yes. I was in my pit. The messing was luxurious compared to earlier ships, that was one of the reasons 21s were so popular, and each gulch had four bunks in it. There's a little curtain you can pull to give yourself a bit of privacy and this particular morning I remember the Officer of the Watch making a pipe for Warren. The lad was in the next gulch to us and I pulled the curtain back, wondering whether anyone was going to give him a shake. They couldn't, though. Because he wasn't there.'

Faraday nodded. In the Nuffield Room, after bowed heads for grace, waitresses were circling with bowls of soup.

'What happened next?'

'There was another pipe, this time for Thimblehunt. That means you all search your own particular areas of the ship. Thimblehunt wasn't a good sign, not as far as Warren was concerned.'

'And after that?'

'The Captain turned the ship around. One of my oppos up in the Commcen told me later he'd been on to *Hermes* for permission. Man overboard, there's a drill you do, special kind of sea search, but by that time it was pretty obvious Warren was a goner. Mid-winter, that far south, he wouldn't have had a prayer.'

Wallace was looking glum. Yates had spooled on through the meal. The dessert courses had come and gone, and the speeches were under way. Yates hit fast forward, then put the machine on pause again. The room was on its feet, glasses raised.

'When guys go overboard, or get themselves killed, you organise an auction. A lot of their clothing and stuff goes back into stores but all the personal items are put up for sale. We call it Dead Man's Kit. The stuff's sold over and over again, doesn't matter what it is, scabby old pair of trainers might fetch twenty quid, maybe thirty, then another thirty from someone else. Same with Walkmans

277

or old cassettes. I remember Warren had loads of Status Quo and AC/DC. Terrible stuff. Raised a fortune.'

'Where does the money go?'

'Normally his wife. In Warren's case, probably his mum and dad.'

'Where was he from?'

'Pompey.'

'I see.'

Faraday couldn't take his eyes off the screen. Absent friends, he thought. And some poor scrap of an eighteen-year-old, adrift in the South Atlantic, either dying or dead.

'Exit tapes next?'

Yates consulted the log the general manager had provided. One camera covered the lobby area outside reception. Another the steps leading down to the street outside. *Accolade*s began drifting away around eleven o'clock, often in twos and threes. Faraday watched them for a moment, then told Yates to pause the tape again.

'You were there in the main bar after the meal?' He'd turned to Wallace.

'Some of the time, yes.'

'Do you remember a particular group? Three blokes? Might have been talking about Coughlin?'

'No.' He shook his head. 'But then I can't remember anyone ever talking about Coughlin. He was like a bad dose of flu. Why would you want to remember something like that?'

'OK,' Faraday went on, 'was anyone talking about the Alhambra?'

'The what?'

'The Alhambra. Hotel in Granada Road. Kind of place you might go for an after-hours drink or two. Run by a sailor by the name of Pritchard.'

'Never heard of it,' Wallace said. 'Or him. That doesn't mean to say no one went on there. The mob's a smaller organisation than you might think. But you're asking me? I don't know.'

Yates hit play again. The Home Club was emptying by now, more bodies making their way into the street, checking watches, looking for taxis, saying their good-byes. Without Pritchard here to mark their card, Faraday knew they had no option but to trawl through the whole list, sixty-three interviews.

'There. Look.' It was Wallace again. He was pointing to a group of departing guests. One of them had his face to camera: lean, fit-looking, hair pulled back into a neat ponytail. He eased himself into a leather jacket and then nodded at another man on his left.

'That's the guy you want to talk to about Warren.' Wallace reached for his membership list.

'Why? Who is he?'

'He was our Joss, our Master-at-Arms. The killick Reg was in our mess, hard bastard, name of Flaherty. The killick Reg works with the Joss. They run the ship, discipline-wise. Whatever's going on, it's their job to know, especially the killick.'

'Was Flaherty there as well? Monday night?'

'Flaherty was killed when the ship went down. That's why the Joss is your man.' He nodded at the screen again and Faraday turned to watch the figure in the leather jacket disappearing down the street. He counted five others with him.

'Is he local? This Joss?'

'Negative. Lives down in Devon somewhere. Hang on.' He had his head buried in the membership lists. 'Here it is. Dave Beattie. Ezentide Quay.' He looked up. 'You know the Tamar Valley at all?'

Eighteen

Winter, on a roll after ambushing Corbett, bought the
flowers from the ground floor shop at the QA hospital.
The woman behind the reception desk had keyed in
Darren Geech's name and traced him to a ward on the
third floor. Winter, suitably concerned, had enquired
about visiting times but she'd referred him to the staff on
the ward itself. If there was a problem with access, they'd
be the ones to know.

Cradling his enormous spray of carnations, Winter
headed for the lifts. Cathy Lamb had phoned Dawn with
the news about Geech. An ambulance had scooped him
up from Somerstown and taken him to the QA. Odd
thing was, he'd been dumped on exactly the spot where
Rookie had received his beating.

Winter loved the touch. Vintage Bazza, he thought.
Not just a lesson for the little knobber but a sweet twist
at the end to bring this whole episode full circle. Had
Bazza's blokes screwed the location out of Geech before
they got down to business? Or had it taken a preliminary
whack or two before he'd volunteered the information?
Either way it didn't matter. Darren Geech's infant career
in hard narcotics was very probably over.

Beds on D20 were supervised from an L-shaped
nursing station at the junction of two corridors. A
harassed-looking sister took a cursory glance at Winter's
warrant card, and a longer look at his arm.

'Been in the wars, have we?'

Winter ignored the raised eyebrow. The flowers, he
said, were a humanitarian gesture from himself and his

colleagues. Young Geech had been through a great deal on their behalf. Where might he find the lad?

The sister indicated a small glassed-in cubicle at the end of the longer of the two corridors. Winter had already spotted the uniform sat outside. The young PC looked up at Winter's approach. A copy of the *News of the World* lay open on his lap. Beside him, on a low table, was the visitor log.

The PC studied Winter's face. He hadn't a clue who he was. Out came the warrant card again.

'What's this, then?' the PC enquired.

Winter gave him the flowers and asked him to sort out a vase. Bewildered by a lapful of mixed carnations, the PC said that access to Geech was strictly limited: inspectors and above, unless through prior arrangement.

Winter looked astonished.

'You didn't get the call?'

'Who from?'

'Major Crimes.'

The PC looked dubious a moment, then shook his head.

'Not a peep from anyone,' he said. 'And I've been here since six.'

'Overtime?'

'You have to be joking.'

'Shit.' Winter wagged his head. 'You wonder some-times, don't you?' He hooked a chair towards him with his leg and sat down. The view through the glass was half-shuttered by a fall of Venetian blind, but from here Winter could make out the hump of a body in the single bed. 'How is he?'

'Fuck knows. I'm just the gate man.'

'You don't go in there at all?'

'Not unless I have to. Hospitals freak me out.'

'Got kids yourself?'

'Yeah, but not his sort.'

Winter offered a sympathetic nod, then told him about

the state of the flat in Somerstown. Blood-soaked jeans in the bath, baseball bat in the wardrobe, and his mum wandering around with an armful of smack. No wonder the kid had got himself into trouble.

Winter leaned over and patted the carnations before getting to his feet.

'Lots of water,' he said. 'Soon as you like.'

The PC gazed up at him. The body in the bed appeared to have shifted.

'You're serious about taking a look?'

'Of course I am.' Winter's hand was already reaching for the door. 'Couple of minutes, max.'

It took a second or two for Winter's eyes to adjust to the gloom of the tiny private room. He stood by the bed, staring down. Geech's face was swollen beyond recognition, both eyes purpled and his nose plainly broken. The guys Bazza used to send the occasional message must have broken his jaw, too, because his mouth was set in a strange rictus, the lips parted in a thin snarl to reveal the remains of his teeth. If you were looking for a single good reason to keep to the straight and narrow, then here it was.

Geech's eyes were open now, the thinnest slits weeping some nameless liquid. A tiny curl of tongue darted out, moistening the bloated lips. Winter bent low beside the bed, trying to coax some sense from the mumbled obscenities. He might have been kidding himself but he thought he recognised the word 'dog'.

'Charlie?' Winter dug in his pocket and produced a small digital camera. 'Safe and sound, son. Sends his love.'

He stepped back from the bed. From a couple of metres, using the zoom, the wreckage of Geech's face filled the viewfinder. A thin dribble of saliva, pinked with fresh blood, had stained the pillow beside his cheek.

He took three shots, the flash erupting in the gloom.

Outside, the PC had got to his feet. One more, Winter thought. The clincher.

Geech's legs were protected by some kind of cage beneath the sheet. The memory of his own injury still fresh in his mind, Winter stepped closer to the bed, adjusting the zoom as he did so. Geech's face perfectly framed, Winter gave the bed a little jolt with his foot. The yelp of pain brought the PC to the door.

'What's going on?'

Winter was examining the camera.

'Couple of snaps,' he said. 'For the file.'

Back in the lift, Winter checked the shots on the tiny fold-out screen. All of them were ample proof that Bazza knew his business but the last image, Geech's ruined face twisted back against the pillow, chilled even Winter. On balance, the kid might have been better off dead. It would take months to recover from a beating like this.

Waiting for a taxi, minutes later, Winter remembered the call he'd been meaning to put in. He fumbled for his mobile and scrolled through the stored numbers until he got to 'Yates'. It took a while for Bev to answer and when he did so, Winter could hear crowd noise in the background. More bloody football, Winter thought.

'Listen . . .' he began. 'It's about young Dawn.'

Willard appeared at Kingston Crescent in mid-afternoon. A pub lunch with Sheila had put him in a better mood than usual and he paused outside Faraday's open office door, jacket hooked over one shoulder.

'Seafood salad. New potatoes. Decent bottle of Sancerre. And change from thirty quid. Not bad, eh?'

Faraday, who'd so far survived on two apples and a Mars bar from the machine along the corridor, didn't pursue the conversation. Instead, he got to his feet and followed Willard into his office. Dave Michaels was already there, sorting through a pile of PDFs on

Willard's conference table. The news from Somerstown was getting worse by the hour.

'Absolutely fuck all I'm afraid, boss. We thought sheer numbers might crack it but no one's saying a word. Couple of dozen blokes on house-to-house and all we get is a load of grief about Geech getting dumped like that. Poor little bunny. They think we're losing it.'

'They're right.' Willard was checking his e-mails. 'We are.'

He glanced back over his shoulder. Faraday wanted to talk about the tapes at the Home Club. With Pritchard off the plot, their only option was to interview every guest at the *Accolade*'s dinner.

'Is that a problem?'

'With four blokes on the strength it might be, yes. We're talking more than sixty of them.'

'Then it's going to take a while, Joe.' Willard had found a message from the Force Intelligence Bureau, up at headquarters. He moved aside and gestured at the screen. Faraday peered at the e-mail. SO11 at New Scotland Yard had come back on the information Corbett claimed to have sourced. There was evidently some kind of surveillance operation under way and Davidson's name was one of many in the frame. The DI in charge was operating out of Streatham nick. Once the smoke had cleared, Willard thought he might be prepared to give *Merriott* half an hour of his precious time, strictly face to face.

Willard had produced a toothpick.

'You talk to that girlfriend of Davidson's again?'

Faraday, irritated by this sudden change of tack, nodded. He and Yates had reinterviewed her yesterday afternoon.

'And?'

'She thinks the relationship's going nowhere and she's bloody upset about it.'

'Surprise, surprise. What's that got to do with us?'

'Everything, sir.'

'How come?'

'Because it confirms she's straight. Naïve, maybe, but straight. She was definitely with Davidson all Monday night. No way was she lying.'

'Not even to protect him?'

'Absolutely not.'

'You're sure about that?'

'Yes, sir.'

Willard studied the toothpick a moment, gave the sharp end a little suck, then dropped it in the bin.

'Must be nice to be so certain, Joe. Wish I had that confidence sometimes. Be good to talk to the Met, though . . . face to face, eh?' His eyes went back to the e-mail.

Faraday fought the urge to argue. In his view, the Alhambra lead was by far the strongest to date. Three ex-shipmates of Coughlin with a skinful of lager and some kind of twenty-year grudge? Didn't that represent a worthwhile line of enquiry?

'Of course it does, Joe. I'm just asking you to keep an open mind. Elimination can be trickier than you think, especially if you're relying on instinct.'

'There were two of us, sir. And we both agreed.'

'Glad to hear it. So where do we go next?'

Faraday began to explain about the tapes again. One of the guests the association secretary had ID'd was the Master-at-Arms aboard *Accolade*. His name was Dave Beattie and he had a place down in Devon.

'You're telling me he's worth the trip? Four hours there, four hours back?'

'Definitely. The guy's job was heading off trouble. And Coughlin was trouble. If anyone knows what happened on that ship, it would have been Beattie.'

'And you really think there's any point going down this road? Twenty years is a long time, Joe.'

'Sure. Of course it is.'

'Two decades? Some kind of debt to settle? Is that what you're saying?'

For a moment, trying to fathom Willard's reluctance to pursue the *Accolade* lead, Faraday was tempted to mention Eadie Sykes and the even longer shadow cast by the Second World War. Sixty years had come and gone since her father had stumbled out of Crete, yet her anger still boiled beneath the images on the tape Faraday had seen. Compared to that episode, the Falklands War was yesterday's trauma, practically newly minted.

'Beattie?' Faraday shrugged. 'Think of it as copper to copper. We're both in the same business, sorting out the bad guys, keeping the peace. Chances are he'll give me a steer, blokes Coughlin had really pissed off. Who knows, he might even come up with names for Monday night, guys who might have ended up at the Alhambra.'

'So why don't you phone him?'

'Because it wouldn't be the same.' Faraday nodded at the e-mails on the screen. 'Strictly face to face, sir. Has to be.'

Bev Yates didn't get to Portchester until late afternoon. A precautionary phone call home had established that Mel was about to drive the kids across to a birthday party in Winchester. As long as the bloody car didn't misbehave again, she should be back by seven. Not that she'd had time to sort out anything for supper.

On the phone, Winter had mentioned something about a domestic. He hadn't gone into any kind of detail but it was plain that Dawn was in need of a little TLC. She'd taken a knock or two over the last couple of days, what with the fire bomb, and writing off the Skoda hadn't helped. Anyone eavesdropping on the call might have assumed that Dawn had been at the wheel – her judgement call, her fault – but Bev had known Winter far too long to fall for such a neat piece of sleight-of-hand. Nonetheless, he was genuinely concerned about Dawn.

Falling for an arsewipe like Corbett was a serious lapse of taste.

She answered the door on the fourth ring and Yates knew at once she was in big trouble. She looked gaunt, almost haunted.

'Hi.' Her voice was flat. 'Just passing, were you?'

'Yeah.'

They studied each other for a long moment, then she shrugged and stood back to let him pass. The sour reek of a recent fire still hung in the hall and when he poked his head round the lounge door, he saw that she'd pushed all the furniture to the back of the room.

'I was going to roll the bloody thing up.' She gestured at the cratered carpet beneath the window. 'Only I never seem to get round to it.'

'You want me to do it?'

Without waiting for an answer, he stepped into the room. Sorting the carpet was the work of a minute. On his hands and knees at the back of the room, he got her to help him move the furniture. Moments later, they were standing on the underlay.

'Should I hang on to the carpet? For the insurance people?'

Yates shook his head. Scenes of Crime had come and gone. Insurance assessors never turned out for less than a five-figure claim. Best get rid of it.

'How?'

'Leave it to me.'

'You're serious?'

'Always.'

She made him tea, then changed her mind and broke out a four-pack of San Miguel she'd been hoarding for months. Infinitely more cheerful, she carried the bottles out to the back garden and fetched a couple of chairs from the lean-to beside the kitchen door. Out of the wind, the sun was warm.

'How's life in the country, then?'

'Fucking awful. Second biggest mistake I ever made.'

'And the first?'

Yates didn't answer. The sun felt wonderful on his face. He sat back in the chair, tipped the bottle to his mouth, took a long pull at the San Miguel, then closed his eyes and sighed. For the first time in weeks, he felt truly relaxed.

'Tell me about Andy,' he murmured at last. 'I don't get it.'

'Me neither.'

'Really? I thought you were . . . you know . . .'

'Shagging?'

'Yeah.'

'We were. Or sort of.'

'Sort of? What kind of shagging's that?' Yates opened one eye, waiting for an answer, but Dawn shook her head. The thing was over. That's all Bev needed to know. She'd spent a bit of time at Winter's, tried to sort herself out over Corbett and now she was back home again, happy never to see the bloody man again.

Yates thought about this for a moment, trying to disentangle what he really felt about Dawn, then decided it didn't matter. They'd been partners on countless jobs, shared cars, stake-outs, fuck-ups, monster bollockings from Cathy Lamb, the lot. Now, sitting in the sunshine on a Sunday afternoon, they might have been brother and sister. He fancied her, of course he did. Once or twice, especially recently, he'd even been tempted to make a move or two, stuffing the leaks in his little boat with something more real than the occasional porn mags that did the rounds in the CID office. At the moment, though, this was nice. Just conversation.

'You know something about Corbett?' he mused. 'The man's a maniac. He's got this thing about a bloke we've been after, ex-con. It now turns out the guy's in the clear but Corbett won't have it. Chases him around, real stalker job, trying to put him back in the frame. Won't leave it alone, won't take no for an answer. Sad, really. Know what I mean?'

The story drove the smile from Dawn's face. She wanted to know more.

'There isn't any more,' Yates said. 'He's bonkers. Deep space. Another galaxy. Take him to a psychiatrist and they'd section him.'

Dawn flinched at the phrase.

'But he doesn't give up. Is that what you're saying?'

'Yeah. In one.'

'Even when it's obvious? When' – she frowned, reaching for the rest of the sentence – 'there's no way he can ever get what he wants?'

'Exactly. Problem is, he looks pretty normal.'

'No.' She shook her head. 'It's worse than that. He looks great. Dresses the part. Drives a big black car *and* a monster bike. Talks the talk. Most women I know would be counting the days.'

'Like you did?'

'Yeah.' She gazed at the bottle in her hand, then shuddered. 'Like I did.'

'So what happened?'

'You don't want to know.'

'But I do, love. I do.'

'Then I'm not going to tell you.'

'Did he hurt you?' Yates was sitting bolt upright now, one hand over his eyes to shade out the sun. 'Physically, I mean?'

Dawn studied him a moment, then turned away.

'That's the wrong question. Physical I can handle. Physical's easy. It's the rest I find a bit tricky.'

'He did hurt you.'

She looked at him again, unblinking this time. Then she reached forward and took his hand.

'You should go,' she said softly. 'Before this gets really silly.'

'You mean that?'

'Yes.'

Yates eyed her, then swallowed the rest of his San Miguel and glanced at his watch. Nearly five.

'What about the carpet?'

'Fuck the carpet.' She let go of his hand. 'We'll sort the carpet some other time.'

Faraday was still in his office when J-J's e-mail arrived. Last time he'd seen the boy, first thing this morning, he'd been sprawled in bed, sound asleep. Now he was at his PC, updating Faraday on the latest addition to their crowded social diary. *Patti's coming down from London to see us*, it went. *Said she could stay the night. What do we do about dinner?*

Patti? For a moment, Faraday hadn't got a clue who J-J was talking about. Then he remembered the Ansel Adams exhibition and the battered Jiffy bag full of snaps J-J had toted back from the Hayward Gallery. Twenty-plus years ago, Patti had been Janna's best friend, a cheerful West Coast girl with a passion for downhill skiing and huge boxes of Belgian chocolates. What might two decades have done to that wide, wide smile?

Faraday had been trying to buy himself time for tomorrow's trip to the West Country. Wallace had given him a number for Dave Beattie. On the phone, the man had seemed happy to see him. Ezentide Cottage was a nightmare to find and Beattie's careful directions filled nearly a sheet of A4. The one-time Master-at-Arms was going out, but thought it was odds-on he'd be back by mid-morning, and in case he wasn't there was a spare front door key under a slate behind the summerhouse. Coffee in the cupboard over the stove. Yesterday's milk in the fridge. Only at the conversation's end did Faraday enquire how long he'd been out of the navy, a question that had drawn a soft laugh.

''Eighty-three,' he'd murmured. 'Couldn't wait.'

Now, hurrying through the paperwork that couldn't

wait until Tuesday, Faraday wondered what might have driven this seagoing policeman back into civvy street so soon after the Falklands. Coughlin, too, had lasted barely a year after *Accolade* went down.

En route home, Faraday stopped at the big twenty-four-hour Tesco at the top of the city. The fish counter looked tempting, but a long-buried memory told him that Patti had once been a veggie and the last thing he wanted to do was hazard what promised to be an interesting evening. With eggs, beansprouts, spring onions, limes, cucumber and a thick peanut sauce, he could put together a huge plate of gado-gado, an Indonesian salad that he and Janna had practically lived on during those first months in Seattle. Memories of the big open-air market down on Pike Place brought a smile to his face, and he ducked out of the check-out queue to add a two-pound box of Belgian truffles to the pile of goodies in his trolley.

Back home, Patti had already arrived. J-J, suspiciously organised, had settled her in the garden with a bowl of pistachios and a bottle of good Chablis he'd pre-cooled in the ice box. Standing unnoticed in the big lounge, Faraday watched the pair of them talking.

J-J rarely made any allowances for other people's unfamiliarity with sign, believing – often rightly – that there was a force and logic to gesture that demolished hang-ups about getting through to the deaf. In J-J's world, communication was party-time and in his view there was literally nothing – no nuance, no implication – that couldn't be transmitted through a bizarre and wholly personal repertoire that was closer to mime than classically taught sign. This was especially evident with people he liked, and watching them out in the sunshine, Faraday knew his boy had taken a very big shine to Patti. The pair of them were like boxers, leaning into a conversation that was wholly physical, all restraint abandoned in the race to make themselves understood. Party-time indeed.

Loath to disrupt this passionate exchange, Faraday

retreated to the fridge for a beer before joining them. Hearing the rumble of the big glass sliding doors, Patti froze, one arm raised, three fingers pointed skywards, turning in her chair to greet the figure emerging on to the lawn.

'Joe.' She got to her feet and ran across to give him a hug. Faraday held her for a moment, unaccountably overwhelmed, aware of J-J beaming at them both. Then he took a tiny step backwards, raising his glass in salute. Patti had taken to dyeing her hair blonde but otherwise this sturdy little woman was just the way he remembered her. Her face was still full of laughter and the passage of time had done nothing to dull the sparkle in her eye.

'Boy looking after you OK?' He gestured across at J-J. 'Only he normally hates strangers.'

The gado-gado was a big success. A huge high pressure system had settled over the southern half of the country, and the three of them ate around a table in the garden, aware of the warm darkness stealing towards them across the harbour.

Patti was entranced by the house and its setting. She was still in touch with Janna's parents, on the West Coast, and she'd seen some of the photos they'd brought back from their occasional visits. But no photo, she said, could possibly have done justice to an evening like this, and with J-J charged with clearing the table, she took Faraday by the arm and led him to the low hedge that fronted the towpath beside the harbour.

The moon was full tonight, a huge white orb the colour of clotted cream, and the rising spring tide lapped at the pebbles on the foreshore. When Faraday tried to take the conversation back to Seattle – remembered friends, familiar hang-outs – she put her finger to her lips, straining to distinguish the separate calls of birds out in the soft darkness.

'What's that? That flutey noise?'

'Curlew.'

'And that?'

'Lapwing. Some winter days, if you're really lucky, you get to see them all together, in flocks. They fly with this odd, flapping beat, so the whole flock seems to windmill across the sky. It's really bizarre, something you never forget.'

'So how come you know all this stuff?'

Faraday smiled down at her, oddly comforted by the question. Last time they'd met, half a lifetime ago, he couldn't have told a stilt from a woodpecker. More than that, he'd seen absolutely no point in peering into this strange hierarchy of feather and fowl, so interdependent, so artfully constructed, so utterly different to the me-first anarchy that now passed for society.

'It was the boy,' he said simply. 'We needed to get in touch with each other, build a bridge. I bumped into someone with the same challenge. Birds had worked for her so I gave it a go.'

'But J-J can't hear.' She gestured out at the harbour. From the darkness, again the haunting cry of a curlew.

'You're right. But that never seemed to matter. We started with pen and paper and loads of books from the library. He got to drawing up to three eagles an hour. That must have been a world record.'

'And you took it on from there?'

'Non-stop, every moment I could. Photos, magazines, videos, I even bought him a stuffed raven one Christmas.'

'Creepy.'

'I know. He loved it. He kept it on the bookcase in his bedroom. Used to talk to it in sign. Can you imagine that? An eight-year-old in his jim-jams? Last thing at night? The light off? Head to head with a stuffed raven?' Faraday laughed at the memory.

'What about the real thing? You take him places? Go scouting for these critters?'

'Of course.'

Faraday leaned against the gate, remembering their first birding expeditions, joint adventures to Titchfield Haven and the New Forest, J-J's bony little hand in his, a thousand pictures come to life. Up in his study, filed carefully away, were the notes and photos from those excursions. Bovver-boy nuthatches in the deep chill of winter. Parachuting meadow pipits in the first blush of spring. Long summer evenings playing games with the butterflying nightjars in a remote stretch of the New Forest they'd practically made their own.

'Great,' Patti kept murmuring. 'You've been a great dad.'

'You think so?'

'Definitely.'

'How can you tell?'

'By watching him. By being with him. By talking to him. He doesn't talk, I know, but he gets through just the same, maybe better than the rest of us. That says confidence to me. And confidence says great parenting. You should be proud of yourself. How many dads and sons have a relationship like this?'

Faraday ducked his head, suddenly ambushed by a thousand memories. Should he tell her about the tougher times? About the umpteen thoughtless cruelties inflicted by other kids, normal kids? About his six-year-old son abandoned on the beach by yelping playmates too busy to spare him the time? Should he describe those moments in early adolescence, the fourteen-year-old J-J bewildered by the changes in his body, no mum to talk to, no elder brother to compare notes with? And might this not be the moment to share the later dramas – J-J's dogged flirtation with factory work, the butt of every practical joker with too much time on his hands? And more recently his doomed love affair with a French social worker, a woman with a taste for more than one man in her bed? On each of these occasions J-J had squandered just a little more of his innocence and his passion for life, and if there was a miracle at all then it lay in the fact that he was still more or less intact, a rock which life's heavier waves seemed unable to budge.

'Sweet boy,' Faraday heard himself saying. 'But hopeless at washing up.'

Later, with the tall French windows still open, they sat in the lounge while J-J produced sheaf after sheaf of photos. Faraday was starting to wonder whether Patti's appetite for moody black and white landscapes might start to flag but she never showed a trace of impatience. On the contrary, image after image won her applause, praise that Faraday found all the more heartening because – in Patti's view – it led straight back to his dead wife.

The way J-J had framed the wreck of an old fishing smack, beached and abandoned on the mudflats across the harbour. The magic he'd conjured from the play of light on one of the freshwater ponds a stone's throw from the Bargemaster's House. Work like this, said Patti, was a voice from the past: distinctive, uncompromising, unmistakably Janna. The fact that it had survived in her son's viewfinder was a small down payment on immortality. The friend she still treasured from those madcap days in the seventies hadn't, after all, been wiped out by cancer. No, she was here, scattered all over the carpet, still speaking to them.

Faraday, who had little taste for excess, put this little outburst down to their third bottle of Chablis. Talk of immortality made him deeply uncomfortable.

'No.' Patti was perched on the edge of the sofa. 'I mean it. Ansel's long gone. Yet every time I pick up another of his shots, I can hear his voice. Take a look at some of the stuff from the Rockies, and he's there in the room with you. No kidding.'

She was on her feet now, scooping up a handful of J-J's prints. At the foot of the stairs, she picked one out, held it at arm's length. Three of Janna's photographs – Faraday's favourites – hung on the wall beside the staircase. Faraday narrowed his eyes. She was right. Same framing. Same compulsive need to marry acute observation with a dig in the ribs.

J-J, sprawled on the carpet, was spellbound. If ever he needed confirmation that his work mattered, that the hours in the darkroom had been worthwhile, then here it was.

Patti returned the prints to J-J. Faraday grinned at her.

'You ought to come over more often, my love.' He stole a glance at his watch. 'You do us no end of good.'

Nineteen

Faraday left early next morning, sinking three cups of tea and scribbling a goodbye note to Patti. Before she retired to bed, she'd presented Faraday with a little gift, a memento from their days together in Seattle. It was yet another photograph, Janna and the young Faraday posed against a distant frieze of snowclad mountains, and she'd mounted the snap in a plain wooden frame that J-J had instantly propped on the shelf where his dad kept his favourite spices. Faraday eyed it now before finishing the note. 'You've made a friend for life,' he wrote. 'And not just J-J.'

Out on the road, the traffic was already beginning to thicken ahead of the morning rush hour. Faraday joined the queue of commuter cars grinding up the motorway that sliced through Portsdown Hill, doing his best to ignore a gathering hangover. The weather was still perfect, the gleam of the Solent away to the left, and as the traffic slowed for the busy Gosport exit he wondered when it might be safe to put a call through to Bev Yates. Normally he would have taken Yates with him to Devon – two heads were always better than one – but it was Willard who had suggested going alone. With the Somerstown job still at full throttle, *Merriott* needed Yates back at base.

Faraday had nearly made Dorchester before he reached for the mobile. Eight o'clock in the morning, Bev should be readying himself for the drive to work. Faraday punched in the number, braking for yet another tractor. When the phone was finally answered, it was Melanie on the line. She sounded harassed. One of the kids was squalling in the background.

'Bev there?'

'In body, yes.'

'Quick word?'

There was a pause. The crying receded. Then the distant roar of a crowd, Bev next door tucked up with the early coverage.

'All right are we?'

'Don't ask. The US of A are beating South Korea. Any more of this and they'll win the fucking tournament.'

Faraday knew better than to pursue the conversation. Half an hour in a Gibraltar bar had cured him of any interest in football.

'Listen,' he said. 'That guy who used to be First Lieutenant in *Accolade*. The one who lives up round your way.'

'Mark Harrington?'

'That's him. Give him a bell first thing. Try and fix to meet.'

'He's up at the MoD.'

'I know. If he'll see you today, go and talk to him. He'll know about Coughlin. Press him on the boy, Warren. And another thing . . .'

'What's that, boss?'

'Ask him for a copy of that bloody report, the Ship's Investigation. We need to know exactly what happened.'

There was a longish silence, and for a moment Faraday wondered whether Yates, too, might be having second thoughts about the relevance of a long-ago war. Then came the roar from the crowd and Yates was back on the line.

'Friedal just stopped a penalty.' He began to laugh. 'Can you believe that?'

Winter spotted the car at once. He was standing in the front room, still in his dressing gown, debating whether or not to tackle the morning post. A council tax demand and a couple of other bills could certainly wait but a holiday brochure for packages in the Greek Islands looked promising. Given the events of the past few days, there might be worse things than a year or two tucked up in some villa on Santorini.

He moved across to the bay window and peered through the gap in the curtains. It was one of the Traffic cars, a marked Volvo, and he thought he recognised the bulky figure behind the wheel. One of the sergeants from Kingston Crescent. Not a good sign.

For a moment, he wondered about getting dressed but then decided against it. Better, at this stage, to play the invalid, the heroic detective who'd risked life and limb in the interests of justice. He checked the Volvo again. The sergeant was flipping through a sheaf of notes on a clipboard. At length, he opened the door and got out, and Winter stepped back behind the curtain as he glanced across at the bungalow before heading for the front gate.

'DC Paul Winter?'

On the doorstep, Winter rubbed his eyes and then stifled a yawn.

'Just got up.' He looked down at the clipboard. 'What's this, then?'

The sergeant studied him for a long moment. He was a squat, thickset man, the wrong side of forty. The frustrations of the job had emptied his face of everything except a stoic interest in the facts.

'The name's Leavis,' he grunted. 'Traffic. We may have met but I don't recall it.'

'And?'

'I understand you were involved in an incident.' He nodded at the plaster cast. 'We need to know what happened.'

'Is this a criminal investigation?'

'Yes.'

'What's the charge?'

'Dangerous driving. We can do it here, contemporaneous record. Or I can take you down the station. In which case we tape it.' He paused. 'You know the drill.'

Winter weighed his options for a moment, then shrugged and stood aside.

'Kitchen's through there,' he said. 'Be handy if you could put the kettle on.'

The sergeant made the tea while Winter ducked into the bathroom for a quick shave. Scraping away with his good hand, he watched his baggy face appear from the whorls of foam. Get the next half-hour wrong, he thought, and his case file would start its journey to the local branch of the Crown Prosecution Service. Worse than that, should a court case be pending he was now convinced that Hartigan would have him back in uniform.

'Sugar?'

'Two.' Winter settled into the chair by the fridge, easing his plaster cast on to the kitchen table. 'Keeping you busy, are they?'

The sergeant didn't answer. He passed Winter the cup and sat down before reciting the formal caution. Winter listened to the familiar phrases then helped himself to a chocolate digestive.

'No tea for you?'

'No, thanks.'

'Biscuit? Bacon sarnie? Only—'

'I said no.'

'OK, OK.' Winter held up his good hand. 'Just asking.'

The sergeant had buried himself in his notes. Winter, staring glumly at the RSPCA calendar on the wall above his head, wondered quite how far the investigation had progressed.

By now, the boffs from the investigation unit over at Winchester would have been to the scene of the accident and then crawled all over the remains of the Skoda, trying to back-calculate the exact sequence of events. On top of that, there might well have been witness statements, passers-by astonished to watch a portly man in his mid-forties turning the quieter reaches of Old Portsmouth into a race track. And as well, of course, there was Dawn Ellis.

The sergeant at last looked up, biro in hand.

'Let's start at the beginning,' he said. 'I understand you were on a job.'

'That's right. Down by the Camber. Little scrote called Darren Geech—' Winter broke off. There was something else he wanted to establish, right off, before he wasted any more of this busy man's time.

'What's that, then?'

'I don't remember any of this stuff too well.'

'Don't remember any of what stuff?'

'Exactly what happened. Don't ask me why. Maybe it was the concussion. Fact is, most of it's gone. Apart from the call, that is.'

'Call?'

'I seem to remember we put a call through to control. Request for a marked car? Isn't that the way we do it?'

'You remember the call but you can't remember chasing the lad?'

'I can't remember anything after he spotted us – and even that's foggy.' He looked regretfully up at the ceiling. 'Red motor? Astra? VW? Yellow? Blue?'

The sergeant sat back. The biro had come to a halt. He gestured at his notepad.

'This isn't much use then, is it?'

'Probably not.'

'You want to have a go?'

'Up to you. I'm just here to help.'

The sergeant gave him a sour look.

'I checked with the hospital,' he said carefully, 'and they told me you'd make a complete recovery.'

'They were talking about this.' Winter lifted his arm

from the table, wincing as he did so. 'And I just hope they're right.'

'They never mentioned amnesia.'

'I'm not surprised. I never told them.'

'You never told them? You never wondered what had happened? How you'd got there?'

'It wasn't that. I knew I'd been driving a car and I knew something had gone wrong because – bang – there I am in some newsagent's fucking lap. But you ask me what happened between the OP and the ambulance and I have to tell you I haven't a clue. Sad, I know. But true.'

The sergeant didn't bother to mask his disbelief. 'No comment' would have been more acceptable than a piss-take like this. For a moment, Winter thought he was going to have a real go. Instead, he glanced at his watch.

'You know the drill from here on? Preparing the case file? Submitting it to the CRS? Deciding whether or not to press charges?'

'Yeah, of course.'

'And you know the view that judges take over obstructive defendants?'

'Of course. Occupational hazard. Pain in the arse for all of us.'

'Just thought I'd mention it, Mr Winter. Might be germane, that's all.'

He gave Winter another look, then drew the notepad towards him again.

'I'm going to write it your way,' he grunted. 'I'm going to say you remember the beginning and the end but have absolutely no recall of anything in between. Fair?'

'Spot on.'

'Good.'

The sergeant sorted a statement form from his clip-board, checked the date on his watch, then began to write. After a couple of lines of careful script, he suddenly looked up.

'That bus, by the way. The doubler-decker down by the Hard. The one you nearly hit.'

Winter gazed at him for a moment, then offered a bemused grin.

'Bus?' he queried.

It was barely mid-morning by the time Faraday got to Plymouth. Dave Beattie's directions unfolded on his lap, he picked his way through the northern suburbs, following the road to Tavistock. There were bubbles of cloud now, away over the distant swell of the moor, and the weather forecast on Radio Four was talking about the possibility of rain before nightfall.

Beyond Bickleigh, he slowed for a turn to the left, astonished at how quickly the city had disappeared. Barely ten minutes from the urban tangle of roundabouts and Londis stores, they were in a world that might have belonged to a different age: lush green fields; dry-stone walls yellowed with moss and lichen; even the glimpse of a buzzard, riding the thermals above a nearby tor.

The road narrowed, then plunged abruptly to the right. Trees on either side splashed the windscreen with shafts of livid sunlight. Winding down his window, Faraday could hear the suck and gurgle of running water. Soon came a bridge, impossibly narrow, and a glimpse of sleek brown pebbles on the riverbed, then the road was climbing again, the trees beginning to thin. From time to time, a bend surprised him, revealing a bungalow hunkered down behind a thickly-hedged bank, or a hint of something more substantial beyond the drifts of cow parsley. From time to time, he saw signs for nurseries, directions in fading blues and yellows that seemed to point nowhere. Rarely had he been somewhere that felt so reclusive, so shut away. This, he thought, was a landscape that turned its back on you, determined to keep its secrets.

Minutes later, realising he was lost, he stopped the car.

A signpost indicated Bere Ferrers, three miles. He drove on, meaning to stop for a decent map. Untangling an area like this with a page of scribbled notes was hopeless.

Bere Ferrers turned out to be a tiny village beside a wide stretch of river. Faraday parked the Mondeo and walked to the water's edge. Returning to the car for his binoculars, he swept the glistening mud flats, tallying cormorant, shelduck and common sandpiper, realising that this was the place that Scottie had mentioned the first time he'd dropped into Faraday's office. Something large and slightly comic caught his eye, standing rigidly to attention beside the eelgrass on the far side of the river. Grey heron, he thought. Then came a flurry of movement, much closer. A pair of wagtails, brilliant yellow, flycatching like mad. Faraday tracked them for a moment through the binos then turned away, a wistful smile on his face. What a place to live.

The village stores lay at the back of a hairdressing salon. Faraday bought an Ordnance Survey map, returned to the car and flattened it on the bonnet. Transferring Beattie's directions to the web of tiny roads, he finally tracked Ezentide Cottage to a stretch of river a couple of miles upstream. He refolded the map and checked his watch. Just time for a little stroll.

A footpath took him up through the churchyard. The weathered granite headstones spoke of generations of families, bloodlines stretching centuries back. One, in particular, brought him to a halt. 'Cholera,' it said simply, '1849.'

Fascinated, Faraday walked on. The path left the churchyard and climbed a nearby hill. More breathless than he cared to admit, Faraday got to the top. Miles away to the south, hazy in the distance, lay a wide stretch of water surrounded on both sides by the dark sprawl of Plymouth. Through the binoculars, he could make out towering blocks of flats, tiny church spires, huge dockyard gantry cranes, and street after street of terraced housing. Pompey, he thought at once. The same huddled lives. The same post-war clutter. The same echoes of spilled blood and hard-won treasure.

He racked the focus on the binoculars, quartering the water. The distinctive coathanger humps of Brunel's bridge lay at the farther end, but closer he could make out the sleek grey shapes of warships at anchor in the tideway. Similar vessels dotted the upper harbour at Portsmouth, frigates and destroyers put out to grass pending some unimaginable catastrophe that might coax them back to sea, and Faraday found himself wondering whether any of these ships might be relics from the Falklands War. Did Dave Beattie ever climb this hill? With a memory or two and a good pair of binos?

Back in the car, Faraday drove north again. Within minutes, aware that he was getting a feel for this shy little patch of God's England, he was back on track. The peninsula lay between two rivers. The biggest of them was the Tamar. On the map, Ezentide Cottage appeared beside the blue, fat, sinuous line of the river, miles from anywhere, a tiny black oblong at the end of a single-track road.

Faraday drove on. The road began to narrow again until there was barely room for the car. More cow parsley. A farmyard or two. Then – slowly – all signs of habitation began to disappear. Minutes later, still bathed in sunshine, Faraday found himself looking at a five-barred gate. Carefully wired to the gate, a sign hand-lettered in red.

'Keep Out. Private.'

Faraday pushed at the gate and returned to the Mondeo. A track swung in beneath thick stands of spruce and pine. The ground fell away to the right, and at the first bend Faraday glimpsed the rusting, upturned body of an old Cavalier, wedged against the bottom of a tree. He was in shade now, and with the window down the air felt cold and damp. Two more bends, and the track petered out. To the left, quarried into the hillside, was a levelled patch of beaten black earth that clearly served as a kind of makeshift car park.

Locking the Mondeo, Faraday gazed down at the thickness of wheeltracks in the loamy earth. A four-wheel drive of some kind, maybe a Land-Rover. Still carrying the binos, Faraday followed a path down through the trees. The cottage came as a surprise, appearing suddenly as the path veered to the left: slate roof, newly white-washed elevations, tiny recessed windows. The garden in front of the cottage stretched down to the water's edge, a patchwork of carefully cropped lawn, shrub-filled borders and – beyond a timber summerhouse – a sizeable veggie patch.

Faraday shook his head, overwhelmed by the isolation, the peace, that this man had created for himself. The cottage was overhung on three sides by trees, yet facing south the front of the cottage was flooded with sunshine. Beyond the slow, green drift of the river, more trees. Could life get any better than this?

It could.

On the far side of the cottage, Faraday found half a dozen chickens in a coop, counted four fresh eggs tucked carefully into a bucket lined with straw, caught the scent of freshly sawn timber from a pile of newly stacked logs beside the back door, knelt to tickle the chin of a pink-nosed tabby, sprawled in the sunshine. In another life, unshackled from the Pompey underworld, Faraday would kill for a place like this.

When he couldn't raise anyone at the front door, he strolled back down the garden. The key, as promised, was under a pile of spare slates to the rear of the summerhouse. With it, black capital letters, was a note. 'Make yourself at home. Little grebe (if you're lucky). Back by lunchtime. DB.'

Faraday, amused, went to the water's edge. Beattie was right. Little grebe were notoriously hard to find. Stand here for hours and he'd be lucky to spot them. Stand here for days and even then they might never appear. But that wasn't the point. How on earth had Beattie known about his passion for birding in the first place?

Winter's call found Bev Yates in Faraday's office at Kingston Crescent. He had a list of *Accolade* interviews as long as your arm to do and so far he was making fuck all progress. Blokes at work. Blokes away on holiday. Blokes too idle to get out of bed to even answer the phone. The job was never in any danger of getting easier, but this one in particular was proving a real bastard.

'Where's Faraday, then?'

'Off to Devon somewhere. Gleam in the eye.'

'Again?'

''Fraid so. How's life on the dole?'

'Very funny. I need to talk to you about Dawn.'

Winter wanted to know whether Yates had been round to Dawn's place. Yates grunted, noncommittal, trying to suss Winter's angle. Was he after gossip? Had he baited some kind of trap? Or might this simply be a courtesy call?

'She's fine,' he said simply. 'As far as I know.'

'Back at work? Only I tried to phone her.'

'No idea, mate.'

There was a long pause. Winter normally hated silence.

'You wouldn't happen to know . . . ah . . .'

'Know what?'

'. . . whether she's had any kind of session with those pillocks from Traffic?'

'Why would she have done that?'

'Because they're trying to stitch me up.'

'Ah.' Yates was smiling now. 'Gotcha.'

He gazed up at Faraday's wall board, wondering how a grown man could live with pictures of birds all his life, then told Winter he was clueless about what Dawn got up to off-duty.

'Really?'

'Yeah.' Yates was enjoying this. 'Really.'

'You didn't talk to her yesterday afternoon?'

'I might have done.'

'And she didn't mention anything about Traffic?'

'Definitely not.'

'Then do us a favour, eh? If you see her, tell her I can't remember a thing. OK?' He paused, then chuckled. 'That's the least you bloody owe me.'

Faraday let himself into the cottage, struck at once by the shadowed bareness of the place. A single worn rug on the cold slate floor. Rough granite walls glittering with mica. A tiny pile of ashes in the fire-blackened hearth. Faraday stood motionless in the gloom for a moment, remembering the CCTV tapes at the Naval Home Club. The function over, a tiny group of *Accolades* had gathered outside on the street. The lean, fit-looking figure in the leather jacket spoke of independence and a certain raw austerity, and if Faraday wanted any more evidence of the life this man had made for himself then here it was.

He looked around, aware of the cat winding itself around his ankles. There were books piled on one of the deeply recessed window sills, pages flagged with strips of torn newsprint. An abandoned copy of the *Guardian*, three days old, lay on the floor beside a battered-looking sofa and there was a saucer of fresh milk, presumably for the cat. Next door, in the narrow little kitchen, Faraday found a single mug upturned on the drainer beside the sink.

There were two other rooms downstairs. One was a bathroom – shower, tub, airing cupboard, plus a single toothbrush in the glass beside the handbasin – while the other room obviously served as some kind of study. There was a desk jammed in beneath the window with a PC and keyboard on top. A reminder list was Scotch-taped to the PC screen and an adjoining trolley held a cardboard box full of files. Below the trolley, tucked against the wall, Faraday caught the dull gleam of a bottle. Famous Grouse. Half empty.

Faraday returned to the screen, peering at the list. The office was at the back of the house and the place was in semi-darkness, but Faraday could make out a number of what he took to be addresses. Each had a date and a sum of money beside it and Faraday began to wonder whether Beattie was making a living as some kind of tradesman. A plumber perhaps, or a carpenter. Stepping back from the desk, he was about to leave the room when his attention was caught by a framed photo hung on the wall. Even in the gloom, the picture was unmistakable. Beattie might have baled out of the navy nearly twenty years ago but in the shape of this single, unforgettable image, the Falklands War had stayed with him. HMS *Accolade*, on fire and sinking, 21 May 1982.

Winter had known Mick Clarence for years. As a young lad growing up on the Somerstown estate, he'd served a successful apprenticeship as shoplifter, housebreaker and occasional arsonist. By eleven, he'd learned four ways of nicking any number of vehicles from Transit vans to upmarket continental saloons, and his hot-wiring skills were in demand with older kids in a position to put serious money his way.

At the age of fourteen, with nearly two thousand quid in a Lidl bag under his mattress, Mick had treated his mum and himself to a fortnight on the Costa Brava. He'd done it on a whim, partly because he fancied the word 'Brava' and partly because he knew something horrible was going on with his mum. As it happened, Lloret de Mar was the very last place she should ever have gone. His mum's alcoholism was totally out of control and three solid days at the hotel bar robbed her of any interest in survival. A man she'd never met before carried her back to her tenth-floor hotel room, raped her, then sat her on the balcony wall before disappearing into the night. According to the local authorities, Elaine Clarence died the moment she hit the faux-marble walkway round the pool.

Back in Somerstown, Mick went to the police. The first detective he met was Winter. He explained what had happened to his mum and begged Winter for some action. Winter did his best, but in the absence of evidence the Spanish authorities said they could do very little. The man must have worn a condom because there was no DNA. And – with the exception of Mick – no witnesses. The boy had been insensible on San Miguel and Bacardi chasers at the time, and with a long list of juvenile offences to his name he'd be an easy target if it ever got to court.

This realisation changed the boy's life. Overnight, incandescently angry, he turned his back on a promising criminal career. He gave up drinking, became obsessional about drugs, hospitalised a slightly older youth he caught giving a couple of Asians a hard time. His one-time mates were baffled by this Robin Hood act but Mick Clarence didn't care. When Anghared Davies, who ran the city's Persistent Young Offender scheme, enquired whether he was interested in coming on board, he leapt at the invitation. Now, nearly seven years later, he was still there, tagged as a Youth Worker, one of the very few grown-ups that errant Pompey kids would ever listen to.

Winter met him at a café in Elm Grove. Wiry, aggressive, crop-haired and watchful, he was indistinguishable from the delinquents and other assorted mushers who were currently swamping the magistrates' court.

Winter slipped a handful of photographs from an envelope. Mick Clarence had never seen the point of small talk.

Now, he glanced at the photos. Turned out they were all the same.

'Geech,' he said.

Winter nodded. He'd been pleased with the digital prints. The bruising showed up nicely, purple shading into black.

'You know what happened?'

'Someone gave him a smacking.'

'Yeah, you're right, but d'you know who?'

'Haven't a clue, mate.'

'Bazza Mackenzie.'

'Really?' Clarence picked up the top print and studied it more closely. For the first time, a flicker of interest. Then his head came up, eyes that never blinked. 'Why?'

Winter kept the explanation brief. Young Darren had been dealing for Bazza. Then had come the run-in with Rookie. Darren, his street-cred at stake, had rounded up a mate or two and given the bastard a battering. By going over the top, and killing the man, he'd seriously embarrassed some of Winter's more senior colleagues. Fire-bombing the house of a serving CID officer, whatever the justification, was the boy's second big mistake. Unable to collar young Darren, Major Crimes were about to turn their attention to Bazza himself. Bazza, less than amused, had consequently gone looking for Darren. Hence the pile of horror pix on the café table.

'You mean he's delivered the little cunt?'

'Yeah.' Winter nodded. 'After a word or two in his ear.'

'So what's the problem?'

'Darren's still facing a murder charge.'

'So go ahead. You know where he is. Charge him.'

'We can't. There's no evidence. We've recovered stuff from his mum's place but she's still blaming it on another kid.'

'Like who?'

'Won't say.'

Clarence hadn't taken his eyes off Winter's face. The perfect detective, Winter thought. Scary as hell.

'You want me to push these round?' Clarence's tattooed hand closed on the pile of prints.

'Yeah. You'll know the names, Darren's mates, the ones who were with him when he did Rookie. Give them a copy each. Tell them Bazza is still itching to sort out Darren's little gang. And then explain how cool it might be to make a statement or two.'

'About what?'

'Darren thumping Rookie.'

'That's grassing.'

'No, it's not.' For the first time Winter smiled. 'Let's call it self-preservation.'

Bev Yates finally got through to Mark Harrington just before noon. *Accolade*'s First Lieutenant had been top of his call list since nine. Now a captain with a desk in the Ministry of Defence, he'd so far resisted the temptation to phone Yates back.

Until now.

Yates was still in Faraday's office. The pad at his elbow was full of names ringed, ticked, or savagely scored through. To date, Yates had managed to arrange just five interviews with *Accolade*s from Monday night.

The phone to his ear, Yates explained the reason for the call. A Major Crimes team were investigating the death of a serving prison officer. Sean Coughlin had once been in the navy. They had reason to suspect a possible connection with an incident aboard HMS *Accolade*, back in 'eighty-two. Captain Harrington might be able to shed some light on this incident. Might he have time for a brief interview?

'I don't understand,' Harrington said at once. 'What kind of incident?'

Yates mentioned Matthew Warren. There was a silence, then Harrington was as measured and business-like as ever.

'I'm not quite with you,' he said.

'We understand Warren disappeared over the side.'

'That's right, he did. Unfortunate to say the least, poor kid. We did our best to find him, of course, but these things happen. Bloody tragic, actually, though I suppose he was spared what followed.'

Yates repeated his request for an interview. Half an hour, max.

'When?'

'This afternoon?' Yates glanced at his watch. 'I can be with you by three.'

'No can do, I'm afraid. Meetings all afternoon.'

'This evening, then?'

'I'm off to Leicester.'

'Tomorrow?'

'Stafford. Then Stoke-on-Trent. I'm on the Recruiting Directorate. You won't believe how understaffed we are.'

Join the club, Yates thought. He pushed the pad away, his patience suddenly exhausted.

'I understand there was a Ship's Investigation into Warren's death.'

'Of course. Standard procedure.'

'So there'd be an official report, something in writing.'

'Undoubtedly.'

'We don't seem able to access it.'

'Really . . . ?' Harrington strung the word out. For the first time, Yates imagined a smile on his face. There was a long silence. Then Harrington was back on the phone. 'Listen. Best I can do is make some enquiries. It won't be today and probably not tomorrow but I'll give you a call back. How does that sound?'

Fucking useless, Yates thought, but the line had already gone dead.

Twenty

Dave Beattie returned to the cottage shortly before noon. Faraday, alerted by the approaching growl of a diesel engine, stepped towards the window with his second mug of coffee, watching an ancient Land-Rover bumping down the track between the trees. Parked-up, Beattie got out. With him was an Alsatian dog. The pair of them paused to examine Faraday's Mondeo, then made their way towards the cottage.

Beattie seemed smaller than Faraday remembered from the CCTV tapes, a lean, slight figure in grubby shorts and a torn blue T-shirt. The T-shirt was blotched with sweat and he paused by the garden gate to stamp the muck and dust from his boots. Glancing up again, the sunshine caught his face. It was an outdoors face, a face weathered by hard physical work. Faraday guessed his age at early fifties, maybe a year or two older. His greying hair was drawn back, a ponytail secured with a rubber band, and he wore a tiny gold earring.

They met at the door. Beattie's handshake was dry and firm. The dog sniffed Faraday up and down while Beattie clumped through to the kitchen. A blast of water from the tap, then the sound of the electric kettle being filled.

'How did you know about the birds?' Faraday had propped himself against the jamb of the kitchen door.

'I gave Derek Grisewood a call. After we talked on the phone.'

'Checking me out?'

'Of course. He said you were all right. Apparently you'd been discussing birds with him.'

Faraday nodded. Grisewood was the manager at the Home Club in Pompey.

Beattie busied himself with a jar of Maxwell House. He wanted to know the purpose of Faraday's visit. Just what was he after?

On the phone, Faraday had simply referred to a major inquiry. Now, he began to talk about Monday night.

'Does the name Coughlin ring any bells? Sean Coughlin?'

'Yeah. Killick chef aboard *Accolade*. We were only talking about him the other day. Arsehole, if you want the truth.'

'So I gather. Maybe that's why he's dead.'

'Dead?' Faraday's news put the ghost of a smile on Beattie's face. 'You mean someone whacked him?'

'Yes.'

'You're serious?'

'Absolutely.'

'You've got a squad on it?'

'Obviously.'

'So how's it going?'

Faraday didn't answer. Instead, he suggested they talk next door, somewhere more comfortable. Beattie followed him into the big living room, settling himself on the sofa with the dog curled beside him. Faraday retrieved his mug from the window sill and took the other armchair.

'I want to talk about *Accolade*,' he began. 'And what happened in the Falklands.'

Beattie frowned. A conversation like this appeared to be the last thing he expected.

'The Falklands was a bummer,' he said. 'We lost the ship.'

'I know.'

'Sure you know. Everyone knows. It's history. It's in all the books. What you don't know is what it feels like.'

'Felt like?'

'Feels like.' Beattie took a long pull at the coffee. 'Something as big as that, you never forget it.'

'Is that why you went to the reunion last Monday night?'

'Yeah.' He looked at the dog. 'Yeah.'

'And that brings it all back?'

'Of course.'

Faraday let the silence grow and grow. From way down the valley, he thought he caught the clatter of a train. At length, he asked why Beattie had left the navy so soon after the Falklands.

'Who told you that?'

'Wallace. The association secretary.'

'What else did he say?'

'He said you'd baled out sharpish. Lost your taste for it.'

'Then you've got your answer.' He nodded. 'I thought you were interested in Coughlin?'

'I am.'

'Then why all this personal stuff?'

Faraday studied him for a second or two. It was a fair question and he saw no point in not admitting the truth.

'Because I'm fascinated,' he said. 'I've never been here in my life. For two pins I'd never go back.' He paused. 'You've been here long?'

Beattie shot him a quizzical look, then ran a finger round the top of his mug. Plainly, Faraday's question was more complex than it sounded.

'Nearly twenty years,' he said at last. 'We were living down in Guzz before, me and the missus. I used to take the kids up here on the boats they run in the summer. I'd seen this place often. You pass it on the way to Morwellham. It was a real wreck.' The memory put a bigger smile on his face. He glanced across at Faraday, then eased the dog off his lap and got up. 'You want to see it? The way it was?'

Without waiting for an answer, he stamped upstairs.

Faraday heard footsteps overhead. Then Beattie was down again, back on the sofa, leafing through a big photo album.

'Here.' He passed the album to Faraday. 'That was the first summer. This time of year. 1983.'

Faraday found himself looking at a building site. The cottage was barely recognisable, scaffolded on two sides, and the garden had disappeared beneath stacks of timber, a small mountain of sand, and carefully sorted piles of slates. A cement mixer stood beside the open front door, a wheelbarrow parked on the plank that led inside.

'You sort all this yourself?'

'Had to. Leaving the navy when I did, I never got the full pension. Plus I'd split up with my missus. Divorce isn't cheap, believe me.'

'So you were living here, as well?' Faraday turned the page. Gaping windows, waiting for new frames. An old tarpaulin, secured with ropes, where the roof had once been.

'Yeah. Took the best part of two years. We managed it in the end, though.'

'We?'

'Me and Rory.' Beattie looked down at the dog and gave it a pat. 'This one's her son, Rory Two, and even he's getting on now. Rory One came from the RSPCA. Useless guard dog but great company. We mainly got by on Welsh rarebit and bean stew. On good days, I might shoot the odd pigeon.'

'What about money?'

'I'd started a little business, just to make ends meet when the bills piled up. Couple of days a week to begin with.'

'Doing what?'

'Gardening.' He nodded at the album. 'Take a look.'

Faraday turned the page. As the cottage slowly emerged from the chaos of those two years, other shots began to intrude: gardens of all sizes, enormous lawns, tiny borders, rows of runner beans, immaculately staked. Occasionally Beattie himself would appear, bent over a spade or filling a watering can, eyeing the camera. Beneath the deep tan, he looked wary and ill-at-ease. Life as a divorcee plainly had its problems.

'You liked it here?'

'Loved it. It was hard at first, like nothing I'd done before, but it gave me what I wanted. The place itself is amazing. Winter, you needn't ever see a soul.'

'And that suited you?'

'Then it did. Now it's just habit. You know something?' He gestured towards his own garden, and the river beyond. 'This valley used to be the Klondike. Hundred years ago, they were digging every bloody thing out of the hills, copper, arsenic, you name it. Stuff went out on barges, down to Guzz, then was shipped off round the world. Miners walked here from West Cornwall, thousands of them, brought their families, made their fortunes. It's all gone now but you can still feel it sometimes. This valley's full of ghosts.'

Ghosts?

Faraday's eye had settled on another shot in the album. Time must have passed because Beattie was looking older, and infinitely more relaxed. He was posed against a backdrop of an exquisitely terraced garden. He had a glass of something bubbly in his hand, while his other arm was draped around a much younger man.

Faraday showed him the picture.

'That's Johnno, my oldest. Still lives in Guzz but helps me out on some of the jobs. That was a couple of years back. Bloke was really chuffed with the garden.'

Faraday remembered the files stacked next door on the office desk. Twenty years of hard labour had obviously paid off. He glanced up, more intrigued than ever by the life this man had made for himself. What wouldn't he give, he thought, for fresh air, silence, and the promise of a good night's sleep?

'Soil good?'

'South-facing, it is. It's moist round here, lots of rain and lots of sunshine. Fruits crop well. You have to watch for arsenic, though, the tailings they left. I could take you places where nothing will ever grow.'

He got to his feet, checked his watch, then drained the last of the coffee. One o'clock, he was due at a pub in Calstock to pick up a cheque. Smalltalk was getting them nowhere. Whatever Faraday was after, now was the time.

Faraday was still leafing through the photo album. Finally, he looked up.

'How about I buy you lunch?'

They went in Beattie's Land-Rover, the old dog wedged between them. The back was full of cuttings and potted shrubs, plants destined for Beattie's current project, and as they bumped up the narrow lane towards the cross-roads at the top, Faraday wondered about the realities of living in a spot this remote. You'd need to be on good terms with yourself, he thought. You'd need to know who you really were.

Calstock was a scruffy collection of houses climbing up the valley beside an impressive-looking railway viaduct. Beattie described it as a village that had never quite managed to become a town, and hinted at a certain degree of lawlessness. Calstock, he said, was the last refuge for hard-core sixties hippies, plus a small army of assorted no-hopers, and gazing out at the narrow-fronted terrace houses, Faraday could believe him. Round one corner, a stained mattress lay abandoned on the pavement. Round the next, someone had spray-canned 'Legalise Smack' across the notice board outside the Methodist Church Hall.

The pub lay beside the river. Clouds were building to the west but the sun was still strong and Faraday elected for a table on the terrace overlooking the river. He bought himself a pint and a packet of crisps and left Beattie to collect his cheque. Downstream, he could see a modest line of yachts, swinging in the tide. Immediately below him, where the muddy water lapped against the pilings, three mallard were quarrelling over the remains of a bread roll.

Bev Yates was still at Kingston Crescent when Faraday finally got through.

'What's been happening?' he asked.

Yates updated him on the *Accolade*s interviews. He'd now managed to get through to more than a dozen survivors from the anniversary dinner and planned to start the interviews this afternoon. One of them sounded especially promising.

'Who's that?'

'Bloke called Gault. Says he knew the boy Warren really well. Took him under his wing.'

'And Coughlin?'

'Knew him, too. Usual story. Complete cunt.'

'Where is this Gault?'

'189 Glasgow Road.'

'*Pompey?*'

'Yeah.'

'And he was at the do on Monday?'

'Yeah. Pal of your bloke, Beattie. Gault was a cook in the navy. Works in the Harvester now, over on the Eastern Road. I couldn't get any more out of him because he was so busy.'

'You've fixed to interview him?'

'Tonight. Mel's going to love it. I'm blaming it on you.'

Faraday smiled to himself. Yates went through the rest of the list. When he got to Mark Harrington, the First Lieutenant, Faraday broke in again. He wanted to know when Yates anticipated the return call.

'It won't happen. I'll put money on it. It's a family thing. We're not welcome.'

'Family thing? Kid going over the side? Suspicious death?'

'Who says it's suspicious?'

'Me . . .' Faraday had spotted what might have been another buzzard, high over the wooded flanks of the valley. 'But you're right. I can't prove it.'

Yates rang off shortly afterwards, leaving Faraday wishing he hadn't left his binoculars at the cottage. For high summer, the pub felt deserted, just a couple of tables occupied. Brilliant, thought Faraday, leaning back in the sunshine and closing his eyes.

Seconds later, the door from the bar banged open and Faraday found himself looking at a middle-aged Hell's Angel, big as a house, with a pint in one hand and a couple of pasties wrapped in napkins in the other. Bare-chested under a filthy denim waistcoat, he commandeered the table next to Faraday. With him was a girl, no more than seventeen. She was blonde and pretty and the cut of her T-shirt left absolutely nothing to the imagination. The side of her neck was livid with love-bites. She settled within touching distance of Faraday and kicked off her sandals. For a moment or two, he put the giggles down to high spirits. Then he realised she was drunk.

Her partner swallowed half the lager, then asked her which way had been best. The girl told him she didn't care. Up the arse, oral, it was all the same to her. She stuck her tongue out and giggled again. The tip of her tongue was pierced, a tiny silver ball nestling amongst the pink folds. She nodded at the biker's ample crotch.

'What about you, then? Fucking loved it, didn't you?'

'Yeah.'

He began to review their morning in bed. Faraday, aware of two elderly women three tables away, shot him a warning look. The biker broke off and stood up. Seconds later, he was looming over Faraday, grease-stained jeans, studded belt, scuffed Doc Martens. Monday morning clearly didn't extend to soap and water.

'You got a problem?'

'Yes. I have.'

'Something get up your nose?'

'Definitely.'

'Like what?'

'You.' Faraday shielded his eyes from the sun. 'You want to compare notes, you should have stayed in bed. You think anyone else is interested in your love life?'

The biker said nothing for a moment. Then a shadow fell over the table as Beattie stepped between them. He eased the biker away, backed him against a window, began to talk very softly in his ear. There was a stillness about Beattie that it was impossible to miss. In situations like these, you'd be foolish not to listen very hard. Faraday caught the word 'fuckwit' before the girl abandoned her drink, grabbed her boyfriend by the arm, and dragged him towards the exit at the end of the terrace.

Beattie sat down.

'Guy's a clown,' he said. 'Means no harm.'

'Really?'

'Yeah. We had words about something else recently. Good as gold as long as you know which buttons to press.'

'Job teach you that?' Faraday realised that he was shaking.

'Yes.' Beattie produced two menus. 'As a matter of fact, it did.'

They had seafood salad with an enormous helping of chips. Faraday, more grateful to Beattie than he liked to admit, insisted on apple pie afterwards and a second pint to wash it down. When he asked Beattie about the realities of being a policeman at sea, the nuts and bolts of the job, the one-time Master-at-Arms gave the question some thought.

'Most of it was being ahead of the game,' he said at

last. 'You've got to tune in, get to know all the buzzes. Every mess was different, different feel, but if you got a handle on the blokes you could spot where the trouble would come from.'

Most of the messes, he said, preferred to sort out problems on their own. Blokes caught stealing, for instance, would be discreetly seen to. Favourite for theft was a heavy steel hatch dropped on the bloke's hand. Broken bones, for sure. Very Saudi.

'Did that make life easier for you?'

'Definitely. I was the official bit of the navy. If it got as far as me, it was normally down in writing. I was Mr Nasty.'

'And Mr Fair?'

'Sometimes. Most skates are good blokes if you give them a bit of a shake. Only once in a blue moon would you come across a monster.'

'Coughlin?'

'A monster.'

Beattie had been warned in advance about the killick chef. A mate of his had been Master-at-Arms on Coughlin's previous ship, a Type 42, and had sent him a brief précis of the delights in store. Amongst the adjectives Beattie remembered were 'devious', 'disloyal', 'nasty' and 'infatuated'.

'Infatuated, how?'

'With himself, his own importance. My mate swore blind Coughlin thought he was Mr Exceptional – great seaman, great cook, great human being – and my mate was right. The fact Coughlin was also an arsehole never seemed to have occurred to him. Funny that. With those kinds of blokes it never does.'

Faraday pushed his plate to one side. Something had snagged in his memory.

'Coughlin used the name Freckler on the internet,' he said. 'Why Freckler?'

Beattie glanced round, then beckoned Faraday closer.

'It's a mess game,' he said. 'Involves human waste. You wouldn't want to know the rest.'

'And Coughlin played this game?'

'Pig in shit. Literally.'

'Friends?'

'None. There were people who were frightened of him, definitely. He had a reputation for losing it, often for no good reason, and you wouldn't want to be around when that happened. That was the shame of it, of course. A ship like that, two hundred blokes, you need to get along.'

Faraday nodded, thoughtful. This was Wallace's account, word for word. Serve alongside Coughlin and you'd never forget it.

'Enemies?' Faraday said at last. 'Blokes with a grudge? Blokes who might have been in Pompey on Monday night?'

For the first time, Faraday felt Beattie's foot touch the brake. So far, he'd been happy to talk about facts. Now Faraday was inviting speculation.

'That's difficult.' Beattie began to toy with the remains of his apple pie. 'There wasn't a bloke on that ship who wouldn't have sent Coughlin home by the next post. But that's not the same as murder.'

The two men studied each other. Then Faraday mentioned Matthew Warren. The boy had gone overboard. No one seemed to know how or why. Faraday had evidence from other sources that he'd been involved somehow or other with Coughlin, same mess, same galley. Was it stretching credulity to speculate about some kind of link between this relationship and Warren's abrupt disappearance?

Beattie took a while to frame an answer. Then he balled his serviette and tossed it into a nearby bin.

'I'm due a meet at half two.' He got to his feet. 'You're welcome to come along.'

*

334

They drove back to the cottage, Beattie working his mobile, calling clients, ordering fertiliser and building materials, putting a call through to his son. He had a big job on just now, the biggest he'd ever tackled, and if he got it right then there'd be more of the same kind of work. Ideally, he'd bin the little jobs, leaving himself a raft of two or three contracts to carry him through the year. That way, he could at last make time for the book he was trying to complete.

'Book?' Faraday was astonished.

'Yeah.'

'About what?'

'This.' They were close to the river again, plunging down yet another narrow track, the water shimmering through the blur of trees. 'The valley. The past. The stuff I mentioned this morning. The guys who fed the lime kilns. The women who broke the ore. The miners who worked the really deep pits. The bargees. What those people must have gone through.'

'And you think there's a market for a book like that?'

'Fuck knows.' He flashed Faraday a sudden grin. 'Who cares?'

At the cottage, Beattie collected a bundle of files from the office. Once a month he took all his receipts and invoices to a lady in the village who'd do his books for him. He slipped the files into a plastic bag, called for the dog, locked the door of the cottage, and then set off along a path that skirted the back of the property before disappearing into the woods. It was suddenly colder here, and Faraday could smell the peaty, slightly sour breath of rotting leaf mould. Beattie moved fast, the dog bounding ahead, following the track as it wound upwards, climbing away from the river. From time to time the dog would raise a covey of birds – pigeons, the odd pheasant – and Faraday wondered what else might be tucked away in this chilly gloom. Was this where the buzzards nested?

'There.' Beattie had stopped.

Faraday followed his pointing finger. Amongst the thickets of bramble and stands of nettles, he could just make out the remains of a square of wooden posts. The wire strung between them had long gone and it wasn't clear what lay in the middle.

'Mine shaft,' Beattie explained. 'Here. Look.'

They scrambled down the hillside, trying to avoid the brambles. Kicking aside the nearest fence post, Beattie rummaged amongst the lattice of fallen branches until he uncovered the opening to a shaft. Faraday gazed into the darkness. If you were small enough, access would be easy.

'How deep?'

'Two thousand feet? Three? These hills are full of holes like this.'

Faraday eased back, still squatting on his heels. He had a number of questions he wanted answering, none of them to do with mine shafts.

'The boy Warren,' he said. 'There was an investigation afterwards?'

Beattie was still gazing at the open throat of the shaft. At length, he took a tiny step back.

'Of course. Had to be.'

'And what did you establish?'

'For definite? Very little. The kid went AWOL early in the morning. He was 06.00 for the wardroom lay-up. Never appeared.'

'Who reported him missing?'

'Coughlin.'

'Really?'

'Yeah. That's no surprise, though. Coughlin would have been the first to realise he wasn't up and about. So off he goes to the Officer of the Watch. From that point on, there's a set procedure.'

Faraday nodded. Wallace had been through the order

of events, each one inching closer to the inevitable conclusion: Warren was no longer aboard.

'You're telling me it was an accident?'

'I'm telling you what happened. We don't know whether it was an accident. That's the whole point.'

'But you'd have had a thought or two, a suspicion. Isn't that what the job was about?'

'Of course.'

'And?'

'And nothing.' Beattie checked his watch, and then whistled for the dog. The scramble back up the hill sucked the breath from Faraday's lungs. It was a full minute before he caught up with Beattie again.

'You had an oppo. Man called Flaherty.'

'Who told you that?'

'Wallace. Flaherty was killed when the ship went down. He was in the same mess as Coughlin and Warren. His job was to keep his ear to the ground. You're telling me he didn't suss some kind of relationship between the two?'

'Sure.'

'There *was* a relationship between them?'

'I don't know.'

'You mean you can't prove it? Evidence it?'

'Exactly.'

'But that doesn't rule it out, does it?'

'Of course not.'

They strode on in silence. The sun had gone in now, and a rising wind was beginning to stir the trees. Faraday was watching the dog.

'Just say Coughlin and Warren were screwing. Not the boy's choice, Coughlin's. Where would they go? Where would they do it?'

Beattie, if anything, quickened his pace.

'That's tough,' he said. 'There was a store up forward where we kept the hawser reels. That was private enough. There were a couple of battery stores and a chain locker midships. They might have been a possibility. Then there was the tiller flat.'

'Where's that?'

'Aft. Above the rudders. There's an emergency steering rig in there, in case the bridge takes a hit.'

'And someone like Coughlin could have gained access?'

'Anyone could. There's access through the main dining room. Or you could climb down through a hatch on the quarterdeck. The place was checked pretty regularly, but it was empty most of the time.'

'So Coughlin and Warren . . . ?'

'Sure. If that's what they fancied.'

'Not they.' Faraday was fighting for breath now. 'It would have been down to Coughlin. The boy had no choice. He was so terrified of the man he just went along with it. Doesn't that sound plausible to you?'

Beattie's steps faltered for a moment, then he stopped altogether. The expression on his face suggested he might have come to some kind of decision.

'We all have nicknames in the navy,' he said at last. 'Warren's was Bunny. Everyone called him that, his mates, everyone. It goes with the surname. Bunny Warren. Coughlin thought it was hilarious. I remember him pissed one night, down in Two Delta mess. Bunny Warren. Fucks like a good 'un. Some of the guys had a ruck about it. That just made Coughlin worse. After that, he called Warren "Fluff".' He paused, bending for a stick and sending it into the trees for the dog. 'The night before he went missing, Warren went to Flaherty, my killick Reg. He wanted to tell him something, fix a time for a private chat. Flaherty said he was very upset.'

'Why?'

'We never found out. Flaherty was really pushed that night, said he'd see him in the morning. By then, Warren had gone.'

'And you've no idea . . . ?'

'None. First thing I did was search the kid's locker. Cases like that, that's what we always do. There might have been a diary in there, some scribblings, maybe a letter.'

'And?'

'Nothing. Nothing I could evidence. Nothing I could put in the report.'

'The report's gone missing.'

'That's strange. There's fuck all in it, just the bare facts. I interviewed Coughlin, of course I did, but he was Mr Plausible when the chips were down. Just said how sorry he was, kid like that, barely eighteen.' He shook his head and eyed the path ahead. 'Bastard.'

Minutes later, they were out in the fresh air again. Across a field lay a country road. Half a mile's brisk walk took them past a tiny railway station, semi-abandoned, and then into a road flanked by a row of forlorn-looking bungalows. The one at the end was called 'Wensleydale'. Beattie knocked at the front door, stepping back into the sunshine. At length the door opened and a woman appeared. She was in her sixties at least, small and plump with a ready smile.

'This is Dorothy.' Beattie lifted the plastic bag. 'She keeps me legal.'

Dorothy peered at Faraday. She had a Yorkshire accent.

'And you are?'

Faraday returned the smile.

'Joe. Nice to meet you.'

She led the way down the narrow hall and into the kitchen. She had a couple of queries to sort out over Beattie's last set of accounts. She fetched a ledger from the top of the fridge and handed it to Beattie. Moments later, she was asking Faraday whether he preferred tea or coffee.

Faraday consulted his watch. Half two. If he wanted to be back at a sensible hour, he ought to think about getting on the road. He thanked her for the offer, then turned to Beattie.

'There's just one other question. I ought to have asked you earlier.'

'What's that?' Beattie was already leafing through the ledger.

'Monday night at the Home Club. We're trying to trace anyone who might have gone on to a hotel for a late drink. Place in Granada Road.'

'What's it called?'

'The Alhambra.'

Beattie frowned a moment, his finger on a line of figures. Then he looked up.

'That'd be me,' he said.

Twenty-one

It took Faraday less than a minute to get through to Willard on his mobile. What had begun as a promising expedition westwards, a chance to tap into Beattie's memories of his months aboard HMS *Accolade*, had abruptly become something very different.

'Joe?' Willard sounded less than pleased to have been hauled out of conference. 'What's the problem?'

'Beattie, sir. Turns out he was one of the blokes at the hotel.'

'Monday night?'

'That's right. Him and two others. All of them pissed. Just the way Pritchard told us.'

'You've got names?'

'Yep. One of them is a mate of Beattie's from Plymouth. Used to be an electrical engineer in *Accolade*. The other is a bloke called Gault. Lives in Milton. Bev Yates has him down for interview this evening. For the time being, I've told him to hold off.'

'And Beattie's account of Monday night?'

'Says they walked to the Alhambra from the Home Club. None of them had been there before but someone else at the dinner thought they'd get late drinks. He was right.'

'And Coughlin made an appearance?'

'Just the way Pritchard described. Called in late, went to the bar, ordered whatever, then saw who else was in and had second thoughts.'

'Did they talk to him at all?'

'Beattie says no. Coughlin was out the door before anyone got the chance.'

There was a longish silence. Faraday could picture Willard in his office, hunched over his desk, the conference abandoned, swivelling slowly left and right in the chair while he decided what to do. In situations like these, he exercised an almost pathological caution, determined to exhaust every conceivable line of enquiry. Absolutely nothing, he always insisted, should be left to chance.

'So what's your feeling about Beattie?' he said at last.

Faraday had been expecting this question. The fact that he quietly admired Beattie – the life he'd made for himself, his strange sense of self-possession – was neither here nor there. The nicest people frequently did the strangest things.

'He's a policeman,' he said simply. 'He's one of us. He knows the way we go at it. He's not one to scare easily.'

'You think he's telling the truth?'

'Some of it, yes.'

'You think there's more?'

'Undoubtedly.'

'Where is he now?'

'Sitting in a bungalow up from his cottage. The place belongs to the woman who does his books. I've told him we'll need a formal interview under caution but he's not keen. Told me he's got a big job on, can't spare the time.'

'And?'

'I arrested him.'

'So where are you?'

'In the woman's back garden. Beattie's sitting in her lounge reading the paper. There's nowhere else I can keep an eye on him until Devon and Cornwall arrive.'

'You've talked to them?'

'Couple of minutes ago. They're sending a car.'

'Then what?'

'You tell me, sir. Either way, we'll obviously need a proper go at him.'

For a moment, Faraday thought Willard was going to lose it. *Hexham*, he said, was on its knees. Geech may have reappeared but they were no closer to binding him hand and foot to the Rooke murder. Geech's mother was still swearing blind that the baseball bat and the jeans had been left by another youth which meant that only witness statements to the beating itself offered the guarantee of a result in court. Now this.

'We've got a choice,' Willard said at length. 'Your end or here.'

'There are two of them,' Faraday reminded him. 'Beattie's oppo is a bloke called Phillips.'

'And you say he's also down there?'

'That's right, sir. Plymstock address.'

'That's two sets of premises, then. Two searches.'

'Yes, sir. Beattie's place I've seen already but—'

'You've been *in* there?'

Faraday had been dreading the question. In evidential terms, he knew he was crazy to have accepted Beattie's invitation to make himself at home in the cottage but at that point the ex-Master-at-Arms had been nothing more than a promising source of information. He'd policed the ship. He'd have known about Coughlin and the boy Warren. The last thing Faraday had expected was his own hand in any final settlement of accounts.

'Well?' It was Willard again.

'His place was where we talked earlier,' Faraday said carefully. 'But it's secure at the moment and we'll obviously need to turn it over.'

Willard grunted his agreement and then broke off to take another call while Faraday eyed Beattie through the tall French windows. Arrest and caution hadn't appeared to have troubled him at all, and in his heart Faraday knew that there was little prospect of a Scenes of Crime search finding anything incriminating at the cottage. The man was far too canny to have left evidence lying around. Indeed, inviting Faraday to help himself to the cottage had been the clearest possible proof that Beattie had nothing to hide. Had that been deliberate? Faraday wondered. Had Beattie been expecting a visit like this? Had he stuffed a bundle of bloodied clothing down a mine shaft and then decided to send a signal or two in advance?

Willard came back on the line and began to muse about what to do with Beattie. Already, Faraday sensed that favourite was to ship both Beattie and Phillips to Hampshire. The Police and Criminal Evidence Act put strict limits on the time available for interview but as long as Faraday kept his distance, resisting the temptation to press Beattie further about events on last Monday night, the PACE clock wouldn't start ticking until both men were booked into a Portsmouth police station. Faraday could, on the other hand, take them down to Plymouth and conduct the interviews on Devon and Cornwall's turf, although he'd need another detective alongside him, ideally someone like Bev Yates. Either way, he was looking at a lengthy wait before they'd be able to get down to business.

'We'll ship them back here,' Willard decided. 'I'll talk to Devon and Cornwall, they've been helpful on a couple of jobs recently. We'll get Beattie's mate nicked and Operational Support can sort out the transport. Devon and Cornwall can do the searches, too. You'll need to brief them.' He paused. 'This other fella . . . Gault. You're telling me Yates has got him down for interview?'

'Yes, sir.'

'OK, tell him Gault's on a nicking. That way we get all three tonight, separate police stations. Have a think about interview strategies and give me a bell once you're on the road.'

The line went dead and Faraday found himself looking once again at Beattie. The beginnings of a friendship had definitely been there, and even now Faraday found it hard to credit the man with murder. He'd quarried out a life for himself deep in this glorious valley. Why hazard all that – the cottage, the solitude, the business – for an arsewipe like Coughlin? Were there really situations aboard ship that would justify measures that extreme? Or did the act of war itself damage men for life? Loosen their hold on reality? Remove the taboo about killing?

The fact that Faraday didn't know came as something of a surprise. He'd often heard fellow police officers, guys at the end of a particularly difficult shift, talk about the job in terms of war. The bombardment of calls, incidents piling up, the shock of finding someone lying in the street on a Friday night with half their face hanging off. Little could prepare you for this and nothing could soften its impact.

Policemen, though, got in the habit of expecting the worst. Indeed, in some ways it almost served as a defence mechanism. But the odd thing about the navy was that most sailors would serve twenty years at sea and never hear a gun fired in anger. There were plenty of exercises, and vast amounts of guile went into making them as realistic as possible, but nothing could prepare a man for the real thing and Faraday had met enough veterans through the years to know that war – organised violence on a major scale – was indescribably horrible. One young officer aboard HMS *Glamorgan*, attacked for the first time by Argie bombers, had stood on the helicopter deck waving the plane away. Didn't the bloody pilot know that firing guns in earnest was liable to hurt somebody?

Faraday smiled at the story. The young officer had later been killed by an Exocet, but his first taste of enemy fire lived on in letters home, the starkest possible evidence that war, once unleashed, turned your world on its head. Had Beattie felt that? Trying to keep the peace aboard *Accolade* as the frigate ploughed its way south? And days later, when the bombs sent his ship to the bottom, had the Master-at-Arms come through the experience unscathed? Faraday, remembering the incident on the pub terrace at lunchtime, rather doubted it. He sensed a violence in the man, unexpended. The biker had felt it too.

The sun had gone in now and rain clouds were building over the wooded hills to the west. Faraday stepped back into the bungalow, checking his watch. The woman who did Beattie's accounts had disappeared into her bedroom, embarrassed by this sudden turn of events, but when Faraday put his head round the lounge door, Beattie was still buried in a copy of the *Daily Telegraph*, as peaceable and untroubled as ever.

For a moment, their eyes met.

'Taking their time, aren't they? Your mates?'

'Yeah. I'll give them another bell.'

'OK.' Beattie was smiling. 'You do that.'

Winter wasn't the least surprised to find Bev Yates at Dawn Ellis's house. Between them, they were trying to wrestle a roll of foul-smelling carpet into the back of Yates's Golf. Winter stood on the pavement, watching.

'Good deed for the day?'

Yates ignored him. With the carpet wedged across the back seats, he slammed the tailgate shut and gave Dawn a peck on the cheek. After a visit to the city dump, he was off to arrest someone. Faraday's orders.

'Is this the Coughlin job? Only I'd heard that laughing boy had it sewn up.'

'Laughing boy?'

'Your mate Corbett.'

'Fat chance. Haven't seen him for days, thank Christ.'

Yates got in the car and gunned the engine. Dawn watched him disappear down the road, then nodded at the house.

'I'm living in the kitchen,' she said, 'if you fancy a coffee.'

Winter followed her indoors, perching himself on a stool while Dawn spooned Gold Blend into a couple of mugs.

'Bev been helpful, has he?'

'Very.'

'Nice of him to take the carpet, too.'

Dawn ignored the comment.

'I had a call this morning,' she said. 'Sergeant from Traffic. He's looking for a statement.'

'Surprise, surprise. So what are you going to tell him?'

'The truth, I imagine.'

'You'll have to remind me, love. I've forgotten.'

'Really?' She glanced up. 'There were witnesses, Paul, probably dozens of them. There's no way you kept below thirty and me lying through my teeth just puts two of us in the shit.'

'Breaking the limit isn't necessarily dangerous driving.'

'Is that the charge?'

'That's what they're after. Dangerous driving could mean a disqual. And that would put me back in uniform.'

'Would that be the end of the world?'

'Yes. Since you ask.'

'Enough for me to lie for you? Put my own career on the line?'

'Lie?' Winter looked hurt. 'Who said anything about lying?'

'That's what it boils down to. I sit down with this nice sergeant, tell him you drove like an angel, what happens then? They have guys who'll be looking at the car, Paul. They can reconstruct the whole thing, you know they can.'

Winter nodded. It was true.

'There's another way,' he said at last.

'What's that?'

'Put the prat from Traffic on hold. You're off sick at the moment. You've got every excuse you'd ever need.'

'Cathy expects me back tomorrow.'

'Delay it. Give her a call. I just need a couple of days.'

'What difference will that make?'

'Christ knows.' Winter made room on the work surface for the coffee. 'But give it a shot, eh?'

Faraday, still waiting for the Devon and Cornwall car from Plymouth, made Beattie a cup of tea. There was no way he was going to discuss Coughlin outside an interview room but there were still loose ends in their wider conversations about the Falklands which intrigued him. This wasn't material for any court of law but in Faraday's head there remained a profound suspicion that this half-forgotten war may have somehow shaped the events of Monday night.

Beattie accepted the tea with a nod, added two spoons of sugar, then returned to the *Telegraph* crossword. Faraday settled himself in the other armchair, gazing out at the garden as the first fat drops of rain blurred the view from the window. The silence stretched and stretched, neither hostile nor embarrassing, but simply an acknowledgement that the situation between them had changed.

'What was it like, then?' Faraday asked at length.

'What was what like?'

'The Falklands.'

Beattie studied him for a moment, surprise laced with something close to curiosity.

'Is that a serious question?'

'Yes.'

'You really want to go back to all that?'

'Yes.'

'And you think I'm the best man to ask?'

'Yes.'

'Why?'

'Because you were down there, obviously, and because you've thought about it since.'

'Like everybody does.'

'I'm sure. So what's the harm in telling me?'

Beattie looked away, turning the proposition over.

'There isn't any harm,' he said. 'I'm just not sure why you want to know. If you're trying to build some kind of case then I'd be mad to help you.' He paused. 'Is this a conversation that needs a solicitor?'

'Far from it. Fighting a war isn't a crime.'

'No?' The smile again, fainter this time.

There was a long silence. The rain was getting heavier. From miles away, a rumble of thunder. Faraday lay back in the armchair and closed his eyes. Finally, he heard the rustle of paper as Beattie put the *Telegraph* to one side.

'If you really want to know . . .' he began. 'The whole thing was weird. Not the going down there. Not even fighting the bloody war. Not even sinking, for that matter. No, it was afterwards. They'd got us out of the water. They'd saved our lives. They'd even found cabins for us on *Canberra*, hot water, civvy food. But we were spare. We were gash. Two hundred blokes and no ship, you're a waste of space. That's hard to take, believe me.'

Beattie's voice was low, a man sharing a secret. Faraday opened one eye. Beattie was staring into space.

'You lost nineteen blokes,' Faraday murmured.

'That's right. And you ask yourself, don't you, you ask yourself why them? Why not me? That's where the weird comes in. War's a lottery. If you're lucky, you die.'

Faraday thought he'd misunderstood.

'If you're *lucky* you die?'

'Yes.' There was a frown on Beattie's face now and his voice had begun to falter. 'You won't believe this but that's what a lot of us felt. We'd no right to be on *Canberra*, all tucked up. Don't get me wrong. The blokes on board were brilliant, really generous, but none of us wanted the stuff they pushed at us. Not at first, anyway.'

'So how did you cope?'

'We didn't. We just sat around, trying to make sense of it all.' His voice tailed off and he turned his face away.

'We transferred to the *QE2* after *Canberra*. That was even more bizarre. There were other 21s on board, other ship's companies who'd gone down, but it made no difference. We were still refugees. Take away your ship, you take away everything. Our clothes had gone, our little knick-knacks, our music, our pride, every bloody thing. All you could think about was the training you'd done, how good you thought you were, how you could handle anything, and then came the great day – bam – and none of it worked.' He looked across at Faraday again. 'That's a killer, believe me, and you know why? Because no one ever tells you the truth. High explosive is fucking horrible. Horrible. And worse than that, you knew you'd blown it.'

'Blown it how?'

'By losing the ship. By losing all those blokes. That wasn't in the script. Ever.'

They sat in silence for a minute or so, Faraday's thoughts about war confirmed. He'd put money on the fact that Beattie had been a hard case. You didn't get to keep two hundred blokes in order by being nice to people. But even the Master-at-Arms had buckled before this savage eruption of violence.

Faraday stirred.

'So what was it like coming home?'

'Bizarre. Bizarre like you wouldn't believe. For a start, *Accolade* was a Guzz ship so most of us lived in Plymouth. We steamed up past the Lizard and they could easily have choppered us off, but no, they wanted to save us for the curtain call, Maggie's War, the big finale up Southampton Water.' He began to laugh, a soft laugh, laughter emptied of any trace of merriment. 'That was unbelievable. We were all mustered on deck, huge crowds, hundreds of boats, Page Three girlies with their tits hanging out, then there was this noise of low-flying jets, and we all hit the deck, flat on our faces, just praying for the noise to go away. Just which clever bastard dreamed *that* up?'

Faraday remembered the live pictures on television: the *QE2* nosing her way through an armada of smaller craft, flanked by fire tugs chucking up great arches of water while the Red Arrows roared overhead. Grand opera, he thought, scored for every front page in the world.

Beattie was describing the welcome now, the band on the quayside, the kids with bouquets of flowers, families and friends pressing up against the crowd barriers. From Southampton, he'd gone back to Plymouth. Down the pub, for night after night, friends and strangers bought him drinks, demanding to know what the war had been like, how it had *felt* to be caught up in it all.

'At first you don't say very much. Then they keep pushing and pushing until you realise that they want the Hollywood version, the *Sun* version, you know, strip cartoon stuff, the wicked Argies, the brave Brits, all that crap, then – if you're like me – you lose it completely, and you sit them down and tell them a story or two, a true story, blokes with no heads, blokes you tried to save, blokes whose faces you'll never forget, and then it all goes very quiet, and your missus has run off to the loo, and your kids are looking at their hands, and you realise that however hard you try, no one will ever understand.'

'Except the blokes you served with?'

'Yeah.' He nodded. 'Them and the Argies. They know, too.'

Faraday remembered the tapes again, the pictures he'd watched at the Home Club. These men will go on meeting until they die, he thought. Because they alone had been there.

There was another long silence. Then Beattie leaned forward in the chair.

'You asked me what the war was like,' he said softly. 'But you know what really does it for me? The bottle of Grouse on the bedside table. That's the Falklands in one.'

Faraday held his gaze for a moment, knowing that this was probably as close to the truth as he could ever reasonably expect, not a bunch of shipmates meeting every year or so, toasting each other until they were legless, but thousands of individual veterans, banged up with their memories, looking for some kind of solace, some kind of peace.

The soft patter of the falling rain was interrupted by a knock at the front door.

'Your mates must be here.' Beattie was getting to his feet, suddenly businesslike. 'Do us a favour?'

'What's that?'

'The dog. Dorothy only puts up with him on sufferance. Couldn't take him to Pompey with us, could we?'

Paul Gault lived in a modest terraced house in the depths of Milton, a tightly knit suburb on the eastern edges of Southsea. Yates had agreed half six for the interview but arrived twenty minutes early. He'd brought Dave Michaels with him, just in case, but he didn't think things would turn sticky.

On the phone, Gault had been extremely accommodating, the flat Pompey mumble laced with cheerful expletives. He'd read about Coughlin in the paper and was happy to spare Yates half an hour of his time. 'You wanna talk about last Monday night?' He'd laughed. 'Absolutely no problem, mush. What I can fucking remember.'

Now, Yates and Michaels walked the ten metres to Gault's house, trying to avoid the worst of the rain. There were two wet gnomes in the front garden and a tiny brass plate on the front door warning about the moggie inside. 'Killer Tabby,' the message went. 'Beware.'

Yates rang the bell. He could hear kids inside and the bellow of a telly at full blast. Then came heavy footsteps down the hall and Yates found himself looking at a bulky, balding man in his mid-forties. He was wearing a string vest tucked into a pair of scruffy shell-suit bottoms and he'd obviously been up in the bathroom because one half of his face was still covered in shaving foam.

'Yeah?'

'DC Yates. This is DS Michaels.'

'Pleased to meet you.' His hand was still wet. 'Bit previous, ain't ya?'

Yates apologised. Maybe Gault would like to get some clothes on. It was wet out.

'I thought we were doing this at home?'

'Change of plan, Paul.' Yates stepped inside and read him the caution. Gault didn't understand a word.

'Suspicion of murder?' He looked totally blank. 'This some kind of wind-up?'

Dave Michaels was already enquiring about the kids. How old were they? Was his wife at home? Anyone available to keep an eye on them?

'No fucking way. They're seven and eight. I'm here until the missus gets back.'

'Where is she?'

'Asda. Shopping. Listen, I'm not with you. What's any of this got to do with me?'

Yates invited him again to get dressed. The quicker they got this thing moving, the quicker he'd be home again. Yates took him by the arm, easing him towards the stairs.

'There's a question of the house, too. Some of our guys will need to take a look round.'

'What for?' Gault tore his arm free. Yates stepped back, wary now. There was an air of sudden menace about Gault that shaving foam did nothing to disguise. 'Listen, I'm asking you guys some fucking questions. You barge in here, accuse me of Christ knows what, you don't think I—' He broke off. Two little faces had appeared around the door at the end of the hall, both girls. Wide-eyed, they watched as the scene developed. Daddy shouting. Daddy upset.

'Inside girls.' He stepped down the hall, shooing them back to the television. The door shut, he turned to face the two detectives again.

'So tell me. What's all this about?'

Dave Michaels, a genius in situations like these, began to explain about the Major Crimes set-up. They were investigating a murder. They had information they were obliged to develop. A number of people could undoubtedly be of assistance. One of them was Gault.

'But why arrest me?'

'Because we have to be sure.'

'Sure of what?'

'Sure that we can sit you down for a while. Have a little chat.'

Gault shook his head, part bewilderment, part anger, then came the squeak of the garden gate, and a plump, breathless, plain-faced woman appeared at the door, laden with Asda bags.

'Paulie?' She was looking at Yates and Michaels. She had a foreign accent, Eastern Europe maybe. 'What's going on?'

'Wish I fucking knew.'

'Mrs Gault?' Michaels again. 'We're arresting your husband. We'd like him to get dressed.'

The woman lowered the bags to the carpet. The word 'arrest' seemed to have robbed her of the power of speech. Dave Michaels stepped forward, the voice of sweet reason, putting a hand on Gault's arm. It really would be best if Gault took himself back upstairs and put some clothes on. Then they'd all be out of here. Gault stared at him, his face inches from Michaels', and for a split second Yates knew exactly what was going to happen next.

For a big man, Gault could move surprisingly fast. Lowering his head, he drove it into Dave Michaels' face.

There was a crack of bone against bone and then Michaels was reeling back towards the front door, his hand to his nose, blood pumping through his fingers. Yates threw himself on Gault and the pair of them fell backwards on to the stairs. They fought for a moment or two, crashing sideways against the banisters. Down the hall, the two kids were screaming. Then came the bellow of another voice, Gault's wife. She was outraged.

'Paulie,' she bellowed. 'Stop it!'

Yates felt Gault make one last effort, then his body went limp. Yates hung on for a moment or two, then eased himself backwards. Michaels was by the door, examining his handkerchief.

For a moment, no one said a word. Then Gault struggled upright on the stairs. He was staring at Yates, fighting to get his breath back.

'My wife thinks this country's fucking wonderful,' he managed at last. 'No secret police. No knocks on the door.' His eyes were still blazing. 'How wrong can you be, eh?'

Twenty-two

Faraday heard about Dave Michaels at Kingston Crescent. Beattie safely delivered to the Custody Sergeant at Central police station, Faraday was sitting in Willard's office, Bev Yates beside him.

'Police surgeon says he'll live,' Willard said. 'Didn't even break his nose.'

Faraday smiled to himself. Willard seemed quietly pleased at the news that Gault had lost it. At least they'd laid hands on someone capable of violence.

Willard was looking at Faraday.

'So where are we now?'

'Beattie's being checked in at Waterlooville. He's insisting on his lawyer, woman from Tavistock. She can't be here until first thing tomorrow.'

Willard grunted. Beattie's oppo from Plymouth was also en route from the West Country. His name was Duncan Phillips and – at Willard's request – a couple of CID from Devon and Cornwall had arrested him at teatime in his Plymstock semi. Under the PACE regulations, the interview teams would have just twenty-four hours to nail down the truth about events at the Alhambra on Monday night, though a uniformed Superintendent could extend that to a day and a half.

Faraday had already done the sums.

'We've got until eight a.m. Wednesday, assuming the extension,' he told Willard. 'So we're really talking tomorrow.'

Bev Yates was doodling notes on a pad at his elbow. First thing Wednesday was the England-Nigeria game, crucial if Sven's boys were to make it into the next round. He glanced up to find Willard looking his way.

'What kind of state's Gault in?'

'No problem. He could do with finishing his shave but apart from that he's fine.'

'You didn't thump him?'

'No chance. He's a big bastard. Thank Christ his missus was there.'

'What about a brief?'

'Gault's settled for the duty. Michelle's on tonight. She's at Central now.'

Willard nodded. Michelle Brinton was a plump, freckle-faced solicitor in her thirties. Oddly enough, she came from the West Country herself, though a couple of years of Pompey crime had given her sharper elbows.

'Joe?' Willard wanted to know about interview strategy.

Faraday took his time, knowing that Willard was old-fashioned when it came to the coalface. Interviews were normally handled by DCs on a squad, but with so many blokes shipped off to the Somerstown inquiry Willard would be pushed to field three teams of two. Under the circumstances, therefore, Faraday was proposing a novel solution.

'We're up against the clock,' he said. 'I suggest we take a crack at Gault tonight, starting ASAP. Go for open account. See what he's got to say.'

'We?'

'Myself and Yates, sir. So far, all we've got to go on is Pritchard. Yates and I both talked to him. It's not much of a start but it saves briefing two other guys.'

Willard saw the logic at once. He was indeed less than keen to put Faraday at the sharp end – Deputy SIOs were supposed to maintain the wider view – but a break-through this abrupt left him little choice. All the other available DCs had just spent a frustrating day toiling up and down stairwells in Somerstown and were in no state to switch back to *Merriott*.

'Forensic are in Gault's place already,' Willard mused. 'Devon and Cornwall are sorting out Beattie and Phillips. They reckon they'll be through the properties by noon tomorrow, first trawl. What else have we got?'

'Phones,' Faraday said at once. 'All three have mobiles. I've talked to Brian Imber already and he'll be on to the TIU for billings first thing.'

'You're telling me we'll get them in time?'

'We might.'

'Fat chance.'

The Telephone Intelligence Unit was housed in Winchester, a specialist department charged with wrestling data from the phone companies. Billings, with the added possibility that individual calls could be pinned down geographically, could change the whole direction of an inquiry but often took days – sometimes weeks – to arrive. Willard had been banging this drum for longer than anyone could remember but so far to no great effect.

'Any previous?'

'Nothing, sir.' Yates this time.

'Brilliant.' Willard threw his pen down. 'So it's really back to our friend Pritchard. All we have is a dead man's word that these three guys were at the Alhambra Monday night.'

'Not at all.' Faraday took up the running. 'It's Beattie who's put them there.'

'I know that. But what else did he tell you?'

'Not much. They went for a drink. Coughlin turned up briefly, then left again. Sometime later, they called it a night and went home.'

'And you think he'll stick to that?'

'I think he'll try.'

Willard revolved in his chair.

'Of course he will, bound to, and that's my point, Joe. It's Pritchard who's telling us they were really pissed off,

Pritchard who has them ranting on about what a tosser Coughlin was, Pritchard who says they were out of their skulls on Lamb's Navy.'

'Bacardi, sir,' Yates murmured.

'Sure, OK, whatever. But we have to be careful here, don't we? Because it seems to me that Pritchard had every reason to give us these three guys. Especially if he whacked Coughlin himself.'

Faraday was staring out of the window at the rain. He'd somehow assumed a consensus that Pritchard was out of the frame. Evidently not.

'I don't think Pritchard got anywhere near Coughlin that night,' he said carefully. 'We should be talking motive and opportunity. He had neither.'

'You think the defence'd buy that? Bloke who admitted being in love with the man? Potty about him? Jealous as fuck?'

'Over what?'

'Who cares? Pritchard was a screaming queen. These blokes are unbalanced. Juries lap that kind of stuff up. And who says he wasn't there? I thought we had a footprint? Evidenced? Plus the man himself, admitting he popped round?'

'We do, sir. But he never got in.'

'I know, Joe. I know. But whose word do we have on that? Apart from Pritchard?'

Faraday wondered about fetching the Scenes of Crime report but decided against it. Willard knew very well that not a shred of forensic evidence connected Pritchard to the inside of 7a Niton Road. As usual, the Det Supt was giving Faraday's cage a rattle.

Yates stirred.

'There's still the taxi,' he pointed out.

'And where are we with that?'

'I talked to Aqua again this morning. The driver who picked the three of them up from the hotel is still in Amsterdam. They gave me his girlfriend's number. She

349

hasn't a clue where he's staying but she says he's back on Wednesday.'

'What time?'

'Early. He's on a KLM cheapie. I checked with the airline. Seven o'clock in the morning, Gatwick.'

Faraday and Willard exchanged glances. Seven on Wednesday morning was dangerously close to the moment the PACE clock finally stopped. The timing couldn't have been worse.

Willard scowled. It was at moments like these, backed into a corner, that he was frequently at his best.

'What if we send you up to Gatwick if we have to?' He was looking at Yates. 'Give ourselves a bit of leeway?'

'Fine, sir.' Yates beamed at him. 'Be my pleasure.'

Winter took a cab to the funfair. Clarence Pier was beside the hovercraft terminal on Southsea seafront, an acre or so of tacky rides plus a cavernous amusement arcade packed full of fruit machines and hi-tech video games. For a quid, you could battle anything from Mike Tyson to the Gulf War. Not that Winter was in the mood.

Mick Clarence, the youth worker from the Persistent Young Offender scheme, had phoned an hour or so earlier. He'd pushed Winter's photos around likely Somerstown contacts but got little response. Then, just minutes ago, he'd taken a call from a lad whose voice he hadn't recognised. The boy had seen the state Darren had got himself into and wanted to know more. He wasn't prepared to give his name, but when Clarence explained about Winter he'd thought a meet might be in order. Winter, tucked up with one of Joannie's Ruth Rendells, wasn't best pleased but knew he had little choice. The visit from the Traffic Sergeant had shaken him more than he cared to admit. Somehow or other, he had to look for ways of turning imminent disaster to his own account.

On the phone, Mick Clarence had mentioned a game

called Formula One Plus. According to his new contact, it was the hottest of the new rides. Winter would find this rendezvous towards the back of the arcade, near one of the fire exits, and he spotted it now, three youths in a gaggle beside it, none of them more than fourteen.

For a Monday night, the arcade was empty. The nylon carpet, cratered with cigarette burns, felt slippery underfoot.

'Who phoned Mick Clarence, then?' Winter saw little point in smalltalk.

Three faces, shadowed under baseball caps, stared him out. Under different circumstances, this situation could have been threatening and Winter found himself wondering yet again what had happened to the nation's youth. In his day, wickedness began and ended at scout camp. These days, you found yourself counting the bodies.

At length, the smallest of the youths nodded at the machine. He was wearing baggy jeans and a Liverpool top. The Nike Air trainers looked brand new.

'You got any money?'

'I might have.'

'We need three quid for starters. One go each.'

Winter eyed him a moment, then found a pound coin. The youth grinned at his mates and slipped quickly on to the bench seat, a child again. Winter had yet to give him the coin.

'How does it work, then?'

The youth explained the controls — steering wheel, fingertip gear shift, two pedals for throttle and brake — then grabbed the money. The console came to life. A choice of options scrolled on to the screen, race circuits from Hockenheim to Sao Paolo. The youth went for Monte Carlo, and then spent a second or two contemplating his choice of weather.

'Heatwave?' One of his mates grinned. 'Well cool.'

'Whose been on this afternoon?'

'Fuck knows. Let's see.'

The youth at the wheel called up a list of current title contenders. Half a dozen names appeared on the screen. The fastest time to date had been posted by someone calling himself 'Iceman'.

'Wanker. I know him. You gonna do this or what?'

The youth at the wheel hit the Go button. The sound effects were deafening. A couple of dozen bright little Formula One cars squatted on the starting grid, maximum revs, then the lights on the overhead gantry flicked to green and the race began. The youths crowded round, sucked in by the noise of burning rubber, and even Winter had to admit to a flutter of excitement. The lad behind the wheel drove with some style, taking the first corner wide and passing a blur of scarlet on the outside of the bend. Seconds later, he was powering along the Corniche.

One of his mates was pointing at a huge white yacht in the harbour, the sundeck at the stern decorated with nubile young flesh.

'Look at the tits on that,' he chortled. 'Well fucking fit.'

The harbour had gone. Next came a tunnel, the scream of the engines suddenly redoubled. Winter waited until a disc of light appeared, ballooning as the car burst into the dazzle of a perfect Monte Carlo afternoon, then he slipped a photo from his pocket, reached forward, and propped it on the screen. There was a scream of tyres as the youth at the wheel braked. Briefly, he fought for control, then threw himself backwards as the car hit the barrier and somersaulted into the crowd.

'Fuck off,' he yelled. 'What's all that about?'

The other two were staring at Darren Geech, his head arched back on the pillow, his face barely recognisable. This was the moment Winter had given the bed a nudge and the agony was unmistakable.

'Been to see him yet? Only it might be wise to hang on a couple of weeks because he's finding it hard to talk.'

The youth at the wheel didn't care. He wanted another quid. Winter ignored him.

'Who made the call to Mick Clarence then? Tonight?'

Two pairs of eyes flicked to the driver. The youth at the wheel was still complaining about the crash. His first lap had been going really well, half a second up on his all-time best. Keep that up, and he'd be untouchable.

'You don't get it, do you?' Winter had retrieved the picture. 'Darren copped this because he upset the wrong people. The wrong people want Darren put away. Unless my lot get some help, the wrong people are going to be looking for more Darrens.'

The youth at the wheel had managed to re-set the game. One of his mates stirred, ignoring the cars on the grid.

'What's that then? This help?'

'Statements. Witness statements. People who might have been around when Darren did the bloke in Fraser Road.'

'That's grassing,' the youth said flatly. 'No one fucking grasses.'

Winter looked at him. Mick Clarence's point. Exactly.

'You're right, son,' he said. 'But there are limits here. What Darren did was out of order. It's not me saying it. It's the blokes he upset. Anyone with half a brain would draw the line at doing what Darren did. Now he's lucky to have even that.'

'What?'

'Half a brain.'

'But what did he do, though, Darren? Apart from that arsehole in Fraser Road?'

'Us. One of us. That might sound like a right laugh to you but we think it's a serious piss-off. And you know what? Bazza Mackenzie happens to agree with us. Some things you do. Some you don't. Problem with Darren, he never knew the difference.' Winter paused, then passed the photo. 'There's a phone number on the back. It's a police number, direct line, a Mr Hayder. When you get through, mention that you've been talking to me. You'd be amazed at how nice we can be sometimes.'

Winter stepped back a moment, letting the thought sink in. The youth at the wheel had emerged from the Monte Carlo tunnel for a second time though Winter could see his heart wasn't in it because the lap time was crap. Aware of everyone watching, he let out a half-hearted whoop and gunned it into the next corner, failing to brake in time to avoid the car in front. The screen suddenly filled with the back of a dawdling Ferrari. This time, the crash was terminal.

'Shit,' he said bitterly. 'Look what you've done now.'

The first session with Paul Gault started at 20.47. It would have been fifteen minutes earlier but Faraday had been involved in a head-to-head with the Custody Sergeant. No way was he going to take responsibility for Beattie's dog. He had nowhere to put the bloody animal since the local authority had taken over responsibility for strays and the last thing he was going to do on a wet Monday evening was take it outside for walkies. If Faraday had been silly enough to cart it 170 miles in the back of his car, then it could bloody stay there.

Faraday, slightly perturbed by the accusatory way the dog kept looking at him, had racked his brains to find a home. Taking it back to the Bargemaster's House was a non-starter. J-J had once been bitten by a collie and gave anything with a bark a very wide berth indeed. That left friends, and in the end Faraday had been driven to give Eadie Sykes a ring. No problem, she said at once. She had the remains of the weekend's joint and it would be a pleasure to see them both.

'Both?'

'You, too.'

Now, Faraday settled into the chair across from Gault, starting the tape machines and announcing the time, date and individuals present. Beside Gault sat Michelle Brinton. A severe black two-piece gave the solicitor a lean, rather London look. Either that, or she'd started taking her gym membership seriously.

Faraday had asked Bev Yates to lead. He started with the obvious, inviting Gault to describe exactly what he'd done on the Monday night. Ignoring the question, Gault launched into a furious protest about the way he'd been treated at home. In front of his wife and kids, that had been a disgrace, totally out of order. The lightest touch on his arm stopped him in mid-flow.

'Just answer the question,' Michelle mumured.

Gault stared at her for a moment. He'd refused point blank the offer of soap and a razor and this decision had given his dark, jowly face a maniacally lop-sided look. Meet this big, shambling man on the street and you'd probably cross the road.

'Monday I was at work at the pub.' He was frowning now. 'Couple of dozen lunches. I'd booked off the evening shift months before. I was home by half three. The missus'll tell you that.'

'So what did you do at home?'

'Put my feet up. Had a couple of tinnies. Watched telly with the kids. Nice it was, knowing I didn't have to go back.'

Around six, he went upstairs for a shower. It wasn't often these days he wore a suit but his wife had ironed it specially and it was on the bed waiting for him. He broke off and the frown returned.

'What d'you want to know all this for?'

'Just tell us, OK?' Yates was making a note. 'We'll ask the questions.'

Gault was close to another outburst but another look from Michelle was enough to return him to Monday night. He'd decided to treat himself to a cab to the Home Club. The walk from Milton would have taken him the best part of an hour.

'The other two hadn't been in touch?' It was Faraday.

'What other two?'

'Beattie and Phillips.'

'No.' Gault shook his huge head. 'But then there was no reason why they would have done. We weren't special mates or anything. Nodding terms, maybe. Nothing more.'

'Really?' Faraday had somehow assumed all three had been close.

'No way. Like I knew them, seen them before, but' . . . he shrugged . . . 'no.'

He'd got to the Home Club around seven fifteen. The bar had been filling up nicely, and he'd sunk a couple of lagers with blokes he knew well, proper messmates, by the time they'd gone next door for scran. That's when he'd found himself on the same table as Phillips and the Joss.

'They were right beside me, know what I mean? I'm not sure who did the table plan but it was crap. Me and my real mates were all over the fucking room.'

'You didn't like Beattie and Phillips?'

'It wasn't that, I just didn't know them. Phillips was a Tiff, worked in the engine room – when does a cook get to meet a Tiff? As for the Joss, he's not the kind of bloke you get rat-arsed with, not unless you've got a death wish.'

'So what happened? Monday night?'

'You want the truth, I don't remember too well. I know we had a bit to drink at the meal. Me and Beattie and Phillips started buying wine between us, house red, not a bad drop, then we got on to whisky chasers in the bar afterwards. They turned out OK, both them blokes. Must have done, otherwise we'd never have gone on together, know what I mean?'

Faraday stirred. He could sense the effort Gault was making to reassemble the evening and he began to wonder about the long-term legacy of an experience like the Falklands. 'The bottle of Grouse on the bedside table,' Beattie had said. And now this, an alcoholic ex-cook having a problem remembering what happened just seven days ago.

Yates wanted to know whose idea the Alhambra had been. Gault shrugged.

'Wasn't mine. I'd never heard of the place. Wouldn't have been the other two, either. They were Guzz lads. Must have been someone else. We were up for it, I remember that much, so we'd have asked around.'

'How did you get there?'

'Walked. I wanted to take a cab but the Joss was for doing it on foot.'

'Call in anywhere en route?'

'Doubt it. It would have been late by then.'

Faraday nodded. So far, everything Gault had said tallied with notes he'd made from the tapes: Beattie on the steps of the club, wrapped in his leather jacket, surrounded by half a dozen others. Two of them must have been Gault and Phillips. He'd check later.

Yates had nudged Gault on to the Alhambra. At this point his memory gave out altogether, until Faraday mentioned Coughlin.

'You remember him coming into the bar at the hotel?'

'Too fucking right I do.'

'Where were you?'

'Sitting down. We had a table at the window end of the bar, manky fucking place. The door was down by the bar itself. Fuck knows how but there he suddenly was, horrible as ever, make your flesh creep just looking at him.' He paused, staring down at his hands. 'I think we'd bought the bottle by then. Bacardi. Phillips' idea. Claimed he'd picked the taste up in Spain getting pissed with his missus. He was all for giving Coughlin a glass, but I remember telling him we should empty the bottle first, then I could smash it over Coughlin's fucking skull. Yeah.'

He nodded, the same abrupt downward thrust of the head that had broken Dave Michaels' nose. Faraday and Yates exchanged glances, aware of the look on Michelle Brinton's face. There were easier clients to defend than Paul Gault.

'Why do you say that?' Yates enquired.

'Say what?'

'Say you'd have liked to have whacked him with the bottle?'

'Because he was a trunker. A trunker's trunker. The biggest fucking trunker of all time. Real shagnasty. And because he made that nipper's life a fucking misery.'

There was a long silence. Michelle was close to interrupting again, trying to bring this particular exchange to an end, but this time Gault just ignored her. Playing it by the book, Faraday – too – should have kept Gault on the rails, insisting he finish his account of what had happened on Monday night, but something told him they were closing on a more important truth.

'Nipper?' he queried.

Gault looked startled.

'You don't know about Matt?'

'Tell us.'

'He was a kid. Our mess. Two Delta. I can see him now, runs ashore, cropped hair, Doc Martens, cut-offs, strutting his stuff, the Marine that never was. Skates don't fool that easy. We all knew the lad was just out the egg. Yeah . . . Mattie Warren. Mr Disco.'

'And Coughlin?'

'Spotted him at once. Easy meat. Easy, easy meat. That's the thing about blokes like Coughlin. They're like animals. They *are* fucking animals. You can see them sniffing the wind. The first time he laid eyes on Warren, he knew he was there for the taking. You did what you could but blokes like Coughlin around, what fucking chance did you have?'

'You got to know the boy?'

'I did, yeah. He was a nice lad. He was pretty fucking clueless but that wasn't his fault, we all have to start somewhere. What he needed was someone to keep an eye out for him. You do your best but . . . fuck.' He lowered his head again, a gesture – Faraday realised – of defeat. Whatever else this man had brought back from the Falklands, he'd never forget Matthew Warren. 'There's a saying in the navy. Everyone like Mattie, all the skins, they need a sea daddy. That was me, believe it or not. I tried to be there for him. My own marriage was down the khazi. I had two kids, a missus who couldn't stand me, a bloke who'd moved in when I was away, and nowhere to fucking go if we ever got through the poxy war. I was Mr Fucked-up, believe me, and the least I thought I could do was try and keep the boy in one piece.'

'You're talking about Warren?'

'Yeah. There was pressure on all of us, we were all cacking ourselves about what would really happen, but young like that, Mattie really took it bad. That's where Coughlin creamed himself. Couldn't get enough of winding the kid up.'

'How?'

'You really want to know?'

'Yes.' Faraday nodded. 'Please.'

'OK.' Gault looked first at Faraday, then at Yates. 'Take the Jack Dusties, the stores blokes, they were in our mess. When we stopped at Ascension, we took on a load of body bags. It's just what you do. You're going to war, you take body bags. Now the great question was *how many* body bags. That's what Coughlin banged on about all the time, how many body bags. Now I knew one of the dusties really well, good bloke, all right, and he told me it was seventy. Coughlin trebled it, *trebled* it, just to wind the boy up. Two hundred body bags, one each. The boy was terrified, never got to sleep at night worrying about all those Argie torpedoes. Two *hundred*? There wouldn't be anyone left on the fucking ship.'

As *Accolade* sped south, life for Matthew Warren got worse. For one thing, according to Gault, he kept picking up little buzzes from the officers in the wardroom. How the French were flying thousands of Exocet missiles into Buenos Aires in the dead of night, and how effective these missiles were supposed to be. None of this mattered until *Sheffield* went down, then everyone – not just Warren – started taking the war very seriously indeed.

'Turned out the blokes in the wardroom were right. The Exocets were fucking lethal. One of them in your galley, and you were history.' Gault was back aboard, reliving those days. 'You ever see the state of Shiny Sheff? The fucking boat was a hulk, burned-out, nothing left, and within hours the buzz is going round, Christ knows how many blokes have been wasted. So what does Coughlin do? He bangs on, day and night, about all this French technology. Heat-seeking, heat-seeking, I can hear him now. And why does he go on and on about the guidance system? Because the fucking missile heads straight for the galley, where the heat is, and that – surprise, surprise – is where Mattie spends most of his working life. Fetching and carrying, flashing up for Coughlin, helping do the washing up, thinking all the time about the next fucking Exocet.'

'But what about Coughlin himself?' Yates was confused. 'Wasn't he in the galley too?'

'Of course he was. And so was I for that matter. Different galley, thank fuck, but same principle. No, the difference with us was that we were older. In my case, to be honest, I didn't care the fuck what happened. In Coughlin's, he thought he was bloody immortal. Just wouldn't happen. Mattie? Like I said, he was cacking himself, just thinking about it.'

Faraday eased back from the table, aware of Michelle Brinton looking pointedly at the clock. This wasn't an interview at all, more a glimpse of what it was like to go to war.

'My client . . .' she began.

Gault put his hand on her arm, a gesture of reassurance. Leave this to me, he was telling her.

'You won't know this, but Coughlin was screwing him.'

'You're sure about that?'

'As sure as I can be, yeah. You don't go to sea for years on end without getting a nose for stuff like that. And Mattie would have blown the whistle, for definite, had Coughlin not scared the crap out of him.'

'You talked to him about it? The boy? Warren?'

'A couple of times, yeah.'

'And?'

'He wouldn't say, but that meant nothing. Coughlin was pulling strings all the time, getting Mattie on night watches, just the two of them in the wardroom galley. Trunker's paradise, that galley. Even the fucking officers knock twice before going in. Tell you something else, too. Flaherty had sussed it. The killick Reg. He was in our mess, not a bad bloke for a Reggie. Shrewd, too.'

Faraday glanced up from a note he was making. Flaherty reported to Beattie. Had the Joss mentioned anything about Warren on Monday night?

'I don't know. He may have done.'

'But when Coughlin turned up at the hotel . . . you must have talked about him afterwards. Didn't Warren's name come up then?'

Gault stared at Faraday, trying to remember. Faraday offered a prompt.

'The bloke behind the bar, the hotel owner, he said you were up on your feet after Coughlin left, giving him the finger through the window.'

'Yeah. I expect he's right. Shame it was just the finger.'

'And that was because of Warren?'

'Yeah, and a million other things, but Warren mainly. Listen,' – he beckoned Faraday closer – 'what you have to understand is what it does to you, something like that.

The kid went over the side. Fuck knows how, we've all got our little theories, but either way he's dead and gone. We should have done better than that, all of us, and maybe he'd still be with us now. That's why I went to see his folks afterwards, did my best like, still do.'

'Still do what?'

'Still pop round, bunch of flowers every May the twenty-first, make the odd call, pay my respects.'

This, too, was news to Faraday. Warren's family were still in Pompey?

'Yeah, absolutely, couple of streets down from me. Dad's a builder and Matt's brother does a bit, too. Ask me, they've never got over it, especially the mum. Poor bloody woman. Son goes off to war and ends up trunked to death.'

'Is that an allegation?'

'No, but I'm marking your fucking card, aren't I? You ask me why we all hated the cunt, I'm telling you. You ask me why he deserved whatever he got, I'm telling you that, too.'

Faraday nodded, accepting the logic of Gault's argument. Then he pushed his notes to one side, and looked Gault in the eye.

'OK,' he said. 'So what do you say if I suggest that you killed Coughlin? That he came into the hotel that night, that you somehow traced him back to where he lived, and that you squared it with him later? Maybe you didn't mean to kill him. Maybe you just meant to settle a debt or two. But that's a bit academic now because either way he died. That means you murdered him' . . . he spread his hands wide . . . 'doesn't it?'

Gault gave the suggestion some thought. Finally, he leaned back in the chair and shook his massive head.

'Definitely not,' he said. 'I'd remember something like that.'

It was midnight before Faraday made it to Eadie Sykes's

seafront apartment. The rain had stopped now, and the air smelled fresher. Faraday coaxed the big old Alsatian out of his car and took him on to the beach for a last-chance walk, crunching down through the pebbles towards the soft lap-lap of the falling tide.

Another hour or so with Gault had failed to progress the investigation one inch. After a wealth of motivation – any number of reasons for wanting to see Coughlin dead – the interview had stalled on what Gault claimed to be the facts about Monday night. They'd all got arseholed at the hotel. Someone had called a cab. And Gault had finally tumbled into bed with his long-suffering missus. Challenged for times, Gault said he hadn't a clue. Accused, once again, of giving Coughlin a well-earned seeing-to, he'd regretfully declined the honour. Given half a chance, he'd have beaten the man senseless. Alas, though, he'd been too pissed.

The Alsatian was nosing around amongst the bundles of drying bladderwrack. Tomorrow, thought Faraday, there'd be a chance to test Gault's account against Beattie and Phillips. Tomorrow, as well, he'd organise for someone to talk to Gault's wife, establish some times, check them against the CCTV tapes and taxi log. That way, fingers crossed, he'd be able to fill in the bits that had fallen through Gault's memory. But what if it all tied together? What if the time-line put all three of them in the clear? Faraday shook his head, watching the dog at last lift its leg. Willard, for one, would be extremely vocal. And that didn't bear thinking about.

Eadie Sykes fell in love with the dog on first sight. In two minds about the fairness of imposing a large Alsatian on this impeccably designer apartment, Faraday was amazed to see her on all fours on the carpet, giving the dog the full treatment.

'Name's Rory,' Faraday muttered. 'Lives in the country.'

'But you've been on the beach, haven't you? All that

nice tar?' She glanced up at Faraday. 'Cupboard over the cooker. Stuff called Vanish. And there's surgical spirit in the bathroom for his paws.'

Between them, they cleaned the dog up. The tar on the carpet, on the other hand, resisted their best efforts. Not that Sykes appeared to mind.

'Rory? Here . . .'

She'd sorted out a makeshift bed in the bay window beyond the sofa, a couple of old blankets and – inexplicably – a stuffed pink elephant that had seen better days.

'Got it when I was seven.' She was back on her hands and knees, playing with the dog. 'We used to have a couple of mutts in Ambrym. They used to kick the shit out of my poor little elephant. He can probably still smell them.' She looked up. 'You hungry?'

She'd made a big salad, tuna, mackerel, boiled egg, with a top dressing of green olives stuffed with anchovy. Much to his surprise, Faraday discovered he was ravenous, the kind of hunger that barely paused for a third glass of wine. At length he collapsed on the sofa, checking over his shoulder for the dog. Rory, to his immense relief, appeared to have settled.

'You liked it then?'

'Loved it.'

Faraday had been telling her about the Tamar Valley: the depth of the peace; the slow brown river flowing past Beattie's cottage; the woods full of interesting birdlife; the knowledge that industrial life had come and gone, leaving this little cut-off promontory miraculously intact.

'You must take me there. Sounds like a film to me.'

'That's the last thing it needs. Can you imagine somewhere that perfect that close to a major city? Doesn't happen. Not round here.'

'Is that a no, then?'

'Not at all.' He watched her sorting out meat for the

dog. 'Just me being selfish. Who'd want to spoil a secret like that?'

'OK. No film. Does that make it better?'

'Much.'

'Is that a yes, then? Little expedition? You and me?'

Faraday smiled. He'd known this woman all of a week, yet already she seemed to have worked out how to square him away. Part of it was his own fault. Saddling her with Beattie's dog was a definite imposition. Yet he was fascinated by the speed with which she'd managed to connect the various dots in his life. First, she'd established squatters' rights over J-J. Now, she was talking of a long weekend in the Tamar Valley.

Not that he objected. Life with Eadie Sykes was so easy, so risk-free. She was every inch her own woman. She had a brilliant job, a flat to die for, and the kind of self-respect that sent her loping along the seafront at God knows what hour every morning. Faraday, if he was anything in her life, was a novelty, the opportunity for conversation and a laugh or two. They'd made love the other night, a coupling that was all the sweeter for being so shamelessly free of any emotional commitment, and afterwards Faraday had slept like a baby.

Now, he sensed something similar in the offing. Nice.

'Coffee?'

'No, thanks.' Faraday smothered a yawn. 'Tell you the truth, I'm buggered.'

'Me, too.' She bent over him, and kissed him on the nose. 'You'll give me a ring about the dog tomorrow? Only I'll need to lay in supplies.'

Dawn Ellis, alone in the big double bed, listened to the pumping of her heart. The phone had woken her up. She'd looked down at it in the half-darkness, flooded with relief when it stopped. Now it was ringing again, and this time she knew she had to answer it.

The clock on the little bedside table read 02.18. Had to be her caller again. Had to be.

At length, she reached down. The phone felt cold against her ear. There was a long silence. She was scarcely breathing, determined to offer not a shred of provocation. Finally, there came a strange laugh, high-pitched, then a voice that chilled her to the bone.

'Bitch,' the voice said. 'You know you'll have to pay.'

Another laugh, sealing the conversation, before the line went dead. Dawn lay sideways in the bed, still up on one elbow. She managed to get the ringing tone back, then her fingers tapped out 1471. There was a click on the line, then a recorded voice offered a number that didn't take incoming calls. Call-box, she thought numbly, settling back against the pillow.

Twenty-three

To Faraday's astonishment, Willard was rather impressed with the opening interview with Gault. He'd listened to extracts from the tapes first thing and had drawn the obvious conclusion.

'The man's a pisshead,' he said. 'And he loathed Coughlin. If that doesn't take us closer, then tell me what does.'

They were in Willard's BMW, driving up the motorway to nearby Waterlooville where the first interview with Beattie was to start mid-morning, as soon as he'd had a chance to confer with his solicitor. Willard had managed to lay hands on two DCs from the Somerstown job. Faraday had already discussed the overall strategy with the Tactical Interview Manager, and also found time to give the two DCs a flavour of the investigation to date. First off, Faraday and the TIM wanted an open account, a step-by-step description of exactly what had happened on the Monday night.

Willard was already looking beyond that.

'Where's the crux?' He eased into the outside lane. 'What do we need to develop?'

Faraday had been pondering exactly the same question.

'I tell you where it falls down,' he said. 'We can put all three of them at the hotel. Coughlin's obviously not flavour of the month. Gault in particular would happily sort him out. The man arrives, takes one look, knows he's not welcome, goes again. Agreed?' Faraday looked sideways at Willard.

'With you.' Willard nodded.

'OK. So where does Coughlin go?'

'Home.'

'Do we know that? For sure?'

'No.' Willard shook his head. 'But it's a reasonable assumption. Niton Road's five minutes away. And it's late.'

'OK. So let's assume we're right. Coughlin legs it home, leaving the three guys banging on at the hotel. There's no suggestion any of them followed him.'

'Pritchard?'

'Specifically said they all stayed drinking. Had one of them gone after Coughlin, he'd have mentioned it, I know he would.'

Willard ducked back into the slow lane and signalled left for the Waterlooville exit.

'You're right,' he muttered. 'How would they know where to find the bastard?'

Bev Yates was halfway to Milton before he remembered about the Scenes of Crime team. Gault's wife and kids had been moved out to hotel accommodation while Jerry Proctor's boys went through their house, looking for evidence that Gault might have been involved in a beating. As soon as they'd finished, Mrs Gault could have the house back but for the time being she and the kids were occupying a room at the Travel Inn on the seafront.

She was sitting in a chair beside the bed when Yates tapped at the door. A taxi had taken the kids to school at half past eight and she'd spent the last two hours watching morning TV.

'Do you mind if I . . . ?'

Yates turned the TV off without waiting for an answer. The kids had left their pyjamas in a pile behind the door and two breakfast trays had been abandoned on the unmade bed. Mrs Gault had obviously made no attempt to tidy up the little room and under the circumstances, Yates didn't blame her. Trying to come to terms with the fact that your husband might have killed someone, you'd have other things on your mind.

'Have they finished yet, your people?'

Yates said he didn't know. A full forensic search could take days but now wasn't the time to tell her that.

'I'll let you know as soon as I have some news,' he said. 'I just need to get a statement off you.'

Mrs Gault didn't appear to understand. She was a big, bulky woman – similar build to her husband – but there was a softness in her face that began to explain Gault's outrage the previous evening. *Accolade*'s ex-chef had found himself a cosy berth with this woman – nice house, lovely kids – until he and Dave Michaels had stepped in from nowhere and wrecked it all. No wonder the man had gone potty.

'Last Monday night . . .' Yates began.

Mrs Gault knotted her hands in her ample lap. Angry, reproachful, it was more than she could do to look Yates in the eye.

'What do you want to know?'

'Your husband went to the function.'

'That's right.'

He'd left early. A cab had called for him. After he'd gone, she and the kids had walked round the corner for a video. *Toy Story*.

'I don't suppose you've got kids.' It was an accusation.

'Two. If I look knackered it's because I am.'

'Girls?' A tiny smile.

'One each. Where we live there's no video store so we have to rely on telling them stories.'

'That's good.' She nodded approvingly. 'Stories are good.'

'Yeah?' Yates's pen still hovered above his notebook. 'So tell me about Monday night. Paul went out. What time did he get back?'

'Late. Very late.'

'You were still awake?'

'I was. I was worried about him.'

'Why?'

'Because . . .' Her eyes went to her lap again. Her husband's a pisshead, Yates thought. And she doesn't want to admit it.

There was a long silence. Yates could hear the whine of a vacuum cleaner up the corridor.

'Does he get violent?' he asked at last. 'With the drink?'

'No, no.' She looked up, colour flooding her face. 'Never violent, no, not Paulie.'

'You're sure about that? Never threatens you? Never comes home off his head and makes life difficult?'

'No. Never. He likes a drink, Paul. Always, he likes a drink, too much he likes a drink, and then sometimes . . .'

'What? Sometimes what?'

'Sometimes he gets . . . you know . . . so he falls down.'

'And Monday night?'

She gazed at him a moment, then offered a small, regretful nod.

'He fell down.'

'What time was this?'

'Late, I told you.'

'How late?'

'Gone two in the morning. I had the light on upstairs. I was waiting for him. I heard the cab come. The driver was kind, helped him to the door.'

'You saw the cab?'

'I was downstairs by then. I had the front door open, ready for him.'

'Was there anyone else in the cab? Can you remember?'

The frown again, intense concentration. Then she shook her head.

'I can't remember. It was dark. I don't know. All that mattered was Paulie, that he was safe.'

The cab gone, she'd tried to get her husband up the stairs but in the end she'd left him on the sofa in the living room, wrapped in an eiderdown.

'What sort of state was he in?'

'Drunk. Very drunk.'

'I know that but . . .' Yates gestured loosely at the space between them. 'Was he hurt at all? Had he been in any kind of fight?'

'*Fight?*' Her voice rose. 'I tell you something about my husband, Mr Policeman. I've never seen Paulie fighting in my life. Not until yesterday. Not until you came into our house. He's like most men. He talks big, talks tough, but he wouldn't hurt anyone. He's not like that. Paulie? *Fight?*'

Yates was still trying to picture Gault sprawled on the downstairs sofa, dead to the world. There were questions here that he had to ask, but already he sensed that she knew the truth about this man of hers: that Gault, behind all the bluster and the booze, was a puppy dog.

Yates leaned forward.

'You went to bed and left him to it.' He took care to spell it out. 'How can you be sure he didn't get up again? Leave the house?'

For a long moment, Mrs Gault considered this proposition. For some reason, it seemed to have distressed her.

'I locked the front door and kept the key,' she said at last.

'You thought he might go out again?'

'Yes.' She nodded. 'Sometimes he does that. A little walk. The fresh air. But that Monday night? No. He stayed on the sofa. Even when . . . you know . . . he should have been in the lavatory, he stayed on the sofa.' She tipped her head back, her eyes swimming with tears. 'He's never been that bad before. Never.'

The first interview with Beattie began at half past ten. His solicitor had made it plain that her client was only too happy to help in whatever way he could but would limit his replies to the circumstances surrounding Monday night. Any discussion of events aboard *Accolade*, in particular concerning Matthew Warren, were off-limits. If the police were interested in any of that, then their questions – in Beattie's view – should be more properly directed to the Ministry of Defence.

'If only,' Willard had grunted, hearing this news.

Now, with the interview under way, Faraday and Willard sat in a small, bare room down the corridor. An audio feed enabled them to monitor the exchanges, a process that plunged Faraday into gloom. Beattie had obviously had a bad night. His voice was gruff, his answers bare of anything but the facts. He'd driven Phillips to Portsmouth. They'd booked into the Home Club, adjoining rooms. They'd met in the bar for a pre-dinner drink. Paul Gault had joined them on table five and they'd sunk a fair amount of wine. Afterwards, more drinks in the bar, then an excursion to the Alhambra. The barman at the Home Club had heard about lock-ins at the hotel. The place might be good for a nightcap or two.

'What was it like when you got there?'

'Crap . . . but it didn't matter. We got stuck in. Gault especially.'

'What were you talking about?'

'I can't remember. Stuff from way back. You talk a lot of old bollocks on occasions like these but I suppose that's why you go.'

They'd been there maybe half an hour by the time Coughlin turned up. Gault had been the one to recognise him. Phillips was all for offering him a drink but Coughlin hadn't hung around. Afterwards, Gault had blathered on about Coughlin, threatening all sorts, but he was too far gone to do anything about it.

'Did he leave the hotel at all?'

'No.'

'Did he leave the bar?'

'Yeah. We'd been at it since seven. No one's got a bladder that big.'

The bloke behind the bar, Beattie said, had obviously wanted them out. They'd shown no interest in going so in the end he phoned for a cab. The cab called first at Gault's place. He'd been in a real state by then and needed help to make it to the front door. The cabby had done the honours and his wife, poor soul, was there to haul him inboard. After that, the cab had taken them back to the Home Club. End of story.

Faraday and Willard conferred about the CCTV tapes. From memory, Faraday confirmed that a cab had dropped two passengers at the club around two o'clock in the morning. On the face of it, the timings were a perfect fit.

Willard pulled a face.

'So when did anyone get the chance to have a pop at Coughlin? Doesn't work, does it?'

Faraday agreed. When the first interview session came to an end, he and Willard sat in the uniformed Superintendent's office reviewing their strategy for the rest of the day. The interviewing DCs had done their best, taking Beattie back over every element in his story, but already it was obvious that the ex-Master-at-Arms had nothing to add. Time after time, he'd met their questions with a stony 'No Comment', and when one of the DCs ventured on to new turf, enquiring about shipboard attitudes to Coughlin, Beattie had refused point-blank to rise to the bait.

From Fareham police station, more bad news. Phillips, Beattie's mate from Plymouth, had made it plain that he'd be suing Devon and Cornwall for wrongful arrest. There wasn't a shred of evidence to connect him to anything as bizarre as a murder. He'd spent a pleasant evening in the company of a roomful of old shipmates, got legless afterwards, and woken up next morning with a thumping headache. Thanks to the Alhambra, his days on the Bacardi were well and truly over but any suggestion that he might have given Coughlin a kicking was totally out of order. Like Beattie, he'd given an account of his movements on Monday night and, like Beattie, he'd now withdrawn his cooperation. With some reluctance, Faraday was therefore obliged to accept the obvious: that another hour or two of 'No Comment' would get them nowhere.

Close to midday, Willard announced his departure. He had an important meeting at the Home Office and needed to be there for half two. There were cars going back to Pompey all the time so maybe Faraday could bum a lift. Heading for the door, Willard paused to take a call on his mobile. He listened for a moment or two, grunted a couple of times, then brought the conversation to a close.

Faraday, wondering whether he should bother monitoring a second session with Beattie, was already on his feet.

'Dave Michaels just took a call from the MOD.' Willard was pocketing the cell phone. 'Vice Admiral Wylie mean anything to you?'

Faraday shook his head. One of Wylie's staff was evidently keen to set up a meeting. The Vice Admiral had an office in Portsmouth and was due down at lunchtime. There was a window in his schedule early afternoon and he'd be grateful for a word or two with a senior member of the *Merriott* team.

'So what does he want?' Willard asked.

Faraday remembered Yates's enquiries at the Ministry of Defence.

'We've been chasing a guy called Harrington. Mark Harrington. He was First Lieutenant in *Accolade* and promised to come back on that missing Ship's Investigation report. Maybe he talked to the brass instead.'

'Yeah. Maybe he did.' Willard glanced at his watch. The meet at the Home Office was suddenly a pain in the arse. 'You'll stand in for me? Find out why they pulled the bloody report? Yeah?'

Faraday nodded. He recognised an order.

'Of course, sir.' He smiled. 'My pleasure.'

Dawn's call found Winter at the city's dog pound, prowling from cage to cage, wondering whether the time hadn't come to get himself a pooch. So far nothing had caught his fancy except a young, pugnacious-looking boxer, who eyed him through the wire before jumping up, throwing his head back, and howling. I'll call him Rookie, Winter thought, and see if he gets the joke.

Dawn was back at work, chained to her desk in the CID office at Highland Road.

'How come? I thought you were going to take another couple of sickies?'

'No chance.'

She told him about the two a.m. call. She hadn't slept a wink since and now she felt like death.

'You get the number?'

'Call-box in Cosham High Street, down by the station. That's why I came in. Reverse phone book.'

'And what time was this?' Winter had his pen out.

'Two eighteen.'

'Leave it to me, love.' Winter was making faces at the boxer. 'I'll be in touch.'

Whale Island lies to the north of Portsmouth's continental ferry port, a lozenge-shaped scrap of land colonised for generations by the Royal Navy. Traditionally the home of HMS *Excellent*, the navy's gunnery school, it had lately become the UK headquarters for Fleet Command.

Faraday crossed the bridge from the city and coasted to a halt beside the guardhouse. A sentry manning the barrier already had a note of his name and phoned through to the Vice Admiral's office for an escort.

Waiting in the warm sunshine, Faraday watched queues of cars disappearing into one of the big cross-Channel ferries. One day, he thought, it might be nice to spring a little surprise on Eadie Sykes. Two return tickets for Le Havre and a week in between for some serious eating.

The escort turned out to be a smart young Wren with a bright smile and terrific legs. Faraday left his Mondeo in the bay behind the guardhouse and together they walked across towards the building that housed the administrative offices. Faraday, she said, was lucky. The Vice Admiral was the busiest, most in-demand boss she'd ever worked for. Laying claim to even fifteen minutes of his precious time was nothing short of a miracle. Faraday, who'd never heard of the Vice Admiral, was tempted to come clean but decided against it. Whatever the navy wanted to get off its chest, it clearly couldn't wait.

'Inspector?' A tall figure advanced across the office, silhouetted by the light streaming in through the big sash windows.

'*Detective* Inspector.' Faraday shook the outstretched hand. 'Pleased to meet you.'

The Vice Admiral was younger than Faraday had expected, no more than his own age. His eyes were nearly black and he had a gambler's smile, at once mischievous and knowing. He waved Faraday towards a comfortable-looking armchair and offered him a cigarette.

'No, thanks.'

Still on his feet, Faraday couldn't take his eyes off the view. This was a perspective on the harbour he'd never seen before, a line of pensioned-off warships lying in the deep-water channel that curled up towards Portchester Castle, and Faraday thought at once of Plymouth, those same grey shapes dancing in the haze.

'Sorry about the short notice. It was good of you to come.'

Faraday at last sat down. Wylie had shaken a cigarette from its packet, and was patting his trouser pockets for a lighter. The ashtray on the low coffee table between them was brimming with discarded butts.

'It's about *Accolade*.' Wylie drew the first lungful of smoke deep into his chest, then expelled it, tipping his head sideways. 'You'll forgive me getting to the point.'

'Of course.'

'I understand you're mounting some kind of investigation?'

'That's right. A man named Coughlin was murdered last week. It's my job to try and work out why.'

'Why or how?'

'How we know. How's easy. Why's more important because why might take us to the killer.'

'And you're getting there? Making progress?'

'Yes.'

The Vice Admiral waited for more but Faraday just smiled. There was no professional guidance he'd ever seen that obliged him to share investigative details with a total stranger.

A moment later, there came a knock at the door. The Wren was back again, this time with coffee. The Vice Admiral was on his feet at once, making space on the table.

'Milk? Sugar?' The Wren had gone.

Faraday watched Wylie at work with a sachet of sugar. Finally, he opened it with his teeth.

'You'll know we lost a lad at sea.' He didn't look up. 'Name of Matthew Warren. I understand you're keen for sight of the Ship's Investigation.'

'That's right.'

'May I ask for what reason?'

'Of course.' Faraday reached for the proffered coffee. 'In cases like these we find it pays to try and get inside the victim's head. To begin with, that may be the only lead we have to go on. And so we go back and back, years back, decades sometimes, putting a life together. You'd be amazed at what we find.'

'I'm sure. We do it with our blokes, all the time. Read between the lines of a man's service record, talk to one or two of his shipmates, and it's all there.'

'Exactly. For us, that kind of research has become a forensic tool. I wouldn't be doing my job if I didn't have Coughlin pretty much taped.'

'And you think you've done that?'

'I think I've made a start, certainly.'

'Enough to take the inquiry in a certain direction?'

'Enough to give us a steer or two.'

'So why your interest in the Ship's Investigation?'

Matthew Warren again. And the winter's night, way down south, when the young steward had inexplicably disappeared.

Faraday began to explain about possible evidence of some kind of relationship aboard, a tiny cancer that might have grown and grown over the intervening years.

'I'm afraid I'm not with you.'

'We think there might have been bullying. Coughlin and the boy Warren.'

'That's possible.' Wylie frowned. 'Of course it's possible. We do our best to stamp on that kind of abuse, and it's much better now than it was, but I'd never claim we're a hundred per cent successful. But forgive me . . .' The frown deepened. 'What's that got to do with this man's death?'

'We don't know.' Faraday smiled at him. 'Yet.'

'But you think there might be a connection?'

'Yes. Abuse is a good word. Maybe Coughlin didn't stop at bullying.'

The Vice Admiral was looking thoughtful now. His coffee lay on the table, untouched. Finally he got up and went across to his desk. The buff envelope was on top of the files beside his PC.

'This is the orginal.' He gave Faraday the envelope and sat down again. 'I'm afraid you can't take it away but you're welcome to read through it.'

Faraday slid the contents on to his lap. Four photo-copied sheets of paper, stapled together. This, he quickly realised, was the Ship's Investigation missing from the archive at HMS *Centurion*. He scanned quickly through the first page, a summary of events.

Warren had been reported missing at 05.48 Zulu. The ship, after seeking permission from *Hermes*, had com-menced a sea search a little over an hour later. By mid-morning, in a rising gale, the search was officially abandoned.

Faraday turned the page, spotting a contribution from the Master-at-Arms. In Beattie's view there were no grounds for viewing Warren's disappearance as anything other than a tragic accident. His Divisional Officer had reported no undue anxieties. To his friends' knowledge, there were no girlfriend problems at home. A search of his locker had revealed nothing untoward. Beattie had signed his report in a small, crabbed hand, making way for a paragraph each from the two officers co-opted to oversee the investigation. Like Beattie, they'd concluded that Warren had been the victim of an unfortunate accident. What contribution he might have made to his own death – by ignoring regulations, by taking an unwarranted risk – was unclear, but there was a measure of sympathy for the rating throughout the ship, and his messmates had responded generously.

'Sympathy?' For the first time, Faraday detected a chink of light.

The Vice Admiral shrugged the word away.

'It's what you'd expect,' he murmured. 'They raffled his tapes, bunged money his way. Normally it goes to the wife but in Warren's case it would have been the parents. Happens on every ship.'

Faraday turned to the final page. The First Lieutenant, Mark Harrington, had respectfully brought the report to the attention of the ship's Captain. He, in turn, had signed it off.

Faraday felt a little jolt of recognition. Commander Jock Wylie. No wonder, he thought.

'Maybe I should have told you earlier.' Wylie could see Faraday's finger anchored beneath the Captain's signature. 'Might that have been more diplomatic?'

'Not at all.' Faraday slipped the report back into the envelope. 'Do you mind if I ask you a question?'

'Delighted. Fire away.'

'Was this why you asked me in?' Faraday tapped the envelope.

'My ship, you mean?'

'Yes. I imagine you'd get quite parental. Especially if she'd gone down like that.'

'Parental?'

'Protective.'

'Of what, exactly?'

'I don't know.' Faraday tried to get a fix on what he was trying to say. 'Her reputation? Her memory? The blokes you served with? It can't be a small thing, losing your ship.'

Wylie gave a little bark of laughter and then stood up. By the time he got to the window, he'd lit another cigarette.

'I've no idea how much you know about *Accolade*, Inspector Faraday, but let's suppose you've done your homework.' He turned back into the room. 'You're right about losing your ship. It hurts in personal terms, of course it does. We lost far too many men. Caused far too much grief. But it goes a lot further than that, especially if you're the one carrying the can. The navy, quite rightly, is unforgiving. They want to know exactly what went wrong. Boards of Inquiry can be brutal.'

Wylie was beside the coffee table, the cigarette smouldering between his stained fingers. He'd shipped home, like everyone else, aboard the *QE2*. The management had given him a palatial cabin on one of the upper decks. His XO had christened it 'The Penthouse Suite'. He'd sat

380

up there for days and days on end, writing letter after letter, to wives, mothers, even – when he knew them personally – kids. And he'd emerged from that personal taste of purgatory with the conviction that there was nothing – *nothing* – more important than a man's family. Not victory. Not honour. Not medals. Not glory. What mattered, what really mattered, were the people left behind. How they'd cope. How they'd adjust. How they'd somehow be able to heal that yawning hole a war had blasted in their lives.

'And Matthew Warren?'

'I was coming to him.' Wylie sucked in a another lungful of smoke. 'That lad didn't go down like the rest of them. It wasn't the war that killed him. But you know something? We did our level best to gloss the difference. And you know something else? I truly believe it worked. The Warrens are a Pompey family. You probably know that. They live out Milton way. And as the years have gone by I think they've come to believe that Matthew gave his life for Queen and Country. We used to hold annual services, remembrance services, on the twenty-first of May, and the whole family – mum, dad, and I think his brother – used to turn up. One year, I've an idea it was eighty-seven, I remember his mother approaching me after the service and telling me that she'd made a sort of peace with herself. Matthew's death had broken her heart, her own words, but now she realised that it was a kind of sacrifice. He was dead, just like the other nineteen were dead. They'd been killed because they'd gone to war. Is that self-deception, *pro patria mori*? It probably is. Does it matter, even in the slightest? No.' The Vice Admiral retrieved the buff envelope from the coffee table, then weighed it in his hand. A moment later, he checked his watch. 'Peace is a precious commodity, Mr Faraday,' he murmured. 'It would be a shame to disturb it.'

Winter had lost count of the times he'd relied on CCTV

footage. With more than a hundred cameras now covering most of the city, he'd raided the tapes again and again for evidence, pinning down a face and a time at a particular location, demolishing the tosh that passed these days for alibis. The on-street cameras were supervised from a spacious control room in the bowels of the city's civic centre. The operation rolled on, twenty-four hours a day, and Winter's favourite shift leader was called Len.

'All right, Paul? What happened to that arm?'

Len was nearing retirement, a wiry little man with the world's worst taste in ties. He had a passion for greyhound racing, and Winter occasionally sorted him out an invite for the local track.

'I'm after Cosham, Len.' Winter was inspecting the big wall map, each camera tagged with a number in red. 'Down by the station there. Number ninety-seven.'

'When?'

'Last night. Two eighteen.'

'No problem.'

Recorded tapes were kept for a month before being wiped. Cassettes with last night's coverage were still on a shelf at the back. Len loaded one into a replay machine, part of a tiny edit suite, and then spun through the footage, pausing to check the digital time read-out. Finally, he beckoned Winter over.

'This what you're after?'

Winter looked at the screen. The length of Cosham High Street lay before him, empty except for a pair of cats stalking each other between the chemist and the Salvation Army shop. For a moment, he couldn't remember where to find the phone-box.

'There.' Len was pointing.

Winter nodded, orientated now. The box was lit inside and a tall figure was bent over the phone, his face shielded. After a while, he began to talk, the briefest conversation, then he put the phone down and turned back towards the street. Winter watched as he retrieved a helmet from the bike parked beside the call-box. Seconds later, his helmet on, he looked directly up at the camera. Then came the raised hand, the middle finger erect. He held the pose for a couple of seconds, just standing there, before straddling the bike and disappearing up the High Street.

Len couldn't take his eyes off the screen.

'What's that about, then?'

'He's sending us a message.' Winter grinned. 'Any chance of a VHS?'

Twenty-four

Faraday was walking Beattie's dog on Southsea beach when Willard rang from London. Faraday had stolen fifteen minutes to duck out of the office and drive down to Southsea. Eadie Sykes, away for the day, had given him a spare key last night and now he was enjoying the warmth of a perfect June afternoon while the Alsatian prowled amongst the damp, shadowed spaces beneath the pier.

'What was he after, then? The Admiral?'

'Vice Admiral.'

'Whatever.'

Faraday, who'd given the same question considerable thought, admitted to his own confusion. On the one hand, it was nothing more than an affable exchange of views. On the other, there might have been an altogether darker agenda. Therein, he supposed, lay the guile of senior commanders like Wylie.

'I may be wrong.' Faraday was trying to keep his eye on the dog. 'But I got the feeling he was warning us off.'

'Doing *what*?'

'He never spelled it out. He's far too clever for that. But he obviously thinks we're trespassing. It doesn't help that *Accolade* was his ship.'

'At the time, you mean?'

'Yes. He was Captain when it went down.'

'So he'd know about Coughlin?'

'And the lad Warren, yes.'

'Shit.' Willard sounded impressed. 'You should have

interviewed him, got it down on paper. What was he up to on Monday night?'

Faraday assumed this was a joke, but Willard wasn't laughing.

'What about the Ship's Investigation? Did you ask him about that?'

'He had it there. He showed me.'

'And?'

'Nothing in it. The lad was reported missing. They searched the ship. Went back to look for him. Then got on with the war.' He paused. 'I get the feeling that if anyone killed Warren, it was the Argies. Everyone seems more comfortable with that.'

'I bet.' Willard broke off to bark at someone, then came back on the phone. 'So why couldn't we find the report in the first place?'

'I've no idea, sir. Coughlin's death may have sparked some kind of review. They knew his file had been accessed so they may have taken a look at what else was lying around.'

'Just in case, you mean?'

'Exactly.' They'd sensed a storm coming, he thought. And they were clearing the decks.

Willard changed the subject. He wanted to know about the Scenes of Crime searches. Compared to Faraday's exchange with the Vice Admiral, this couldn't have been simpler.

'Nothing.'

'Nothing at all? All three properties?'

'Nothing at Phillips' place. Some traces of old blood in Beattie's kitchen, probably animal. They're happy to send it up to Lambeth but they're talking pigeon or rabbit.'

'And Gault?'

'Clean as a whistle, except for the sofa.'

'What did they get from the sofa?'

'Urine stains. Someone seems to have pissed on it.'

'Like who?'

'Yates says Gault. According to his missus, Gault spent Monday night on the sofa. Full to the brim and totally legless.'

'Great.' Like Faraday, Willard had drawn the obvious conclusion. A man who couldn't make it to the loo was hardly likely to have battered someone else to death. 'What do we do about the cabby, then? Still worth getting Yates up to Gatwick?'

Faraday was watching the Alsatian. He'd emerged from under the pier and was now splashing around in the shallows. He should have brought a towel, he thought. Otherwise Eadie's flat was in for the full beach experience.

'Joe?'

'I don't know, sir. Part of me says it's a waste of time. But then' . . . he shrugged . . . 'we've come this far, we might as well be absolutely certain.'

'That's my feeling, too. Get him up there first thing tomorrow.'

Winter took the chance on reappearing in the CID office at the Highland Road nick. Signed off by his doctor, he had no business venturing on to police property but he was determined to have a word or two with Dawn Ellis. He found her sitting at her desk beside the window. Half a dozen other DCs were bent over their PCs, tapping in data from their pocketbooks. No one appeared to register his presence.

Winter looked round, knowing at once that he'd be lost without the comforts of this little world. The piles of uncompleted CPS files. The scribbled Post-its gummed to PC screens. The trophy headlines, ripped from pages of the *News* and pinned on the wall board over the big catering-size tin of Gold Blend. One of them, to his consternation, featured a crumpled Skoda embedded in the remains of a Queen Street newsagent. 'Hot Pursuit,' someone had scribbled across the photo. 'The Movie.' Unkind, thought Winter.

'What are you doing here?'

It was Cathy Lamb. She was standing in the doorway, nursing a stack of files.

Winter began to mutter about an address book he'd left in his desk drawer. Numbers he couldn't do without. Just happened to be passing.

'Bollocks, were you.' Cathy nodded back along the corridor. 'Come with me.'

Winter followed her to the DI's office. She shut the door and told him to sit down.

'What's the matter with you, Paul?' she said at once. 'You've put Dawn in an impossible position. First you bloody nearly kill her. Now you're asking her to perjure herself. Does that strike you as fair?'

Cathy meant it. He'd rarely seen her so angry. He spread his hands wide. Abject surrender.

'They're going to take my job away, Cath. Put me back in uniform.'

'So they bloody should. And not before time, either.'

'What?'

'You've spent half a lifetime getting away with it, Paul. Now they think they've nailed you.'

'Who's they?'

'You want a list? Hartigan, for starters. You've always made him uncomfortable. Then there's a couple of thousand guys in Traffic. You know what they feel about us. Scruffs and layabouts. They can't wait to put you away.'

'Uniforms.' Winter did his best to sound dismissive.

'Sure. But the law's on their side. And they know it.'

'What about Willard?'

'I haven't a clue about Willard. Willard's in orbit as far as I'm concerned, way out of my league. I think he'd probably miss you, if only for the laughs, but I'm guessing.'

'What about you?'

'Me?' She looked at him for a long moment, refusing to commit herself. Then she turned away.

'You've been good to Dawn,' she said woodenly. 'And I appreciate that.'

'I thought you said I'd nearly killed her?'

'You did, but that's not what I'm talking about.' She glanced round, angry again. 'As you well know.'

Winter nodded, remembering the afternoon Cathy had dropped round to the bungalow in Bedhampton, offering her own support to Dawn. He'd watched them through the kitchen window, locked in conversation. Cathy knew as much about Andy Corbett as Winter. Probably more.

Now, she perched herself on the edge of her desk. Life in the office had put a bit of weight on her big frame.

'He phoned again,' she said. 'Can you believe that? Middle of the night? After everything else he's done to her?'

'I know.'

Winter produced a VHS cassette and passed it across. He'd been meaning to show it to Dawn but sensed that this was better.

'What's that?'

'Footage from one of the CCTV cameras. Cosham High Street.'

'Last night?'

'Two o'clock in the morning.'

'Corbett?'

'Clear as daylight.'

'Definitely him?'

'No question. His bike's there, too. Numberplate, everything.'

Winter's hand was back in his pocket. An audio cassette this time. Cathy gazed at it.

'You've been having chats?'

'Afraid so.'

'With Corbett?'

'Obviously.'

'And?'

'If you think I'm in the shit, you should listen to that.'

For the first time, Cathy smiled. She was still staring at the little cassette.

'May I?'

'It's yours.'

She picked up both cassettes and slipped them into her drawer. The sight of her turning the lock gladdened Winter immeasurably. He looked up at her, sensing they'd reached a bend in the road.

'You've been a prat, Paul. And that's being charitable.'

'I was chasing a murder suspect, Cath, a kid half the bloody city were trying to find. What was I supposed to do? Give him a little wave and let him get on with it? Of course I chased him. That's what blokes like me are for. We're detectives. We go after the bad guys. And when they run, we run after them.'

'But there are procedures, Paul. Regulations.' She waved a hand across the clutter on her desk. 'Don't tell me you don't know about all this stuff.'

'Of course I know about all this stuff. Christ, I spend most of my life trying to get round all this stuff. It's all this stuff that's made the job so bloody impossible. It's all this stuff that keeps blokes banged up next door when they should be out on the street. The fun's gone out of the job, Cath, you know it has. It's just paperwork now, and covering your arse. That's why people are so pissed off. Jesus, Cath, the suits should be *pleased* with me. I'm the one guy in this organisation not queuing for early retirement.'

'Finished?'

'No. I haven't. I've got a case here. I know I have. OK, I'm a bad boy. OK, I cut the odd corner. But in the end we should be talking results – and you don't put Darren Geech away by filling in forms.'

'But you lost him,' Cathy pointed out. 'And nearly killed God knows how many people in the process.'

'Like who?'

'Like Dawn.'

Winter stiffened in the chair. Cathy had backed him against the wall, he knew she had, but he had a right to be angry as well. Angry about vindictive, po-faced Traffic sergeants trying to put him away. Angry about what had happened to the job. Once upon a time, blokes like Winter would have been given a bit of credit. Now they were an embarrassment.

'Maybe Hartigan's right,' he said. 'Maybe it's time I went, jacked it in completely. That might make it sweet for everyone. Including me.'

'You mean that?'

'Of course I fucking don't.'

'Then why say it?'

'Because it's hard, Cath. And because so much of it is bollocks.'

She nodded, saying nothing. Then she glanced at her watch.

'Hartigan wants me in for an off-the-record chat,' she muttered.

'About what?'

'You.'

At Kingston Crescent, Faraday found the Major Crimes suite in a state of some excitement. Nick Hayder emerged from the tiny kitchen at the end. He had three polystyrene cups in one hand and a bottle of Sainsbury's champagne in the other.

'What's happened?'

'You won't believe it.'

'Believe what?'

Faraday followed Hayder into his office. Two DCs were already in there, big grins. One of them was Andy Corbett.

Hayder shut the office door with his foot. He passed the cups around, then nodded at the phone.

'Took a call round lunchtime,' he said. 'Kid by the name of Hollins. Comes off the Somerstown estate. Claims to have seen Geech putting the boot in the afternoon Rookie got it. Not just that, the boy was happy to talk about it.'

'On the record?'

'Yep.'

Hayder was pouring the champagne. Corbett took up the story.

'We were straight round there.' His eyes went to the file lying on Hayder's desk. 'Kid put it all in writing. Full witness statement. And not just him, either. Two other little scrotes as well.'

'Saying what?'

'Saying that Geech did it.'

Faraday couldn't believe it. Getting anyone off the estates to answer their front door was a major result. Securing a signed statement was an urban miracle.

'They're happy to go to court? Testify against Geech?'

'So they say.'

Faraday looked from one face to another. The billion-dollar question.

'Why?'

Hayder shrugged. Sometimes you had a lucky day, he said. This was obviously one of them. He glanced at the two DCs. Corbett was shaking his head.

'I put it down to legwork. That and some fucking good decisions from the top.' He offered Faraday a cold smile, then gestured towards Hayder. 'Great guvnor.' He tipped his cup in salute. 'Great team.'

Back in his own office, Faraday found himself looking at a message from one of the management assistants. A London number beneath a name he didn't recognise. DI

Pannell? The name was underlined twice, with a scribbled 'Urgent!' beside it.

Faraday phoned the management assistant.

'Streatham nick,' she told him. 'Something to do with intelligence.'

Faraday remembered now. This was the DI in charge of the surveillance operation, the mates of Andy Corbett who were keeping tabs on Ainsley Davidson. The last couple of days, Faraday hadn't given the young ex-con a second thought. Now, with the *Accolade* interviews bogging down, he might conceivably be back in the frame. The thought filled Faraday with gloom. Corbett, next door, was already toasting one success. The prospect of another triumph would be too much to bear.

Faraday put the call through. After a while, a woman's voice.

'I wanted to speak to DI Pannell.'

'I am DI Pannell.' She sounded icy.

Faraday introduced himself. Pannell recognised the name at once.

'It's about Ainsley Davidson,' she said flatly.

To her evident regret, she'd been volunteered for a meet. If it was to happen at all it would have to be tonight. Under the circumstances, she'd prefer it if Faraday didn't come to the station. Sorry about the short notice but the job had gone crazy.

'Where, then?' Faraday decided he had to go. 'My shout.'

She named a wine bar in Streatham High Road. Early evening, say half seven, would be best for her. Green Berghaus anorak and a black shoulder bag with half her life inside it.

'One thing I didn't mention.'

'What's that?'

'I have to be away by eight. Just in case you were thinking of making a night of it.'

She rang off, leaving Faraday holding the phone. From Hayder's office next door, the sound of laughter.

It was the work of minutes for Winter to seal one of his spare audio cassettes in an envelope and slip it into the internal post. It wasn't that he lacked faith in Cathy Lamb. On the contrary, he knew that she'd use every ounce of her newly acquired authority to try and make Corbett pay for what he'd done to Dawn. But internal procedures were famously slow and Winter wasn't at all sure that a form existed for a wanker like Corbett. No, far better to give him a little push, a tiny preview of the difficult interviews to come. That way, fingers crossed, he might get the hint and bugger off.

A colleague at the next desk watched him addressing the envelope to Major Crimes.

'Job application?' He cocked an eyebrow.

'Yeah.' Winter was still shielding Corbett's name. 'Sort of.'

Faraday took the train to London, sharing a table with three yachties. Two of them were men his own age, seamed faces, deep tans, and as the conversation developed it was clear they'd been away for some time. The talk was of Caribbean anchorages and the gumbo in some beachside bar on Martinique, of the price they'd had to pay for a fill-up of fresh water and the storm they'd weathered on the passage home. Staring out at the neatly hedged fields, Faraday could see Eadie Sykes in a setting like that, and by the time they got to Waterloo he'd begun to wonder whether she needed a mate. There were times when the job got on top of him, and this was very definitely one of them.

The interviews with the three *Accolade*s, he knew for virtually certain, were going nowhere. Sessions after lunch had quickly hit the buffers. Neither Beattie nor Phillips was prepared to add anything to their previous accounts, and Gault was showing serious signs of alcohol withdrawal. His replies to the simplest questions were fevered and rambling. All he wanted was another glass of lemonade.

Given this obvious lack of progress, Faraday had encountered some difficulty making the case to the uniformed Superintendent for a twelve-hour PACE extension. Only the prospect of case-breaking new evidence from the Aqua cabbie, the guy Bev Yates would be intercepting at Gatwick airport, had persuaded the Superintendent to OK the extra twelve hours. The man might have overheard an incriminating conversation. He might have been asked to make a detour to Niton Road. He might even have found blood in the back of his cab next morning. On the point of leaving his office, Faraday had been halted by the door.

'But what happens if these three guys are in the clear?' the Superintendent had wanted to know.

'Don't know, sir. I imagine we go back to square one.'

Streatham High Road was thick with traffic when Faraday finally made it from Balham tube. Buses and lorries were backed up as far as he could see, and the air tasted foul. It was still hot, hotter than Portsmouth, and he was glad of the air-conditioning when he finally ducked into the wine bar.

To his surprise, the DI was already there, perched on a bar stool beside the coffee machine. The green anorak was folded on her lap and she was leafing through a copy of the London *Evening Standard*.

'You're early,' Faraday said.

She glanced up. She had a striking face – blue eyes, wide mouth, fringe of blonde curls – but her complexion was pallid and she looked like she needed a good night's sleep. She made space between them, pushing back the adjacent stool with her foot.

There was an open bottle of red beside the ashtray on the counter. She indicated the other glass.

'It's a Merlot,' she said. 'I took the liberty of putting it on your tab.'

'No problem.' Faraday reached for the bottle. 'Do you have a first name?'

'Chris. And yours?'

'Joe.'

They sparred uneasily for several minutes, Faraday waiting for the wine to kick in. She'd been on division as a DI for the best part of two years, trying to stopper the usual bottles. They agreed that shoplifters were a pain, kids worse and nuisance jobs worst of all. By the time she got to her recent intelligence posting, Faraday was glad he didn't live in South London.

'So how long have you been on intelligence?'

'Three months. Moved over early spring.'

'Like it?'

'Love it.'

Faraday knew that now was the moment they'd get down to business. It wasn't that this woman begrudged him a decent conversation. It was just that her job was hectic enough already without having to make room for some provincial dipshit from the sticks.

'This is off the record, right?'

'Absolutely.' Faraday had expected nothing else.

'OK. We've been interested in Davidson for a while. We followed him through the prison system and we knew his release date before he did. Though he even tried to fuck with *that*.'

She didn't bother to hide her irritation. Ainsley Davidson had plainly been a handful, with his relentless campaigning to win himself an appeal.

Faraday poured himself some more wine. Pannell covered her glass with her hand.

'Did you see him inside at all?'

'Never.' She shook her head. 'I was tempted sometimes but no, we waited.'

'And?'

'Made contact when he came out. Davidson had been driving for some serious criminals, made quite a name for himself. Odds on, he'd be back in the same company. Criminals are like anyone else, creatures of habit. Don't you find that?'

Faraday nodded. Too right, he thought.

'You ran Davidson yourself?'

'No. I've got a team of DCs, nothing massive. One of them looked after Davidson.'

'And Davidson was happy to go along with you?'

'Yeah. More than happy. That should have wised us up, really, but you get a result and you just want to keep the stuff coming in. It was good quality, too, intelligence we could check out, names we recognised. It seemed more than promising.' She paused, staring down at her empty glass. 'I suppose that was a clue, too.'

'Clue to what?'

'Clue to Davidson's little game. He'd taken decent money off us by this time, four figures, the little shit, and then we got a whisper from another source and we realised what he was up to.'

'Both ends against the middle?'

'Exactly. There was no question he was back in bad company. Christ, we'd encouraged that and had the videos to prove it. No, turned out he'd been straight with them from the off, blown himself completely, and everything we had down on tape – jobs they were planning, dates, times, locations – was all fiction. It sounded great, really kosher, but they'd probably rehearsed it all a million times. Straight fucking pantomime.'

'You'd wired Davidson?'

'Of course. Little bastard even flogged the mike and transmitter. Hi-spec kit. Cost us a fortune to replace.'

'And nothing at the end of it?'

'Absolutely fuck all. The targets must be pissing themselves.'

'And Davidson?'

'Disappeared.'

Faraday permitted himself a chuckle. It was a good story, the stuff of wry CID legend, and even Pannell had the grace to smile. Entrapment turned inside out. Game, set and match to Mr Davidson.

'You know why he screwed you around?'

'Yeah.' She'd just checked her watch. 'He hated us. Hated the screws inside. Hated anything in a uniform. Thought he'd been fitted up.'

'My understanding was he *had* been fitted up.'

'You're right. But not by us. He went down on a GBH charge, ran down a woman on a crossing, lucky she didn't die. Only he wasn't the bloke at the wheel. The guy driving was the brother of the bloke who runs the firm. Davidson had nicked the car in the first place and his prints were all over it. They were happy to let him take the fall.'

'And he was back with these guys?'

'Yeah, but not happy.'

'Why not?'

'Because they wouldn't come across. No down payments on future jobs. No compensation for seven years of his life. Nothing to say thank you for letting them into our little secret. They knew we were paying him and they left it at that.'

'How come?'

'They didn't trust him. They knew they'd fucked him about over the GBH charge and they thought he was setting them up. So it was wait and see time.'

'Absolutely no money?'

'None.'

'Or favours?'

'Like what?'

'Like sorting out a screw he hated? In Portsmouth.'

'You're joking.' Pannell laughed at the thought. 'These guys are careful like you wouldn't believe. Whacking screws is bad shit. Whacking screws brings half the bloody police force round your neck. Why would they want that kind of grief?'

Good question, thought Faraday. He swallowed a mouthful of the Merlot. Now the tricky bit.

'There's a DC called Andy Corbett,' he said. 'You'll know him.'

Pannell nodded. The laughter had left her face.

'What about him?'

'He's been back recently, talking to some of your guys, maybe even talking to you. He's used your intelligence to make a case against Davidson. A screw Davidson loathed got murdered. Corbett's keen to put Davidson away for it, or at least Davidson's buddies. You must know all this. That's why you're here.'

Pannell had produced a packet of Marlboro Lights. Faraday shook his head when she offered. She lit the cigarette and then ducked her head behind the cloud of smoke.

'This is difficult,' she said at last.

'Why?'

'Because it isn't something I should be telling you.'

Faraday sat back, knowing better than to interrupt. At length, she changed her mind about the wine, emptying the remains of the bottle into her glass.

'Corbett was with us for three years. He got married during that time. I knew the girl. She'd been a temp in Traffic, real looker. They were engaged before anyone even realised what was going on. A bunch of us went to the wedding.' She watched Faraday's face. 'The marriage lasted less than a year. After the wife, Corbett started with other women. A couple were in the job. Finally, one or two of them put their heads together, compared notes.'

'And?'

'Turned out Corbett got off on weird stuff.'

'Violence?'

'Absolutely . . . but not what you or me would mean by violence. We're not talking ten pints of Stella and a punch in the mouth. It was much more creative than that. He put real thought into it. Not just violence but humiliation. Once you understood, you could see it in him. The way he handled the job. The way he handled other people. Corbett has to be top dog. Come what may.'

Top dog? Faraday was looking beyond her, at the blur of faces crowding into the bar. This wasn't Corbett she was describing. This was Coughlin.

'Control,' he murmured. 'This is all about control. Me first.'

'Yeah.' She nodded. 'And fuck everyone else.'

Too right. Faraday was frowning now. Something still bothered him. If the intelligence on Davidson's criminal friends ruled out any kind of favours for the young ex-con, then how come Corbett had been so convinced they might have sorted out Coughlin? Had he made it up?

'No.' Pannell expelled a long plume of smoke. 'He talked to the lads. They hate him. They know about his funny little ways and they'll do anything to set him up.'

'So they fed him this stuff? Is that what you're saying?'

'Sure. As soon as they knew what he wanted, what kind of case he was trying to make, they took him down the pub and let him buy them lots of drinks.'

'In return for . . . ?'

'Whatever he wanted to hear. It's all non-attributable. You know that. There wasn't any chance of come-back.'

'And you think Corbett believed them?'

'I think Corbett didn't care. If it made the case, it made the case. All he had to do was make a dramatic entrance and brag about his Met friends. He's into the big time. You must have noticed.'

Indeed. Faraday was trying to attract the barmaid's attention. Another bottle of Merlot would go down very nicely indeed. At length, she caught his eye.

Faraday felt a pressure on his arm. It was Pannell.

'Not for me.' She sounded genuinely regretful. 'I have to go.'

'That's a shame.' Faraday was holding up the empty bottle and signalling for another. 'I'm beginning to enjoy this.'

Twenty-five

Next morning, Bev Yates was up at half past four. He slipped out of the house, pausing by the car to savour the first blush of sunrise. An hour later, on the motorway and tuned in to the latest match analysis from the Far East, he was wondering quite how efficient KLM might be in keeping to their schedules. He'd talked in advance to the uniformed duty inspector at Gatwick, and had secured access to the landing pier. By arrangement with BAA security and a cheerful Dutchman in KLM's traffic office, he'd be allowed on to the inbound plane. The cabby's name was Vaughan. An office alongside Immigration had been made available for the interview. With luck, they'd be through by the time the England–Nigeria match was due to kick off.

At the airport, Yates left his Golf in the short-term car park and paused on the walkway to call a pre-assigned number. A woman from BAA security met him on the main concourse. She had good news. The KLM flight had already left Schipol and would be arriving fifteen minutes early. He had time for a Danish and a cappuccino before she'd escort him airside. Yates gave her a smile, then touched her lightly on the arm as she turned away.

'Where would I find a television?' he enquired. 'Afterwards?'

The KLM flight touched down at 06.53. Yates, waiting at the end of the arrivals pier, was first on to the aircraft. The senior steward had already identified the cabby and led Yates down the aisle towards the rear of the aircraft.

'Mr Vaughan?' The man looked up in surprise, first at Yates, then at the proffered warrant card. 'You got a moment?'

Vaughan was a thin, sallow-faced man with haunted eyes and a disastrous haircut. A long weekend in Amsterdam appeared to have robbed him of the power of speech.

'What's this, then?' he said at last.

'Nothing you should be worried about. Do you have any hand luggage?'

Yates escorted Vaughan off the aircraft. Minutes later, they were sitting in a small, bare office with a square of one-way glass in the door.

Yates explained the background. He was investigating a major crime. A man had been murdered in Pompey. He wanted Vaughan to think back to Monday night.

'Monday night just gone? I was over in Amsterdam.'

'No, the Monday before that – or early Tuesday, rather.'

'Fuck me, don't want much do you?'

Yates offered a prompt. It had been two in the morning. He'd gone to the Alhambra Hotel in Granada Road and collected three guys, one of them pissed out of his skull. The cabby gazed into the middle distance. He'd picked up hundreds of fares last week, each one blurring into the next. Past eleven o'clock it was rare to find anyone who wasn't legless.

'These were middle-aged guys,' Yates said. 'Ex-skates. Two of them wanted to go back to the Home Club. The other one you dropped in Milton. He was off his face. You had to help him into the house.'

The cabby frowned. Something had snagged in his memory.

'Big guy? Heavy?'

'That's it.'

The frown deepened. He was trying really hard.

'Glasgow Road? Milton?'

'Spot on. 189.'

'Yeah.' He nodded. 'So what's the question?'

'I want to know what happened.'

'You what?' Vaughan looked bewildered.

'Just talk me through it. You picked these guys up?'

'That's right. The Alhambra, Granada Road, like you said.'

'Then what?'

'I dropped the big guy off. Terrace house. His missus was at the door.'

'And afterwards?'

'We went to the Home Club.'

'No detours?'

'No.'

'You're sure about that?'

'Yeah.'

'What were the guys talking about?'

'Talking about? You've got to be joking. A week ago? How the fuck am I going to remember that?'

'Did they mention a name at all? Bloke called Coughlin?'

'No idea, mate.'

'Straight back to the Home Club, then. Is that what you're saying?'

'Yeah. Definitely.'

'And you'll make a statement to that effect?'

'Yeah.' He shrugged. 'Why not?'

Faraday was asleep when Yates got through.

'Listen, boss. I've talked to the cabby.'

'And?'

'Fuck all. He picked them up, dropped them off. No surprises. OK?'

The phone went dead and it was several seconds before Faraday was able to focus on the clock beside the bed.

07.31. He rubbed his eyes, trying to ease the pain. Waiting for the train at Waterloo, he'd treated himself to a pint of Spitfire and a couple of Scotches. Two Nurofen last thing had been a lifesaver but he still felt dreadful.

Willard answered the phone surprisingly quickly. Faraday, still propped up on one elbow, told him about Yates. In his view, there were no longer any grounds for hanging on to the *Accolade*s. They were free to go. Willard grunted his approval and told Faraday to sort it with the Custody Sergeants.

Faraday returned the phone to the bedside table and then eased himself out of bed, knowing that he had to get some fresh air in his lungs. Out on the harbour, a lone figure in a smallish yacht was taking advantage of the ebbing tide. Couple of minutes, he'd be out through the narrows and away. Lucky bastard, thought Faraday, hunting for a pair of jeans.

It was gone nine before he got to Kingston Crescent. Three miles on the towpath beside the harbour and a full fried afterwards had stilled a little of the thunder in his head. Calls to the Custody Officers at Central, Waterlooville and Fareham had already authorised the release of all three prisoners, and Faraday left a number for Beattie. He'd no idea how the man was going to make it back to Devon, but whatever happened he ought to take his dog. The Alsatian was still at Eadie's place, and Faraday still had the key.

Willard had been at his desk since eight, locked in conference with Nick Hayder. Willard had already had a lengthy conversation with the Crime Correspondent on the *News*, confirming the breakthrough on the Somerstown murder, and there now appeared to be every chance of an optimistic in-depth feature highlighting a welcome change of mood amongst hard-core youths on the estate.

From Willard's point of view, this was a perfect result. More and more, top management were emphasising the links between crime and social exclusion – and here was a textbook example of painstaking detective work successfully undertaken in a difficult and challenging neighbourhood. Hayder's squad, said Willard, had managed to turn the tide of apathy and aggression on the estate. The kids were not, after all, beyond salvation. Fundamentally decent, three of them had chosen to come forward and volunteer statements.

As the morning wore on, there were rumours along the Major Crimes corridor that Paul Winter's hand might lie behind this surprising outbreak of civic duty. There was even word that the youths concerned had mentioned him by name but no one was quite sure why. The younger DCs thought this was bollocks and said so but Faraday, still nursing the remains of his hangover, wasn't so sure. Winter was a past master at ghosting into other people's investigations. More often than not, he caused a great deal of confusion, but the results – as Faraday knew only too well – could occasionally be startling.

Not that Willard paid the slightest attention. As far as he was concerned, making the case against Darren Geech had been a scalp for Major Crimes and a memo to that effect landed on the desk of every DC involved in Operation *Hexham*. Andy Corbett taped his to the corridor wall facing Faraday's office, a gesture that Faraday treated with contempt.

The call from Beattie came shortly before noon. Under the circumstances, Faraday thought he sounded remarkably sanguine. He was in Southsea and he wanted his dog back. Faraday glanced at his watch. Anything to get out of the office.

'Where are you?'

'In the middle. By the shops.' There was a pause on the line. 'Store called Knight and Lees?'

Faraday told him to hang on. Five minutes and he'd be down there to pick him up. Blue Mondeo, X reg.

Beattie was waiting on the pavement outside the big

department store. He hadn't shaved and he looked tired, but there was something in his eyes that spoke of a deep satisfaction. Only on the seafront, slipping into a parking bay across from Eadie Sykes's flat, did Faraday break the silence between them.

'Dog's been fine,' he said.

'Good.' Beattie was gazing out across the common. 'I used to come down here years ago. Saturday nights mainly. Runs ashore.' He frowned. 'The Birdcage? The Pomme d'Or?'

Faraday nodded. The clubs had been closed for years, but in his days as a young beatman he'd policed them both. He began to hunt for stories, little anecdotes that might raise a smile, but quickly realised that Beattie wasn't remotely interested in the past. The silence between them stretched and stretched. Then Beattie looked across at Faraday.

'No grudges, OK?' He extended a hand. 'In your shoes I'd have done exactly the same thing.'

'You mean that?'

'Yeah. I might have been tougher . . . but yeah.'

Faraday hid a smile and shook the proffered hand. For some reason, he felt flooded with relief.

'I'll get the dog,' he said. 'You hang on here.'

Upstairs, Sykes was out again. A note on the carpet inside the front door established that Rory had gone running with his new mistress at dawn and was now knackered. He'd had a big breakfast and a little nap but might need another walkies before lunch. The note ended with a line of kisses, a gesture which further brightened Faraday's morning.

Back in the street, Faraday handed the dog over to Beattie. For a moment or two they stood awkwardly on the pavement, not knowing quite what to say, then, on the spur of the moment, Faraday gestured at the pub across the road.

'Fancy a spot of lunch. My shout?'

Beattie gave the invitation some thought, then shook his head. He'd take the dog for a stroll on the Common, then he was off to the station. The Custody Sergeant at Waterlooville had given him a rail warrant. There was a through train at two. He wanted to get home.

'Of course.' Faraday turned to the car. 'Just a thought.'

Beattie bent to the dog. Then he squatted on the pavement, ruffling the fur behind the Alsatian's ears, making friends again. The dog licked his hand.

Faraday was in his car. He wound down the window.

'Good luck,' he said simply.

'Sure.' Beattie was still making a fuss of the dog. 'Listen. If you're ever down our way again, time to spare . . .' He glanced up, looking Faraday in the eye. 'OK?'

'You're telling me Corbett sold us a dummy?'

Faraday was back in Willard's office. He'd been through the conversation in the wine bar with DI Pannell, and the Det Supt hadn't been slow in drawing the obvious conclusion.

'I think he was over-hasty, sir. Ambition's not a sin but he ought to be more careful.'

'Don't fuck about, Joe. The pillock was trying to snow us.'

'You might be right.'

'I am right. The point about intelligence like this, you can make any case you want. He was grandstanding. You were right all along. What else did she tell you?'

Faraday had spent the last hour or so debating where to draw the line on Corbett. It gave him a deep personal pleasure to know that his instincts about the young DC had been right, that the man really was an arsehole, but fellow officers' private lives were no concern of Willard's, not unless they got in the way of the job. At length, he shook his head.

'Nothing,' he said.

'You're sure?'

'Absolutely.'

'And you're telling me this DI knew Corbett pretty well?'

'Yes.'

'And she was happy to talk about him?'

'Yes.'

Willard gave him a last chance, then pulled open a drawer. Faraday found himself looking at two cassettes: one video, one audio.

'Cathy Lamb brought these over. I haven't been through them myself, but if what she told me is even half true then Corbett's out of here. Harassment? Sexual abuse? Date rape?' He sighed. 'You know something, Joe? You're too bloody straight for your own good.' He got up and went across to the window. 'So what are we going to do about Coughlin?'

Faraday was still looking at the cassettes. At length, he straightened in the chair.

'You want the truth, sir?'

'Dare you.'

'I haven't a clue.'

The billing on Gault's mobile phone came in five days later. Brian Imber, in his office at Havant police station, phoned through with the news.

'Gault made a call that Monday night,' he said. 'From the hotel.'

'What time?'

'Twelve nineteen.'

'Did he get through?'

'I assume so. It lasted a couple of minutes.'

Faraday was fighting to remember the exact chronology of events that Monday night. Already he was dealing with another murder, a Southsea housewife who was denying taking the kitchen knife to her errant husband. Coughlin, just now, felt like history.

'Remind me.' Faraday was reaching for a pen. 'Had Coughlin paid his visit by then?'

'Definitely. Pritchard tried to phone him at twelve two. Gault's call was after that.'

'And the number?'

'It's local. You want to take a guess at the address?'

'No. Tell me.'

'217 Kingsley Road. Subscriber by the name of Warren.' He paused. 'That's the lad's mum and dad.'

Faraday's call found Bev Yates in the Southsea Waitrose. Lunchtime, he was doing the weekly shop.

'Do you remember Gault mentioning making a call from the hotel that Monday night?'

'No.'

'You're sure about that?'

'Positive. We asked him in that first interview and he said no. Check the tapes if you want.' There was a pause, then Yates laughed. 'Means bugger all, though. He was so bladdered he couldn't remember anything.'

Faraday was already on his feet. His next meeting on the Southsea stabbing wasn't until two thirty.

'You finished the shopping? I'll be outside in ten minutes.'

217 Kingsley Road was a modest, neat-looking terrace house in a quiet street on the eastern edge of the city. There was a poster for a church rummage sale in the downstairs window, and the front door had recently had a new coat of paint.

Faraday paused on the pavement. This bottom end of Kingsley Road overlooked a tiny, tucked-away corner of Langstone Harbour known locally as the Glory Hole. Once used as a dumping ground by various branches of the armed services, this muddy little backwater was rumoured to be a soup of heavy metals but Faraday was in no position to know the truth. It certainly offered a nicer view than most locations on the island and Faraday could think of worse places to live.

Turning back to the house, he wondered whether anyone would be in. There were no real grounds for supposing that Gault had said anything worthwhile, but gone midnight was a strange time to phone and whatever tiny light this call might shed on the investigation might just be worth the drive across.

A second knock brought a woman to the door. She was large and untidy, a stained beige cardigan pulled tight over a flower-patterned dress. She stared at the proffered warrant cards.

'Police?'

'CID.' Faraday introduced himself, then Yates. Something in this woman's face told him that the visit hadn't come as a surprise. 'Are you Mrs Warren?'

'That's right.'

With some reluctance, she invited them in. The house smelled of recent baking. They followed her into the small back room. She didn't invite them to sit down.

'What is it, then?'

Faraday explained that they were making enquiries about the death of a Sean Coughlin. Did the name mean anything to her?

She shook her head.

'Never heard of him.'

'He was in the navy a while ago, around the same time as your son. Can't recall the name?'

'My son's dead,' she said at once.

'I know. And I'm sorry.' He paused. 'Sean Coughlin? You're sure the name rings no bells?'

'No.' She folded her arms over her bosom. 'I'd remember a name like that.'

Yates was looking at a couple of framed photographs on the mantelpiece. In one of them, a young naval rating was posed against a line of railings, glimpses of the sea in the background. The lettering around his cap read HMS

Raleigh. In the other the same youth was on a quayside, framed by the looming mass of a warship. In both shots – with his toothy grin and his jaunty, stuck-up thumb – he looked impossibly young.

'What about Paul Gault?'

The mention of Gault at last brought a smile to the woman's face. Paulie she knew well, lovely man, always cheerful, tried to keep an eye on Mattie, tower of strength.

'He brings me flowers every twenty-first of May,' she said. 'Some of those amaryllis this year, beautiful they were, I thought they'd last for ever.'

'Do you see him often?'

'He pops round occasionally, just to see if we're OK.'

'Does he ever phone?'

'Once in a while, yes.'

'Did he happen to phone last week? Monday? Late?'

Mrs Warren went through the motions of trying to remember. Then she shrugged.

'I've no idea. I don't know.'

'Were you here that Monday night?'

'Yes. I'm always here.'

'But you don't remember a call? Past midnight?'

'No. Maybe there's been some mistake. No one phones that late.'

Yates stepped into the conversation.

'We know there was a call, Mrs Warren. We know it happened. We know exactly when it happened. And we even know how long it lasted. Was there someone else who might have taken it?'

'No.' She was anxious now. 'There was only me.'

'And you don't remember taking a call? Nineteen minutes past midnight?'

Faraday could hear the ticking of a clock. This woman knew something. It was there in her face, in the way her hands kept returning to the same button on the cardigan, twisting and twisting. She wanted them to stop asking her about this wretched phone call. Better still, she wanted them to leave her alone, to go away, to get out of her life.

'Just tell us,' Faraday said gently, 'what Paul said.'

'I . . .' She took a deep breath and then shook her head. 'I can't remember.'

'It was Paul?' Yates this time.

'Yes.'

'What did he want? At that time of night?'

'It was nothing. It was silly. Just, you know . . . nothing.'

'But what did he say? It's important, Mrs Warren. We wouldn't be bothering you otherwise.'

She looked from one face to the other, trapped. Then a hand reached backwards, blindly, feeling for the arm-chair. Yates helped her sit down.

'You know, don't you?' Her voice was barely a whisper. 'Women can tell, they can read men like a book.'

'Tell what, Mrs Warren?'

Briefly, she tried to get up again but gave up the struggle. Then she nodded at the open door.

'Look in the kitchen. There's a letter on the side, behind the cake tin.'

Yates disappeared. When he came back, he was carrying a blue envelope.

'Is this it?'

'Yes. Go on, read it.' She made a brief, despairing gesture with her hand, then leaned back and shut her eyes. She wanted no further part of this.

Yates handed the letter to Faraday. It carried the Kingsley Road address but no stamp. He weighed it in his hand for a moment, sensing that they'd finally found the key to Coughlin's death.

'Is this from your son? Matthew?'

'Yes.' Her eyes were still closed.

'When did you get it?'

'Twenty years ago. It was the last letter he ever wrote us. That's why I never opened it. I couldn't bear to hear his voice again. Not until . . .' She frowned. 'Not until I thought I was ready.'

'And when was that?'

'Nearly a month ago. The twenty-first of May.'

Faraday looked at her a moment longer, then unfolded the letter. It was like an aerogram, a single sheet of paper with a front panel for the address. It began innocuously enough, big loopy scrawl, stuff about the passage south, about Ascension, about painting out the ship's number. The weather, Matthew said, had been getting colder by the day and twice they'd depth-charged whales by mistake. Then, after a one-line space halfway down, came a sudden change of tone.

If you wanted the truth, he wrote, life aboard was a nightmare. He was in a mess with thirty-six other blokes. One of them was a cook. His name was Coughlin. He worked in the wardroom galley which meant being with him day after day. He'd never leave you alone. He was a big bastard and he made you do things that were wrong, things that made you want to throw up. Lots of times he'd thought of going and telling someone about it – the Divisional Officer, the Master-at-Arms, maybe even the Captain – but he knew that would be asking for trouble because Coughlin was bound to find out and after that he'd be a dead man. He couldn't explain how horrible this bloke was. It made him sick just thinking about him. He'd made his life a misery. And what made it worse was not knowing what to do about it. So now he was hoping against hope that something might come along and sort it all out. A couple of Argie bombers, maybe. Or an Exocet. The letter petered out on the next line. After the scrawled signature, the boy had added three kisses.

An Exocet?

To Faraday, with a son of his own, the letter was truly shocking. It amounted, in essence, to a suicide note.

Whether Coughlin had physically dumped the young steward overboard or not was immaterial. Hands-on or otherwise, the fact was that the older man had driven this woman's son to his death. Not at the hands of the enemy, but at the vicious whim of a messdeck bully with a taste for young boys.

Faraday gave the letter to Yates. Mrs Warren was staring up at him.

'Who really took the call that night?'

'My husband.'

'He'd read this letter?'

'Of course he had. He read it after I opened it. It broke his heart. Like it's broken mine.'

'Did you talk to anyone else about it? Anyone from the navy?'

Mrs Warren hesitated a moment. Then she nodded.

'I phoned Mr Wallace. He's in Drayton, runs the association. He's been good to us, like Paulie.'

'And you read him the letter?'

'I told him what was in it.'

'And what did he do?'

Once again, there was a pause.

'I think he talked to the First Lieutenant,' she said at last. 'I think Mr Harrington was the person he got on to.'

Faraday glanced at Yates but Yates was still deep in the letter. This was why the Ship's Investigation had gone missing, Faraday thought. The tight little family that were the surviving *Accolade*s had closed ranks and were doubtless deciding exactly what to do. Not that either Wallace himself – or, indeed, the Vice Admiral – were going to share the contents of this letter with a stranger. No. Both men, in their separate ways, had marked Faraday's card. But there was a deeper and more complex loyalty here that only the *Accolade*s themselves would understand. Because that's what war did to you.

Yates passed the letter back to Faraday. A tiny shake of the head. Faraday refolded the thin, blue paper, trying to imagine how you'd ever cope with a bombshell like this, a cry for help that twenty years had done nothing to mute.

'What about your husband?' he said gently. 'What did he do about it?'

Mrs Warren was crying now, her pale cheeks shiny with tears.

'He talked to Paul. He wanted to find Coughlin, you know, find an address for him.'

'And Paul told him?'

'Paul didn't know.' She fumbled for a tissue, and then blew her nose.

'What about Wallace? Wouldn't Wallace have known?'

'Paul tried but Wallace hadn't got an address. Coughlin never came to any of the services, never kept up.' She was gazing at the letter. 'Not surprising, really.'

'So your husband didn't have an address until Monday night? Until Paul Gault phoned?'

'No.' After the call came in, she said, her husband had left the house within minutes. An hour or so later he was back again. His boots had blood on them. His jeans, too. When she asked him what had happened, what he'd done, he wouldn't say a word.

'What happened to the clothing?'

'I burned it.' She gestured hopelessly towards the back garden. 'White spirit.'

'The boots?'

'They went into the Glory Hole.'

Her husband had left early the next morning, taking the van with him. He'd packed some spare clothes, and taken stuff from the larder, cereals and biscuits mainly. She'd heard from him a couple of times since but she'd no idea where he was. He said they were sleeping in the van, the pair of them. He sounded pretty rough.

'Pair of them?'

'My husband's a builder. Warren and Son. Malcolm's

disappeared as well. He lives round the corner, Sheryl and a couple of nippers. She's like me. Out of her mind with it all.'

'They both went round to see Coughlin?'

She nodded, her eyes moist, saying nothing.

Faraday glanced at Yates, then left the room. From the kitchen a door opened on to a tiny square of back garden. In one corner, he found a circle of flattened earth and a scattering of ashes. He gazed down at it for a long moment, unable to rid himself of the image of the Vice Admiral, bent over the coffee table, the cigarette smouldering between his fingers. The man had been more right than he'd known. The war they'd fought had cast a long, long shadow. After twenty years, this woman hadn't lost one man from her life but three.

Faraday looked up to find Yates at the kitchen door. He, too, had spotted the ashes.

'Scenes of Crime?' he muttered.

Epilogue

Ten days later, Faraday took the road back down to the West Country. He'd taken the precaution of phoning ahead, making sure that Beattie would be at home, and when the ex-Master-at-Arms had asked what lay behind this latest visit, Faraday had told him not to worry. There were one or two details he needed to sort out. Nothing that Beattie himself wouldn't have done.

· Past Dorchester, Faraday ran into torrential rain. Crawling along behind a lorry, he thought of Willard at Kingston Crescent, supervising the final preparation of the *Merriott* file prior to submission to the Crown Prosecution Service. Warren and his son had walked into a Midlands police station after a fortnight's misery in the back of a Transit van. Whether Warren's decision to give himself and his son up had been prompted by a phone conversation with his wife wasn't clear, but either way it made no difference. Both men had held their hands up to assaulting Coughlin. They'd never meant to kill him, but now he was gone they had no regrets. Forensic tests on ash residues from Warren's back garden had been disappointing but under the circumstances, with two signed confessions on file, Willard had organised a modest celebration.

Faraday, pleading a prior appointment, hadn't turned up. His first solo Major Crimes had been a troubling experience. Procedurally, he hadn't put a foot wrong. He'd explored every line of enquiry, put all the ticks in all the right boxes. In Willard's absence, he'd been punctilious about the Policy Book, and with the Det Supt back at the helm, he'd finally achieved a result. Given the circumstances surrounding Matthew Warren's death, it was highly likely that the CPS would settle for manslaughter charges on the basis of the two confessions, but whatever happened the interests of justice had been served. But was that the end of the story? Faraday thought not.

The Vice Admiral had, in the end, been right. Peace was a precious commodity and so was a family as troubled and vulnerable as Matthew Warren's. By doing his job, and by doing it well, Faraday had shattered both. Given exactly the same circumstances, he couldn't think of a single decision he'd take differently, but that bleak knowledge gave him no comfort whatsoever. A death like Warren's would haunt you for ever.

Beattie, two hours later, was pleased to see him. He put the kettle on and produced a tin of home-made scones. The Alsatian loped in from the garden and gave the visitor a sniff.

Faraday explained about the Warren family. Beattie didn't appear to be the least surprised.

'You're telling me you knew?' Faraday had helped himself to a chair by the fireplace.

'I'm telling you nothing.'

'Off the record?'

Beattie smiled to himself and called the dog over. The big, old Alsatian padded across the slate flagstones and made himself comfortable on the sofa beside his master. Beattie tossed Faraday another scone from the open tin at his feet. With jam and little whirls of clotted cream, they were delicious.

'Off the record, there's not much left to tell,' Beattie said carefully.

'How about Coughlin's address? I'm still not clear how Gault found out. You were all in the hotel. Coughlin came and went. No one followed him. He's not in the book because I checked. And Pritchard would have been the last person to part with the address.'

The dog was licking jam off Beattie's fingers.

'Pritchard was nearly as pissed as Gault,' Beattie said. 'He made a call out in the hall then left his mobile behind the bar.'

'And Gault accessed the directory? In his state?'

'No.' Beattie offered the dog a dot of cream. 'I did.'

'*You* did. Why?'

Beattie ignored the question, so Faraday went at it a different way. Pritchard's mobile had been behind the bar. Beattie had gone to the trouble of retrieving Coughlin's details. What happened next?

'I wrote the address down, brought it back to the table.'

'And Gault saw it?'

'Must have done.'

Faraday, sensing regret, leaned forward in the chair.

'Did you know he'd phoned the boy's parents?'

'No.'

'He didn't do it from the bar?'

'No.' Beattie shook his head. 'He went out for a piss a couple of times. It doesn't take long to make a call like that.'

'Are you sorry he made it?'

Beattie thought about the question. At length, he permitted himself a tiny frown. Irritation, as well as regret.

'Yes,' he said, 'I am. Gault was out of his head. The last person he should have phoned was the lad's father, putting it on him. You know what I'm saying?'

'Of course.' Faraday nodded. 'But what about Coughlin? If Gault hadn't seen the address, what would *you* have done . . . ?'

Faraday let the question tail away. Matthew Warren's letter, twenty years unread, had lodged in his brain. The thought of an eighteen-year-old boy praying for an Exocet was grotesque.

Beattie stirred.

'There's something else you ought to know,' he said. 'About that Monday night?'

'About the war. About *Accolade*. The evening we were hit, I was down in the S and S mess. That's Two Delta. Coughlin's mess. Warren's mess. We were at Condition Zulu, fully closed down, then we got the word on the inbound raid. At that point, wherever you are, you hit the deck. The Argie Skyhawks were visual, seconds away.' He paused, then reached across for the dog. 'The first bomb hit aft. You could feel the whole ship lifting beneath you, the weirdest sensation. Then the PWO called a second aircraft, which made sense because those bastards always came in pairs.'

He turned his head towards the window, gazing out at the rain, and Faraday wondered just how many times this man must have relived *Accolade*'s final moments. Would you ever share an experience like this with anyone else? Or did you spend twenty years keeping it under lock and key?

'We had Seacat on the 21s.' Beattie laughed softly. 'The Marines used to call it Seamouse. That tells you everything. They let one go, you could hear it blasting off, then some brave soul had a pop with the Oerliken, and then – bang – we were stuffed. You just have no idea. You just can't imagine what's happening. One moment you're lying there, cacking yourself. The next you're in some movie. There's smoke everywhere. The ship's listing. The bulkhead's gone. There's a big fire down below. Fucking grade A chaos.'

He looked down at his empty plate. At this point, he said, the drills kicked in. He knew guys had been hurt, had to have been, and so he went looking. One guy had lost it completely, didn't know where he was. Beattie gave him a couple of smacks and shoved him towards the ladder. Another bloke, Taff, was obviously dead. Then he spotted a third body, the other side of what had once been the bulkhead. This guy turned out to be alive, wrecked but alive. He was a big guy, too. Beattie tried to get him to help himself but knew he was past it. Getting him out was a two-man job. At least.

'And you were by yourself?'

'No. There was one other bloke down there. Barely injured at all.'

'And?'

'I tried to get him to help, yelled at him, ordered him, but no way was he interested. In fact it was worse than that. He wanted to fight me.'

'*Fight* you?'

'Yeah. The guy I was trying to get out was none of his business. Me? I could fuck off. The guy flat on his back? He was a goner.'

'So what happened?'

'I did my best by myself.' He looked Faraday in the eye. 'And I failed. Guy's name was Rory. Plymouth boy. Big family. And you know something? Not a day has gone by without me thinking about him. Between us, me and the other bloke, we could have got him out. No question.'

'So who was he? This other bloke?'

Beattie tipped his head back, staring at the ceiling, and for a moment Faraday swore he detected a smile. Then Beattie's hand found the dog again.

'Who do you think?' he said softly.